HIGH LONESOME SOUND

JAYE WELLS

"The earth has its music for those who will listen."
-Reginald Vincent Holmes

1

PREPARATION FOR BURIAL

Ruby

THE BEAR WAS CRYING AGAIN.

In the cold hours before her sisters demanded breakfast or Daddy got back to drinking, Ruby Barrett lay in bed and listened to the cub down the road holler for its mama. The high, pitiful wails didn't enter through her ears; they shredded through her middle like icy fingers. Once inside, the sounds crawled up under her ribs and throbbed like a second heart.

The mean old Plott hounds down at Junior Jessup's farm answered each of the bear's cries with howls that sounded like hell's own choir. When she'd first asked Daddy about the bear, he said Junior kept it caged near the dog runs to train the hounds for hunting season come deep fall.

"If Junior's in a Christian mood maybe he'll send some of that bear meat our way for the winter," he'd added.

"But isn't it illegal to take a cub?" she'd whispered.

Instead of answering, he'd punched her. After living in that house for eighteen years, she should have known better than to sass him. These days, the only sure things in her life were Daddy's fist, the crying bear, and the Mama-shaped hole in the world.

After he'd hit her, she'd washed the blood from her mouth in the cracked bathroom sink. She sent her anger down that drain, too, because her sanity depended on staying numb.

The memories faded away, just like the bruises eventually did, leaving her alone in the dark with the rain beating on the clapboards like tears and the cold so hard like a winter grave.

That morning, they were gonna bury Mama.

The thought created a crack in the dam she'd built around her heart. She swiped at the first couple of tears, but soon she couldn't stem the tide anymore. Her sobs weren't as loud as the bear's, but they sounded and felt just as hopeless.

Squeezing her eyes closed, she listened hard for the song. She yearned for the sound of wind whispering secrets through the trees and the distant rumble of highland thunder. Mama had been the one to teach her how to listen to the mountain's music. But when Mama died, so had the songs, and now the only music in her life came from that terrified bear cub.

Without the mountain to tell her its secrets, she had no choice but to turn to God for help. "Please, Jesus," she whispered. "Bring me a miracle."

In all her life, she'd only known two people who escaped Moon Hollow. The first was Jack Thompson, but even he hadn't lasted a full year at college before he lost his scholarship and moved back to his mama's trailer. Last time she'd talked to him, he'd said he was looking into work down in the mines. Might as well have said he was buying a plot up on Cemetery Hill, which is right where her mama, the only other escapee, would be buried that very morning.

"Please help me leave this place." Something deep in her chest, some burning knowledge that was not of the brain but of the heart, told her that if she didn't find her song, Moon Hollow would become a tomb and she'd be buried alive.

But Jesus didn't answer her prayer that morning. The only response came from down the road.

She wondered if the bear had watched its mama die, too.

Like lightning, an image appeared in her head of Mama's whole body shuddering as death asked her to dance. The jerky steps of that morbid waltz represented the surrender of Rose Barrett's body and soul. The remembered smell of cinnamon and grain alcohol from the spilled apple pie moonshine—a perfume she now would always associate with death—filled her nostrils. She swallowed hard and pushed the ugly memory back down into the dark vault where she hid all of her ghosts.

Funny, she never remembered hearing that bear cry once the sun was high and the dew baked off every blade of grass. But at that moment, in the dark, in the cold dark, the world felt impossibly small and filled with the terrible realization that the only thing worse than those cries was knowing that soon enough they, too, would fall silent.

2
REMAINDERED

Peter

THE BOOKSTORE USED to be a temple where he'd communed with the gods of story, but now it felt like a crypt where his dreams had gone to die. The musty scent of old paper and binding glue, once so dear, now repulsed him, made him ashamed.

He pasted a smile on his face for the old woman behind the counter. Last time he'd been in for a book signing, she'd predicted big things for his career. Now she barely met his eyes as she waved. "Mr. West," she said in a patronizing tone.

He scanned the store to see if any fans might poke their heads over shelves to catch a glimpse of famous horror author, Peter West. But there were only two other people in the store—a five-year-old boy and his mother, who was too busy forestalling a tantrum to be impressed by the arrival of an almost-big-time novelist.

The woman behind the checkout desk busied herself

placing stickers on copies of the latest blockbuster horror novel from that hack author Hollywood loved. All the reviewers called him, "a natural storyteller," which every *real* writer knew meant he couldn't write his way out of a grocery list, but he still sold a metric ton of copies, regardless of his lack of talent. Peter took a deep breath and dismissed that old rant because the only way to shut up that voice was to drown it with whiskey.

"Mr. West?" What's-her-name—Gladys? Gertrude?—was talking again. "I said, it's been too long."

Understatement of the century. Oh, he knew she was referring to how long it had been since he'd visited to buy books. But he also heard the unspoken judgment about how long it had been since he'd published a new novel. "Been busy," he lied. "Working on something new."

Her smile was too polite to be sincere. She went back to stickering the hack's books. Grateful for the excuse to escape, he ducked into the regional lore section. At least it wasn't the local authors area, where he'd be faced with seeing how few copies of his last book they carried—or worse, discovering that they'd already remaindered the few copies they'd had.

The thought reminded him of the time he'd gone out back to smoke during a signing at a Barnes & Noble in Chicago. The Dumpster in the alley had been overflowing with the novels waiting to be pulped after the covers had been stripped to return to the publishers for refunds. The unbound pages lay in the rain, bloated and naked as corpses.

Wicked Ink Book Store in Raleigh, North Carolina, was one of the few independent bookstores in the southeast that had yet to show any signs of shuttering. They thrived on a robust special order business of devoted horror fans. All the biggies signed at Wicked Ink, and every fan of the genre knew the store's name. He still remembered the first time he'd signed there. Only five people had shown up, but he'd been grateful for the opportunity and that anyone was reading his work at all. What a desperate asshole he'd been.

He half-heartedly scanned the shelves for interesting titles, but his mind was busy planning what he'd say to Renee.

The call had come in a few days earlier. As usual, he'd ignored the ringing phone, but that time she'd left a message. Short and polite, it had asked him to meet her at the store at ten on Wednesday morning. She didn't say what she wanted to discuss, but he knew.

It had been a year. Plenty of time for her to realize her mistake and swallow her pride. The choice of a bookstore for the meeting had been his first clue. They'd met in a bookstore twenty-five years earlier at UNC Chapel Hill. He'd offered to buy her the book in her hand, which had turned out to be a romance novel. She hadn't argued when he put that book back and selected a copy of *The Haunting of Hill House* by Shirley Jackson instead.

"But I don't like horror," she'd complained.

He had wanted to suck that pout right off her lips. Instead, he'd leaned in and said, "You will by the time I'm done with you."

As he read aloud the passage about Eleanor Vance's cup of stars, Renee took him into her mouth for the first time. That's when he knew it was love.

These days, he wasn't sure he'd ever really understood love at all, but after twelve years of marriage and a nasty divorce he sure as hell had intimate knowledge of hate.

He passed the shelf dedicated to the lore of North Carolina's coast and moved toward one labeled, "True Ghost Stories of Appalachia."

How should he play it? She'd be coy about it, of course. Try to blame him for what happened. Bring up the fling with his

T.A. at Meredith College. He'd remind her it was just the once, but, Christ, he was a male professor at an all-girls college, he should get credit for having screwed only one—or three, he'd silently amended—of them. Next, she'd bring up his drinking and the way he'd disappear into his office for days on end. She never did understand the demands of the creative life—the burden of his imagination.

He ran a finger over the spines. The words and colors blurred together until the wall morphed into a great mosaic of ideas. Where were all those writers now? They were non-fiction sorts, which meant they probably had day jobs as technical writers or copywriting advertorials. He couldn't judge them, not really. The only thing keeping him from declaring bankruptcy was his adjunct salary at the college. Meredith had fired him after the incident in the library with the T.A., but Wake County Technical College wasn't too picky about who taught basic comp to budding HVAC specialists.

At random, he pulled a book from the shelf. The cover showed an illustrated night scene of a full moon over a mountain cabin with a few pairs of predators' yellow eyes looking out from the dark. The title was *Appalachian Hauntings*. Peter fanned the pages and stopped at random. The chapter he landed on appeared to be about stories of ghosts living in the coalmines of southwest Virginia.

The bell over the door announced a new arrival.

"Peter?"

With a finger holding his place in the book, he turned toward Renee's voice. "Hey," he said too eagerly.

She didn't smile and her eyes narrowed a fraction, as if it allowed her to see through his façade. "You okay?"

He laughed. "Sure, sure. I was just reading." He held up the book. She barely spared it a glance.

"You look good."

Here we go, he thought. Play this cool. Think Marlowe, *The Big Sleep*. "And you look like trouble, sweetheart."

Her expression cooled. "Coffee?"

"Sure." He smiled and let his gaze wander down her body. She stepped back, telling him she didn't take it as a compliment. Okay, maybe not Chandler. She was always more of a Nicholas Sparks girl, anyway, but damn him if he was going to spout that saccharine dialogue. Maybe he could meet her halfway with some Tennessee Williams or Fitzgerald. Yeah, that was it. Renee certainly had Daisy Buchanan's beauty and depth. Of course, in this version he'd play Nick Carraway, not that pathetic sap Gatsby.

"Peter?"

He looked up to see Renee already halfway to the coffee stand. He brought the book with him, as a sort of totem. Maybe he'd tell her he was doing some research for a book he was writing. *Oh, I can't talk about it yet. You know how it is. Don't want to jinx it.*

She ordered a cup of tea with cream and sugar. He asked for dark roast, black. They took their drinks to the small bistro table, one of three in what passed for Wicked Ink's version of a coffee shop. While she stirred her tea, he sat back and waited for her to figure out how to begin.

She used a small wooden stirrer, moving in smooth clockwise circles. Orderly and neat. When she was done stirring, she tapped the stick three times before setting it on a napkin, which she folded once, twice, three times. Finally, she looked up and met his gaze. He smiled a smile that said, *we'll get through this together*.

It had been—what? Six months since their last conversation. Hadn't that been such a joy? He still carried a faint bitterness on his tongue from the words he'd spoken that day when she'd called to yell at him to "just sign the papers already, damn it—put us both out of this misery." Well, signing the papers might have put her out of her misery, but it had been the start of his.

He hadn't been able to write a word since.

"Thanks for meeting with me today," she said finally. Instead of looking at him, she stared at the steam rising from her tea.

"I'm surprised you still had my number."

She smiled with infinite patience—the kind she'd never shown when they were married. "Of course I had it. But you made it pretty clear last time we talked that you weren't too interested in keeping in touch."

The names he'd called her goose-stepped through his memory. "Sorry about that. I wasn't in a good place."

She nodded, a queen indulging a beggar. "You seem to be in a better one now."

He returned her nod, accepting the lie.

She raised the cup to her mouth and blew away some of the steam. "Allison called." She took a dainty sip. "She's worried."

"Don't know why she would be."

"Don't you have a book proposal due?"

He laughed. "My deadlines are no longer your business. She shouldn't have called you."

She mumbled something he didn't quite understand. Frowning, she removed the tea bag from the cup and set it aside. The liquid spread across the napkin like a bloodstain.

He dipped his head to catch her eye. "Speak up, Renee."

"I said, she called me about something else. Something besides you. While we were speaking, she asked if we were in touch. I told her I'd try to reach you."

Despite the heat from the mug warming his palms, coldness crept up his arms and across his shoulders. "What would my editor be calling you about that didn't have to do with me?"

The silence that followed wasn't dead, exactly, but it was definitely terminal.

He got in her line of vision, forcing her to look at him. "Renee?"

"I have some news." Her tone was synthetic, overly bright, like her smile.

She once told him her daddy spent thousands of dollars making sure his little girl had a mouthful of perfect white teeth. The neon brightness of that smile had always reminded Peter of Las Vegas. He hated that town.

"I've sold a book," she said.

No words had chilled him so much since the first time she'd used *divorce* as a verb. "What? What book?"

Renee scanned the store for potential witnesses. That's when he realized why she'd requested this location for her big reveal. She knew he'd be too conscious of his reputation to throw a scene in a bookstore.

She cleared her throat, and in that brief sound he heard a chorus of guilt so loud it would have drowned out the Mormon Tabernacle Choir. "A memoir."

If he avoided sudden movements, maybe he could keep the rage at bay long enough to win this conversation. "A memoir about what, exactly?"

The laugh is what did him in. The nervous giggle that admitted her guilt at the same time it attempted to dismiss his anger. "Just a thing I wrote ... about my life."

"I know what a fucking memoir is, Renee." His whisper came out as a hiss. "What I meant was, what part of your life is so interesting, so fucking compelling that you felt moved to commit it to paper and sell it to my God-damned editor?"

"You don't get take that tone with me anymore." Her gaze darted around the store. At that moment, the guy came out from behind the curtain separating the coffee bar from the back room. She relaxed.

Peter raised his hands in conciliatory gesture instead of speaking again and hoped that would be enough to encourage her to continue. He didn't trust himself not to scream.

"I—It's just about living through a …" She trailed off.

"A what?" Menace crept into his tone again but didn't care. He needed to hear her say it. "Living through a what?"

Her hand toyed with the wooden stirrer. "Remodeling the house and what came after."

He closed his eyes to enjoy the poison of his fury. "What came after?" He opened his eyes again and leaned forward. "You mean how you destroyed our marriage?"

Renee leaned across the table, meeting his gaze with a go-to-hell twinkle in her baby blues. "No, Peter, this is non-fiction."

If he hadn't already wanted to kill her, he might have admired the comeback enough to want to take her to bed again. "How much they paying you to make a fool of me?"

"It doesn't matter." She answered too quickly for the real answer to be insignificant.

"Hardcover?"

"Yes." She smiled, a pure, acidic *screw you*. "A big autumn release next year."

Renee in hardcover. He'd entered some Kafka-esque alternate reality.

"Let me guess—you're getting the full nine. Book tour, fifty thousand copies—"

"A *hundred* thousand plus placement on the front table of every major bookstore in the country."

He wanted to vomit. "Of course. Tell me, what did I do that was so evil that you needed to shame me publicly?"

Her hand tightened on the cup. There was still a faint indent on her fourth finger where his ring used to live. She didn't answer him, so he switched to offense.

"You've been around the business long enough to know that a hundred thousand books in print ain't a guarantee of shit."

"I still have a better chance of hitting a list than you've ever had, *sweetheart*."

His hand tightened on the table. He wished it were her neck —the long, ivory column that used to arch when he kissed it. The throat that would produce such lovely sounds when they made love. Now he wanted to bruise it until she begged his forgiveness for laughing at him.

"Peter?"

"What?" He looked at a spot just above her right ear. The air beyond it had a hazy quality, like looking down a long, hot stretch of road in August.

"It's not fun, is it?"

"What?"

"Having someone you trusted using your life as material for their stories."

The road burst into flames. Maybe if he were lucky, the heat would singe his wife's perfect blond hair and char the smirk off her perfect face.

"Believe it or not, writing this memoir wasn't about you. It's about me needing an outlet to process everything. Surely you, of all people, can appreciate how healing writing can be."

He pulled his attention away from the mirage of Renee burning *auto-da-fé*-style. "Is that what your self-help books told you?"

Her smile was too cold for a woman he'd just imagined burning at the stake. "You can blame me all you want for ending our marriage, but I gave you what you wanted—to be left alone to play God to your imaginary people. They're so much easier to deal with, aren't they? You can boss them around and kill them off if they don't behave."

"You're right, as always, sweetheart. Real humans are far too fucking needy—and too quick to stab you in the back."

"Then you should be happy." The final word exited her red lips with ironic bitterness.

"How do you figure?"

"Because you pushed away everyone who needed anything from you." With that, she tossed back the last of her tea and rose. "Call your fucking editor." She laid a five on the table and pushed it toward him. "For the tea."

He stared at the money she'd earned by selling his secrets to New York.

The guy at the coffee stand and the woman behind the counter watched Renee go. Judging from their too-casual expressions, they'd heard every word. The only way it could have been more humiliating would have been if Renee had kicked him in the balls literally instead of just figuratively.

He pushed back his chair to leave so he could go somewhere and feed his anger with some cheap whiskey. His elbow knocked into his coffee. "Shit!" The brown liquid splashed across the cover of the book he'd brought to the table. He grabbed napkins from the holder and attempted to mop up the worst of the spill.

"Yo, dude," the guy behind the counter called. He wore a Tar-Heel-blue T-shirt, and his eyes had the glassy sheen of a liberal arts major. "You're gonna have to buy that."

Peter looked up. "Huh?"

"The book." He nodded at the swollen pages. "You spilled on it so you gotta buy it."

He wanted to snap at the kid. Ask him if his parents were proud they'd paid a hundred grand for an education so their sweet boy could serve coffee for six bucks an hour and use deplorable grammar. But the last thing he needed was for this punk to tweet that Peter West came into the store and acted like "a total douchebag" or whatever kids were calling assholes these days.

"I was going to buy it anyway," he lied.

THE BOOK LANDED on the passenger seat with a wet plop. Peter slammed the door and gripped the steering wheel. Hot breath scraped up and down his throat. He wanted to turn the key and drive the car right through Wicked Ink's front door. He closed his eyes and imagined his bumper pinning the college kid's body to the espresso machine. Coffee and blood would spray on every book in the place. He laughed, wondering how much his bill would come to for all those ruined books. Maybe he could ask Renee for help covering the damages.

The giggle that escaped at that thought sobered him right up. He'd be damned if he allowed Renee West née Broussard to drive him into the nuthouse. No, what he needed was some old-fashioned poetic justice. Not the violent kind. Even though his mind sometimes felt like the most vicious place on earth, in reality, he didn't have the gumption to carry out any real violence. He preferred to keep it on the page. Less chance of arrest that way.

Renee thought she'd bested him at his own game. But he knew how things worked. His ex-wife had about as much writing talent as a chimpanzee throwing shit at the wall. First thing Allison would have done after reading the piece of trash would have been to hire a ghostwriter to punch it up. He could hear Allison now, telling some eager young writer working for pennies to "clean up this shit show of a manuscript."

No, Peter was the writer in the family. Renee might sell a lot of copies, but she'd never be able to out-write him. The question was, how did he prove that to her?

Through his windshield, he looked at the storefront. Posters advertising upcoming book signings filled the windows. He knew a couple of the authors they'd scheduled. He'd signed with one of them, Rex Franklin, at a convention in Dallas a few years earlier. The guy had gotten famous for writing novels based on true crimes. Peter asked if he felt limited by the facts of the stories he was telling. Rex laughed and lit a cigar. "Hell, no. These are novels. I just use the true stuff as a jumping off point. I change the names of the real victims and stuff and just run with it."

Peter had always trusted his imagination to provide ideas for his novels. He'd had horrible nightmares as a child that still plagued him when he'd had too much to drink. Those dreams alone had provided enough fodder for three novels. But now he rarely had any dreams at all, and the words that once had come so easy had dried up.

Coffee seeped from the pages of the folklore book and into the cheap fabric of the passenger seat. He'd bought the sensible compact sedan from a used-car lot after he'd sold his Range Rover to help pay for his divorce lawyer. Rex had a brand new Mercedes with heated leather seats that he'd paid for by telling other people's stories.

He picked up the book and ignored the odor of dark roast and wet paper. He ignored the slippery wetness of the cover and the way the pages rippled. But he could not ignore the quickening in his middle when he opened the pages to the section he'd read earlier—the part about the mysterious happenings in the coal mines.

He quickly read the story, which talked about a town in southern Virginia called Moon Hollow. There was an image on the front page of that chapter of a church with a shard of twisted metal instead of a cross on the steeple. It looked like the sort of place a bestselling horror story might be set. Rex's words came back to him. *I just use the true stuff as a jumping off point.*

He tossed the book in the seat, threw the car in gear, and backed out of the lot. All thoughts of the bar he'd planned on camping out in that afternoon evaporated. Instead, he steered his car in the direction of NC State's research library. On his way, he finally called his editor.

3
THE SCREAM

Ruby

THREE WEEKS after they buried Mama, Ruby got the girls ready for church. She oversaw Sis and Jinny putting on their best dresses, which also happened to be their only dresses. In a fit of twelve-year-old rebellion, Sissy had insisted on doing her own hair. Ruby didn't argue because she had her hands full braiding eight-year-old Jinny's corn-silk strands into braids. After warning them not to mess up their nice clothes, she sent them to watch TV, took a deep breath, and went out to the back porch.

Cotton Barrett sat in a rocking chair on the pitted wood of the porch. The roof leaked something fierce, but he didn't seem to notice the cold water dripping on his creased face. A cigarette smoldered in his left hand. Judging from the length of the ash, the old man had forgotten all about it. However, the empty liquor bottle in his right hand proved he hadn't forgotten about the white lightning he'd been nursing all night. Ruby hesitated on the threshold and took in the bluish cast to his face, which was punctuated by dark brown stubble.

"Daddy?" She wasn't sure if she'd chosen the soft tone so she wouldn't startle him or in the hope that he'd not hear her at all.

Those glassy eyes blinked once, twice before slowly tracking in her direction. The whites of his eyes were a sickly yellow shot through with red.

She swallowed. "We have to be getting to church soon."

No response.

"I pressed your shirt. It's on the bed with your Sunday britches."

He blinked heavily.

"Daddy?"

His mouth opened, but instead of a response, a whimper escaped. The sound should have made her feel something—a shiver up the spine or the dark bloom of her own grief or maybe the icy-hot sensation of pity deep in her gut. But after weeks of keeping the family together while he slowly fell apart, Ruby wasn't capable of feeling anything for him. The minute Mama died, something inside Ruby died, too.

While Daddy climbed into the bottom of a bottle, she'd taken care of her sisters and kept the bills paid and the house as clean as she was able. While he slept off a bender, she'd picked out the plain pine casket that became her mama's home for eternity.

Another sob followed the first and his body crumpled forward. The cigarette butt fell to the puddle at his feet and hissed before dying. Something hot and sharp snapped inside her. Searing heat burned off the cool detachment. She wanted to lunge at his throat and shake him 'til his brain rattled in his skull. But, even angry, she knew better than to get within arm's reach when he was in this mood.

Instead, she repeated, "We've got to get to church."

"Ain't goin'."

"You have to. If Deacon Fry—"

"Fuck Deacon Fry! He don't know what I'm goin' through."

"But you already missed two services." As a deacon in Christ the Redeemer Church, he was required to attend all services except in the case of illness or acts of God. Deacon Fry might forgive one or two absences on account of grieving, but three strikes equaled a sin. According to the head deacon, worship cured all of life's problems and washed all of a man's sins away.

"You have to go," she said.

His jaundiced eyes cleared and took on a darkness that scared her. "What did you say, girl?"

She swallowed hard. "Daddy, I—"

He rose faster than a man whose blood was eighty-proof should move. She bolted like a spooked animal. Before she'd made it two steps, iron hands caught her arms and swung her around. He jerked her roughly toward his face. His breath stank of whiskey fumes and something more rancid and sinister, like a rotting soul.

She held her breath and braced for the smack. No child grew up in Moon Hollow without knowing the sting of leather to flesh. But Daddy didn't remove his belt or raise his fist. Instead, he smiled like a snake. "You're getting too big fer yer britches, girl."

"Please," she whimpered. "I didn't mean to make you mad."

"I don't answer to you or Deacon Fry. If he asks where I am, you tell him one of our animals got loose." He shoved her away as if he couldn't stand the sight of her. "Take off that makeup before you go. I won't have no daughter of mine looking like a whore in the Lord's house."

She stumbled toward the safety of the kitchen. The creaky screen door slammed behind her. She grabbed a flour sack towel from the counter. Two years earlier, Mama had embroidered delicate yellow flowers along the edges. Now, Ruby shoved it between her lips. The dry fabric sucked the spit from her tongue. She bit into the cotton folds so hard her gums ached.

With the scent of Mama's lemony laundry detergent filling her nostrils and the curses of her drunken father filling her ears, she screamed until her lungs burned.

4

CROSSING THE THRESHOLD

Peter

Pine trees cast long shadows over the mountain road. Up here, the air was cooler, and recent rains intensified the sharp green scent of pine and the earthy perfume of wet leaves. He leaned an elbow out of the open window and turned up the radio. The reception was getting spotty, and the only station coming in clear was playing Hank Williams. It was the kind of music that made him long for a dark bar, a cold beer, and a lonely woman, but he hadn't seen a building, much less a woman, for miles.

The map he'd bought at the gas station in Asheville, the last major town he'd seen before crossing the border into Virginia, lay in a heap in the passenger seat. The cashier had asked where he was headed. When he said the name of the town, the old man had smiled and shook his head. "That map ain't going to do you no good. Must be a hundred hollers hidden up in them hills."

He bought the map anyway because it made him feel like he had a plan.

The car cruised around a wide bend in the road. Rhododendrons were just starting to bloom alongside mountain laurels at the bases of oaks and tulip poplars. The trees created walls of green that offered only brief glimpses of the rise and fall of hills as far as the eye could see.

He pressed harder on the accelerator. He wanted to fly.

Fly toward the story he'd come to find. But, more importantly, away from the worries he'd left behind in Raleigh. Renee lurked five hours behind him in the house they'd restored together in the Inner Beltline. He'd refinished the hardwoods himself and tiled the bathrooms under her gimlet gaze, but the sweat equity hadn't earned him forgiveness or a new key after she'd changed the locks.

Behind him farther still was New York, where his editor crafted emails and filled his voicemail with requests for book updates. After the initial conversations about the new story idea and his promise to deliver it by the end of the summer, he'd avoided contact. He convinced himself his creativity needed free rein, but really it was because Allison insisted on bringing up Renee every time they spoke. Her apologies rang hollow without a promise to cancel the memoir, or at least give him the right to read it before it hit the shelves.

He lifted his cell phone from the passenger seat to check if she'd called again, but, seeing the No Service warning, he laughed and tossed the damned thing onto the floorboards.

The lack of a signal prevented him from pulling up the written directions from the owner of the cabin, but he'd memorized her email.

Look for the wooden Moon Hollow sign and turn right. Follow that road until you see the church. You can't miss it.
—*Lettie Bascom*

He'd found the listing for the cabin in Moon Hollow a couple of weeks earlier. When he'd called about renting it, the

Bascom woman had sounded old enough to be Methuselah's mother, but she'd informed him that she had the only property for rent in the area. She'd gone on to demand letters of reference and a hefty deposit in cash to secure the two-week rental. But the place had looked perfect for his purposes, and he'd been feeling adventurous, so he'd jumped through her hoops and got his agent to write the recommendation.

"Are you certain you want to spend time alone in the wilds of Virginia?" His agent, Bill, had stuck with him through his early success and more recent slump. He was of the old school of career-building agents who believed you don't just dump a client because they were going through a rough patch. Plus, Bill was the majority partner in the agency, so he could do whatever the hell he wanted—including keeping a loser on his list. Still, Peter's ego didn't love being kept on the roster out of habit or, worse, pity.

"It's the only way this book's going to get written," he'd said. "Raleigh's too haunted for me right now. Besides, I won't be alone. The cabin is five minutes from town. I'll be back in a couple of weeks with the start of a bestseller for you."

He had to be back in time to teach summer school at Wake Tech. As much as he hated the necessity of that job, it would keep him afloat until his book hit it big.

"All right, Peter. I'll send the letter." A heavy sigh had come through the line. It was the same sigh that had preceded Bill informing him that sales of his last book hadn't met expectations.

He rounded a bend and saw a wooden sign on the right side of the road up ahead. The writing was so faded that he had to pull over and get out to read it.

When he stepped out of the car, his loafers gritted against the dirt and pine needles. He paused and listened. The complete silence of the mountain pass pressed in on him. His chest tightened with something close to dread, which confused him. Silence should feel peaceful, shouldn't it?

He wrote off the feeling as the by-product of having lived in cities for most of his life and approached the plywood sign. Red paint formed the words *Moon Hollow* and underneath that *Psalm 55:23*.

A narrow gravel road broke away from the highway about fifteen feet from where he stood. Surely that wasn't the road into town.

He got back in and inched the car forward to peer down the road. The tunnel created by the trees on either side of the shadowed lane prevented him from seeing where it led, but it didn't look like the sort of road one would take into a town. He put the car into gear and continued down the highway to find a proper exit. But two miles later, he gave up and turned back around.

He stopped the car beside the sign and watched it, as if it might suddenly offer up new information. In the mottled light, the drips of red paint on the sign looked like blood. His hyperactive imagination had helped him get three books published, but when it came to his life off the page, it was a nuisance. Since he wrote horror, a lot of people expected him to be a scary guy, but in reality, he was a bundle of neuroses camouflaged by a large ego. He spent most of his time terrified of the real world—a hazard of the fiction trade. In his books, he was the fickle god who could create or destroy according to his whim. The stark contrast between the control he had in his fictional worlds and his utter lack of power in the real world made time spent in the latter almost unbearable.

Still, that biblical sign was the sort of detail that made his imagination fire off like a bottle rocket. He grabbed the pad of paper he kept for such occasions and jotted down the chapter and verse for later.

It really did look like blood.

He closed his lids and rolled his eyes back and forth as if to wipe the image from the screen, but when he opened them again, those letters still spooked him.

Rebelling against his bastard of an imagination, he put his foot on the pedal. The car jerked, sliding on the gravel. He flipped on the headlights to fight the deepening shadows and pressed on toward Moon Hollow.

After about a quarter of a mile, the gravel gave way to dirt. Deep grooves in the surface indicated regular use by other vehicles. Half a mile later, the road curved sharply and gravel gave way to proper paving. As he emerged from the cover of the trees, he found himself at the top of a hill and began a slow descent into the valley. A few buildings and a church squatted in the hollow between two large hills, and on the way down, a few roads veered off with signs warning trespassers away. House-shaped shadows squatted among the thick trees and hills, but the closer he got to town, the nearer to the road the houses had been built.

It was still early, about eight in the morning, but a couple of porches along the way already featured gray-haired sentinels who waved arthritic claws as he passed. He waved back and felt some of his worries evaporate. So far, Moon Hollow seemed like something out of Rockwell's America.

A few shops lined the main road, but they failed to grab his attention. How could they when they competed with the church at the dead end of the only road in town?

According to his research, Christ the Redeemer Church had been the first structure built in Moon Hollow—even before Jeremiah Moon's house, which reportedly still stood further up the mountain. At the time, the population of Moon Hollow was five —Jeremiah, his wife Annie, and their three children—two boys and a girl. The youngest boy, Ian, died during a typhoid outbreak in 1887. Despite his relatively small family for the era,

Jeremiah built the church large enough to accommodate a congregation of nearly one hundred.

Once word spread across the mountain that Moon was building the church, people came to get a look at what folks in the region were calling "Moon's Folly." But strangely, the men who came to gape and tease were quickly charmed by the charismatic Jeremiah Moon and soon found themselves with hammer in hand. Thus, by the time the church was completed, it already had a full congregation.

The church was a marvel of mountain ingenuity. The wooden pews and altar were all carved from local hardwood. Thick pine trunks stripped of bark and polished to a high gloss criss-crossed overhead in the chapel. The original church didn't have glass windows but thin vellum covers that reportedly let in sickly sepia light. But the true masterpiece was the huge metal cross attached to the roof.

According to local lore, Jeremiah Moon had forged the metal himself. It had taken four teams of horses to hoist the massive cross to the roof, but once in place, it inspired several witnesses to fall to their knees and cry. More acerbic historians claimed the true miracle was that the wooden roof could support Jeremiah Moon's enormous ego. Still, once the church was complete, the population of the town exploded to ninety-seven in the span of a year. Times were good, spirits were high, and the future looked bright for the town that eventually became known as Moon's Hollow—later shortened to Moon Hollow— in honor of its founding father.

Peter knew this basic history and had seen a grainy black-and-white photograph of the church taken from a distance. None of this prepared him for seeing it in person. The structure before him bore little resemblance to descriptions he'd read of the original church. Over the years, as the population of the hollow grew, additions were added on to the main structure. The residents in charge of each expansion had cared little about architectural consistency. Some of the sections were covered with vinyl siding or patchwork shingles or cinder block. The original wooden chapel stood in the center of this hodgepodge. The gleaming pine of its glory days had blackened with time, and red stained glass replaced the original vellum. Still, the architectural anomalies and time-weathered pine weren't what captured Peter's imagination as he rolled toward the church.

Instead of a cross on the roof, there stood a massive hunk of twisted black metal, which scraped the sky like a scythe.

Peter squinted at the tip of the steeple. "What the hell?" he whispered.

The pitch-black metal sparked wickedly in the morning light. The grainy picture he'd seen didn't do it justice. He wasn't a religious man, but he associated churches with crosses and this odd detail unsettled him.

He braked the car at the intersection directly across from the church. After a few moments of idling at the curb, a horn's sharp retort shocked him from his study of the steeple. A battered blue pickup truck quivered in the rearview mirror. He waved and pulled out of the way, but instead of going around him, the vehicle pulled up even with his window.

A man with a time-eroded face and a cigarette hanging from thin lips stared at him through the passenger's window. Peter rolled down his with what he hoped was a nothing-to-see-here smile. "Sorry about that. I was admiring the church."

"Hmmph," the old man said, unimpressed. "You got business here, son?"

Peter hesitated. "I'm supposed to be renting a house on Bascom Road. Don't suppose you could point me in that direction?"

The man's face cleared as if Peter had spoken some secret code. "Ah, you're that author fella! Lettie had to go see about her sister in Blacksburg for a couple of days. She left the keys for ya at the church office with the deacon. You can pick 'em up after services."

He'd expected there to be some attention from the townsfolk over his temporary residence in Moon Hollow, but he hadn't expected everyone to be in on the arrangements he'd made. "My name's Peter West."

"Bunk Foote." When the man raised his arm, he touched the brim of his baseball cap with a double-pronged prosthesis instead of a hand.

"Nice to meet you," he said, avoiding the urge to stare at the metal pincers. "What time is church over?"

"Depends on how long Deacon Fry's sermon goes." The old man chuckled. "You can park 'round the side of the church. See ya in there."

As the pickup pulled away toward the lot, Peter realized that the old man expected him to attend church. He considered ignoring the assumption and killing time until services let out. But something told him the entire town would know he'd arrived the instant Bunk Foote parked and got inside the church, so his absence at services would definitely be noticed.

With a resigned sigh, he put the car in Drive and pointed it toward the lot where Bunk already leaned against his truck and waited for him.

5

A WOLF ENTERS THE FLOCK

Deacon Fry

THE BLUE RIDGE MOUNTAINS had been around longer than men—longer than most beasts, too. Lots of stories had been written about the bad luck of the people there. Poverty, illiteracy, illness, accidents, and tragedies. Some said the land itself was cursed. Others believed the mountain people were the victims of government and industry more interested in raping the hills than helping the people who lived and loved and lost there.

But Deacon Fry knew the real reason: The devil lived in those mountains.

He was not a man who believed in pretty metaphors. Fanciful talk was for women and children. Real men spoke in concrete language and trusted logic more than feelings, except when it came to faith in God. Men didn't speak of things that scared them, either. That was why he had never told anyone what really happened in the woods when he was eight years old.

But for some reason, as he looked out over the congregation

that Sunday morning in May, memory of that long-ago winter haunted his memory.

The sun so bright through the trees' blackened bones. The smoky, cold air scraping in and out of his lungs as he struggled to climb over deadfalls. The shouts of his little brother, Isaac, begging him to slow down—*please, Virgil—Virgil, I'm gonna tell Ma!*

When evil showed itself, its face was like a television screen blizzard that buzzed with static. His eyes burned and his bladder surrendered and his mind whispered a single word: *Evil*.

"Deacon Fry?"

A throat cleared at his shoulder. Pulling himself back to the present, he shifted his attention from the hymnal he'd been pretending to study to the face of Deacon Smythe.

"We're ready for you, sir." Smythe's jowls quivered as if he was bracing himself for a reprimand. Sweat seeped through the cheap cotton of his shirt. He was not an elegant man, but he was malleable, which made him useful.

"Thank you, Brother Smythe." He strode toward the pulpit. On his way, he spared a glance for Reverend Peale, who was already half-asleep in his chair. At seventy-three, the good reverend found the rigors of watching over such a large flock exhausting, which was why the generous Deacon Fry had insisted on taking over delivery of the weekly sermon.

At the pulpit, he took his time opening the Bible his daddy had given him on his eighteenth birthday. He cleared his throat and lifted the glass of water to prepare his voice for delivering the Good Word. As he raised the glass, he let his gaze roam over his church.

His wife, Sharon, sat in the front row. The sun coming through the red stained glass tinted both her bleached hair and the lace collar of her dress pink. Beside her, their daughter, Sarah Jane, leaned to whisper something to Jack Thompson.

All the girls of a certain age in Moon Hollow—as well as some of the older women who should know better—giggled whenever Jack walked by. The former quarterback of the county high school had the All American good looks of a young man whose glory days were already behind him. He'd been dating the deacon's daughter for several months. According to Bob Truman, the foreman at Big Stone Gap Mining Company, Jack would be starting his new job in the mines that very afternoon. Sharon believed it wouldn't be long until he popped the question. Deacon Fry had never prayed so hard for something *not* to happen.

Dragging his gaze from Jack, he noted Ruby Barrett and her little sisters in the row behind his family. Once again, their father hadn't joined them for services, despite the fact that Sissy and Jinny would be singing during that day's service. It was time to go have a chat with Cotton. Too many people were whispering about the man's overindulgence. He couldn't continue to be given a pass on account of his grief. Rose Barrett had been dead a full month. Not long enough for the man to forget, but long enough for him to make an effort at living again.

After a moment, he realized several members of his congregation were shifting restlessly in the pews and casting glances toward the rear of the chapel. He scanned the area until he spotted the issue.

The stranger was wearing a T-shirt in the house of the Lord. Lettie had told him the author she'd rented her cabin to would be arriving that day. Lettie being Lettie, she'd ignored his advice to forgo renting to a total stranger. Now, seeing him slouching in the pew as if he were in a bar instead of church, the deacon was inclined to believe his predictions were justified. How could he be expected to trust anyone who earned money by selling lies?

Over the heads of the deacon's flock, the author met his gaze without flinching. Clearly it would be up to him to rid the town of that man's bad influence. He closed his Bible and stuck the sermon he'd prepared back in his coat pocket. It was time to start letting the author know he was not welcome in Deacon Fry's town.

"This morning I'd like to talk about the dangers of inviting the devil into our lives."

6
GHOSTS OF COMFORT PAST

Ruby

WHEN THE TIME came for Jinny and Sissy to take the stage, Ruby nudged them out of the pew like a proud hen. But once they stood before the congregation, her pride morphed into something that made her ashamed. Bright green envy choked her pride like kudzu. Used to be, it was her standing up there singing hymns while Mama smiled so proud at her from the pews.

She clasped her hands in her lap and smiled at Jinny, who was looking her way for encouragement. Sissy stood tall and raised her chin as if daring the congregation to look away. She didn't have the high, clear voice Ruby and Jinny had inherited from their mama, but she made up for it with a stage presence that rivaled any popstar diva.

The song was one of Ruby's least favorite hymns. The girls sang the first verse together, and the rest of the congregation joined in for the chorus. Ruby mouthed the words because it was too painful to listen to her own voice. Her song sounded wrong and lonely without the mountain or her Mama to sing harmony.

As the hymn reached its end, Sissy's voice cracked on a high note. Ruby's smile didn't slip a bit—even when Sarah Jane swung around with her accusing eyes. Sarah Jane's scorn was nothing new. For some reason, she'd targeted Ruby as her favorite victim ever since kindergarten. Her snide comments and passive cruelties caused a lot of tears for young Ruby, but now that they were older, she couldn't understand why the town's sweetheart bothered. Sarah Jane had everything: blond hair, a pretty face, and the money and influence that resulted from being the only child of the town's most important man. The money and power didn't impress Ruby much, but the hair and the face had earned Sarah Jane the one thing Ruby secretly coveted most.

She stared at the back of Jack's perfect golden head perched above a set of broad shoulders. She wasn't blind to his looks, but she knew a side of him that few others in town had ever seen. She had no right to but, sometimes, when she felt so small and alone that it felt like she'd disappear altogether, she wished for that secret Jack to come and make her feel seen again.

The first time she met the secret Jack, it was just after his daddy died. They'd been eight years old, and she found him crying down by the river. He had escaped the post-funeral party at his mom's trailer to go mourn in peace. When she found him, he was slumped on a rotting log as he sobbed into his hands. Before she could back away he looked up and caught her. She expected him to yell at her for seeing him so weak. She'd never seen a boy cry before, and every time her daddy got upset he let blows fall instead of tears. So when Jack asked her to sit with him, she'd been too taken aback to answer. He asked again and scooted over to make some room for her.

After she joined him, they'd talked a little bit about his

daddy, but mostly they just sat in companionable silence and watched the water rush by. When he started crying again, she reached for his hand. He squeezed it hard but she didn't complain. Being there with Jack felt so good, she hummed the river's song for him until the sun went down and they had to run home.

After that evening, Jack went back to his buddies and Ruby went back to her books, but sometimes she caught him looking at her with soft eyes. She never pretended those glances were filled with anything other than gratitude for the kindness she'd shown him. Eventually, Jack found football and began his ascent to athletic godhood, and the soft looks stopped altogether once his status earned him the favor of Sarah Jane Fry.

On the day of Mama's funeral, Ruby had gone back down by the river seeking comfort. She wasn't sure how long she cried there, alone, before he came, but once he was there, she realized she'd been waiting for him the whole time. He put his arm around her shoulders, and she held on tight while grief tried to sweep her away like a river current. He didn't sing to her, but he whispered promises that everything would be okay and she believed him.

After the sun went down, he took her hand and walked her home. By the mailbox at the end of the driveway, he kissed her cheek and smiled a smile that made her believe in happy endings again. But then he'd strolled off into the shadows and never looked back.

In the weeks since that night, she hadn't seen him much. She kept waiting for those soft looks to start again, but they never did. The few times he looked her way during church, his eyes had looked normal and his smile friendly, not soft, not filled with promises like she'd hoped they'd be.

The girls' song ended and Deacon Fry joined them on the

altar steps. "May you all go in peace, and may your words and your deeds be guided by Christ Almighty."

"Amen." Ruby's whisper was swallowed by the enthusiastic responses of the entire congregation.

Ruby stood with everyone else. The deacon led her sisters down the aisle and Reverend Peale followed at a meandering pace with the help of Deacon Smythe. People began shaking hands and saying their goodbyes so they could begin the process of leaving. In the front pew, Sarah Jane embraced her mother while Jack turned to shake hands with Bunk Foote. When that was done, Jack caught her eye and smiled. "Girls sounded real good, Ruby," he said. "Sure do miss your singing, though."

Heat bloomed in her cheeks and words tangled on her tongue. Was he talking about the song she hummed for him down by the river?

"It's been a couple of months since you sang at services," he added.

Realizing he'd been talking about religious hymns and not secret mountain music, she cleared her throat. Under the wash of embarrassment was the thin ice of shame. "I'm too old now," she lied.

"Jack?" Sarah Jane's hands wrapped around his waist and she turned to join the conversation. "We need to get going if you're going to be there on time."

To Ruby, he said, "I'm starting my new job in the mines today."

"Are you nervous?"

Jack's daddy had died from black lung after working every day of his adult life in those mines. She really wanted to ask if he were scared but resisted. It was the sort of question she'd only have the courage to ask if they'd been alone by the river, not in the middle of church with the whole town eavesdropping.

He tipped his chin and opened his mouth to say something,

but Sarah Jane interrupted. "Of course not. He's excited. Right, Jacky?"

Jack winced. Ruby wasn't sure if it was because of the nickname or the fact she'd just answer for him like he was a baby. "Actually, I'm excited *and* nervous."

Suddenly, inexplicably, she was scared for him. Before she could think better of it, she reached out and touched his hand. "Just be careful, okay?"

He froze, looking down at their hands. Before he could react or she could take it back, Sarah Jane grabbed her fingers and pulled them away.

"I swear, Ruby, you're such a downer." Her laughter was grating and forced. "This is a huge opportunity for Jack."

Ruby felt embarrassed for Sarah Jane and sorry for Jack. He still hadn't said anything but he refused to look at either of the girls.

"Anyway," he said, "they train us real good so we'll be plenty safe."

Sarah Jane changed the subject. "Where is your daddy today?"

Ruby's insides went cold with shame. "He's not feelin' too good."

Instead of letting it go, Sarah Jane said, "Hungover, you mean."

"Sarah Jane," Jack said in a warning tone.

"What? It's true, right?"

Ruby pulled herself taller and looked the bitch in the eye. "I need to go find my sisters. God bless you, Sarah Jane." To Jack, she said, "Good luck." She tried to convince herself he needed the luck for dealing with Sarah Jane his whole life, but deep down she understood the real threat to Jack was down in the mines. That's where her daddy's problems started. Now, his lungs were as black as the coal he'd hauled for twenty years, but at one time he'd probably breathed as easy as Jack did now with his healthy pink lungs and life spread out before him like a golden promise. She prayed Jack would be one of the ones who got out before the blackness crept in.

She longed to go to the ridge and ask the mountain for a sign, some glimmer of hope, but the mountain had fallen silent. Besides, lately she'd come to learn that hope was for other people. So she marched away, leaving Jack to deal with the consequences of the fate he'd chosen.

7
TESTS

Peter

PETER HAD HOPED to escape before the service started and come back later to get the key, but then that deacon had speared him with a suspicious glare and started in on his sermon. The words still tainted the chapel's air like a stealthy fart.

When a man starts imagining he's the source of creativity he starts thinking of himself as a god and that's when the devil comes a-callin'.

To say he wasn't looking forward to shaking the man's hand was an understatement, but he needed his key to the cabin. If Bunk were right, there'd be no escaping an introduction to Deacon Fry.

When the service concluded, he sat in the pew while the parishioners filed out. The words of the final hymn, which had been sung by two rugrats, still echoed in the chapel.

> *Would you be free from the burden of sin?*
> *There's power in the blood, power in the blood;*

Would you o'er evil a victory win?
There's wonderful power in the blood.

Hearing those words coming from two little girls had sent a creeping chill up his neck. No one else in the congregation appeared to be disturbed by it, which told him that sort of thing happened all the time.

Part of him wanted to get out of the pew and escape into the sunshine, but he knew he'd get stuck waiting in line to meet the deacon. So he sat, waited for his turn, and observed the good people of Moon Hollow. Everyone who passed by stared openly at him, as if he were a freak in a sideshow. The idea struck him as funny, since he wasn't the one who sang about blood and believed art was the devil's playground.

There's wonderful power in the blood.

As he watched them file past, he realized that each of those suspicious faces was lily white. His own white skin meant he wasn't used to being an outsider, but in Moon Hollow he wasn't just an outsider—he was *the stranger*. Maybe that's why it was unsettlingly easy to imagine what might happen if a stranger with the wrong skin color stumbled into town.

Talk about the makings of a horror novel.

He would have jotted down the idea, but even he wasn't enough of an asshole to think that was his story to tell.

The only resident who didn't stare at him on the way out of the chapel was a mousy teenager who stormed down the aisle without a look in his direction. Her demeanor reminded him of a librarian who'd just told off some unruly kids for being too loud. Her indignant posture was the most remarkable thing about her, but she looked so determined he found himself looking over the crowd for the poor soul she'd just told off. He didn't see anyone who looked especially indignant or wounded, though, so he gave up and went back to enduring more stares and wondering how long it would be until he could escape to the privacy of his cabin.

Remembering the sign he'd seen on the road to town, he pulled out the pocket notebook where he'd jotted down the chapter and verse number. He pulled a Bible from a shelf in the back of the pew and flipped through until he found Psalm 55:23.

> *But you, O God,*
> *Shalt bring them down into the pit of destruction.*
> *Bloodthirsty and deceitful men shall not live out half their days;*
> *But I will trust in thee.*

He slammed the Bible shut and shoved it back into the shelf.

That gem, along with the lyrics of that creepy hymn, would make itself at home in the dark place in his head where he kept all of the props for his personal horror matinees. It was his safe place—had been since he could remember. His subconscious, where he played with his imaginary friends—or characters, as he called them as an adult. It was the room of miracles where all his best ideas appeared like images on a cave wall; and the place of evil, where he imagined all the worst things that he could never speak about in public.

A throat cleared nearby. A woman with blue-gray hair wearing a pink polyester suit and white shoes waited to speak with him. Her spectacles—they were too prim to call glasses—reflected red sparks from the chapel's stained glass.

"Mr. West?" Her voice was surprisingly strong for such a petite package. "I'm Mrs. McDuffy—Deacon Fry's assistant." She said this last part as if Peter should be very impressed with her title.

Her hand felt cold and bony, like a bird's claw. "Pleased to meet you."

"If you'll come with me, I'll introduce you to the deacon and we'll see about getting your key."

After that sermon, he was about as eager to meet the deacon as he'd be to make the acquaintance of the guy who'd given him his first one-star review. "I'm sure he's very busy. You can just give me the key and I'll meet him another time."

Her smile was as warm as an ice cube. "I'm afraid that's not possible. The deacon has the key on his person."

"Of course he does." He held out a hand. "After you."

Her eyes narrowed and she hesitated, as if she suspected he was tricking her somehow. But when he stood very still and put every ounce of sincerity he possessed into his smile, she finally executed a curt nod and walked back out of the pew and marched up the aisle.

Peter kept his shoulders loose and his gait easy. Yet, his entire left side felt hot from the attention of the remaining congregation. Now that he was on the move, they sped down the aisle because everyone, it seemed, wanted to witness the moment when Deacon Fry met the stranger.

Too soon, he emerged from the sanctuary and into the cramped vestibule. The light from the open double doors leading outside blinded him temporarily. By the time he reached the door, he regained enough vision to see the hulking silhouette in the doorway. He blinked and waited behind Mrs. McDuffy while the deacon finished speaking to a young couple.

Deacon Fry appeared to be in his mid-sixties judging from the wrinkles around his eyes and mouth. He had a skull covered in glorious white hair, thick and luxurious as the pelt of an artic fox. Actually, now that Peter thought about it, the man's pinched nose reminded him of a fox's snout, too.

The deacon's hand rested possessively on the girl's shoulder. Though clearly in her late-teens, she'd twisted her brunette hair into a bun and wore a dress that would have been more appropriate on a schoolmarm. The way she looked up at him made Peter wonder if he was her father. It was just as likely she admired him because of his position in the church, but her nose, though not as pronounced as the deacon's, had a familiar point. Despite her conservative get-up, there was something about her posture that hinted at a wildness under all that calico.

The young man with them had a corn-fed physique. Peter couldn't see his face clearly, but the way all the girls passing him cast glances under their lashes suggested the kid was the town hunk. Judging from the coldness in the older man's gaze as he listened to something the boy said, the town hunk had set his sights on the deacon's daughter, but the deacon wasn't too thrilled by the prospect.

Once the young people were gone, Mrs. McDuffy stepped in front of the old couple who were next in line. She didn't even look at them or apologize for the slight, and they didn't raise a stink. They simply waited patiently in the vestibule's unnatural silence.

McDuffy spoke in a low tone, which lifted the deacon's gaze in Peter's direction. He felt a sudden urge to cover himself—to shield his sins from those eyes.

"Mr. West!" Deacon Fry's voice cut through the heavy air like lightning.

Peter wasn't a religious man, so it wasn't the deacon's position in the small church that had him jumping to action. However, he recognized the sound of power and the promise of retribution in a man's voice. He'd heard it enough growing up to still be a little afraid of it, even though he was a man full-grown himself.

The deacon's hand was not large, but it had a firm grip. Peter met the man in the eye and met that grip with equal pressure. "Deacon Fry, it's a pleasure."

Their hands separated and they squared off under the gaze

of maybe a quarter of the parishioners looking on. Something told Peter the rest of the town would hear of this moment before sundown.

Closer now, he noticed another distinguishing feature on the Deacon Fry's face—a patchy scar in the center of his forehead. The light coming through the open doors hit the shiny surface of the pink skin.

"Our Lettie said you were renting the old Bascom Road cabin for a spell."

Peter forced himself to stop looking at the scar. "Yes, sir."

"A book, she said?" the deacon prompted.

"A novel."

"May I ask what brought you to Moon Hollow for such a project?"

"I needed some peace and quiet to focus on my work," Peter lied. Something told him that sharing that a book of hauntings and folk tales brought him to town would only invite scorn—or suspicion, more of it, anyway, from the good deacon. "Lettie's cabin came up on a website that advertises mountain rentals. It looked perfect."

"Where do you hail from, Mr. West?"

"Peter, please. I live in Raleigh."

"Hmm. Never been, myself."

"It's lovely this time of year. But not nearly as beautiful as Moon Hollow. Quite a charming town you've got here."

Instead of pleasing the man, Peter's praise made his eyes narrow. Before he could respond, Mrs. McDuffy came forward and whispered something in the deacon's ear. When she retreated, he turned back to Peter. "I'd love to keep chatting, Mr. West, but I have a luncheon appointment with the Deacon Council. Come by my office tomorrow morning, say, 10 a.m.?"

"Why?"

The deacon paused, as if unused to being questioned. "So we

can get to know each other, of course. I'm very interested in this novel you're writing."

"Oh? Are you much of a reader?"

The corner of the deacon's mouth lifted a fraction, but it didn't look like a smile at all. "Of course! My favorite authors are Matthew, Mark, Luke, and John, Mr. West." He held out his hand, and this time, when Peter shook it, the grip was punishing. "See you in the morning."

Peter could not think of a meeting he'd ever looked forward to less.

"Wait," he said, "the key?"

"We don't lock doors in Moon Hollow, Mr. West." The deacon half-turned to acknowledge the question. "We pride ourselves on that."

Peter gritted his teeth against the string of curses just itching to jump out.

"Until tomorrow, Mr. West." With that, he turned to greet the couple behind Peter, which left him with no choice but to slink out of the church and let the good deacon have the last word.

8

IN THE BELLY OF THE BEAST

Jack

THE HARD HAT weighed as much as a boulder. Jack adjusted the brim and checked the switch that would turn on his headlamp. His gloved fingers fumbled with the mechanism a couple of times before the reassuring click sounded, but the sunlight swallowed the meager beams. He turned toward Old Fred. "My light workin'?"

Old Fred smiled, revealing gray teeth interrupted by large black voids. He dipped his chin in response to the question before asking one of his own. "Ya nervous?"

Jack shook his head. "No, sir."

Old Fred elbowed him in the ribs. "Bullshit. E'eryone's scared their first time. Nothing ta be shamed of."

His chin rose. "I'm not everyone."

A phlegmy chuckle escaped the broken picket fence of Fred's smile. "That ain't a football helmet, son. The mines don't care how many touchdowns you scored."

The reminder of his glory days caused Jack's chest to tighten.

A slideshow of his greatest victories on the field rushed behind his eyes. Then, slower, the first day at Virginia Tech. The classes that moved too fast for him to follow. Eating candy bars in his dorm room while those who could afford a food plan enjoyed hot meals in the dining hall. Getting cut from the team because he'd failed two classes. "Besides," coach had said, spitting a long stream of shit-brown tobacco at Jack's feet, "your legs been weak lately." Then, the agonizing drive away from campus, watching his future slip further and further out of his reach in the rearview.

The whistle cut through his recollections like a steam burn.

"Time to go." Old Fred tugged on Jack's sleeve and walked toward the tram.

For the first time, Jack wondered if it had been wise to sign up for deep mountain duty. Most rookie miners got the safer, and lower-paying, jobs—scraping coal into buckets in shafts closer to the surface. Dangerous deep mine work paid more, which meant the veterans got first dibs. But Jack had been given his pick of jobs. Some of the other miners had muttered under their breath. He heard them but pretended not to. They weren't wrong to resent him. He resented him too. His daddy had toiled for years to earn his place in the deep mines. But one word from the mine foreman's buddy, Deacon Fry, and Jack had been handed the plum job.

The tram resembled a steel centipede. Each single-person car was no wider than a man's shoulders. Jack ducked into a car halfway down the line. All around him, the other miners chatted about sports or the weather. None of them seemed the least bit concerned about the prospect of plunging thousands of feet into the earth. He couldn't imagine ever getting to the point when he'd feel casual about something like that. All the dark and the cold down there, like a grave. The choking air that turned a man's lungs to coal and buried him long before his time. Had his daddy promised himself the job was only temporary, too? Or had he simply resigned himself to spending his life digging his own grave?

Jack settled his butt on the hard seat and placed his small cooler between his boots. After church, Sarah Jane had presented him with the red Igloo filled with sandwiches, chips, cookies, and sodas. "Daddy says all the miners need lots of calories down there."

He'd accepted the gift with a smile, but he didn't tell her that "Daddy" had lied. Miners took food with them for the same reason they stored emergency oxygen tanks down in the tunnels.

Old Fred was in the car in front of Jack. He turned around and flipped his thumb up. Jack returned the gesture. He didn't bother pretending to look excited.

"Respirator," Old Fred called. He watched until Jack checked the gauges and gave him another thumbs up. Jack noticed Old Fred's respirator hung from the back of his rig, instead of in a spot where he could easily reach it once they were down the shaft. The old man had been working the mines more than thirty years. He probably hadn't breathed oxygen that wasn't tainted by coal powder or cigarette smoke since the Reagan era.

The tram jerked into motion. He started but caught himself. A quick look around confirmed that none of his coworkers had seen him. Only the mountain, with its hole that gaped like an empty eye socket, had witnessed his fear. He wondered if that was worse.

Closer to the entrance, the air was thick with coal dust. It coated the inside of Jack's nose and gritted against his teeth. He pushed the respirator over his mouth and pulled his goggles down over his eyes to protect them from the sting. The lenses of the eyewear distorted his vision until it appeared as if he were swimming through murky water.

The tram's wheels squeaked against the metal track, and the rocking motion didn't do much to settle Jack's nerves. Inside his gloves, his hands sweated and rubbed against the nubby grain of the interior. The eye socket loomed ahead, like a sightless Cyclops. He closed his lids to block out the image and took a deep breath of filtered air. When he opened his eyes again, the entrance was closer, and the opening looked less like an empty eye and more like a hungry mouth.

The tram reached the opening with both agonizing slowness and nerve-wracking speed. One moment, sunlight spilled into the tram from both sides, and the next, the hole swallowed all light, sucking him down into its cold, black throat.

The watery shadows conjured a memory of the first time he dove into the old swim hole near Moon Hollow. His friend Dinkus had dared him—double-dog dared him—to jump first. When he'd hesitated on the edge of that deep chasm of cold dark, Dinkus called him a pussy. If there had been one thing that scared Jack more than that swimming hole, it was being a pussy.

The water had punched him like a fist in the chest, forcing the air from his lungs. Water flavored with dirt and algae filled his mouth and choked him. A split second of complete fear passed—I'm drowning! Oh, God!—and then his legs had kicked and kicked, scissoring through the frigid water until—Thank God, thank you, sweet Lord!—his head had broken the surface into the light. He would never forget the benediction of warm sun on his face while his lower half shivered in the icy, dark water.

But now, no matter how hard Jack kicked and prayed, he wouldn't see the sun again for a long time. His first shift lasted from noon until 10:00 p.m. He expected that by the time he emerged from the mine, he'd be just as relieved to see the moon as he'd been to see the sun that day twelve years earlier.

Inside the main tunnel, support beams reinforced the rock walls and ceiling. Christ the Redeemer Church had a vaulted ceiling, too. But in the mines, instead of the Lord's Supper, the worshippers took coal as communion. Like those tasteless wafers Reverend Peale handed out, each lump of coal promised future salvation in exchange for their sacrifices.

The tram paused for the large metal door leading into the tunnels to open, and then it rocked forward through the gate into the underworld. Once the tram made it through, the massive door closed behind them, blocking out all natural light.

They descended into the working tunnels, where halogen lights glared along a large conveyor belt that belched coal up to the surface. As his car passed, one of the men looked up. The respirator and goggles concealed the man's identity. He realized that the man couldn't identify him either. The mines made strangers of them all.

We're drones. Drone ants, maintaining the hill. Only instead of working for a queen, we toil for kings of commerce.

The man at the conveyer belt didn't wave or nod. He just lowered his head as if he'd not seen the tram grinding past.

The lights disappeared as they pressed on farther into the earth.

Jack realized he was trembling, and it had nothing to do with the tram's vibrations.

The wheels clicking and clacking and the loud drone of generators created a wall of sound. He retreated into himself, where the only noise was the beat of his heart echoing in his ears. How many times had he run onto a football field with that primal rhythm pounding against his eardrums? Back then he'd associated the sound with victory, but now he could only think of drowning.

"Pussy!" Dinkus shouted in his memory.

Something welled in his center. It was the place where he

always found his resolve on the football field in the fourth quarter when the score was not in his favor. It was the birthplace of grit, and Jack called upon it now to steel his nerves.

Dinkus hadn't known shit about grit. That asshole had died in that damned watering hole three years later after he'd drunk too much of his daddy's moonshine. He'd hit his head on an outcropping of rock and sunk to the bottom. Jack always wondered if Dinkus had died instantly or if he'd tried to swim for the surface. If there was one thing he'd learned in his life, it was that there were two kinds of people: sinkers and swimmers.

Losing his ride had felt a lot like sinking. Moving back into his mama's trailer had felt a lot like drowning, too. It was only after Sarah Jane threatened to break up with him that he realized it was time to start pushing for the surface again. She'd been the one to suggest a job at the mines. Her daddy could call in a favor. It wouldn't be for too long, she'd promised. Only until he could afford to buy her a ring and maybe buy a nice little plot of land for them to live on as husband and wife.

Jack might be a dumb jock, but he wasn't stupid. He took the job, but not for the reasons Sarah Jane wanted. He had his own plan. Once he had enough money saved, he'd convince her to run away with him. If she refused, he'd just go alone and transform himself into the kind of man she couldn't refuse. But staying in Moon Hollow wasn't an option.

He sat up straighter in the tram. Whatever surprises those mines held couldn't be worse than the prospect of spending the rest of his life under Deacon Fry's thumb. He'd put his head down and do his duty, and he'd know that each lump of coal he stole from the earth was a down payment on his freedom.

9

DARK MOON INTERLUDE

When night falls in Moon Hollow, mists roll in and blanket the hills with quiet. If the moon is round and full, shadows dance on the edges of vision. But on moonless nights, all is shadow.

There was no moon on Peter's first night in town, and the quiet mists surrounding the cabin porch seemed to have eyes. As he rocked in the metal glider, the porch's uneven boards creaked, and the trees responded with groans and whispers.

When he'd come to Moon Hollow, he'd yearned for silence as a sailor longs for the sound of the sea. But now, sitting alone with the aggressive shadows and the seeing mist and the audible lack of human white noise, he realized he didn't like it at all.

He considered playing music while he read, but he resisted the urge. Something in his gut told him the racket might invite attention he didn't want. There were no neighbors within sight of the cabin, but there was that palpable sense he was not alone.

He picked up the book of folklore he'd brought with him. Since he'd bought it on that day with Renee, he'd read every story—some more than once, but he felt no closer to knowing what story he aimed to tell. He hoped that soaking in the scenery and talking to the locals would inspire him.

Sitting alone in the dark with stories about demons and malevolent faeries made his restless imagination shift into overdrive, but he felt no particular urge to write. Instead, he had an overwhelming desire to gather his things, throw them in his shitty car, and leave Moon Hollow far behind in the rear view.

It was only the nauseating promise of shame that kept him rooted. How could he face his life if Renee won because he was too scared of the dark to write his own story?

So on he sat, rocking and listening to the night sing its dark songs.

———

HIGH ABOVE TOWN, on a lonely ridge reached by a solitary logging road, Granny Maypearl stepped out the back door of her cottage. Her old coon dog, Billy, brushed past her ankles and lumbered down the steps to look for chickens to vex in the yard. But the chickens were all dreaming in their coop, so he plopped down in the dirt to wait for his mistress to finish her business.

Maypearl looked up at the sky, which had plenty of stars but no moon. She took a deep breath and waited for the night to share its secrets.

She bent down and set a basket on the top step. A dark moon always made the mountain spirits go looking for trouble. To stay on their good side, she'd prepared an offering to leave on the back steps. The cookies and small crock of wild cat should do the trick. With Decoration Day coming soon, it was important to stay on the spirits' good sides.

She stepped off the porch and walked across the chicken yard toward the tree line. She didn't bother with a flashlight to guide her way. The path had been forged by her own two feet over the decades, and she could step over each root and log with her eyes closed. Billy followed along more slowly, his sensitive nose easily distracted by the scent of mushrooms and a lichen-covered log that served as multi-family housing for woodland creatures.

Mist tickled her ankles all the way to the small bridge that spanned the narrow stream. She stepped onto the rough-hewn boards and turned her face to the west.

Her eyes closed and her hands rose into the cool night air. The wind kicked up and swirled around her, making her thick gray hair dance around her head like the mountain mist. The air smelled of green water, brown earth, and the steely tang of ozone that always accompanied the mountain's song. The wind whispered confidences in her ears. The water babbled below, eager to share its secrets, too. Maypearl listened to them all.

When she opened her eyes, she smiled and ruffled Billy's shaggy coat. "Company's comin'." She blew out a breath to still the quickening in her belly. "Someone's leaving us, too."

Billy chuffed out a low bark. She looked out toward the inky darkness. Given what she'd learned, she half-expected to see a specter moving among the black trunks, but the mountain was too old to worry about mortal time. It could be hours or a few days until the portents came to pass. Either way, she'd best start preparing.

"Tomorrow, we've got to make some pie," she said to Billy, "and prepare for another funeral."

―――

IN THE BIG house on the main rise above Moon Hollow, Deacon Fry looked out over his town. With no moon to reflect off the rooftops and all the businesses closed, the buildings seemed to disappear into the shadows and the mist. He wondered if this was the same view Jeremiah Moon enjoyed as he looked out over the town two hundred years earlier. Either way, he had faith his ancestor used the same word to describe the buildings and all the souls in them: Mine.

On his desk, a stack of papers waited for his attention. That author fellow, Peter West, grinned up from the top page. In the headshot, he wore a tweed blazer with a black turtleneck and smiled at the camera like he was having impure thoughts.

He looked like a man used to female readers hanging on his every word. Lots of men, too, hoping some of his cool would rub off on them.

The devil never appeared in a homely costume, did he?

The cup in the deacon's hand held coffee. He normally didn't like to indulge in caffeine after sundown, but that night was an exception. From the moment that writer walked into his church, a weight had settled in his chest. The mass wasn't large, but, like a tumor, it didn't need to be large to be dangerous. No, he realized, it wasn't like a tumor at all, but a small black seed. If he wanted to prevent that seed from blooming into a predatory vine, he'd have to expunge Peter West from the garden altogether.

He took a sip and savored the bitterness. He'd have to be careful about how he handled Mr. West. Yes, very careful. A man who made his living off manipulating people with words could cause a lot of trouble for a town of God-fearing people.

———

Up on Cemetery Hill, a shadow moved among the tombstones. This specter didn't glide or float over the ground; he staggered and cursed, and the fumes emanating from his clothes were quite flammable.

Cotton Barrett tripped and skidded to his knees in front of a weathered headstone. "Shit."

He leaned in to look at the inscription. The words blurred

and doubled. Cursing, he fished in his pocket for the lighter, a Zippo given to him by his pappy. The steel wheel snicked once, twice before catching. The flame coated the headstone in an orange glow that reminded him of Halloween. The stone was so old the engraving had been eroded away by rain, wind, and age. He squinted and held the lighter closer, but only could make out an image of a cherub and the dates 1812-1813. He slapped the metal lid closed to tamp the flame and burned his fingers in the process. "Fuckin' thing."

Standing was no longer an option, so he crawled. His progress over the graves was hampered by frequent pauses to drink from the bottle in his hand. Pine needles and twigs dug into his knees, but he didn't care. The firewater had numbed his skin, but physical pain didn't compare to the ache in his heart. Some agony even alcohol couldn't numb.

"Rose," he cried. "Rose!" The words scraped his throat, leaving it raw. Tears blinded his vision, making the cemetery a kaleidoscope of grays and blacks. There was no light here. No color. No hope.

"Rose."

Exhausted, he collapsed on a mound of earth and rolled over on his back. The pebbles covering the grave dug into his spine. He ignored them and pulled the bottle to his dry lips. The alcohol burned his skin as it spilled onto his face. His tongue darted out to catch every drop.

He opened his eyes. Through the blurry shapes of trees rising over him, a single bright spot glowed. Not the moon. Damn the moon, anyway. No, that light was special. That light was his beautiful Rose.

He looked up from the grave of his life and yearned toward the Rose light shining her love down on his body. "Rose," he whispered.

His left hand lifted toward the light, but he couldn't touch it.

The light and Rose were beyond his reach. Tears spilled freely from his eyes to mix with the whiskey on his cheeks.

He rolled over on his side, like a child, and cried his grief on the grave of his dead love, Rose.

———

RUBY CURLED up on the bench created by the attic dormer and didn't miss the moon at all. There were plenty of stars to keep her company as she pondered the arrival of the stranger into her small life.

The first time she'd seen him he stormed out of the church like a dark star simmering against the daylight.

The midmorning sun had caught his dark hair and lit up his face like old paintings she'd seen in some of her picture books. He'd been frowning, but that only made him more mysterious, like a man who thought serious thoughts. Edna, who owned the Wooden Spoon and served as Moon Hollow's official gossip, told Ruby that his name was Peter West, and he was a genuine writer. But she didn't know all that at first. In the first moment, in the first glimpse of that man, all she knew was that her world, normally dull and muted, snapped into sharp focus and became saturated with color.

She was old enough to recognize that her awareness of him was at least partly sexual. She'd never done *it* before, but she'd known pleasure by her own hand. Those breathy moments in the dark of her attic, the gasp like a tiny death rattle, the way she seemed to float up from the mattress. Afterward, anchored by the damp quilts, the dull thump of shame arrived, but it never could quite erase the curious thrum of power under her skin. Yes, she knew pleasure, but she also understood there was more to be understood. If it felt that good alone, what sort of magic could be conjured with twice the energy?

But that didn't feel like the real reason she'd been so fascinated by the author.

No, the stronger, more urgent and true sensation was a hunger of the heart. She'd lived in the same town with the same people for all of her living life. Peter West's arrival had pierced the bubble that kept her trapped inside her small world. She guessed if he could come into her world so easily maybe it wouldn't be as hard as she thought to visit his world, too.

Sitting in her room with the stars shining in the distance, she let herself imagine who she'd become if she left Moon Hollow.

JACK WAS TOO FAR BELOWGROUND to know there was no moon. The hostile darkness crept in through his ears and mouth and spread like a suffocating shadow down his throat. The only light in his world was a white-hot spotlight of pain in the center of his chest. The darkness couldn't penetrate that sharp, electric agony. He knew he'd been unconscious until only a few moments earlier, but he couldn't remember how he'd been knocked out.

He remembered wandering through maze-like shafts looking for his crew. Somehow, he'd gotten separated from Old Fred and the others. He'd heard some giggles in the dark and suspected it was an initiation rite they imposed on all the rookies. But after several minutes trying to find his way back to them, the laughter had died and only oppressive silence remained.

He'd felt his way through the dark by running his hands along the uneven walls until the surface gave way. Somehow, he stumbled into a new chamber. He recalled the air smelling fouler and a drop in temperature. He'd just been about to turn back when a solid weight slammed him into the rock wall. The blackness had swallowed him for a while, but now that he was awake he felt no closer to understanding what really happened.

The only thing he knew for certain was that he was alone and seriously wounded.

Shadows shifted; a whisper of air brushed his cheek. A low, rumbling growl pierced the silence.

Cold penetrated the fog of half-consciousness. Not the cold one would expect so far down in the earth. Not a damp cold of the grave, but a dry chill that began in his center and radiated outward—the creeping blue frost of fear.

His thoughts swam through the dark trying to find relief. If he just tried hard enough, he'd emerge from the nightmare waters to the blessed light of reality. He yearned for the surface toward an image of Sarah Jane's face. If he were a good boy and tried real hard, he could inhale her sweet scent like oxygen, and taste the salvation of her lips.

From the edges of his hearing, another growl—mechanical in its intensity but too erratic to be anything but animal. Closer now. Moist air hit his face with the acrid smell of rotten eggs and putrefied flesh.

Sarah Jane. Swim, son! Swim harder. There isn't enough air.

Pressure on his side. More fetid air. Not oxygen, but the breath of death. He swam harder. Sarah Jane!

Another growl knocked him in the face like a fist. He opened his eyes, and through the watery dread he finally saw it.

The beast had two black eyes set in a snowstorm face.

Jack sucked in a breath to scream.

He never exhaled again.

10

THE THIRST

Cotton

THE BASTARD SUN was coming up. There was no place for warmth in his world now. No desire for light. Cold and dark were his friends—and whiskey. Shadows were quiet, at least. Not like his head. In there, banshees screeched until he burned them away with whiskey. A baptism by fire.

His old coat needed patching at the elbows, but no one was around anymore to do the mending. Ruby didn't know a needle from her ass, but damned if that child wasn't looking more and more like his Rose every day. Looking at the girl's face made black spots block out his vision as if he'd stared straight into the sun.

They said absence made the heart grow fonder, but in his experience, absence only made his heart feel like an angry mule had kicked it.

He pulled his hunting cap farther down to cover his ears. The empty jugs went into the truck bed. If he worked all day, he might get enough moonshine made to last him another week or two. He'd have to keep it stored somewhere safe, though. If Ruby found out he was hoarding whiskey she'd give him lip, and then he'd have to bust hers.

It's not that he liked hitting women. It's just—well, it was easier than listening to them squawk all damned day.

He shoved his rifle into the passenger's side floorboard and blew heat into his hands before turning over the ignition. The truck coughed and wheezed in the damp air. He didn't worry about the racket waking the kids. Ruby was already awake. He knew she thought she fooled him into thinking she was still asleep when he looked in on her. Her eyes had been closed, sure, but her hands had been clenched into fists on the quilt. Girl never was any good at playin' possum.

The truck's engine finally rumbled to life like an old man waking from a nap in his favorite chair. He patted the dashboard, threw the gear into Drive, and took off down the gravel road.

His hands shook on the steering wheel and the pounding in his head sounded like a hammer beating on a metal barrel. He wasn't sure if his body was paying for the bender he'd enjoyed the night before or if it was anticipating the new one he was about to begin.

He wasn't even sure what day it was or how long it had been since Rose died. He rubbed at his stinging eyes. Too many, that's how many. Ever since he'd come home to find the county ambulance in his driveway, time had warped and folded back on itself and wrapped around him until he suffocated. But he was sure the time that had passed had nothing on the hell of days stretching before him until he could join her in the grave.

Swiping at the wetness on his cheeks, he muttered, "God damn it."

The banshees screamed again. He needed a drink, but all he had was a truck full of empty jugs. The sun continued its steady climb. The bright streaks of orange and yellow shouting over the ridge stabbed his eyeballs. The dashboard clock told him it was coming on six thirty. It would take him another half an hour to the logging road and another twenty minutes of climbing to reach his refuge.

The banshees kept hollerin'. The pounding behind his eye sockets provided a rhythm section for their devil's song.

He couldn't wait an hour.

Six thirty in the morning.

Too early for the liquor store. But old Edna would be open and ready to serve muddy coffee to the early risers of Moon Hollow. Old Edna used to take a shine to Cotton. Maybe if he smiled and asked real nice, she'd donate a beer or three for his journey.

He turned his truck toward town.

THE WOODEN SPOON sat on the opposite end of town from the church. Thank God for small miracles, he thought. He didn't want to get anywhere near that church and risk running into Deacon Fry. Lord knew the man would probably hear he'd stopped into the diner, but by the time he found out, Cotton would already be in his hidey-hole and the alcohol would be simmering in his gut.

Just as he'd hoped, the lights were already on in the diner. No cars were parked in front, though, which meant none of the regulars had made it in yet. Perfect. He could get in and out without having to see the pity in their eyes and know that the minute he left they'd start whispering.

Cotton parked the truck on the side of the diner instead of the front. Before he got out, he took a look in the rearview. His hunting cap was pulled down low over his eyes and made them look like two dark voids on his face. Black holes.

He ripped off the cap and tried to finger comb out the worst of the cowlicks. He hadn't showered in—how long had it been? Anyway, the grease helped plaster the strands to his skull. There wasn't anything to be done about the whiskers or the deep pockets that sat under his eyes. He ripped the old pine tree air freshener from the rearview mirror and rubbed it under his armpits and over his shirt. Satisfied he no longer smelled like a three-day dead critter, he jumped out of the truck.

His ankle buckled under him. Damned thing. Probably he'd just stepped wrong. He hadn't had a drink in about four hours so he wasn't drunk at all. Or drunker than his baseline, he amended silently, and saluted the rising sun with his middle finger.

Catching his breath, he straightened up and focused real hard on walking a straight line to the front door. Through the window, he saw Edna behind the counter refilling napkins into metal dispensers. He grabbed the door handle and pulled, but the door didn't open.

The rattling glass caught Edna's attention. She started and jerked around with a hand to her ample bosom. When she saw it was him, she hurried around the counter. Cotton smiled and waved. Nothing to see here. Just a friendly neighbor stopping in to beg for some predawn hooch.

She worked the dishtowel over her hands as she walked. Her smile was polite but curious. Cotton wasn't surprised by her surprise. Ever since Rose died, he hadn't come to the diner. Hadn't gone anywhere, really, except his moonshine shed and the house.

"Cotton!" Edna said as she opened the door. "Ain't seen you in a coon's age. How you doing?" Her overly cheerful tone was one he'd heard from every woman in Moon Hollow since the funeral. The happiness was always tinged with rust-colored pity.

"Mornin', Edna. Can I come in?"

She hesitated, but the smile remained firmly in place. "I don't open for another thirty minutes, but I don't see why not. Can I get you some coffee?"

Only if it's got whiskey in it, he thought. "Sounds good."

He followed her inside. Her ample rear end stretched the bonds of her polyester pants and her orthopedic shoes squeaked on the linoleum tiles. It was a damned shame the way she'd let herself go over the years. Back in high school, all the boys chased her like hounds in heat. Now they just wanted her for her blue-plate specials.

His Rose never let herself balloon up. Not even after giving birth to his daughters or Ruby. He remembered how proud he always felt to have her on his arm as they walked into church each Sunday. He loved the way her slim hips swayed under the simple homemade dresses she preferred. He knew it wasn't right to lust after her in church, but his hand always found its way to her inner thigh during that self-righteous prick's sermons.

"... Ruby and the girls doing?"

He looked up, realizing he'd missed the first part of her question. Didn't matter much. Every time he ran into one of Moon Hollow's women, they asked about the children. Their questions always held a hint of judgment, as if they didn't believe he was capable of taking care of his family without a woman around.

His hands were shaking again. He shoved them under his thighs on the stool at the counter. "They're doing good," he said, giving his pat answer.

Edna nodded, as if he'd answered correctly. "I'm sure Miss Ruby is a big help."

An image of Ruby's stricken face after he'd grabbed her arm

the other morning tweaked his conscience. "She sure is." His tone was forced even to his own ears.

Edna set a mug of coffee in front of him. "You hungry?"

He licked his dry lips. "I'm good," he said. "Listen, Edna. I—" He stopped himself, wondering if he'd jumped the gun. Edna's expression was open and trusting, but it didn't hold that eager-to-please sparkle he was looking for.

"Go on," she prompted.

"How are your cats?"

Edna's smile grew. She launched into a story about how one of the little fuckers had fallen into the toilet. Cotton eyed the counter behind her for anything that might have a kick. She used to serve alcohol after five o'clock to the dinner crowd, but a year earlier Deacon Fry, in his other role as Moon Hollow's mayor, *encouraged* the town council to pass an ordinance outlawing the sale of spirits in Moon Hollow town limits. Since then, the bottles that used to line the back of the counter had disappeared.

But Cotton knew Edna had to keep a stash somewhere.

" ... and then Stumpy—that's my bobtailed cat—jumped on top of the sink and turned on the tap himself!" She chuckled. "I swear that cat's a genius." She beamed as if her cat's intelligence was inherited from her side of the family.

"That's great," Cotton said with forced enthusiasm. "Tell me, you got anything to warm up this coffee?"

Edna looked at his still-steaming mug. "It can't be cold already."

He leaned in with a conspirator's smile. "No, I meant something a little ... stronger," he whispered.

Edna glanced toward the entrance as if she expected to see Deacon Fry darkening the doorway. When she looked back at Cotton, her expression was wary. "'Course not. Stopped carrying the stuff last summer. You know that."

Not the answer he wanted, but he wasn't disheartened. "You sure you don't have a wee nip of something stashed somewhere 'round here?" He smiled the same smile he used to flash his Rose whenever she pretended to be mad at him.

"Cotton," she began, "have you been drinking already this morning?"

He snorted. "'Course not! What do you think I am?" *An alcoholic, am I, maybe—who cares?* "It's just nippy outside and I have to head up the mountain this morning to check on some land. Thought a little shot of something might keep me warm."

Edna's wariness dissolved into something colder, unwelcoming. "Can't help you. Maybe it'd be best if you left." Her voice shook, but her expression didn't waver.

He threw up his hands. Damned unreasonable woman didn't have to get all uppity. "Well, shit, Edna. We were just having a friendly chat." Maybe she kept it in the storeroom. Or the office. If he could just get her back there—

"I said it's time to go, Cotton." She'd moved toward the phone next to the cash register and placed a dimpled hand on the receiver.

He knew she wouldn't be calling the law. No, she'd call Deacon Dickhead and have him come to give Cotton a talking to. No doubt, the bastard would love the chance to shepherd Cotton back into his flock. And suddenly sobriety was a lot less scary than sticking around for that torture.

He pushed off the stool. "Relax. I'm goin'." He heard the petulance in his tone but didn't care.

"You need to git yourself back to church, Cotton."

Cotton pictured her as a ventriloquist's puppet. His mind flashed an image of Deacon Fry reaching a magical arm all the way across Moon Hollow and shoving his hand up Edna's backside to control her mouth.

A high-pitched cackle escaped his lips. Edna's mouth froze

open and her eyes widened, as if, too late, she realized she was alone with a man who could easily overpower her and force her to show him where she kept the secret stash of liquor. Her hand spasmed on the receiver and it was at her ear before the echoes of Cotton's laughter disappeared from the air.

"Go!" Her sausage fingers stabbed at the buttons.

His skin felt cold and hot. Shame and anger mixed like grain alcohol and flame in his gut. He wanted to tear her skin off. He wanted to shower the diner's walls in her blood. He wanted to kick her face in until those eyes looking at him with fear and disgust were destroyed. He wanted to burn down the diner—hell, the whole fucking town. He wanted to stomp the mountain into ash and piss on the pile.

He wanted to die.

He didn't remember running out the door. He didn't remember opening the truck's door or turning over the engine. Tires spun out on loose gravel and the truck's rear fishtailed through a sharp curve on the road out of town. He snapped to just in time to right the wheel. Heart clawing up the back of his throat, he pointed the truck toward the road leading up-mountain.

But instead of seeing the sun rising over the peaks in a riot of color that celebrated the glory of God Himself, Cotton only saw Edna's face reflected in the windshield. Her fat fucking face.

That bitch, that bitch, that BITCH!

His hands shook with sober palsy and his eyes felt as if they were vibrating in their sockets. He just needed to get to his shed and then everything would be fine. Maybe he'd be able to find a jug with a little bit of hooch inside. Yes, just a few drops. That's all he needed.

Didn't they understand? No, of course not. No one understood.

While Ruby and the girls cried and carried on at the funeral, he'd had to be the strong one. A man had to keep it together. A man had to be strong for his family. It was only afterward that the pressure of his grief fractured him from the inside. The only glue keeping those shards of himself together was 90 proof, and the longer he went without a drink, the larger the cracks and fissures grew. He knew that if he allowed sobriety to take hold, he'd shatter.

Ashes to ashes, dust to dust.

There'd be nothing left of him to bury beside his Rose. The pieces of him would just rise into the wind and be swept away—gone forever. And wouldn't they love that? For him to just disappear.

He white-knuckled his hands on the wheel and closed one eyelid to be able to focus on the road.

But inside, in the secret dark hole sitting next to his heart, a lonely voice chanted the same words over and over just as they had for the last month.

Come back to me, Rose. Back to me, Rose. Rose, come back to me comebacktomeROSE. Rose? Come back!

11

PAUPER'S BREAKFAST

Deacon Fry

THE NEXT MORNING, dreams from a restless night's sleep chased Deacon Fry down the stairs. Vague images of dark caves and screams alternated with scenes of him at the pulpit wearing a devil's costume. He'd spent a portion of his night reading the contents of Peter West's most recent novel, *Devil's Due*, which was likely the source of the disturbing dreams. After witnessing the sick contents of that man's head, he was more determined than ever for their meeting that morning to mark the end of Mr. West's tenure in Moon Hollow.

But first, breakfast. His daddy, God rest his soul, always said a man should eat like a king at breakfast, a prince at lunch, and a pauper for dinner. It was just one of several life lessons his mama had taught him, and following his advice was one of the ways the deacon honored his father, the great Reverend Seamus Fry's memory.

When he reached the dining room, Sarah Jane was already seated at the table. She looked down at her hands, which were clasped next to an untouched glass of orange juice. She looked up when she heard the creak of the floorboards announcing his arrival.

"Good morning, Daddy." Her dejected tone made him want to turn tail and go right back upstairs. He prided himself as a pious man, so he never could reckon why the good Lord saddled him with a daughter. While his friends had fine, strapping young men to carry on their family names and make their daddies proud, he had to suffer through the emotional traumas of fathering a girl.

Father, why hast thou forsaken me?

His lips twitched at his little joke. Luckily Sarah Jane didn't see it or he would have had to deal with her hurt feelings over that too. "What's wrong, Buttercup?"

She sighed. "It's Jack, Daddy. He was supposed to call me last night after he got off his shift, but I haven't heard from him."

He'd forgotten that yesterday had been the boy's first night working the mines. He'd put a word in for the boy for an office job at the mining company, but Jack had insisted he wanted to get his hands dirty and learn the job from the ground up, so to speak. Some people considered that type of ambition admirable, but to him, it stank of pride and willfulness. He told himself his dislike of Jack had nothing to do with the boy's trash family or lack of resources to take care of Sarah Jane. Boy like that thought dating the deacon's daughter would better his station in life. Boy like that thought he deserved a higher station that he was born into. But the deacon had no intention of letting his daughter be the star to which Jack Thompson tied his future.

Still, it wouldn't do to show any sort of smugness over the boy's missteps. If Sarah Jane even suspected her daddy didn't approve of their match, all their fates would be sealed.

"Mining is hard work, honey. He probably dove headfirst into his bed when he got home."

She nodded absently. "I know—it's just Jack always calls me no matter what."

He reached across the table to pat her hand. "I'm sure he'll call as soon as he wakes up."

"You're probably right." She frowned into her juice.

He smiled, ignoring the lack of conviction in her voice. "Of course I am." He squeezed her hand one last time before he leaned back. "Now, where's your mama?" He flapped his napkin out with a flourish before tucking it into his lap.

"She went to meet Ethel. They were going to deliver some baked goods to that writer."

He froze with his glass halfway to his mouth. "She what?"

She nodded, oblivious to the storm gathering across the table. "They said that since he got in on Sunday when the store was closed he probably didn't have any proper food on hand in the cabin for breakfast."

"But what about my breakfast?" he mumbled.

"She left some oatmeal on the stove." She rose and kissed her father on the cheek. "I need to get dressed."

"Where are you going?"

"I'm working in the library today—remember?"

"Oh, yes—that's right."

She paused and tilted her head to look at him with a worried expression. "You okay, Daddy?"

He forced a smile. "Peachy keen, darlin'."

But inside he was cursing Peter West seven ways to Sunday. The man had only been in town less than a day, but he was already upsetting Deacon Fry's orderly life.

―――

HE DECIDED to walk to the church that morning. The air was heavy, as if it might rain later, but in the meantime the sun was streaking through the morning sky like God had been finger-painting.

He chuckled at his whimsical thought. After eating breakfast, his mood had improved. He was determined to make the most of the day that the good Lord had given him. He saw now that he'd been childish in his worries about that author.

What's the worst Peter West could do, after all? The good people of Moon Hollow were rooted in the land and in their faith. They wouldn't be easily won over by a slick writer with a liar's jawline. Besides, if he got his way—and he usually did— by sundown Mr. West's visit would be nothing more than an unpleasant footnote in the town's history.

The deacon's house sat on a rise above town. He decided to take a trail through the woods to the church since the road wound in a meandering path down the hill. The canopy rose above him and the dappled sunlight coming through the leaves brightened his mood even more. Was there any place on earth where man felt closer to God than in nature? Men like Peter West might prefer the manufactured order of the city that allowed city folk to pretend they were the pinnacles of existence. But he personally felt comforted by the large scale of nature and its untamed majesty. Here it was clear that men were at the mercy of God. Only sinful men had anything to worry about in the woods.

Dry leaves rustled. He pulled himself away from his musing to look in that direction. The vastness of the woods and the number of trees made pinpointing the exact location impossible. Probably just a rabbit or squirrel searching for breakfast. He pursed his lips and whistled a tune. A mockingbird in the distance echoed his song.

A stick cracked. He had not moved on the packed earth of the path, so something else created the sound. Leaves rustled somewhere behind him. His step quickened before he made a conscious decision to do it. He looked around for signs of animal life. Most of the small critters would hide during the day, especially if a human were moving through the woods. But something larger might not. Bears were still filling their bellies after winter's hibernation, and sometimes deer wandered close to town to forage.

Another twenty feet down the path, it dog-legged toward the river. The sound of the babbling water reached his ears over his puffing breath. He convinced himself it was the brisk walk that made oxygen feel harder to come by. But ever since the stick cracked, gooseflesh had broken out over his skin and his heart was galloping like a spooked horse. For a moment, he was back in the woods on that winter morning, but he reminded himself, no, it was May and he wasn't that boy any more.

He walked faster.

Down near the creek, the path veered sharply at the riverbank and went another half a mile before it reached the church. But down by the water, the tree cover was heavier and sun harder to come by. He convinced himself the chill was due to the shade.

Another shuffle of leaves sounded behind him. A loud crack —more than just a cracked stick—a whole branch this time. Something large. But no sound of footsteps or breathing.

He looked over his shoulder. A shadow flashed in the corner of his eyes. A trick of light, probably. Please, Lord, let it be a trick of light.

His breath came out in a puff of steam, as if it were January instead of May. His teeth were chattering in his skull. And when the low growl reached his ears, he knew it was no bear.

Fear sparked the memory of the Thing With No Face that attacked him as a child. The bright void of that non-face. The harsh frost of the air. The vacuum where his lungs should have been. Suddenly the entire forest felt evil.

"No!" he shouted. He could not let the Thing With No Face get him again.

He took off running like a much younger man, and agility borne of terror carried him over a log fallen across the path. Yet, the chill chased him, brushing his neck. A low, mean laugh reached his ears.

He stopped running, as if barred from continuing by some outside force. His body spun despite his desperate thought that he must flee. He looked back up the path.

A shadow stood at the bend where the path broke away from the creek. His first thought was that the Thing With No Face had found him again. Then, the light shifted and fell on the stranger's face. It was swollen and covered in blood, but there were discernible features, not a solid plane of static like all those years ago when Isaac—no, not now—can't think of Isaac now.

"Hello?" His voice cracked.

An unearthly laugh escaped the broken jaw of the man. A laugh too large for the body it came from. Too dark to be human.

Run. Run!

His feet would not move.

The man moved instead. His step brought him into a lone beam of light cutting across the path and illuminated the ruined face.

"Jack?" Deacon Fry breathed. "Jack, is that you?" It was hard to tell. Both eyes were swollen and the jaw hung open and useless. But the build was similar to Jack's and the sandy hair— though clumped dark and wet with something he assumed was blood—certainly looked like Jack's. Plus, he wore the distinctive blue uniform of a miner, even though it was torn and covered in dark stains he refused to believe were blood.

"Are you okay, son?" He took a hesitant step forward. Some part of his brain was still working but it wasn't in charge. His fear center screamed at him to flee even as his civilized mind urged him to offer aid. "Son?" he said. "What happened to you?"

One minute the man who might be Jack stood in the path with his limbs held at unnatural angles. The next instant, a blur, like rage in motion, shot through the air. The deacon only had time to flinch before the air filled with the foul perfume of blood and something darker—the stench of voided bowels; and the sharp crack of freezing air surrounded him like an ice storm. His mouth opened to scream.

Before any sound could emerge, the foul smell and the cold disappeared. Sudden silence pressed in on his skin like the hand of Death itself. Nauseated and trembling, he ran to the one place he knew evil could not find him—Christ the Redeemer Church.

12
RIVER SONGS

Ruby

SUNDAY'S RAINSTORMS left the forest floor soggy and the river riled up. Sitting alone on the bank, Ruby closed her eyes and listened to the water's agitated music. The sound of water rushing over rocks and pressing against the banks wasn't the deep song of the river spirit. That song was lost to her now.

The scents of water and earth reminded her of when she was young and she and Mama snuck away to meet Granny Maypearl in the forest. The three of them had spent many blissful afternoons combing the woods for ginseng roots and other ingredients Granny would use in her tinctures and potions. When their baskets were full, they'd sit by the water's edge and wash away the dirt caked under their nails.

If she focused real hard, she still could feel her mama's body pressed against her right side and Granny's pressed to her left, the shock of cold water on her skin, and the brown muck dissolving to reveal pink fingertips. Mama's hands always dwarfed Ruby's as she cupped them to scrub away the last of the dirt. As their heads bowed to their task, she could see every line on Granny and Mama's faces. She remembered the way the edges of Granny's eyes crinkled when she smiled and then she'd wink at Ruby like they shared a secret.

Hadn't they? Hadn't Mama warned Ruby to keep the meetings by the river secret? Hadn't she warned Ruby that Daddy would be angry if he ever found out?

A flash of violence cut through the warm memories. Daddy's fist flying through the air. Mama's lips slick with red. Sobbing screams echoing up the staircase and haunting her in the dark.

Ruby shook off that memory and sank back into the nicer one. Granny's voice whispering, "Don't fall in, Rubybug, or the river spirits will steal you away to make you their queen."

The sun cast motes of pink light behind her eyelids. She smiled and absorbed the warmth of its rays as fuel for the memories.

Once they were clean, three generations of Maypearl women would sun themselves like contented lizards on the riverbank's sweet grass. Granny always brought a slice of strawberry and rhubarb pie for Ruby. Nothing ever tasted as sweet as that pie eaten in a sunbeam with the river serenading them.

Then, her belly full, Ruby would lay her head in Mama's lap and ask Granny Maypearl to tell her the story of the mountain spirits. Even though she'd told Ruby the story dozens of times, Granny would always smile—revealing crooked teeth stained sepia from her hand-rolled cigarettes—and say, "All right, Rubybug."

Ruby remembered the way the sun would glint like magic off Granny's silver hair and how her eyes would twinkle even brighter.

While Granny settled in to tell the story, her mama would close her eyes and gently caress Ruby's hair. Sitting there like that, looking so peaceful, Ruby believed her mama was the most beautiful woman in the world. With a contented sigh, she'd let her eyes close, too, and swam in the memory of Granny's words.

———

LONG AGO, back before our kin came to the mountains from the land ruled by faeries, these hills were home to the mountain spirits. They lived here for millions of years and took care of the mountains and the river and all of the creatures and plants in the forest. Eventually, Indian folk found the mountains and made them their home, too.

At first, the spirits were afraid because they'd never seen people before. But the Indians loved the mountains and respected the land. The spirits grew to love the people, but they were sad because they couldn't speak with them. Oh, the spirits tried, but the people didn't hear the river songs or the secrets they whispered on the wind.

But there was one girl. Her name was Galilani. She was the daughter of a powerful Cherokee Gigahu, or Beloved Woman. One day, when she had seen six winters, she walked alone by the river. This river right here, in fact. The spirits of the water sang as they did every time people came to visit, but the melody sounded discouraged because no one ever listened.

But that time, the girl knelt by the bank and tilted her ear toward the water. Excited, the river sang faster until its music filled the entire forest. And then something amazing happened: the girl began to sing back to the spirits.

The spirits were overjoyed. Not only did Galilani understand the song, she also sang back to the river, which had never, not once, in the river's long life ever happened before.

Galilani visited the river every day to sing with the water. Soon, the other mountain spirits learned of her gift and began to communicate with her, too. The wind spirits whispered their secrets in her small ears. She'd smile and whistle along with the breezes. The tree spirits swayed their large trunks and their leaves danced in the wind. Galilani danced with them, showing she understood.

Eventually, Galilani went to her mother, the Beloved Woman, and told her of the things she'd learned from the spirits. Her mother was a wise woman and did not make fun of her daughter for what others would dismiss as creations of a child's imagination. The Beloved Woman listened and she shared what her daughter told her with her people. They heeded the lessons and began to honor the spirits. Almost immediately, life for the Cherokee people became easier. The more they honored the spirits, the more abundant their crops became, the easier life became on the mountain.

All the while, Galilani continued her visits to the river, the forest, and the bluffs where the wind made her hair dance. The girl grew into a woman, and, as a woman, she was revered among her people. Eventually, her mother grew too old to lead, and Galilani took over as the Gigahu of her people. Her people loved her and so did the spirits. Life was good.

Eventually, new people came to the mountain. White men. These men pretended to be friends with the Cherokees. They learned the lessons of the people about how to survive on the mountain, but they did not believe their stories about the spirits who should be respected. Still, Galilani and her people were happy to share the mountain's teachings with the white men.

But the white men didn't believe in the mountain spirits. They only believed in one spirit who lived high in the sky. According to the religious leaders who spoke for the white man, the sky spirit told them that the world belonged to white men to do with as they pleased.

Galilani became worried about their new friends. They carried guns and had no respect for the mountain. They said the mountain belonged to them now, and that the Cherokee needed to leave.

As the days grew cold, she went to the river to sing with the spirits, hoping they would provide guidance. But the river was frozen and the spirits refused to sing. She sang all day and all night, but the river didn't respond.

The next day, she went to the trees and danced, but the trees had gone still and their branches were bare.

On the third day, she went to the bluff and called on the wind and the great mountain spirit, but the air was still and the mountain refused to acknowledge her.

Galilani cried and raised her face to the sky, where the spirit of the white man lived. If her own beloved spirits would not speak to her, perhaps this other spirit would help her. She raised her voice to the sky and shouted to the sky spirit to tell the white men to let her people stay.

The sky spirit did not answer.

13
CRYING OUT IN THE WILDERNESS

Deacon Fry

BY THE TIME Deacon Fry made it to his office, the shock was wearing off but cold sweat still coated his chest. When he burst through the door to the reception area, Mrs. McDuffy looked up from her desk and half-rose in shock.

"Deacon? Are you okay?"

His breath caught and swallowing it felt like shoving a boulder down his throat. "I—"

She stood the rest of the way and rushed around the desk. "You're pale as a ghost."

He put a hand to his forehead as if he could judge his paleness by touch alone. His fingers came away wet. He shook his head. "I saw something in the woods." His voice sounded too high and young. Shame bloomed in his chest. He was a grown man. A pillar of the community. But there he was acting like a boy who'd seen the boogieman.

Had he seen a ghost? *Again.*

He shook off the thought. "I'm okay. I'm fine. I just—my imagination tricked me."

She rushed over to the small refrigerator in the corner and removed a bottle of water. By the time she placed it in his hand, his breath wasn't so labored and his heart didn't feel like it wanted to escape through his sternum. He uncapped the water and took a long swallow. The icy water burned his throat, but he welcomed its bite because it was real.

"That's better," Mrs. McDuffy said. "Now, do you want to tell me what's got you all het up?"

He pulled a deep breath in through his nose, relieved that the oxygen had an easy path down that time. "I was walking through the forest—the path from the house. Something jumped out and spooked me." He looked up to gauge her reaction. She smiled politely; her concern had dissolved into the practiced practicality with which she approached every situation in life. "It was probably just an animal, though," he added quickly.

But it looked like Jack.

"A deer?"

He shrugged. "Probably."

But deer don't stand on two legs or laugh like demons.

She patted his shoulder. "Well you're here now, and you have a busy morning to take your mind off the incident."

He shook himself mentally and stood straighter. He'd momentarily forgotten himself—who he was. Deacon Virgil Fry didn't let a silly deer spook him.

Even if the deer really had looked like a man. Like Jack. Like Jack covered in blood and smelling of rot and evil. Oh God, what was that smell?

"Deacon? Did you hear me?" She was talking again.

Right. Focus. The thing in the forest was a deer.

"Say that again," he said.

"I said, Peter West should be here soon for your meeting."

He'd forgotten. But now that she'd reminded him, his mood lightened. He found his spine and hardened his resolve. It was good to have focus. He should be grateful to Mr. West for providing him a distraction from what happened in the fore—

No, focus.

"That's good," he said to Mrs. McDuffy. "I have a few calls to make before he arrives. Let me know when he gets here."

Her relieved smile meant he'd managed to sound like himself again. "Yes, sir. I'll bring your coffee in a moment."

He went into his office, but left the door open behind him so she could bring his coffee in when it was ready.

His office sat on the south side of the church building. Before the deacon had been elected head of the Deacon Council, it had belonged to Reverend Peale. But once he'd finally managed to get himself elected as head of the council, he'd taken over the space. It had taken some convincing with the reverend, but eventually he'd agreed with the deacon's opinion that he'd be more comfortable in a smaller office in the back of the building.

A massive wooden desk and an equally scaled leather chair dominated the room. Behind the desk, an expensive cherry wood credenza held all of the deacon's important papers, and lording over those papers was a massive picture window.

He went to it and looked out at his view. Cemetery Hill loomed in his peripheral vision, but the forest dominated the view. He stared at the cutting green of the tender leaves, which trembled on ancient branches.

Normally, gazing out at nature brought him a measure of peace. It made him feel more in control of nature's chaos to view it from behind glass. But looking out that morning, the green felt somehow aggressive. He softened his focus until the image blurred into a large miasma of poison green. But it was worse when he tried to make out individual leaves. The dark spaces between the leaves appeared like tiny, black eyes staring at him.

Was the thing out there, watching him?

Just a deer.

"Here you go!" Mrs. McDuffy called in a cheerful tone.

He started and whirled around, nearly colliding with her. He caught himself short of tipping over the steaming mug in her hands.

"Oh!" she gasped.

He caught her by the forearms to steady them both.

"Sorry," she said, automatically assuming the blame.

It took a moment to collect himself, but having his back to the window was worse than facing it. The creeping green pressed against his shoulder blades and coated his skin with dread. But it wouldn't do to let Mrs. McDuffy see his reaction.

He took the coffee with a smile. "Let me know when West arrives."

Once she'd left, he turned to approach his desk once again. This time, he averted his eyes from the view. The more he thought about it, the more he realized he preferred to drink his coffee from the love seat on the far side of the room. He grabbed his leather bound calendar and went to sit on the sofa.

He took a sip of coffee and winced at the watery flavor. Mrs. McDuffy never had figured out how to brew a proper cup. He'd never corrected her because some perverse part of him didn't want to admit that he liked his coffee to taste like jet fuel. It seemed an indulgence not fitting a man of his position in the community.

He opened his calendar to look over the same schedule he'd reviewed that morning at the breakfast table. Nothing had changed, but the distraction allowed him to gather his thoughts and compose himself for the coming confrontation with Mr. West.

His fingers felt stiff, so he wrapped them around the warm ceramic and leaned back. He looked at the low pile beige carpet on the floor, at the acoustic tiles on the ceiling, at the taupe walls. On the wall parallel to where he sat, he found a few moments of thoughtful contemplation while gazing on the painting of John baptizing Jesus in the river. John the Baptist was the deacon's personal hero—besides Jesus, naturally. Even though he was not an ordained member of the church, he considered himself a secular version of the apostle. He guided the flock of his church and was a role model for how to live a pious life.

The deacon had not been born to elderly parents. But his younger brother, Isaac, had been considered a miracle when their mama gave birth at the age of forty-five. He also was not the one who performed the church's baptisms in the river. That job belonged to Reverend Peale.

They hadn't had a proper community baptism in a couple of years. Lately, the old reverend was growing too feeble to wade into the rushing waters. However, Deacon Fry liked to think the people of Moon Hollow were baptized every day in the purifying waters of his guidance and tough love.

As both the secular leader of the community and the spiritual mentor, he also understood how John the Baptist must have felt being the "voice of one crying out in the wilderness"—the moral wilderness, that was. His sacred duty was to encourage his flock to do what was right, even if what was right wasn't easy.

Meditating on the similarities between himself and his hero went a long way to calm his nerves. He settled back into the sofa's plush cushions and didn't even notice the taste when he took another long swallow of his coffee.

From the outer office, comforting noises reached him as Mrs. McDuffy went through her morning routine. She'd shut the door after her, so the sounds were muted, like relaxing white noise. He lay his head on the back of the sofa and closed his eyes, enjoying his return to equilibrium.

Only a thin sheet of glass separated him from the creeping, patient woods.

A deer. Just a deer.

A loud buzz shattered the silence.

Eyes flying open, he jerked upright. The sound had come from the phone on his desk. Before he rose to answer it, pain and heat spread on his thigh. He made a disgusted sound and slapped at the spilled coffee as he walked toward the desk. The phone rang twice more before he answered.

"What?"

A pause. "Sir, Bob Truman for you," Mrs. McDuffy said in a stiff tone. "He sounds upset."

He cursed silently but softened his tone when he responded. "Put him through, please."

"Bob?"

"Virgil? Oh, shit, Virgil—you've got to get down here."

He wasn't used to hearing his given name in the church, much less having it uttered in the same breath as a curse word. However, the foreman at the Big Stone Gap Mine wasn't one of his flock, so he let it pass.

"Calm down," he snapped. "What's wrong?"

"The kid, sir. The kid ... he's dead."

He heard the words, but his body refused to process them correctly. His attempts to deflect them caught him so off guard that he forgot not to look toward the window. By the time he realized what he was doing it was too late. The green captured his gaze and wouldn't let go.

"Virgil? Did you hear?"

"What kid?" He was too entranced by the wet, black trunks and the sharp green leaves he barely heard the slightly drugged tone of his voice. Something moved in the tree line. A branch rustled; the tender leaves trembled.

Just a deer.

"The Thompson boy—Jack."

His voice dried up in his throat, and tendrils of cold fear crept around his heart.

"Listen to me, Virgil," Bob snapped. "Jack is dead!"

He'd heard the man, but at that moment, a figure crawled out of the tree line.

All he could think about was how it was such a thin sheet of glass and such a short distance separating him from that thing with the bloody, broken-jawed face and those burning eyes.

The phone dropped from his hand.

"Virgil?" Bob Truman's tinny voice rose from the floor. "God damn it, Virgil!"

A scream was born and instantly died in his throat. His vocal cords froze. His limbs hung heavy as lead. Helpless but horrified, he could only stare at the thing—the man—the man who was definitely not a deer, who looked like Jack but Jack was dead.

Oh, God, no.

The thing did not walk toward him or move at all, but its—his—stillness felt far more menacing.

The trees had to be a good fifty yards from where he stood. Yet when that ruined mouth began to move, he could hear the words as clearly as if Jack Thompson were standing right behind him.

"Revelation's comin', Virgil."

Bob's voice continued to scream from the phone. The thing—the Jack-thing—laughed. The sound was so close it seemed to echo inside the deacon's head, crawl down his throat, and attach itself to the chambers of his heart, where it echoed like the toll of a funeral bell.

14

ALLIES

Peter

AS HE APPROACHED Christ the Redeemer Church, Peter whistled a tune he didn't immediately recognize. It felt right on his lips, so he kept at it all the way along the sidewalk.

A car roared to life in the church parking lot to his right. He didn't pay it much mind until the vehicle—a black boat of a Cadillac—screeched out of the lot. The tune he'd been whistling swung low and back up before cutting off. It all happened so fast, he didn't get a good look at the driver, but something in his gut told him only one resident of Moon Hollow drove a Caddie.

Now why would Deacon Fry drive off like a bat out of hell when he had a meeting with Peter?

Determined to find out, he jogged toward the church's front door. Once inside, he followed a series of arrows that pointed him down red-carpeted hallways toward the church's main office. Inside the doors, he found Mrs. McDuffy sitting behind her desk and speaking into a phone in a fierce whisper. He caught the words *accursed mine* and *God bless* before she cut off her words and looked up. Her hand clawed the receiver as she watched him expectantly.

"Good morning, Mrs. McDuffy," he said. "I have a meeting with the deacon at ten."

She sat up straighter and spoke quickly into the phone. "Have to call you back, Edna." She slammed the phone down, cleared her throat, and clasped her hands neatly on the desktop. "I'm afraid he was called away on an emergency."

"Oh dear. I hope it's nothing too serious." What kind of emergency required a deacon? A crisis of faith? Peter bit his lip to hide the smirk that jumped to his lips. "Will he be back soon?"

Mrs. McDuffy adjusted her glasses. "I'm afraid he'll have to reschedule the meeting at a later time."

Peter rocked back on his heels and feigned a look of disappointment. "I'm sorry to hear that."

"Now," she said, "if you'll excuse me, I'm quite busy."

She glanced meaningfully at the phone. Most likely the work keeping her busy was spreading news of whatever happened to the network of gossips in town. He wanted to press her for details, but he figured he'd probably hear what happened if he just walked across the street to the mercantile and struck up a conversation with a local.

With that, he backed out of the room and all but danced toward the exit. Judging from the electricity buzzing in that office, whatever happened to call Deacon Fry away was big news —and most likely not of the positive sort. He should have felt guilty for benefiting from some other person's misfortune, but he couldn't help but feel like he'd just escaped the noose. If it kept Deacon Fry out his hair long enough for him to get his story then he'd send up a prayer for the poor soul whose misfortune had become Peter's lucky day.

Back out in the sunlight, Peter stared up Moon Hollow's main street looking for something to do. At ten a.m., one might expect even a small town to have some activity in what passed for the business district, but that morning, the only soul Peter West saw on Main Street was old Bunk, who sat in a rocking chair on the front porch of the Moon Hollow Mercantile.

The shop sat on the right side of the road about halfway up next to the post office and across from an old log building with a sign out front indicating it was the library. The fact the town even had a library was a source of both surprise and delight to him. The last thing he'd expected to find in Moon Hollow was a building dedicated to the written word. He made a mental note to check it out after chatting with Bunk.

Bunk raised a hand and hollered, "Well if it ain't the city boy."

Peter climbed up on the porch. "Mornin'."

"Thought you writer types only came out at night." He accepted Peter's hand for a shake.

"Nah, that's vampires. Real writers work all hours."

"That mean you don't have time to sit a spell?"

Peter pulled up the other rocker. "As it happens, my schedule just opened up for the day."

"Did I see you come out of the church?" Bunk asked, knowing very well that's exactly where he had been.

"Was supposed to meet with Deacon Fry, but something came up."

Bunk sat back with his hands on his belly. "What sort of something?"

He shrugged. "I suppose if it's important you'll hear about it soon enough."

Bunk's laugh had years of unfiltered cigarette smoke behind it. The sound reminded Peter of his grandfather, who'd smoked two packs a day out in his garage workshop while he worked on the old cars he restored. When he was a kid, Peter would spend hours watching Pop's greasy fingers fiddle with engine parts while a cigarette hung from his lips.

"Lettie said you was renting the cabin to write a book."

"That's right."

"What sort of story you working on?"

"Not sure. That's part of the reason I'm here—to find a story."

"What makes you'll find one in Moon Hollow?"

He wasn't ready to tell Bunk the real reason any more than he was ready to admit it to himself. Mostly because he'd tried not to examine the motivations too closely when he'd made the decision. He'd told himself he was following his muse. But he told Bunk something else, which was equally not-quite the whole truth. "I found a story about Moon Hollow in a book on mountain legends. Figured a place with such an interesting history would be the sort of place I'd find a good story."

Bunk huffed out a breath that was neither quite a rebuttal nor acceptance of the statement.

They fell into an easy silence. Buck rocked back and forth, and Peter propped his feet on the porch's railing. There wasn't much to look at on Main Street, but the quiet had its own sort of charm in the daylight. He didn't expect to find his story on that lazy morning, but you never knew where or when inspiration would whack you upside the head. Wasn't that how he ended up in Moon Hollow? He wondered where he would have ended up after his fight with Renee had he not spilled coffee on that book.

A bar, probably. Some dive with a jukebox that only played Patsy Cline. Without a story to keep him out of trouble he probably would have spent the rest of his days there, chain smoking and nursing cheap beers while "I Fall to Pieces" played on an endless loop.

He shook himself because that image held more appeal than it should have.

"You all right, son?"

"Yeah." He cleared his throat and leaned back in the chair. For a few moments, they rocked in companionable silence. Once again, the silence made Peter uneasy.

A girl was walking up Main on the opposite side of the road. Her head was down and she had several books clasped against her chest, like secrets. She moved quickly and something about her posture tickled a memory that he couldn't quite place.

"Who's that?" he asked.

Bunk squinted and raised his hand to his eyes as if to shade them from a nonexistent glare. "Ah, that there's Miss Ruby Barrett."

"She looks familiar. Was she at church yesterday?"

Bunk laughed. "The whole town was there." He paused. "Well, 'cept for Ruby's daddy."

Before Peter could ask about Ruby's daddy, Bunk raised his hook. "Mornin', Ruby!"

The girl jumped and looked up like she'd been caught doing something wrong. From his vantage point, Peter could make out bright eyes and a pointy little nose. He realized then that she was the girl he'd watched march down the aisle in church. What had happened to her since then that made her so nervous?

"This here's Mr. West!" Bunk called.

Ruby looked toward him but not directly at him and tipped her chin. Then she turned on her heel and escaped into the library's front door.

"Don't mind her," Bunk said, "she's a bit touched." He tapped his forehead with his hook.

"Really?" The day before she hadn't looked *touched* so much as pissed. And that morning, there'd been no mistaking the intelligence in her gaze—nor the fear. Ruby Barrett wasn't crazy —she was scared.

"Runs in the family, I'm afraid," Bunk said.

For some reason, he didn't want to gossip about the girl with the bird's features and the fear in her eyes. It felt wrong somehow—too cruel. Instead, he looked down the street toward the church and changed the subject. "What happened to the steeple?"

The old man spat a stream of brown juice into the dirt. "That legend wasn't in your book?"

Peter frowned and shook his head. "Will you tell it to me?"

15

JOB 28:28

Ruby

SHE RUSHED INSIDE and threw her purse on the old church pew that sat inside the library's front door. Luckily, that snotty Sarah Jane wasn't in sight, but it was only a matter of time until she came out and stuck her nose in Ruby's business.

She hadn't been ready to see Peter West again. The minute he looked at her on the street, she became convinced he could see all the thoughts she'd had about him the night before in her bed. A man like that *knew* things about girls. Way more than girls like her knew about men, anyway.

She blew out a long breath and tried to get her heartbeat under control. The only thing she was thankful for was that no one had seen her act like such a baby. If Sarah Jane had been around she never would have shut up about the way Ruby's cheeks went up in flames.

Speaking of Sarah Jane, Ruby needed to get busy before she returned and started asking questions. But now that she thought about it, it sure was strange that she saw Peter when she was on her way to the library to look for his books. Would he be pleased to find out that was her mission or would he think she was awkward and weird like all the boys in Moon Hollow?

What if he came into the library and found that they didn't have any of his books? Would he leave town? For some reason that scared her more than the idea he might think she was weird.

She pushed off the door and went to the fiction shelves on the far wall. It was the smallest section of the library, and its contents were carefully selected to exclude any contents that might compromise the good people of Moon Hollow. But sometimes, books were donated that Sarah Jane was too lazy to vet properly or else they came in when old Widow Farnsworth was volunteering and she "accidentally" forgot to throw out the shameful books.

She was on her third fruitless pass of the W shelf when a throat cleared nearby. She looked up to see Sarah Jane smirking at her. They were the same age, but Ruby always felt like a little girl next to the deacon's daughter. She stood and smoothed a hand over her jeans, which had smears of mud from her trip into the forest. But she pushed the brief spurt of self-consciousness away. Sarah Jane Fry might be the princess of Moon Hollow, but she had never heard the river water sing or known the blessing of the spring breeze whispering secrets in her perfect shell ears. That thought made Ruby unbearably sad for her.

"What are you doing?"

"Looking for something to read."

A nasty smile spread across Sarah Jane's pink lips. "If you're looking for one of Widow Farnsworth's sex stories, you're wasting your time. I cleaned all those out three days ago and burned them in the barrel out back."

The mental image of flaming books inside a metal coffin

made Ruby's stomach cramp. Her mama taught her never to waste nothing, and it seemed even sex books deserved better treatment. "Wasn't looking for no sex books," she said. "For your information, I was looking to see if we had any of Peter West's novels."

The metallic edge of Sarah Jane's laughter cut deep. "You've got to be kidding. The stories he writes are worse than the sex books."

How did Sarah Jane know what was in the sex books? Did she and Jack do those things? The thought made Ruby sick to her stomach. Sarah Jane had already blabbed to the whole town that once Jack saved enough money from his new mining job, he was going to buy her a big diamond. The way Ruby figured it, a boy wouldn't condemn himself to working in the mines for girls who didn't do the sorts of things found in sex books.

She immediately felt ashamed of her unchristian thoughts. "What do you know about Mr. West's books?"

Sarah Jane leaned in and whispered, "They're about demons and killers. Daddy says that man's a devil worshipper."

Ruby'd never met a devil worshipper, but the man she saw rocking with Bunk didn't look like he believed in much at all—good or evil. "Don't be stupid, Sarah Jane. He's a guest in our town. Least we can do is have one of his books in our library."

At the word "stupid" Sarah Jane's face went from smug to downright mean. "You're the stupid one, Ruby Barrett. If Daddy has his way that man won't be here long enough to even find this library."

The phone at the front desk began to ring. Sarah Jane shot Ruby one last pitying look before pushing away from the wall to go answer it. When she spoke into the receiver, her greeting was so syrupy sweet it gave Ruby a toothache.

Dismissing her tormentor, she turned back to the shelves and stared at the spot where Peter West's books should go. It wasn't right, that absence. She looked toward the doorway that led to the library office, where the computer Sarah Jane used to order new books was located. One week a few months back, when Sarah Jane had the flu and the Widow Farnsworth was off visiting her sister in Lynchburg, Mrs. Fry had asked Ruby to pitch in at the library. Part of her duties that week had been to order a new set of children's Bibles for the Sunday school class. The password for the system was "Job2828."

She looked toward the desk where Sarah Jane was deep in conversation. "Going to use the restroom," she called. Sarah Jane rolled her eyes and turned her back, which gave Ruby all the permission she needed to see through her plan.

16

THE STEEPLE STORY

Peter

Bunk adjusted his arthritic bones into the rocker's cane seat, as if settling in for a while.

"This is the story my daddy told me, and he said his daddy told him. It's been about seventy years since he told me, mind, but I still recall the basics, I reckon," he began. "Musta been fifty years after the War of Northern Aggression—"

Bunk was too busy looking into the past to notice Peter's amusement at his word choice.

"—back then, the church was the only building in town. Lots of people had homesteads in the holler or farther into the hills, but there were no businesses to speak of. You can imagine what it looked like coming round that bend." He pointed his cane toward the place where the road into town curved out of the hills.

Peter looked around, trying to imagine the valley back then. The descriptions he'd read said the church's steeple had been huge, and judging from the twisted hunk of metal that stood there now, it was easy to imagine the size. He tried to picture what it might look like to a farmer from the highlands to come around that curve and see the church shrouded in mountain mist and towering over the emerald grasses that carpeted the valley. "Must have been quite a sight."

Bunk made a noise with his lips that Peter took for agreement.

"Anyway, the story goes that one hot July night an awful storm broke over the valley. Real gully washer, as my pappy used to say."

Bunk must have been eighty if he was a day, and hearing him refer to his father that way delighted Peter. An image of his own father flashed in his mind. Charles West had been all hard angles and cold distance, and, while Peter had several choice names for the man, calling him "Pappy" would have earned him the patented West glare and a shoulder colder than the tundra.

Bunk was looking to the sky, as if seeing it as it had been that stormy day more than a hundred years ago. "The rivers breached the banks in no time. Lots of folks left their houses for higher ground. But one man refused to leave." He lifted his rheumy gaze and there was a spark of mischief in the in his eyes. "Guess who."

"Jeremiah Moon?"

A rusty laugh escaped Bunk's mouth. "Nah, boy. Old Jeremiah Moon had passed on to his final reward by then. Nah, this was Alodius Fry."

"Fry? Related to the good deacon, I presume."

Bunk grunted in the affirmative. "His great-granddaddy. But you weren't totally wrong to bring up old Jeremiah. Alodius was his grandson, born of his only daughter, Rebecca who married into the Fry family. In fact, as long as the church has stood, there's been a Fry man acting as pastor."

"Pastor? Why is the current Mr. Fry only a deacon, then?"

Bunk's shrug was effortless but meaningful, Peter thought. There was definitely a story there, but he had to tackle one mystery at a time or risk alienating himself from his first friend in town.

He pulled out his notebook and pen from his pocket and jotted notes. "Okay, so the Moons and the Frys merged and that started a family line that leads all the way to Deacon Fry," he said partially to himself. Keeping up with the long and tangled roots of Moon Hollow genealogy wouldn't be easy. Peter knew he didn't necessarily need to be accurate about the family trees of the residents to tell his ghost stories, but he found himself fascinated for reasons beyond those of a writer on the hunt for inspiration.

Bunk watched his note-taking without comment. When Peter was done, he continued. "Yes, sir, it was old Alodius Fry who refused to abandon his church. But he sent his woman and youngins away with another family. Two other men stayed behind to help Alodius sandbag the church. I reckon if they hadn't nobody would have any idea what happened that night. Hell, as it is, there're two different stories of what happened."

"Two?"

"I suppose there was really three stories, but Alodius Fry refused to tell his side of what happened that night." He let that comment hang there for a moment before continuing.

"The first story goes like this: Round about midnight, the storm reached its strength. The wind was a-howlin' and lightning streaked across the sky constantly. For some reason, Alodius ran out the church doors right as the clock struck midnight. The other men ran after him to pull him back into the church. Before they could, a monster branch of lightning cracked out of the sky and attacked the steeple."

"That's all?" Peter asked, disappointed. "Lightning struck it?"

"Like I said, that's one story."

As impatient as Peter was to find out the rest of the story, he couldn't help but be amused and impressed by the man's skills at building suspense. He wondered if Southern men were genetically predisposed to being storytellers or if it had something to do with the languorous heat that primed them for spinning yarns.

After a moment, Bunk leaned forward. "The second story, well now, that's a different thing altogether. I can't say for sure it's the true story, but it's the one we don't often tell strangers on account of we don't want to scare 'em too bad."

Peter chuckled. "Then why are you tellin' me?"

Bunk's mouth pursed as he feigned deep thought. "I reckon it's because you write them books and such. Figure a fella like you can appreciate a good demon story."

Now they were getting somewhere interesting. "A demon?"

Bunk shot him a sly look—the hook had been baited by an expert. "Yessir."

Peter leaned forward with his elbows on his knees. "Do tell."

"The second story starts out the same as the first. Lots of rain, river overflowing. Three men stay behind." Bunk pulled a cigarette pack out of his pocket. He offered it to Peter, who refused despite wanting one more than he wanted air. "Only this time, something different happened around about midnight.

"According to the fella who told this story, Alodius spent a lot of time on his knees in the church that night. While the other two scrambled to place sand bags and reinforce the windows, the pastor prayed hard. And not just normal prayer, neither. He was a-swayin' and a-hollerin' like a man in the throes of some internal war. Then, right around midnight, he fell real silent and lifted his head. One of them men said he was covered in sweat and looked real pale. Anyway, he walked straight to the church's doors and threw them open. Rain splashed into the church and all over Pastor Fry, but he stood in the doorway with his legs braced and his face turned up to the sky. Just as the clock struck midnight, he screamed, 'Come and git me, demon!' Then he ran out into the night.

"Them other two, well, they thought old Alodius done lost his damned mind. So they ran out to grab him before he could drown in all that rain. But when they went outside, they found Alodius facing down something, well, I suppose they'd describe it as something pure evil."

Bunk paused to check Peter's reaction.

"Go on," he urged.

"According to the men who were there, the beast was more'n seven feet tall. Had black skin and red eyes and horns out to here." He extended his gnarled hands and arms like branches of a tree. "Alodius told his friends to go back inside the church but they didn't listen. They just stood on the steps gawpin' at the demon. They swore after that the spot where the demon stood wasn't raining at all, but all around him the rain and the wind whipped up something fierce.

"The demon pointed a finger at old Alodius. He said, 'Leave this mountain, human, or be damned for all eternity!'" When Bunk spoke in the voice of the devil, he affected a deep tone and his eyes widened like a spooked horse's.

"Now, old Alodius was married to a woman known all over the mountain to be as mean as a polecat. Facing down a demon didn't faze him one bit. He pulled his Bible from his coat pocket and held it toward the dark figure. 'Be gone from this sacred ground, demon!' Right then, a large bolt of lightning shot out of the demon's extended finger. It hit the steeple with a deafening crash."

Bunk looked in the direction of the steeple in question. Peter's gaze followed obediently and he took in the twisted hunk of black metal as the old man continued his story.

"This is where the story branches off into two directions,"

Bunk said. "According to one man, after Alodius watched the house of the Lord attacked by evil, there awoke in him a faithful rage that flared hotter than the fires of Hades. His whole body shook with anger and his eyes blazed like a man possessed. He ran at the demon with his Bible in front of him like a weapon. Alodius shouted at the devil in a language neither of them could place. I guess it was like them preachers who can speak tongues, you ken?"

Peter confirmed he was familiar with the practice.

"Anyway, whatever Alodius said made the demon take a few steps back. He cowered under the waving Bible, which glowed like red fire in the stormy night. He beat that demon with his Bible until Old Scratch ran off with his pointed tail tucked between his legs." Bunk chuckled and shook his head.

The mental image amused Peter, but Bunk had mentioned two sides to this particular story. "What's the other version?"

Bunk's expression sobered. He spat into the dirt and took a swig of his beer. "The other fella said Alodius didn't fight the demon. According to him, Alodius made a deal with the devil to save Moon Hollow."

A car's horn blasted nearby. Bunk and Peter jumped out of their seats. Chest thumping, Peter turned to see an old blue pickup idling in front of the store. He'd been so caught up in Bunk's tale that he hadn't noticed the new arrival.

"God damn it, Earl, you like to give me a heart attack!" Bunk called to the man behind the wheel.

A mesh John Deere cap emerged from the driver's window followed by a weathered face cracked with a crooked-tooth smile. A creaky laugh escaped the man's mouth before he answered. "Serves ya right for gossipin' like an old hen!"

Bunk grumbled under his breath and leaned back in the metal chair. Peter kept his gaze on the man limping their way. He had the look of most of the men of a certain age in Moon

Hollow. A few strands of white hair clung to his sweaty forehead over a face as rutted as freshly tilled earth. Peter thought that if he counted those troughs like the rings of a tree he'd have a pretty good estimate of the man's age.

The new arrival tipped his hat at Peter. "Afternoon, Mr. West."

He didn't recognize the man from church, but since the whole town had been there, chances were good he simply overlooked him among the crowd. Still, he wasn't surprised the man knew his name. Everyone in Moon Hollow had apparently gotten his life history within fifteen minutes of him pulling into town. "I'm afraid we haven't had the pleasure, Mr. —"

Bunk spoke up. "This here's Earl Sharps. Owns the Christmas tree farm on Evergreen Road."

Peter rose to shake Mr. Sharps's hand. "Christmas tree farm, huh?"

"Yessir." Sharps propped a boot on the edge of the porch as if laying claim to it. "'Course business is a little slow this time of year so I also run a small store selling jams and local craft goods to the tourists off the highway."

Peter hadn't seen the store or the farm on his way into town, so he assumed they could be found on the other side of Moon Hollow.

Sharps continued before Peter could come up with a suitable response to his previous comment. "What you talking about? You two had your heads together good and tight when I pulled up."

"I was telling Mr. West here about how our steeple got its makeover," Bunk said.

"Why you telling this man old wives' tales?" He turned to Peter. "Don't let Bunk here fill yer head up with wild stories and nonsense. He'd convince you the sky was purple if you listened.

I'm sure an important writer like yourself got better things to do with yer time."

"It's precisely because I'm a writer that I was enjoying our talk," Peter said. "Wild stories are my business, Mr. Sharps."

The man stilled and narrowed his eyes. Peter wasn't sure exactly what it was about Sharps that got his back up, but he'd instantly disliked the man, and his patronizing attitude toward Bunk had done nothing to redeem his first impression.

"That may be, Mr. West. It may be. But Bunk here got other business t' tend to this afternoon." To Bunk, he said, "Need you to come on with me. There's been some trouble at the mines."

Peter's story-hound nose couldn't resist the whiff of drama. But before he could ask what had happened at the mines, Bunk replied.

"Welp," Bunk exhaled the word as he pushed himself off the chair, "guess that's that then."

Something in Peter's gut tightened—some deep, unknowable source was telling him if he didn't get the rest of the story about Alodius Fry and the demon right then that he'd never get it. "But I was hoping you'd finish—"

"C'mon now, Bunk," Sharps spoke over him. "Deacon's waiting."

If the deacon was involved in the trouble at the mine, Peter definitely wanted to know what was happening. But his instincts told him to keep his mouth shut. Bunk had been friendly enough, but judging from Earl's tone whatever happened at the mine was town business, which meant it wasn't any of Peter's.

"Later." Bunk said the word low and quick, as if he'd hoped Sharps hadn't heard him. But his boss had definitely heard, and looked ready to intercede again.

It grated Peter's nerves to see Bunk cower under Sharps' intimidation. His instincts told him to make a scene. According to his ex, that's what he was best at, right? Despite what she'd said, there was one skill Peter excelled at even more than throwing one of his "temper tantrums," as she'd called them. Like a lot of writers, Peter was an expert at reading people. And right then, his read was telling him that Sharps was a lackey, and that forcing the issue with him would only get back to the real power behind this play—his new friend Deacon Fry—and encourage stronger tactics in the future.

He stepped out of the way to give Bunk an escape route. "See ya soon, Bunk."

The old man paused and met his eyes. Despite his obedient demeanor, a spark of rebellion made Bunk's eyes twinkle with mischief. "Count on it, city boy."

17

THE FIRST REBELLION

Ruby

As Ruby turned toward the door leading into the library's office, her limbs felt not her own. She walked past the bathroom door and went, instead, toward the desk where the library computer buzzed under a humming fluorescent light.

That was her hand clicking the mouse on the icon for the library's ordering system. Her cold fingers typed Peter West's name into the search box. And, finally, it was her fingertip that clicked on the button to confirm an order of five copies of each of his three novels to be delivered to the Moon Hollow Public Library on rush order.

Once it was done, electricity buzzed under her skin. It was sort of like the feeling she'd had seeing Peter West for the first time—the thrill of the forbidden.

No one ever beat Sarah Jane at anything. No one was allowed to. The unspoken rule of Moon Hollow was that if you're going up against a Fry, you'd best lose or they'd make you sorry you was ever born. Sarah Jane might be the prettiest girl in town and she might have the most handsome boy, but in a few days, she'd have to explain to her father, who funded all of the purchases made by the library, why she'd ordered fifteen books written by a known sinner. As far as victories went, it wasn't much, but to Ruby, at that moment, it felt like everything.

"You fall in?" Sarah Jane's voice carried back to the office. Ruby jumped out of the chair and ran toward the restroom door, but before Sarah Jane could come closer, the bell over the front door dinged.

"Hi, Mama!" Sarah Jane called.

Ruby ran the rest of the way to the bathroom door, which gave her a view of the main library room. Sharon Fry's eyes were red and she wrung her hands together as she walked toward her daughter.

"What's wrong?" Sarah Jane stood frozen halfway to the door. Her mother's face was white as marble with thin veins of black mascara crawling toward her trembling jaw.

"Mama?" Sarah Jane whispered.

"Oh, honey." Sharon rushed forward and grabbed her daughter in a hard hug. Sarah Jane laughed but the sound was hollow, as if she was unused to such displays of affection from her mother. "It's Jack."

Snakes writhed in Ruby's stomach; the warm thrill of rebellion gave way to chilly foreboding. "Oh no," she whispered. "No."

In the other room, Sarah Jane's posture had gone stiff. "What about him?" Her voice was high, bordering on hysteria. "What about Jack?"

Sobs burst from Mrs. Fry's mouth, and now it was Sarah Jane's turn to hug her mother, as if she were the child. "Calm down and tell me what happened," she demanded in a tone that sounded a lot like her father's. Her delicate fingers with their pink-tipped nails curled around the older woman's arms and shook her. "Tell me!"

"He's ... oh, Sarah Jane, Jack's dead!"

Sarah Jane's scream was so loud and so long that it reached every dark nook and dusty cranny of the library. But Ruby barely registered it as her knees gave out and she collapsed to the ground.

18

WRITER'S BLOCK

Peter

IT TOOK LONGER than Peter expected to finally hear the details of what happened in the mines. He'd spent most of the day wandering around town, walking the trails leading into the woods. He'd taken a two-hour nap on the hammock of the front porch—a luxury he'd never experienced before but hoped to repeat as often as possible while he was in town. He drove into Big Stone Gap to buy some food and alcohol. Most of his evening was taken up ignoring his email and staring at his word processing program's blinking cursor. It taunted him like a bully.

Whacha gonna write, pretty boy? How you gonna hit the list if you can't even write one fucking word? Where'd your mojo go, hot-shot?

Last time he'd talked to his therapist, she'd warned him not to force it. "Remember, Peter, the subconscious is like a crab. The more you poke at it the more it's going to refuse to come out of its shell." At the time he wondered why he paid so much to a woman who came up with such awful similes.

The steeple. The steeple—the story's in the steeple. Wait, no. There's power in the blood. That's how the hymn went, right? There's power in the blood. But was there a *story* in the blood?

Vampire stories were so 2009. Every writer who liked affording groceries had moved on to zombies, or hell, they'd abandoned horror altogether and started writing young adult novels. Those jokers were getting huge advances and movie deals. Young adult—like that strange girl Ruby. Was there a story about her? But what could be written about a backwoods girl with minimal education who had no ambition or prospects in life. Jesus, it was depressing.

But she'd been scared.

What did a mountain girl have to be afraid of? Amorous cousins?

No, that was too stereotypical. Lazy-assed hacks relied on stereotypes. Real writers focused on authentic details, not generalizations.

He fisted his hair in his hands and pulled, as if the move might encourage much-needed blood circulation to his brain.

There's power in the blood.

What if she was scared of a secret being revealed? What sort of power did Ruby Barrett carry in her blood?

He paused and tapped his pencil on the legal pad he kept next to his laptop. "Mountain magic. Power in the blood."

A knock sounded at the screen door. He jumped at the unexpected sound, and his elbow clipped the glass of bourbon he'd been nursing. It fell to the scarred vinyl flooring, where it bounced without breaking but spilled its contents all over his shoes.

"Shit," he said before he remembered himself.

A salty chuckle came from the door followed by the screech of the screen's ornery hinges as a woman let herself in like she owned the place. He realized that meant she was probably

Lettie Arbuckle. He rose to his full height and turned toward her.

She had the ruddy complexion of a heavy-drinking Anglican preacher. She wore a purple tank top under a pair of camouflage-print overalls. Her feet were shoved in a pair of brown rubber boots with strips of mismatched argyle socks peeking out. The sides of her gray hair were pulled back in daisy barrettes. The only other adornments on her were a pair of glasses with smudged lenses and a cross hanging around her neck from a chain that was probably once gold-colored but which had faded into a tarnished pewter color.

"Sorry, ma'am," he said, hoping the apology would suffice for the spill as well as the liquor.

"Aw, hell, no use crying over spilled bourbon."

"Pour you a glass?"

"About damned time you offered."

Just like that, Lettie Arbuckle became his favorite resident of Moon Hollow. He grabbed a dishtowel from the counter and threw it at the small puddle.

While he poured, she settled herself into one of the metal chairs and rested her hands on her belly. "See you settled in okay."

"So far so good." He handed her a glass.

She tipped her chin in thanks before taking a belt from the bourbon. It was cheap stuff he'd bought at the ABC store in Big Stone Gap.

"Sorry I wasn't here yesterday when you got in. I was visiting some kin 'round Blacksburg."

"Bunk told me. It's no problem." He took his own seat and settled back, mirroring her posture. They fell in a companionable silence. He had questions he wanted to ask about the town and the cabin, about her history, but he refrained. Lettie struck him as the kind of woman who didn't like wasting words. So they drank and the old cuckoo clock on the wall ticked the seconds away.

Finally, she set her glass on the table. "You heard we had some trouble at the mine today?"

"I knew something happened but not what. Nothing serious, I hope."

She clucked her tongue. He realized he hadn't heard that done in years. "Sad business. A boy named Jack died down the mine. First day on the job." She leaned forward to whisper, as if speaking out loud was a sin. "They didn't find all of him."

Peter moved in until their two heads were as close together as co-conspirators. "What do you mean?"

"I just heard when they went down to git him he was real tore up."

Demons in the mines. The phrase from the Appalachian folklore book that had sent him on this journey popped into his head like a revelation.

"Did he fall down a shaft?" He asked this because it was the obvious question, but he really wanted to know if the body betrayed any sign of demonic attack. What the hell would those be anyway? If he were writing a story about it, there'd be black burns on the skin, maybe a mocking stigmata. And symbols. Yes, symbols written on the mine's walls in the boy's blood.

"... one of the deepest mines they don't use no more," Lettie was saying. "Can't figure out how he got down there."

"Did a forensics team—"

Before he could finish the question, Lettie started hooting. "Forensics? Son, this ain't New York City. All we got is a sheriff and deputy that work out of an office fifteen miles away. The sheriff came by to help get the body out, but the only investigation will be done by the mining company to be sure the boy's family can't sue them. Jack ain't the first man murdered by the mines, and sure as hell won't be the last."

Despite the numbing effects of the bourbon, he could have sworn he felt every individual cell in his skin vibrated with excitement. He couldn't wait to get this down on paper, but until Lettie left, he needed to play it cool so she wouldn't think he was a psychopath. Normal people didn't understand why writers got excited about gruesome mining accidents or the prospect of demonic possession. Hell, he wasn't sure he understood it either.

"How old was he?" he asked.

"Nineteen. Such a shame. He was real famous 'round here on account of him being the star quarterback at the high school. He even got a scholarship to Virginia Tech, but he didn't make it six months as a Hokie before he ran home with his tail 'tween his legs."

"Why?"

"Don't rightly know. His mama won't speak of it. You want my opinion, he couldn't handle the big city."

Peter was pretty sure Blacksburg, Virginia wouldn't count as the "big city" to anyone but a resident of a backwater as small as Moon Hollow.

"So he came back to work in the mines?"

"Oh, he resisted that for a while," she said, "worked some odd jobs. 'Course he wants to marry Deacon Fry's girl, so the mines were really his only choice to make enough money to earn her hand."

"Wait, you're telling me that the dead boy in the mine was Deacon Fry's future son-in-law?" Peter realized then that Jack's death was likely the reason the deacon never showed for their meeting that morning.

"That's right." Her tone lowered, as if she was telling secrets. "Not that I like to gossip, mind, but there folks around here who was surprised the good deacon even let that boy near his girl."

"Well, I sure am sorry to hear about the town's loss. Do you know when the funeral will be?"

"That ain't been decided yet. Decoration Day's coming, so that needs to be taken into account." She spoke as if talking to herself. "Of course they could just combine the two."

The folklore book had mentioned the mountain tradition of having an annual "Decoration Day" where the community came together to honor their dead. He assumed it was sort of like Memorial Day, only instead of honoring veterans they celebrated all their deceased kin. "What exactly happens at a Decoration?"

"Oh, they're real fun. First, the men clean up the cemetery and make it look real nice. All the ladies make paper flowers to decorate the graves. Reverend Peale always says a few prayers and we eat at big picnic right in the cemetery."

"I'd like to see that," he said.

She pulled away and brought her glass closer. "Actually that brings us to why I came to talk to you. I'm afraid I'm going to have to cut your rental short."

"What do you mean cut it short? We have a contract." He rose and walked to the computer bag next to the recliner in the living area. He pulled out the contract and waved it in the air for emphasis. "I prepaid for two weeks with the option of adding more."

She didn't appear ruffled by his agitation. "I understand, but that was before."

"Before what?"

"Before Jack." She said it as if it were the most obvious thing in the world.

He softened his tone because he figured Lettie was the kind of woman who wouldn't put up with being sassed. "Can you please explain what that has to do with me staying in this cabin?"

She hefted herself from the chair with a groan. Her right

hand touched her hip, as if the move had tweaked her sciatica. "I'll give you your money back."

The quickening in his chest felt a lot like panic. "No. I can't leave. Not yet."

She frowned at him. "Why not?"

Because I haven't felt this excited about writing in months. An outcast girl with magic in her family line? Demons in the coal mine? Picnics in cemeteries? Pure story gold.

He kept his tone even, so as not to betray his eagerness. "I told you when I rented the place. I'm writing a book."

"Don't see why you have to be in this particular cabin to do that. There's motels in Big Stone Gap."

"Whether you understand it or not isn't the issue. We have an agreement and I paid you for two weeks."

She pursed her lips and looked him over. Then, to herself, she muttered, "I told him."

Peter stepped closer and forced her to look at him. "Who—Deacon Fry? Did he tell you to get rid of me?"

"No, I—" She cleared her throat and backed up a step. "Look, I'll honor your contract, but don't be surprised if you don't last the full two weeks." The words weren't delivered in a threatening tone that implied bodily harm if he stayed, but she sounded fairly confident in her prediction.

He lowered his voice, a trick he'd learned while teaching writing at the community college in Raleigh. Students always ignored raised voices, but a lowered voice worked like magic to get their attention. "Why does Deacon Fry want me gone, Lettie?"

She licked her lips. "You're gonna have to ask him that. Thank you kindly for the drink. If you need towels or anything, just leave a note on the door and I'll take care of it when I stop in to clean."

"Oh, I don't need you to clean—"

A shrewd little smile lifted the corner of her lips. "You were so hot about following our contract, right? I promised maid service three times a week." With that, she turned and walked to the door, leaving him to stare after her with a slight case of vertigo from her mercurial shifts in tone.

"Hey, Lettie?"

"Mmm hmm?"

"Am I in danger here?"

She paused with her hand on the doorknob and watched him for a full ten seconds before answering. "No more than the rest of us."

19

THE REUNION

Ruby

THE BACKPACK over her shoulder held a bologna sandwich, a can of pop, and Daddy's pistol. The old logging road hadn't been used in decades, but the ruts still dug deep into the earth. Ruby stumbled over the grooves and rocks and dodged low-hanging tree limbs.

The canopy above was dense, and the lack of sunlight made it feel cooler than it had been when she'd set out from the house at ten o'clock that morning. Late enough for Daddy and the kids to be well away, but not so late that she risked getting stuck in the woods after dark if her mission took longer than expected.

It had been ten years since she'd last traveled this road. Back then, Mama had held her hand and guided her around the obstacles while telling her fairy tales about the wee folk who lived in the woods. Ruby's memories of her last visit were hazy. What she did remember started out happy—a warm kitchen, feminine laughter, a cup of milk and Granny Maypearl's pie— but it hadn't ended that way. Mama always told her to keep their visits with Granny a secret, but she didn't recall ever asking why. She'd just seen the whole thing as a grand adventure through the woods to the warm little house that always smelled of cinnamon, dried herbs, and Granny's rosewater perfume. After they'd stopped coming, Ruby's adventures were reduced to hiding under her covers at night as the thunder noises of Daddy's shouts and the lightning sound of fist to flesh echoed downstairs.

Ruby tripped over a large root and cursed. What would Daddy say if he found out? Would the thunder and lightning come back?

She shook her head. Daddy spent his days so drunk he'd never be able to follow her up the road. The only way he could find out is if she told him. Or Granny did.

But she'd never tell him, and Granny definitely wouldn't. Whenever Granny'd spoken of Daddy, she called him "that man." She'd never questioned it as a child, but since then she realized Granny could have called him much worse.

She hesitated. A sudden feeling of foreboding draped over her shoulders. What if her memories of Granny weren't real? In her head, the woman who'd given birth to her mother was a perfect being. All warm, papery skin and an easy, gap-toothed smile. She of the delicious cookies and the great stories. But Ruby had grown up to realize that the people we love in memory can be monsters in reality. Hadn't she idolized her daddy as a child?

Ruby began walking again. Regardless of who the real Granny Maypearl was, she was her only hope. She approached the last bend of the logging road, and saw the little house squatting on a rise. Time had shrunk the house. The harsh mountain winters had stripped shingles from the asymmetrical eaves but the shape still reminded Ruby of an old witch's hat. The dooryard was swept clean and a large willow tree drooped dramatically near the picket fence. Ruby remembered hiding under its branches as a girl and pretending she was queen of the faeries and the shady spot was her kingdom.

The old porch was bowed and chipped, but still had the same haint blue ceiling and window frames it had a decade earlier. She remembered Granny explaining that the blue color confused ghosts because they couldn't cross water. She never did learn the significance of the red paint on the door or why the chimney pot was purple, but knowing Granny Maypearl the choices weren't random. The large bundle of dried rosemary and basil on the front door was fresh and a hand-tied broom leaned against the doorframe, ready to sweep away evil at a moment's notice.

Standing on that porch with the sharp green scent of rosemary filling her nose, Ruby felt like she was eight all over again. Her heart quickened and her hand knocked before her mind was ready to announce her arrival.

Ruby thought back to the last time she'd seen Granny Maypearl—or thought she had anyway. Deacon Fry had stood at the head of Mama's grave speaking about the kingdom of heaven. Ruby's swollen eyes had been staring into the dark hole. Mama never was afraid of the dark, but she couldn't stand the idea of her sweet mother sleeping in that pit for the rest of eternity.

She'd looked up to the gray sky, hoping the change in scenery might chase away the tears. A flash of red in the tree line beyond the cemetery distracted her.

The figure behind the tree hadn't been much more than a shadow. But sometimes the heart knows things the eyes can't see, the ears can't hear, and the lips can't speak. She knew who the stranger in the trees was, and once she acknowledged the truth of it, her curiosity was replaced by a gut-chilling fear.

Then, as if the woman in the woods could hear Ruby's

emotions, she emerged just enough to show her face and lifted a gnarled hand to her lips. Luckily, Daddy had been too busy white-knuckling Mama's handkerchief to his heart to notice the unwanted guest. By the time Ruby looked back toward the trees, her grandmother was gone, as if she'd dematerialized.

After her first knock didn't receive a response, Ruby knocked again. However, this time, her ear picked up muted sounds coming from around the back of the house. Curious, she climbed off the porch and skirted the rue and purslane bushes at the base of the steps.

A chicken coop dominated the rear yard. The hens wandered around pecking at corn and each other for entertainment. Inside a small paddock, a sullen goat methodically chewed hay and watched her with condescension. The smell of dust and feathers and feed tickled her nose. She continued on past the animals toward the stand of trees on the edge of the chicken yard.

A small stone shed was nearly camouflaged by the thick vines of kudzu smothering the stone walls and weathered tin roof. Ruby remembered the workshop from her previous visits but she'd never been allowed entrance. Mama always said it was Granny's potting shed. But even at that age, Ruby had known that there was something special about it.

A small chimney puffed a lazy ribbon of smoke, which meant Granny was probably inside. Still, Ruby listened from the edge of the wood for sounds that might tell her whether Granny would welcome or reject her presence. After a few moments of silence punctuated by chicken clucks and the rattle of wind through the leaves, a faint feminine curse reached her ears. Mama had always fussed at Granny for using colorful language around Ruby, but it was one of the things she loved most about her grandmother. It made her seem more honest than other adults who pretended to be saints around kids even though they were devout sinners when young eyes and ears weren't around to witness.

By the time she reached the door, she was feeling braver. This had to work. It just had to. And when you have no other choice, you don't have the luxury of fear.

She didn't bother knocking. The wooden door—painted red to match the one on the main house—opened soundlessly and allowed a cloud of herb- and wood-smoke-scented air to escape. It was darker inside the shed, and so she stood on the threshold for a moment until her eyes adjusted to the gloom. Before they did, a hand snatched her and jerked her inside the shed.

"Git in here! You're gonna spoil it."

She blinked at a small wrinkled face that resembled the apple head dolls the older ladies in Moon Hollow use to make for the girls. The face seemed smaller than it was due to the wild tangle of white hair curling around Granny's head like cotton batting. "I—what?"

Granny put her gnarled hands on her hips and stared up at Ruby as if the girl was forgetting a conversation they'd never had. "The potion."

Ruby scanned the room. She'd been imagining a witch's workshop right out of Grimm's fairy tales, but there wasn't much magical about the workroom. On the walls, several shelves were lined with old mason jars filled with an assortment of items ranging from mismatched buttons to rusted nails to colorful sections of ribbon. Instead of a cauldron sitting over a fire, there was an old woodstove with a dented saucepan set on top. The only other items were a worktable and a stool covered in chipped turquoise paint.

"I always thought you made moonshine out here," she said, almost to herself.

Granny made a disgusted sound and waved a hand. "Shit, girl, this ain't Prohibition anymore. It's cheaper to buy hooch from the package store in Big Stone Gap than to brew your own spirits."

"Daddy makes his in a still."

"Your daddy is a dumb ass." She stirred the concoction three times widdershins and tapped the wooden spoon three more times on the lip of the pot. "Nah, this is just a simple salve for Reverend Peale's eczema."

"Oh." She had no idea how else to respond. She'd expected there to be more awkwardness when she arrived, but Granny was talking like they'd just seen each other yesterday. "Aren't you surprised to see me?"

The old woman tilted her head. "Not a bit."

"Why not?"

Granny snorted. "The wee people told me you was coming to visit."

At Ruby's confused look, the old woman cackled, exposing the impressive gap between her front teeth.

Ruby took a few more experimental steps into the workroom. The floor creaked underfoot, and she had to duck down a bit to accommodate the low ceiling. The air was thick with the scents of vinegar and eucalyptus. Seeing Granny bent over the pot reminded Ruby of the days when she and Granny would make pies together. Sometimes she'd let Ruby roll out the dough and would patiently explain her secret recipe. "When you get married, Rubybug, make sure to give your husband pie as often as possible to keep his disposition sweet." Then she'd would smile a secret smile and start whistling.

Ruby had never met her grandfather, but Granny always wore a locket that held a black and white picture of him. Whenever she'd spoken of him, she'd take the locket between her thumb and forefinger and give it three rubs before laying it back against her breast.

"Well?" Granny Maypearl's voice cut through the memory. "What you want?"

Something about her knowing tone put Ruby's back up. "Didn't the wee folk tell you?"

The corner of her grandmother's mouth twitched. "You sassin' me, Ruby Barrett?"

She raised her chin. "Yes, ma'am."

Granny cackled again. "Good girl. I was afraid growin' up in your daddy's house would make you timid."

Ruby frowned. "Why?"

"Because living with that man broke your mama."

The words hit Ruby in the gut. "No—"

Granny waved an impatient hand. "That girl of mine used to be wild. She used to dance and sing in the woods. She used to throw open her arms and shout her truth to the world. She was alive—a ball of pure energy."

"Mama still sang and danced," Ruby challenged. "You just weren't around to see it."

"What you mean by that, girl?"

Ruby crossed her arms. "You didn't let us come back here."

"That what she told you?"

Ruby shrugged.

Granny took a step forward, and when she spoke her voice was pitched low and hard. "Or did your daddy tell you that?"

"No," she said. "I just knew."

Granny pulled back. "Well, you don't know nuthin', child."

"I know you never came to see us or let us come back."

Granny stared at her for a long time. It might have been the heat in the room that made her cheeks red, but Ruby thought it was more than that. Unfortunately, the lost decade between them prevented her from knowing if the flush was caused by shame or anger.

"Truth is, your daddy found out about your visits with your

mama and refused to let you come back. It was right after she found out she was pregnant with Sissy, and he beat her real bad. She almost lost the baby, but instead of leaving him, she decided it was safer just to cut ties with me."

Ruby's stomach twisted. Her sweet, brave mama wouldn't have been that cowardly. "But—no, Mama would have told me."

Granny shook her head. "Your mama didn't want you to hate that man."

Ruby was silent for a few moments. She didn't want to admit out loud that Mama hadn't gotten what she wanted. Even though her grandmother's dislike of her father was never in question, it felt disloyal somehow to admit her own negative feelings where he was concerned. "Why didn't he want us coming to see you?" she asked finally.

Granny Maypearl turned to stir the pot again. She tapped the spoon three more times before setting it down and wiped her hands on her apron. "You hungry?"

She didn't understand why she felt relieved her question had been ignored. "Maybe a little." Her walk to the little house up the mountain had burned off the cereal she'd had for breakfast.

"Well, come on then." Granny shooed her toward the door. "I made a pie for ya."

Once again, Ruby wondered if Granny had been telling the truth about expecting her arrival. Mama told her once that Granny had what she'd called "the ken"—a talent for knowing things. She'd said that all the women in their family had it. But if that was the case, why hadn't Ruby known her mama was going to die?

With that thought chasing her, she escaped the dark workshop for the safety of sunshine. She walked ahead, not waiting for Granny to catch up. When she reached the back door, she let herself inside. Funny how quickly she felt like she had the right to make herself at home.

The door led into the kitchen at the rear of the little house. The appliances were dated but so clean they sparkled in the mid-morning sunshine from the window over the farmhouse sink. The kitchen table's long wooden planks were shiny with age and showed decades' worth of dents and scratches. Out of habit, she took her normal spot in the center of the bench facing the stove. She used to sit there every time she visited to watch Granny cook.

Almost as soon as she'd sat, Granny bustled through the back door. She nodded at Ruby, as if she approved of the seating choice and continued to the fridge. From it, she removed a jar of milk. "Just milked Petunia this morning."

Ruby drank cow's milk at home, but she had fond memories of the tangy milk from Granny's goat. "Petunia's still alive?"

Granny smirked at her. "Nah. The old girl passed away five years ago. This is Petunia Two." She poured milk into a glass jar before turning to cut a large slice from the pie sitting next to the stove. "How the youngins doing?"

Ruby wasn't ready to talk about them yet. She wanted to get a feel for Granny before she launched into the reason for her visit. "What kind of pie is that?"

Granny's hesitation was brief but noticeable. Ruby tensed, waiting to be questioned. A woman who knew things surely had already anticipated the real reason for her visit. But instead of pressing the issue, Granny came to the table with the milk and the pie. "Strawberry rhubarb."

"That's my favorite."

"That's why I made it."

Ruby looked up from the pie to check if Granny's expression matched her knowing tone. But the woman just smiled at her, as if she was simply enjoying being able to spoil her granddaughter again.

"Thank you," Ruby said. For some reason her eyes started to

sting. This all felt so ... familiar and comforting, but she was keenly aware of her mother's absence. The void was palpable, tugging at her chest and making the blood push against her skin. To cover the unwelcome emotion, she lowered her head and focused on finding the perfect angle to capture the first bite of her pie.

"She visits me."

The words were spoken quietly, but they hit Ruby like a fist between the eyes. She paused with her fork sunk halfway into the pie.

"Your mama," Granny clarified.

Metal clanged against wood. Ruby ignored the dropped fork and the gooey smear on the table. She didn't say a word because no word existed to capture the exact combination of horror and joy those words conjured.

"Started the night she died," Granny continued. "I was sleepin' when a sound woke me. I opened my eyes and there she was standing in a beam of moonlight. I scrambled out of bed thinking one of you children was sick and she needed my help." She shook her head at herself. "But then I realized I could see straight through her, like she was made from cloudy glass."

"Maybe you were dreaming," Ruby said.

"No, ma'am, I was not," she said. "My Rose was here just as sure as you're sitting in front of me now. I tried talking to her, of course, but she just smiled at me."

"What time was this?"

"'Round eleven. Why?"

Ruby swallowed to wet her dry throat. "Mama passed at ten forty." A time that was now eternally cursed to Ruby. Even if she wasn't near a clock when that minute passed each night, she felt a dip in her middle, as if gravity suddenly doubled. Then, at ten forty-one, the world righted itself once again.

Granny leaned back in her chair. "How'd it happen?"

The pie she'd been looking forward to earlier now smelled sickly sweet with an undertone of rot. She pushed back from the table.

"Ruby." Granny's voice wasn't soft like she'd expected. Instead it was sharp, like the tip of a knife. "Did your daddy kill your mama?"

Ruby turned her back to the woman. "Coming here was a mistake."

"Maybe so, but you're here, so we're going to see this through."

"Daddy wasn't even home." Ruby took a deep breath to settle her nerves. "Doc said it was a heart attack."

Granny didn't respond immediately, but the sound of her rising from the table filled the otherwise silent kitchen.

A framed sampler hung on the wall. The fabric was yellowed with age, but Ruby had no problem reading the words stitched from faded blue thread: *Curses, like chickens, come home to roost.* The words blurred through the film of tears.

Granny placed a warm hand on her shoulder. Ruby closed her eyes. The move made several tears run down her cheeks. "Was the doc right?" Granny asked in a whisper.

Ruby shrugged.

The hand disappeared and she missed its soft pressure. Gathering her courage, she opened her eyes. "I couldn't save her."

"From the heart attack?"

Her throat stung but she forced a single word through the tightness: "After."

The old woman's face paled. "What do you mean?"

Ruby turned away from her grandmother and swiped the tears from her face. "Nothing. I just—I was the only one home."

The silence had mass and weight. The sensation of being watched by eyes that saw too much was almost unbearable.

"Ruby," Granny spoke slowly, "did you try to resurrect your mama?"

She turned so fast she bumped into the table, knocking over the glass of milk. Granny's gaze didn't waver from her face. She wanted to run. She wanted to fly away from that little house, away from Moon Hollow. Away from the horrible memories of her mama's sightless eyes. Away from the shame of knowing she couldn't use her song to save the person who mattered most.

"I don't know what you mean." Her voice shook, betraying her lie.

"Young lady, this is your granny you're talking to. I know all about your raisin' gift."

Ruby's head came up so fast her head swam. "What? Even Mama didn't know about it."

"Your mama was a good woman, Ruby. She had her own gifts, but she threw them away."

She moved to the sink and pulled a flour-sack cloth from the counter to mop up the milk. Ruby knew she should offer to do it for her, but her hands were shaking and her limbs felt like sand bags.

"One time, when you was four, your mama left you with me for the afternoon. She had a doctor's appointment that she didn't tell your daddy about. Anyway, you and I were out in the woods, hunting roots when we came across a dead mouse. I told you to leave it be, but you didn't listen and went to kneel next to it. Before I could snatch you away, you started to sing to it. A few moments later, the mouse hopped up and ran into the woods like you'd just woken it up from a nap. But I saw it before, Ruby. The damned thing had been dead as a doornail."

"I don't remember that."

Granny crossed her arms under her breasts. "Don't matter whether you do or not 'cause I'm bettin' it wasn't the last time you did it."

Ruby thought of the other tiny rodents and birds she'd raised over the years. It had been her secret super power—one she'd never even told her mama about. Lot of good it had done her. Shame made her skin clammy every time she thought about how she could raise a dumb bird that barely mattered but not her own mama, who meant everything.

"Well?" Granny wasn't going to let her squirm out of answering.

"I used to be able to do it, but not anymore."

"Since when?"

"Since Mama died," she whispered.

"I knew I should have started training you back then. But your mama said you weren't ready. She promised when you got older that we could begin, but then—"

"But then Mama stopped bringing me around?"

"Anyway," Granny said, "you said something changed since your mama's passing?"

She wanted to ask her more questions about why they stopped coming up the mountain to see her, but Granny clearly wasn't keen on talking about that. "The mountain won't sing to me anymore."

Granny leaned her elbows on the table and put her face real close. "Are you still singing?"

She shook her head and looked at the floor. "What's the point?"

Granny leaned back in the chair and pursed her lips, like she was puzzling over a riddle. "You don't hear the mountain song at all or just during your bleeding?"

Ruby pulled away. She hadn't seen her grandmother in close to a decade. She had fond memories of their afternoons together, but that had been a long time ago. They were basically strangers now. Strangers didn't talk about such things.

Granny Maypearl swatted her arm. "Now don't go gettin'

squeamish on me. I wiped your rear end when you was a baby and your mama's before that." She stared hard at Ruby, daring her to argue. When she didn't, Granny nodded. "So which is it?"

Ruby swallowed the lump in her throat. "I can't hear the songs anymore, so I don't sing anymore."

Granny nodded, as if this confirmed a suspicion she'd had. "It ain't no surprise, is it? Losing your mama like that. Wouldn't have happened if you'd had the proper training. When a girl becomes a woman, there's rituals need done." She sucked on her teeth for a moment. "There's no help for it now. We just gotta start from where we at."

"What do you mean? Start with what?"

"Your training, of course! We have a lot of time to make up for if you're gonna learn the ways of our women."

She held up a hand. "I'm not here for training."

"Whether you came here for it or no, you're getting it. It's past time."

Ruby rose from her seat. "There's no point in training me because I won't be here."

Granny leaned back in her chair and regarded her granddaughter for a good long time. "Where you gonna be, then, girl?"

Ruby shrugged and looked down, suddenly embarrassed. "Away."

"Away." Granny snorted. "You got more of your mama in you than I suspected."

"That's right." She raised her chin. "But Mama never left. I will."

A snort escaped the old woman's mouth. She leaned forward with a hand on her knee. "Oh, she left all right."

"When?"

"Don't know as much as you think." Granny shook her head and crossed her arms. "Your mama left this town when she was seventeen. Thought she was going to use that voice of hers to become a big time star. She crawled back here six months later after calling me collect for bus money. She was married to your daddy a month later."

Ruby frowned so hard an ache appeared between her eyes. "She would have told me—"

"No, she wouldn't have. Every woman's got secrets she keeps from her daughter."

"Why did she come back?"

"Because the world ain't nice to young girls with stars in their eyes."

They stared at each other for a long moment, neither willing to back down. The kettle on the stove whistled, as if calling a time-out. Granny got up, but Ruby knew she was losing the battle. She'd gone to the little house up the hill to ask a favor and now she was messin' it up by being ornery. If she didn't watch it, she'd leave without getting what she came there for, and probably earn herself a heap of extra trouble on top of it.

"I'm sorry," she said, finally. "I just—I miss her so much my chest burns."

Granny kept her back turned, but her head dipped as if to acknowledge the words. She busied herself pouring hot water into two chipped mugs. She removed a couple of jars of herbs from a shelf next to the stove and sprinkled them in. Ruby wanted to ask what sort of herbs she was using, but thought better of it. She didn't want to make Granny think she was curious about root work nor offend the woman by making her think Ruby didn't trust her not to put something suspicious in her drink.

Finally, Granny spoke. "So why'd you come?" She brought the mugs to the table.

No more putting it off, Ruby realized. "I, um, mentioned I'm planning on leaving?"

Granny nodded and blew the steam from the top of her mug.

"Well, I was hoping you'd look in on the girls while I'm gone."

She stopped blowing the steam. "Wait, when you said you was going I thought you meant in a few years. Long after the kids would need watchin'."

"I'm going as soon as I can. Maybe end of next week." Lettie had told her that was when Peter's rental was up.

"You're making a terrible mistake." Granny carefully set down the mug. She shook her head. "No, this is not good at all." Something in the old woman's voice made the hair on Ruby's arms prickle.

"I'll be fine. I have a little money saved up and I'll find some sort of work when I get to Raleigh." She took a sip of her tea to cover her nervous smile. The flavors of sassafras and sourwood honey hit her tongue.

"Raleigh? Why on earth would you go there?"

Ruby realized that Granny hadn't been to town to hear the latest gossip. "There's a visitor in Moon Hollow. An author. He's here writing some new book. When he leaves, I'm going to catch a ride with him."

Granny got real quiet, but the atmosphere in the kitchen shifted as if a low-pressure system was developing between them. "You're a damned fool, then."

She didn't respond. Granny would tell her all the reasons she was foolish whether she asked for them or not.

"Any grown man who'd take a young girl away from her home ain't got *helping* on his mind. He'll use you and he'll abandon you. Then you'll drag yourself home, hoping things will return to how they used to be. But you will never be able to come back, not really. Part of you will always remain out there." She pointed toward the door to indicate the world outside of Moon Hollow. "And the parts that's left? The pieces of you that you don't lose to that man, they'll be shattered like a mirror—a fractured image of who you used to be and who you could have become if you stayed."

Ruby looked her grandmother in the eye. "I am not my mama."

Granny shook her head. "This ain't about your mama. It's about men and girls. You think he's some knight in armor's gonna take you on an adventure?" Her laughter had a mean edge to it. "He'll show you the world and make you someone else, someone you can be proud of being? But it don't work like that, Rubybug. It never works like that."

She crossed her arms and stared down at her muddy shoes. Granny went silent for a few moments, thank the Lord. What did she know about men, anyway? Long as Ruby could remember, Granny had lived alone up on this mountain. After her man died, she'd given up on love. Surely, now she was too old to remember the type of yearning Ruby carried in her belly. The urge to wander and to know a different sort of life. The need to spread her wings and fly. And, yeah, the desire to have a worldly man find something beautiful inside her, a small spark that he'd nurture into a flame.

Oh, how she wanted to burn.

Granny cleared her throat. "Listen, child, I know you think what's waiting for you outside these mountains has to be better than what you got. But you haven't learned all you need to here."

"I got my diploma." Not that Granny had bothered showing up to the ceremony.

"I ain't talking about book learning. This mountain has things to teach you."

Ruby snorted. "It's had eighteen years to teach me. Besides, I told you, it stopped talking to me."

"You just forgot how to listen." She took Ruby's hand. Her skin felt like wrinkled paper, thin and dry. "Not with your ears, child—with your soul. The song comes from inside. Until you learn that, you ain't ready to leave."

She pulled her hand away and rose. "I ain't asking for your permission. You're not my mama."

"What's brought this on now? Your mama passed a month ago."

Ruby pursed her lips. She'd managed to set aside her grief over Jack long enough to do what needed doing, but now, she faced having to acknowledge his loss. It felt like turning to look a ghost in the face.

"Ah," Granny said. Her chair creaked as she leaned back. "This is about that Thompson boy, ain't it?"

Ruby's head snapped up. "What do you know about it?"

She shook her head and smiled. The smugness in her expression made Ruby feel impossibly young and naïve. "I may live up on the mountain, but I know what goes on in that town." She tipped her chin toward the wall next to the fridge, where a harvest yellow wall phone hung. "Edna called me last night. She was burning up the phone lines to all the ladies in the region, I suspect." She paused and her smile faded. "Were you sweet on that boy?"

Ruby jumped out of her chair. "No! It wasn't like that. He was my friend."

Granny nodded but showed no judgment on her face. "He was too damned young to die. Too young for that mine too. It swallows men whole and spits 'em back out broken. Just like your daddy."

Ruby's breath heaved in and out of her chest as if she'd run up the mountain. "Don't you talk about my daddy or Jack. You don't know them." She sucked in a deep breath and released it slowly to calm her pounding heartbeat. "And you don't know me. If you won't pitch in with Sissy and Jinny I'll find someone who will, but I am going to leave. You can't stop me."

Granny rose with aching dignity. She gathered the mugs and put them in the sink. Without turning to look at her granddaughter, she finally spoke again. "I'm not saying *I* won't let you leave." She turned and placed a hand on the counter, as if suddenly needing extra support. "Truth is, the mountain won't let you go."

20

THE BITTER MOURNING

Deacon Fry

SARAH JANE HAD BEEN SCREAMING all night. It was as if the concussion of her breaking heart had shattered her bones, too.

He tried to stay out of the way. Nothing he could do to take away her pain. No way to fix it. So he hid in his office and left the soothing to Sharon. But after several hours of hearing his daughter scream and wail he started to understand why some men escaped the world through alcohol. Take Cotton Barrett, for example. That man started drinking the instant his Rose's funeral was done and hadn't stopped since.

Of course, in addition to being subjected to Sarah Jane's pain, he was doing his own grieving. Even though he hadn't loved the idea of Jack becoming his son-in-law, he thought Jack had many fine qualities. He was too damned young to be dead. But who was he to question the Lord's plan? God had seen it fit to take Isaac and now He'd called Jack home, too.

The deacon sighed and leaned back in his chair. Through the study's window, he looked out on the mountains. In the distance, he could just see the outcropping of Crying Rock. Legends had it that once upon a time, a young Indian girl threw herself off that rock because she couldn't stand the thought of having to leave the mountain when the white folk drove her tribe out.

Lots of people talked about that story with romantic tones. But to him it was just more proof that young women were prone to histrionics. As if his thought conjured it, a fresh volley of wails rushed down the hall and into his office. He slapped his hands on the desktop and pushed himself out of his seat.

A few moments later, he opened the door to Sarah Jane's room. Tears ran down his wife's cheeks as she rocked their daughter's trembling body. Overnight, his beautiful girl had devolved into an apparition, her skin opaque and her eyes, bloodshot and haunted.

"Enough." He didn't shout the word. He didn't plead.

Both women blinked up at him. They were pitiful.

"Enough fussing and carrying on," he continued. "There's work to be done."

The bloody specter from the forest had vexed his dreams all night. His gut told him that the only way to ensure he never saw that thing again was to get the burial done quickly. That's why he'd spent most of the previous day holding Nell Thompson's hand as she planned her son's funeral. She'd wanted to wait a few days, but he'd encouraged her to get it done as quickly as possible so as to begin the healing process.

"Virgil," Sharon said, "she needs time."

"We have a lot to do for the viewing tonight and the funeral tomorrow," he said. "Best to keep busy than to sit around stewing in your tears. There'll be plenty of time to mourn once Jack's put to rest."

Mentioning the boy's name had been a mistake. The instant she heard it, Sarah Jane dissolved into her mother's arms. Over her head, his wife glared at him like he was the worst sort of monster.

He pressed his lips together and prayed to the Good Lord for patience. How nice it must be to have the luxury of indulging every feeling and avoiding responsibility because emotions got in the way. All he knew was that while the womenfolk got to sit around hollering and brining themselves in tears, he had to drive to the funeral home to make sure all the arrangements were coming along. He also had to write his eulogy for the funeral and figure out how to inspire the people of Moon Hollow to believe that Jack's death had been part of the Lord's plan.

But he couldn't say any of that to them. He'd learned a long time ago that trying to reason with his wife and daughter would test even Job's patience. So he just backed out of the room and got on with the business of putting Jack Thompson's broken body to rest.

21

ENEMIES

Peter

THE MORNING after his second night in Moon Hollow, Peter headed down to the town's only diner for breakfast. He wouldn't admit it out loud, but part of him was hoping he'd find out some more gossip about the dead boy while he was there.

The night before, after Lettie left, he'd spent an hour jotting down ideas for a novel. He hadn't written any actual prose, but the germ of an idea had grown into something with a little bit of mass and shape. He was always careful not to impose too much structure on an idea early. Best to let it germinate and grow organically. He was hoping some time at the diner might be the fertilizer his little idea needed to bloom into something real.

Every stool along the counter was taken and two of the booths were packed with bodies, and when he walked in, every one of those people turned to look at him. He'd been expecting as much so he simply tipped his chin and said "Mornin'" before continuing in like he had a right to be there.

He slid into the booth closest to the ones that were already filled because it offered the best opportunities for eavesdropping and gave him a good view of the rest of the diner. Once he was settled, everyone went back to their conversations but in hushed tones that seemed designed to keep the interloper from listening in.

It took fifteen minutes for Edna—he knew her name because of the nametag—to wander over with her order pad. "Get ya something?" Her expression was blank but her eyes were swollen from recent tears.

"I'm sorry but I didn't get a menu."

"You gotta read the board." She pointed toward a chalkboard hanging next to the counter. It listed a few typical breakfast items, but nothing he couldn't have made for himself at the cabin.

"I'll have coffee, bacon, and toast."

She paused. "No eggs?"

"No, thank you."

She shook her head in a way that implied this choice marked him as a suspicious character. "Suit yourself." She tapped her pencil on top of her pad. "How long you in town for, Mr. West?"

"Peter," he corrected. "I've rented Lettie's place for two weeks."

She nodded. "Where's home?"

"Raleigh."

Her eyes widened, as if he mentioned some exotic locale. "Lettie says you write them scary books. That true?"

"Yes, ma'am."

"Hmmph. I don't care much for reading. I'd rather sit and talk to real people."

"I hear you. Being in that cabin was getting kind of lonely. It's nice to have someone to chat with."

"Well, I'm afraid most of us ain't in a real chatty mood this morning." She leaned in to share secrets. "Did you hear about poor Jack Thompson?"

He leaned in too, inviting her confidences. "The boy in the mine? Lettie told me." He shook his head. "Such a shame."

Edna put her pad to her chest. "Terrible to lose someone so young. Especially with Jack being such a hero in these parts. The whole town's broken up."

"Lettie said she wasn't sure about when the funeral would be," he prompted.

"They're doing a visitation tonight and the funeral is tomorrow."

"So soon?"

"Nell—that's Jack's poor mama—told Mrs. McDuffy who told me that the deacon convinced her that doing it quick would be best. Help us all start healing instead of dragging things out."

"I'm sure the deacon knows best."

She nodded. "We're blessed to have his guidance through hard times."

"Edna," called a male voice.

Peter looked over to see Earl Sharps, the man he'd met with Bunk the day before, standing by the counter expectantly.

"Oops, better get back to work," Edna said. "I'll get you that coffee in two shakes of a lamb's tail."

"I'm in no hurry," he assured her.

As she scurried off to talk to Sharps, he sat back in the booth and watched the other man take her by the arm to whisper something in her ear. Her gaze flashed in Peter's direction and she shook her head. Finally, Sharps released her and she disappeared back into the kitchen. The man retook his seat and turned his back on Peter, but the man's awareness of his presence was as palpable as the booth springs poking his rear end.

He removed his notebook from his pocket to jot down some notes. As he wrote down his observations about the diner and the people in it, his brain analyzed the odds of getting run out of town if he attended the funeral. His conscience told him that crashing a man's funeral was the height of inappropriateness, and his sense of duty argued that he'd come to Moon Hollow to work, not to get involved in the town's dramas. Still, he was curious to see how a town like this one handled tragedy. It was in times of stress that people's true character came through, and he was intensely curious to see what Jack Thompson's death brought out in this place and its people.

He'd become so caught up in writing his musings that he didn't notice Edna's return until she set a coffee mug on the table.

"Food'll be up in a minute," she snapped and walked away.

He watched her go, realizing belatedly he should have covered his notes. Had she seen the words he'd used to describe her? He couldn't imagine most people would be thrilled to see someone making notes about their appearance and personality based on a two-minute conversation.

Ed Sharps patted her arm as she walked by. That's when Peter realized that her change in demeanor hadn't had anything to do with his writing, but was the result of pressure from the deacon's henchman to give the new stranger in town the cold shoulder. The problem was, Ed Sharps didn't understand something fundamental about human nature—and Peter's personality specifically. Acting like there was something to hide only made him more determined to investigate.

Ed Sharps also didn't understand that the worst thing he could do at that moment if he wanted Peter gone was to approach him. But that's exactly what happened.

The man got off his stool and sauntered over. The cup of coffee in his hand was fresh and steaming thanks to Edna. "Mr. West," he said by way of greeting.

Peter took a nice long sip of coffee before responding. "Morning, Ed."

The other man's mouth tightened at his familiarity. "May I?"

He tipped his chin toward the other booth. "Suit yourself."

Once Ed was settled he made a real show of trying to look casual, as if he was just being friendly and not preparing to issue the threat he'd come over to deliver. "I spoke to Lettie this morning. She said you were asking some questions about Jack Thompson."

Peter frowned. "That's a bit of a mischaracterization. Lettie told me about how he died and I—"

"We're private people here in Moon Hollow. I sure hope you're not planning on using our tragedy as fodder for your little stories."

Peter had expected ham-fisted threats and posturing. Ed's directness threw him off. "I can assure you it's not my intention to make money off anyone's pain."

It wasn't exactly a lie. After all, if he ended up including a death in the small town in his novel, the cause would most likely be supernatural in nature, not a mundane mining accident. Thus far everything he'd heard about the Thompson boy's death pointed to it being an accident—a rookie miner on his first day making a dumb mistake, nothing more. Ed didn't understand that everything writers hear, see, or experience becomes material for stories. It wasn't that they wanted to take advantage of people's misfortunes so much as they were inspired by them. He was pretty sure if he explained that to Ed or anyone else in Moon Hollow he'd get run out of town with a bunch of torches and pitchforks at his back.

"Still, I think it would be best for you to leave."

There it was. He wondered if Deacon Fry had made Ed rehearse his speech in front of a mirror first. "Or what?"

"Or nothing. I ain't threatening you, Mr. West. I'm simply

stating facts. The town's hurting right now. We need to come together to help heal, and, frankly, you're not one of us. Your presence is a distraction we don't need."

Peter rubbed his lower lip and considered. "Look, I'm not leaving. I paid for two weeks in that cabin and I intend to get my money's worth. But I can promise you that I will stay away from the visitation and the funeral. I need to focus on my writing anyway."

Ed linked his fingers together around his coffee mug. "See, we got ourselves a problem, Mr. West, because I got no reason to trust you."

"Fair enough," Peter said. "I got no reason to promise you a damned thing, either, but I have no desire to stir up problems. I'm damned sorry that you're all in pain, and I have no desire to add to it. However, I have a right to be here and I intend to stay until my rent is up."

"I can call Sheriff Abernathy."

Peter chuckled. "And tell him what? I'm not breaking any laws."

Ed leaned forward with a hard look in his eyes. "You city fellas think you're so smart, don't ya? Folks that grow up on the concrete don't know nothing about the laws of the mountain. If I call Sheriff Abernathy, he'll run you out of town just because you don't belong. It ain't about breaking laws or not. It's about doing what's proper according to our ways."

Peter leaned forward, too. "Ed, I know you're acting on the authority of Deacon Fry, who by the way is also not the law—"

Ed snorted. "He's the mayor, Mr. West."

Peter paused. "What?"

The other man smiled, clearly pleased to have surprised his adversary. "That's right. He's been mayor for a decade now."

He held up a hand. "Why does he go by 'deacon' if he's the

mayor? Surely holding elected office would trump the ecclesiastical one."

Ed frowned liked he didn't quite follow all the words. "That's the problem. You think the law of man outranks God's laws. He goes by 'deacon' because being a servant of the Lord is more important."

Peter leaned back, shaking his head. "Mayor. I can't believe it."

"Your own lack of faith isn't my problem, Mr. West. Point is, one call from Deacon Fry and Sheriff Abernathy'll come running."

By that point, Peter became aware of the silence surrounding them. He looked around to see all eyes on their booth. For the first time, it hit home that he might see the people of Moon Hollow as unworldly hicks, but they saw him as an actual threat. People who felt threatened were liable to do all sorts of desperate things to get rid of the menace. He might not have done anything illegal, but that didn't mean they wouldn't stoop to breaking laws to get rid of him.

"I think we've gotten off on the wrong foot here. I don't know what I've done to offend you or Deacon Fry, but I swear I am only here to get some work done in peace. There's really no cause to get the sheriff involved. I just want to be left alone, and in return I'll stay out of everyone's business."

Ed thought this over for a moment. He finished off his coffee and stood up before answering. "All right, then, but we'll be watching you, Mr. West."

"There's no need, but I understand."

But the thing was, he didn't. Not really. For some reason he'd been able to convince himself that the unwelcoming attitudes of the deacon and his flunkies was just sort of what people in small towns did. He'd seen that dynamic in dozens of films and books, hadn't he?

Problem was, he had a bad habit of seeing everyone as potential characters in his stories and not as real people. Real people were scary. He couldn't control them, for one thing. Real people were unpredictable and selfish and prone to fits of illogical behavior. He'd have to be more careful now. Stay in his cabin for a couple of days. Hopefully, Deacon Fry and his flunkies would be too busy burying that boy to give him any grief.

He stood and threw a twenty on the table. He'd lost his appetite anyway. But when he got to the door, he heard his name and turned. Edna was standing by the counter with a plate in her hand. "Your breakfast, Mr. West."

He opened his mouth to respond, but Ed beat him to it. "Mr. West needs to be going. Ain't that right?" He openly challenged Peter with his gaze.

He wanted nothing more than to lay that man low with a perfect come back. Certainly he was capable of such a thing. Words, after all, were his greatest weapon. But his talk with Ed had been a bit of a gut check, so instead of launching a verbal attack, he simply nodded and slipped out the door. As he walked down the sidewalk, he felt about ten kinds of coward, but men who wielded words as weapons had to be careful when their adversaries carried shotguns.

22

SKELETONS

Ruby

The morning after her visit with Granny Maypearl, Ruby opened the door to the attic, which was right next door to her room. She usually tried to pretend the attic space didn't exist. It was musty and dark in there, and the crates and boxes inside held so many ghosts now that Mama was gone. But after everything Granny had told her, she couldn't resist the urge to go find out if the old woman had been telling the truth.

The space was still as dank as she remembered, but there were way more cobwebs than her memory had told her to expect. She flipped on the flashlight and shined it at the cardboard boxes under the dormer. She'd put them there herself a few weeks earlier after Daddy had told her to pack all of Mama's things or else he'd throw it all away.

Since she'd packed those boxes herself, she knew they didn't contain any clues to what happened during Mama's time away from Moon Hollow. She turned toward another wall, where old trunks and crates were piled to the rafters. She opened the first trunk and found her daddy's old mining helmet inside. It had been five years since he'd retired from the mines because of his lungs. Although, these days she wondered which was blacker—his lungs or his heart?

The next box was full of old baby pictures of her parents and black and white photos of relatives going back a couple of generations. A girl with crooked braids in one picture stood alone on the bowed porch of a tiny house. She held a fiddle in her hand. Her face was dirty but she was smiling and had a determined twinkle in her eyes. Ruby turned over the picture. It said *Rose Maypearl, age 12*. She flipped it back over and studied her mama. The woman she'd known rarely smiled and looked more resigned than determined even on a good day.

The next picture she pulled out was of Granny Maypearl. It had been taken back before she'd been anyone's granny. Her hair hung in a long, dark braid over her shoulder and she squinted at the camera while she smoked an old corncob pipe. She recognized the expression because she'd seen it on Granny's face at least three times the day before. She placed both photos in her pocket and closed the box to continue her search.

Footsteps on the stairs warned her of the arrival of one of her sisters. "Ruby?"

"In here," she called. She put the next box she reached out of the way because it was labeled in her mama's neat script, *R's baby things*.

"Ruby," Jinny whined, "Sissy hid my shoes again."

She opened the next box. That one held dusty Christmas decorations. She closed it and pushed it aside. "Tell her if she doesn't give them back, she can't watch cartoons after school."

"She don't listen to me."

"Doesn't," Ruby corrected. "Wear another pair then."

"But they're my favorites."

Ruby sighed and turned with her hands on her hips. "If you

don't want to wear other shoes then you're going to have to figure out how to convince her yourself."

"But—"

"I don't want to hear it. I got more important things to do than play referee for you two."

Jinny crossed her arms. "What're you doing up here, anyway?"

"None of your business."

"What's got you in such a bad mood?"

She hadn't told her youngest sister about Jack's death. Sissy was old enough that she'd heard about the death at school the day after it happened, but Ruby had made her swear not to tell her sister. They'd just finally gotten to the point where Jinny didn't wake up every night screaming for Mama, and Ruby was afraid the news about Jack might cause her to backslide.

So instead of telling Jinny the real reason she'd been so crabby for the last couple of days, she told her a half-truth. "I can't find something I need."

"Can I help?" Her tone was so hopeful that Ruby didn't have the heart to send her away.

"Sure. Why don't you look through those boxes over there." The ones she pointed to were the ones she knew contained the girls' old toys.

As expected, Jinny was delighted to find her old toys and immediately got busy playing with them. With her occupied, Ruby got back to work looking for her mama's past.

She found it five minutes later in an old trunk at the bottom of a pile of old coats. The shoebox looked innocent enough, but when she opened it, she found brochures from a few Nashville tourist spots, an old journal with a picture of a kitten on the front, and a cardboard jewelry box with a charm bracelet inside. She lifted the last item and saw that the single charm was shaped like a guitar with the word "Nashville" creating the neck of the instrument. There was also a small disk with the letter "R" written on it linked in the chain. At some point in the past the metal has been silver in tone but now it was tarnished.

"What's that?" Jinny asked.

Ruby looked up but hid the bracelet in her clenched palm. "Just an old piece of junk."

Luckily, her sister's interest dissolved quickly in favor of digging through the box in front of her for clothes for the naked doll in her hand. Ruby tucked the bracelet in the pocket of her jeans and moved to the journal.

There was a small clasp with a tiny lock holding it closed. Ruby rooted through the shoebox for the key, but came up empty handed. It wouldn't be too hard for her to pick a lock like that with a bobby pin or a paperclip, but she still felt frustrated. She knew that the answers she wanted were inside that journal but if she rushed out and started trying to pick the lock, the girls would get curious and try to see what she was doing.

She knew it was selfish, but she didn't want them to know what she was doing. The Mama that she was looking for existed long before Sissy and Jinny came along, and it would be a few years yet before they could relate to the almost-woman their mother had been when she left Moon Hollow. But to Ruby it felt like a message left for her by the past-Mama to help her make decisions about her future.

She placed the journal back in the box and closed the lid. "Put them toys away and come on."

Jinny looked up from wedging a tiny plastic shoe on her doll. "Can I take them with me?"

Ruby looked down at her little sister. Most of the time, she had the typical older sister feelings toward the girls. They were always annoying her and she sometimes wished Mama and Daddy had made her an only child. But ever since Mama died and Ruby became the woman of the house, she developed a new protective instinct toward them. At moments like these, she felt sorry for them. Ruby had gotten her mama for eighteen years. But Jinny was only eight and Sissy was twelve. Now, they both had to grow up without Mama's warm hands to guide them or her soft voice saying just the right thing when they were upset.

Looking down into Jinny's small face with the freckles sprinkled across her nose—Mama always called them "angel kisses"—Ruby realized it was up to her to be the warm hands and soft voice for her sisters now. Except she wouldn't be able to do that if she left.

Could she really count on Granny being there for them? She hadn't been there for Mama—or any of them—all those years. Granny claimed it was her daddy's fault, and she believed he might be the reason for the fight that started the separation, but the way she saw it, she couldn't imagine any mother turning her back on her daughter because of a silly fight.

"Ruby?" Jinny said. "You okay?"

Ruby cleared away the knot in her throat. "Yeah."

Jinny held up the doll with its ratty hair. It wore one shoe and a shirt but didn't have any pants on. Something about that half-naked doll made her incredibly sad.

"You can take the toys."

As her little sister whooped with joy, Ruby clutched the shoebox in her hand. She'd wait until the girls got off to school to read what was inside. If she were lucky, she'd find something to help her make up her mind about whether to stay or to go. She no longer knew which outcome she was wishing for.

23

THE VISITATION

Deacon Fry

THE DICKEY FAMILY had been burying Moon Hollow's dead for generations. Some of the other towns in their section of Wise County used Perkins Funeral Home in Big Stone Gap, but Deacon Fry refused to let any of his people give business to those Episcopalians.

He arrived at two o'clock to prepare for the visitation. Angus Dickey IV, the current director of the funeral home, was technically in charge of the visitation, but he wanted to be sure that everything was just right for Jack.

The funeral home sat across the town limits from Moon Hollow in Norton. The single-story building had no windows and the pitched roof looked too large for the structure and pressed down on the bricks like an oppressive hand. A green-striped awning on the side of the building hung over the old hearse, which Angus's daddy, Angus III had purchased in 1985.

Before he opened the front door, he took a deep breath to steel himself in case Nell was lying in wait. Ever since Jack died, the woman had stuck on the deacon like bird shit on a tree branch. It wasn't that he didn't feel for her, but she was as depressing as a raincloud on Easter morning.

"Deacon!"

His hand spasmed on the door handle. Too late to back out and run. He tightened his lips into what he hoped was a smile and let the door close behind him.

Grief had bowed her shoulders and sucked all the life from her eyes. A few strands of hair framed her face, which was as cracked and dry as a creek bed after a six-month drought. She'd never really recovered after her husband, George, had died ten years earlier from the black lung. He had worked the mines for twenty years before they'd killed him. Her son hadn't survived a day down there.

"You're here early," he said.

She pushed a strand of hair back. "Wanted to be sure everything was right."

A flare of annoyance bloomed in his chest. That was his job. He placed a hand on her shoulder and squeezed. "Angus puts on a nice event. Jack's in good hands."

What was left of him, anyway, he thought, but immediately regretted it. Now was not the time for unchristian thoughts. Still, Angus had been pretty detailed in his description of the state of what was left of the body when it had come in.

"I swear, Virgil, it looked like what's left after a pig pickin'. Must have been a bear or something hunkered down in that shaft."

He pushed that conversation from his mind and focused on the mixture of hope and despair in Nell's expression. "Why don't you go home and lay down? People won't be here for a few hours yet."

She hesitated. "I cain't leave him." The words came out sounding like she was seeking permission to do just that.

"Sure you can. I'll be here with him until the viewing begins. You probably haven't slept a wink."

"I don't know if I could. Every time I close my eyes, I see him." She shivered. He knew exactly how she felt, but didn't mention the dreams he'd been having.

"At least go freshen up. A bath and a clean dress will help you feel more comfortable for the viewing."

For a couple of hours that evening, family and friends would stop by to pay their respects and tell stories about Jack. Nell had originally wanted to stay overnight at the funeral home with Jack's body, but he and Angus had talked her out of it.

"You'll feel better if you let yourself rest a spell."

"Maybe you're right," she whispered.

He lifted the corner of his mouth in what he thought of as his I-know-what's-best smile. It worked well on women because they were so eager to have a man think for them.

She promised to be back before Angus moved the coffin into the viewing room. As the door closed behind her, he let his smile fade. He'd tried to convince her to skip the viewing altogether, but she'd insisted on sticking with tradition even though the infernal coffin had to remain closed. They could have done a nice wake with Jack's picture framed on the table and some flowers. But now they'd all be in that room with the closed coffin and the boy's mangled remains inside like some sort of grim surprise.

He grabbed his box and continued into the funeral home in search of Angus. After finding the funeral director's office and the other rooms on the main floor empty, he gave up. Most likely, Angus was down in the basement doing last minute work on Jack's remains to make them ready to sit out for several hours. He didn't even consider going down to find out if his theory was true. He had no interest in seeing what was left of that boy with his own two eyes.

Instead, he went into the visitation room. A central aisle divided two columns of pews that could accommodate most of the population of Moon Hollow. At the front of the room, a raised stage held a podium and a platform for the coffin. In front of the stage, Angus had already set up a handful of chairs for Nell and her kin to sit on while receiving visitors. Along the right side of the room, long folding tables had been erected to hold all the food and drink the mourners would bring.

Traditionally, the viewing was not a time for grief. Instead, it was like a party where people shared stories about the deceased and celebrated their lives. There'd be plenty of time for wailing and hollering at the funeral the next afternoon up on Cemetery Hill. But at the visitation, the deacon's job was to redirect anyone who was having trouble keeping their feelings in control out into the lobby so they'd not upset Jack's family.

He began distributing prayer books to the pews just in case someone visiting decided they needed comfort from the Good Word. He didn't like the visitation room. It looked like a chapel but it didn't feel like one. This room was cold, sterile. His own church—the one he considered his, anyway—was always filled with colorful light from the stained glass and the ladies' auxiliary kept the chapel full of flowers and beeswax candles. The visitation room, however, smelled like the carpet needed a good vacuuming and didn't have any decorations or flowers. He couldn't totally blame Angus for that last part. Nell couldn't afford flowers to decorate the room. He made a mental note to call his wife and ask her to bring some clippings from their rose garden when she arrived later that evening.

He was halfway up the aisle when he heard a noise that sounded like the doors to the room opening. He kept to his work but called out, "You all done?"

No answer.

He paused and looked up. The doors were closed and Angus

wasn't there. He was still alone. He slid another book into the pew's shelf. It was no wonder he was hearing things. The funeral home always made him feel uneasy. Not that that was anything unusual. He figured it'd be unusual for a fella to feel totally at home around all them bodies and such. That's why he was always careful around Angus. Even if the man had started out sane, the deacon couldn't imagine that sniffing all them chemicals and handling dead bodies was good for a man's mind.

The noise again. But the door at the back of the room remained closed. However, when he turned he saw that the door near the platform was open. That door led to the back hall where the elevator down to the embalming rooms was located. It was open wide, like someone had propped it open to bring in a coffin.

"Angus?"

His heart fell into a trot. It was possible he'd forgotten the door was open when he walked in. But no, it had been closed. He knew it.

"Hello?"

No response. Thinking that maybe Angus had opened the door and then realized he'd forgotten something and ran to grab it, he relaxed a fraction. But he still went to check it out.

"Angus?"

The back hallway was darker than the visitation room had been. The air was colder there, too. The air smelled different there—putrid. Maybe it was his imagination but he wondered if it was from the fumes creeping up the elevator shaft.

"Anyone there?"

At the end of the hallway, a thin line of light near the floor indicated the position of the elevator doors. He focused on that beacon and moved forward, past several open doors leading to other visitation rooms, an office, and a restroom. Each were dark as mine shafts.

A loud grinding sound filled the dark corridor—the elevator churning up from the basement. He froze, his stomach tight with indecision. His rational mind rejected the fear immediately. Obviously it was just Angus on his way up. But his deep mind, the one that never walked past the cemetery on a new moon, whispered sinister theories in his ear.

The temperature dropped. His hands shook on the prayer book he'd carried with him out of the visitation room. The weight of the Lord's words should have been a measure of comfort against his wicked imagination, but his throat still tightened on the first notes of a whispered prayer for protection.

Gears ground against metal. His heartbeat pounded in his ears and bile boiled up the back of his throat. The sliver of light from the elevator shaft changed from warm yellow to corpse blue.

It's Jack.

"Oh God, no," he whispered. He lifted the hymnal like a shield.

Grinding, the gears grinding like sharp teeth devouring bone.

Virgil.

The whisper seemed to come from outside and inside all at once and the voice that said it was not his own. He spun to look back down the hall. He was alone.

Repent, Virgil.

A sob tore from his throat. "What? Oh God, protect me."

His knees wobbled. He fell back against the wall for support. He wanted to curl up and sob like a little child. It was so dark and he was so alone.

A high-pitched, lunatic's laugh echoed through his head. *You're not alone.*

"What do you want?" he shouted. "Tell me!"

Silence. Blue light creeped like frost across the floor. Cold air burned his throat, his lungs. His heart pounded like a prisoner against the cage of his ribs. Pressure built from inside, like madness.

Revelation.

One word, four syllables—a world of terror. Because when that single word echoed through his brain it conjured memories of a winter day. Bare branches scraping a steel sky. The river an indifferent witness. Blood on his hands. A deep, dark well swallowing his secret.

Before the voice or the memory could totally break him, a loud bell dinged in the hallway. The tension in the air popped like a balloon. The elevator doors opened to reveal Angus standing behind a long, wooden box.

His knees gave out. Angus called his name, but the word sounded as if it had been shouted under water. He ignored the call and tried to quiet the voice in his head.

Revelation, revelation, revelation.

A damp palm slapped his cheek. He shook himself and snapped his attention toward Angus's ugly but concerned face.

"Virgil? By God, you scairt the hell outta me!"

He blew out a long breath and let his head fall back to rest against the wall. "What happened?"

"Them elevator doors opened and you was standing there looking like you'd seen your own ghost. Then you dropped to the ground. I thought you was strokin' out or something." He squinted, as if he could gauge the deacon's health by sight alone. "You sure you're okay?"

He swallowed the lingering lump of fear and pushed it way down. Indigestion. That's all it was. His damned wife's dog food casserole that he'd eaten because she'd been too busy carrying on with Sarah Jane to fix him a sandwich. "Ate something bad, I reckon."

Angus chuckled, as if he'd suspected as much all along.

"Hoo boy, I was worried. I've had lots of dead'uns in here, but I ain't had nobody die *in* the funeral home. Wouldn't that just beat all?"

He pressed his lips together to prevent himself from telling the man to shut up. Just shut up. He needed quiet. He needed to get the hell away from that hallway and—

His attention drifted to the coffin just outside the elevator.

He needed to get out of that hallway and as far from that building as he could.

"I need to go home," he said, more to himself than Virgil. "Can you call Deacon Smythe? Tell him I fell ill and he needs to come tend the flock for the visitation."

Angus hesitated. "Sure thing, but you sure you're okay to drive?"

Nothing hurt, except for a dull ache at the base of his skull from dealing with Angus. He pushed himself up the wall until he stood. His legs wobbled a little, but it was nothing some fresh air couldn't fix. "I'll be just fine."

He placed a reassuring hand on Angus's arm. He had to get out of there before Nell returned. If she caught him in this condition, he wasn't sure he'd be able to get away without snapping at the poor woman. "Just need to get home and let the missus fret over me a little."

"You want me to call her?"

"Don't worry her. Thanks, Angus."

He walked away before the man could open his fool mouth again. Instead of taking the direct route all the way down the hall to the lobby, he detoured through the visitation room. Behind him, the squeak of wheels told him that Angus had begun wheeling the coffin into the room. He picked up his pace. Death thickened the air and smudged every surface. He had to get out.

When he finally burst through the doors back into the lobby, some of the tension in his chest eased. He took several quick steps toward freedom. He could already taste the blessing of fresh air on his tongue before he reached the door.

His palm and fingers curled around the handle, but before he could open it, a painting next to the door caught his eye. He'd seen the small picture of Christ holding a baby lamb dozens of times, but, that day, something unsettled him. He released the handle and stepped closer to get a better look.

An entire flock of mature sheep gathered around the Savior's legs as He cradled the lamb. It was meant to be a comforting image to mourners, a happy reminder that their loved one had joined Christ's flock in heaven. Something, though—he couldn't put his finger on what was wrong.

A rush of air swept in as the door opened. "Deacon Fry?"

He didn't look toward Deacon Smythe; he was too busy studying the image. The man's cloying cologne reminded him how he'd longed for fresh air, but first, he needed to figure out—

"Deacon Fry?" Smythe's tone veered toward a whine. "I brought the food the ladies' auxiliary cooked for the viewing."

Smythe's words evaporated inside his head before they took on real meaning. He stepped closer. He reassured himself that the sheep looked normal and that Christ's robes were pristine as ever. The sky in the background was cheerful blue, and the Savior's face was serene. But then, a detail in the background he'd not noticed before caught his eye. While the foreground was a cheerful scene of Christ and his flock, in the background there was a grouping of tombstones.

"Sir? Where do you want me to set up?"

He fumbled with his jacket pocket and removed his readers. Slipping them on his nose, he moved closer until he was only a few inches from the painting.

"Should I ask Mr. Dickey instead?"

There were three tombstones—one in front and two behind.

Only the front appeared to have writing on it. He squinted at the tiny letters. Instead of a name inscribed on the tombstone, there was a single word.

"Revelation," he whispered.

"Huh?"

He jerked away from the painting. In his haste to escape it, he barreled over Smythe.

"Hey! Where you going?"

Without answering, he threw open the door and ran into the parking lot. Once he was by his car, he bent over with his hands on his knees and sucked in three great gulps of sweet mountain air.

He got inside the car because it felt safer there. He gripped the steering wheel. Despite what he'd told Angus, he had no intention of going home. The thought of being around all those tears and the damned neediness made him want to hit something.

He needed help. Someone who could tell him why a ghost might be haunting him despite his doing everything right. Wasn't he setting up the viewing? Hadn't he spent the morning writing a eulogy for the boy? Yet the ghost was still upset.

He needed help, but the only person he could think of who could do the job was the last person he ever wanted to ask for a favor. He looked in the rearview mirror at the funeral home. The building seemed to throb with menace.

He turned on the ignition, and drove off without deciding where he was headed. He figured the good Lord would guide his wheels in the direction he was meant to go. He just prayed that wherever he ended up, the ghost wouldn't find him.

24

PETALS AND THORNS

Granny Maypearl

THE WILD ROSES spread their petals to the sun. Overnight, the large bush on the eastern corner of the house had offered up a dozen hot pink beauties. Come June the branches would be weighed down with hundreds of blooms, but right now she only needed a few handfuls.

The previous night she'd dreamt of crows gathering against a bloody sky. She'd woken with a dry throat and her left knee ached something fierce. Trouble was comin' to Moon Hollow, and she needed to prepare. Once the rose petals were simmering in rainwater she'd collected during a dark moon, she'd begin the process of washing down the front door and sweeping the threshold.

While she collected roses, Billy lay on the porch. He'd been restless all morning, sniffing at corners and growling at the windows like intruders were loitering in the woods, but he'd finally found a warm shaft of sunlight that had lulled him to sleep.

The petals felt like silk on her fingers. She paused in her harvest to bring one to her nose. The scent reminded her of her own granny—Granny Bell—who'd worn rosewater perfume every day of her livin' life. A generous hug from her always brought with it the scent of flowers and freshly risen dough. Bell had taught her how to use food as medicine and spent hours drilling her in the garden about the proper use of herbs and plants for different ailments. Granny closed her eyes and took another wistful sniff. Roses were a sign of spring and hope, but the reason she needed them was definitely the stuff of deep winter and dread.

Billy's low growl warned her of someone's approach. Distracted by the noise, she didn't notice the thorn on the bush until it impaled itself in her fingertip. She yelped and pulled the injured finger to her mouth. The flavor of copper spread on her tongue in the same instant the man emerged from the woods.

She had the shotgun in her hand before she'd made a conscious decision to grab it. Over the long barrel, she finally took her first good look at the visitor. He'd stopped just past the edge of the trees. He raised a hand to push the straw hat back from his brow. The sunlight bounced off his white hair, which fell across the scar on his forehead.

She lowered the shotgun from killing height to her hip, where it would still serve as a warning to mind his manners. "Damn it, Virgil. You scared the tar out of me!"

"Mornin'," he called. His sweet-tea tone was far too friendly to be natural.

"What you doin' way out here?"

He walked several feet forward. She adjusted the shotgun on her hip. He stopped. "There's no reason to be ornery."

She watched him. The silence filled with memories of sixty years of haunted history between the good deacon and the mountain's only witch. Of course, she wasn't a witch at all, but a granny woman, skilled in folk remedies. That never stopped him from tellin' his parishioners she was a bride of Satan, though. 'Course, his parishioners were also her best customers. Not that she's tell him that and risk his wrath.

Finally, the smile on his lips tightened into a pucker, as if he'd belatedly realized he'd put a little too much lemon in that sweet tea. "I need some advice."

A laugh escaped her like a bird shooting out of the underbrush. The sound disturbed Billy, who woofed as he came out of his slumber. "That'll be the day."

He stabbed the walking stick into the dirt a few times. "You got any of that apple pie shine?"

"Thought you didn't drink."

He sighed. "For the business I come to discuss I'm willing to make an exception."

She sucked her teeth as she looked him over for signs of trickery. Virgil Fry had been born with a silver tongue in his mouth, but he rarely used it on her. He learned real early that she was immune to his verbal sorcery, which was why he'd done his best to turn everyone against her. Hell, she hadn't seen the man since Rose's funeral, and she wasn't even sure he'd known she was there.

"Maypearl, please," he said. "I need yer help."

It was the naked pleading in his tone that decided her. She'd known Virgil her whole life, but that had been the first time she'd heard a lick of vulnerability in his voice.

She grabbed her basket of rose petals. "C'mon, then."

25

HOODOO

Deacon Fry

THE OLD BAT had made him beg. When he'd finally admitted to himself that he was setting out for her house, he'd been prepared to jump through some hoops. She'd always enjoyed making him squirm. Back when they were in school, when all the other kids would shrink away from him, Maypearl always stood a little taller and watched him with those gypsy eyes that seemed to see right through his skin and into the dark spots in his bones.

The steps creaked under his boots and that old hound dog gave him the side-eye. The only way he could have felt less welcome would have been if she'd hung a *No Deacons Allowed* banner over her door.

He shouldn't have come.

"Well," the old bat yelled, "you comin' in or what?"

He leaned his walking stick by the door and stepped inside. The scent of dried herbs tickled his nostrils. The damned placed smelled like a hippie hideout. Looked like one, too. Colorful quilts covered the sofa and chairs. Beads hung from every doorway. Each window had some sort of colorful geegaw or doodad hanging from their frames to sparkle in the afternoon sun. All of this confirmed his suspicions that Granny Maypearl's famous visions were the result of smoking drugs.

Of course, her pagan ways also made her the only person in Moon Hollow who could advise him about his predicament. The good Lord sure did have a warped sense of humor sometimes.

She wasn't in the living room. "Where'd ya go?"

"Kitchen." The muted reply came from a doorway on the far side of the room.

The room he entered was larger than the living room by double. Something was steaming inside a large pot on the stove. Dried bundles of herbs hung from hooks in the room's corners. A large window over the sink let in enough light to give the room a cheerful feeling, but it couldn't dispel the constant chill he'd carried in his bones since the day Jack died.

Maypearl stood at the stove. Humming to herself, she placed a small pan on one of the gas burners. She poured some liquid into the pot from a chipped ceramic pitcher. Then she took a handful of pink petals from the pocket of her apron and added those to the pot.

"What you makin'?"

The long, gray braid down her back twitched as she turned to peek at him. "Rose water."

"Hmmph." He'd suspected her of cooking some sort of devil's potion, but she'd just been making some toilet water.

"I got tea."

"I'm fine." He didn't trust any tea that came out of that old witch's kitchen. He noticed she hadn't offered him any of her famous apple pie moonshine like he'd asked for earlier. Knowing her, it hadn't slipped her mind.

"Suit yerself." She turned back to the stove.

Why didn't she ask him already? "May I sit?"

The braid twitched again as she shrugged.

He pulled a chair from the table and lowered his aching joints into the hard seat. He'd be paying for that long walk up the mountain for the next few days. Still, he maintained a dignified posture so the old witch wouldn't forget who she was speaking to.

Except she wasn't speaking to him, was she?

He cleared his throat.

She tapped a wooden spoon on the lip of the dented copper pot. Turning from the stove, she wiped her hands on her apron before taking a seat at the table. Once she settled, she placed her hands in her lap and watched him. He tried not to squirm like a young boy being held back after class by the schoolmarm.

"You heard about Jack?"

She pressed her lips together but nodded. No words. Didn't she know she was supposed to say something now? That she was supposed to help him through this? Did she think it was easy, him coming here?

"Funeral is tomorrow."

She pulled a sprig of some herb from a mason jar on the table. It looked like a tiny Christmas tree branch. She lifted the spiky twig to her nose and inhaled, as if trying to fill every tainted space in her body with a clean scent.

"You going?"

She looked up and smiled. "Would you let me in that church if I wanted to?"

The words sounded uncomfortably like she was daring him to lie to her. "You could come to the cemetery." He paused. "Like how you came down for Rose's services." He'd seen her hiding behind the tree trunks, trying to blend into the shadows.

Her expression didn't change. "Of course I did. Rose was my heart."

The words were simple and spoken softly, but they hit him directly in the center of his chest. He licked his lips. He should never have mentioned Rose. That trail led to tricky ground.

"Anyway," he said, shifting on his seat.

"Did you come all the way up here to invite me to the service, Virgil?" The patronizing patience was gone. He definitely shouldn't have brought up Rose.

"I think I will take that tea after all."

She watched him.

He grabbed a stem of the green herb from the jar and sniffed. The green scent reminded him of the shrub his wife kept by the back door of their house.

"Virgil?"

"Yes?"

"Why are you here?"

He tossed the herb on the table. Now or never. "You ever seen a ghost?"

Her frown deepened. At least she didn't laugh at him, but, then, that's why he'd come to her. Out of everyone in Moon Hollow Maypearl was the last one who'd make fun of someone for believing a bit of hoodoo. "Maybe so," she said, finally. "Have you?"

He shrugged. "Could be."

"Jack's?"

Hearing his name like that, so soon after he'd mentioned the ghost, so soon after he'd seen the ghost, made his skin feel too tight. He shrugged because he worried speaking might summon the spook directly into that kitchen.

She leaned forward and looked at him over the rim of her spectacles. "When?"

"Few times."

"Where?"

Everywhere. "Here and there. Last time was," he paused to sigh, "was just a bit ago at the funeral home."

"Tell me what happened." Her tone was all-business, a professional getting down to work.

He told her most of it. Told her about the hallway and the scent of blood and the cold, cold air. But he didn't mention the word that had haunted his brain ever since the specter whispered them into his ear.

Revelation.

He was almost done telling her the parts he was willing to share when a hiss sounded from the stove. The water in the pot had boiled over to sizzle on the hot burner. She rose from her seat and removed the pot from the flame. As she pulled down a sieve from an overhead rack, he caught her face in profile. Her features were pinched tight, as if she was concentrating on more than just pouring the rose water through the strainer. Had she heard stories like his before? She'd betrayed very little expression while he spoke, and when she'd asked questions, her tone was quiet, not afraid or suspicious.

"Anything else happened?" Her back was toward him as she worked with the rose water. It made answering easier.

"Just dreams."

She nodded. "Anyone else besides Jack in the dreams?"

He started to tell her no, but stopped. The image of Jack dancing in fire and blood had vexed him all day, but now that they were talking about it, new elements of the dream revealed themselves in flashback. It was as if her question had opened a door on the rest of the dream. But he couldn't tell her everything. No one could ever know everything. "Rose was riding on a crow's back through the graveyard."

Maypearl froze and spun slowly to look at him. "You're sure?"

"Yes. There was also something about a bear down in the mines, but I think that was just because of something Angus said."

She set down the bowl of pink water and wiped her hands on her apron. "What did he say?"

He leaned back in his chair and clasped his hands over his belly. "Oh nothin'."

"I can't help you if you're not honest." And there was that look again; he could feel it probing inside him, trying to find all his shadows.

He sighed. "Angus said when they brought in Jack's body it looked like an animal had gotten hold of him. A bear, maybe."

She frowned. "Bears don't go into the mines."

He ran a finger over the table's scarred wood. "He was found in an abandoned shaft. One of them the kids climb into from the woods?" To fornicate, he thought. Sin holes, he called 'em. "Angus was thinking maybe Jack disturbed a sleeping bear by accidentally breaking through a shaft wall."

"But the mine shafts are too deep for—"

He spoke over her. "Anyway, that's all the dreams I been having."

She clucked her tongue and turned toward a cabinet. Pots clanged together as she rummaged through the shelves. Finally, she pulled out two small bottles with sprayer lids. She filled each with rose water. Once the second lid was screwed into place, she spoke again. "It's about time for Decoration Day."

"Is it?" He concentrated on the herb he now recognized as rosemary, and he began stripping the little spikes off one at a time.

"You know damned well it is. It's already mid-May. Usually it happens earlier in the month."

The unexpected question made him stop torturing the rosemary. "What does that have to do with Jack?"

She snorted and waved her hand to dismiss the notion. "A proper Decoration is more than a picnic in the cemetery and you strutting around like the cock of the walk giving speeches about temperance. It's about honoring the dead and making sure we do right by them."

He tossed what was left of the stem onto the pile of broken leaves on the table. With a sigh, he leaned back in his chair. "Maybe we'll skip it this year. Town's going through enough with Jack and your Rose only a month ago."

"Jack and Rose are the reason you have to do a Decoration, Virgil. The proper rites must be observed."

He shook his head. "Don't go spouting your pagan mumbo jumbo to me, woman. Rose received a proper burial according to our customs, as will Jack."

"Your own daddy oversaw the Decorations for years. He respected the traditions. You saying he's a pagan, too?"

"Watch your mouth. My daddy was a good man. If he followed the rituals it was only because it was tradition, nothing more."

She crossed her arms. "Yeah, well, your daddy never asked me if I saw ghosts with fear in his voice."

He rose abruptly. "This was a bad idea."

"No, the bad idea was not doing the rituals like you was supposed to. Jack died during the dark moon."

He stared at her because he had no idea how to respond to such a random statement. Finally, she took mercy on him and explained.

"Spirits get restless when there's no moon. If proper precautions haven't been taken, bad things can happen."

He wanted to ask what sorts of things, but then he remembered he didn't believe in any of that stuff. He shouldn't have come. He just was having an episode was all. Lack of sleep and stress were playing games with his mind. Didn't help that his own home had been filled with wailing and carrying on ever since Sarah Jane found out her beau had died. He just needed to get a handle on things again. Once the funeral was over, things would get better. "I need to leave."

She didn't try to stop him, but she thrust one of the bottles of rose water into his hand. "Here."

He frowned down at the bottle. "I'll give it to Sarah Jane." Maybe it would make her stop sobbing for five seconds, Lord willing.

"It ain't for Sarah Jane, you old fool—it's for you."

"I—"

"Spread it around every window and door leading out of the house for protection."

"Sounds like magical bunk to me." He tried to hand the sprayer back to her, but she resisted.

"Don't think of it as magic, so much as aromatherapy. The scent is calming and promotes peace."

He paused in his effort to force her to take the bottle. Peace and calm were two things his house could definitely use. He unscrewed the cap and sniffed the water. The soft scent was pleasing and he felt an easing of tension that had gripped his neck ever since he saw that unspeakable thing in the woods. He replaced the cap and stuck the bottle in his pocket. He didn't thank her for it because that would mean acknowledging he'd accept a gift from a heathen witch.

He turned to go without another word. But just before he escaped the kitchen, she spoke again. "You want them ghosts gone for good, you gotta do the magical bunk."

Pausing on the threshold, he turned to look at her. "I'm not saying I'll do it, but what would it entail, exactly?"

She didn't smile. For that he was grateful. "If you want to be rid of the haint that's vexing you personally, you gotta get yerself a tater. Don't wash it and don't peel it. Cut it in half and hollow out a little bit of the meat. Put something of Jack's inside. Don't have to be anything special—just something he owned. Reseal the tater with two long nails and bury it near his grave."

He made a raspberry sound with his lips. The idea that the evil thing he'd seen would be scared away by a damned potato was the funniest thing he'd heard in weeks. "I'm wasting my time with this blasphemy."

She shrugged. "This ain't going away, Virgil. There's forces at work in these mountains that your Bible can't begin to tame."

"You dare speak such heresy?"

"I'm speaking the truth." She shook her head sadly. "You can keep lying to yourself, but that won't stop what's coming. You don't want to protect yourself from it? Fine. But if you want to save Moon Hollow, you're going to have to do a proper Decoration."

Instead of arguing, he simply tilted his chin, hoping she'd read it as a simple acknowledgement that he'd heard her. As he walked out the front door and down the steps of the porch, the rose water sloshed in his pocket. He hadn't decided whether or not he'd go through with Decoration Day, but Granny Maypearl hadn't laughed when he'd told her about the ghost. If anything, his story seemed almost to verify something she'd suspected on her own. He hated the idea that he was playing right into her paranoid beliefs, but he was feeling pretty paranoid himself.

As he walked away from the house, he decided he'd see how things went at the funeral. But just in case, he was going to see if they had any potatoes at home.

26

TESTING THE BEAD

Cotton

MOONSHINERS JUDGE the proof of their whiskey by shaking it in a large clear glass jug. The bubbles that form are called "the bead." Large bead that dissipates quickly indicates high alcohol content. A fine bead that disappears slowly means the proof is lower.

To Cotton, Rose's death had tested the bead of his family. Shaken up, they each staggered around, bumping into each other. Ruby's feelings were big but they popped fast. But Cotton's bead was finer—more brittle—and taking much longer to disappear.

Another test involved fire. Moonshine was poured into a spoon and lit. If the distillate was safe the resulting flames would be blue. Tainted batches burned yellow. If a radiator coil poisoned the batch with lead, the flame would have a reddish tint. A common refrain among mountain folk was, "Lead burns red and makes you dead." But if methanol was to blame, the flame would burn invisibly.

Cotton's own flame test had produced mixed results. When Rose had first died, he'd burned bright red with rage. But once his anger had burned away, the invisible poison that remained was far deadlier.

He couldn't remember how he found out about Jack's death or when he'd decided to go to the funeral, but there he was again up on Cemetery Hill grieving someone else who died too soon.

Deacon Dickhead was jabbering on and on about the Lord's plan. Cotton looked at all the people gathered around the grave. Most of them were crying and nodding their heads like they bought his bull. Didn't they always? Virgil Fry could tell them it was God's plan that they all take a leap into the river and they'd trample each other to be the first in the water.

"It's not for us to understand why God called our friend Jack home. It's for us to trust that when it is our turn to join him in heaven we will know that our deaths were also part of a larger plan. It is for us to serve our God and each other so long as we have breath in our bodies and faith in our hearts."

Cotton snorted. The people nearby looked up, but he ducked his chin to make it look like the noise had resulted from grief instead of scorn.

Christ, he needed a drink.

It didn't help that Jack's grave was only a few rows away from where his Rose was buried. He looked that direction and saw that the mound of dirt had settled and had already spouted a few wayward weeds. He needed to remember to pluck them before he left.

"Reverend Peale?" Deacon Fry walked over and helped the reverend shuffle over to the edge of the grave.

Cotton was surprised that the deacon even allowed the reverend to say the prayers. He'd always treated the old man like a child. Didn't give the man an ounce of respect even though he was the real holy man in Moon Hollow. Only man Deacon Fry respected anyhow was hisself.

Once the prayers were done, Nell Thompson was guided to the edge of the hole. Deacon Fry took her elbow and helped her scoop a handful of dirt into the grave. The woman's sobs echoed off the tombstones and the trees and rose up into the mountains like black-winged crows.

Her grief made him feel funny, so he looked away. On the far end of the cemetery, there was a statue of an angel that marked the grave of Jeremiah Moon. When he'd died, all the townsfolk pooled their money to have it carved. Now, it was considered one of the town's greatest treasures, along with the crooked steeple. But to Cotton it was creepy, all covered with moss and dirty. Angels should be clean.

Nell let out a wail that made the hair on the back of his neck prickle. Pulling his attention from the angel, he looked toward the woman who looked ready to jump in the ground with her son. He resented her ability to grieve in public. When Rose died he'd had to hold it all inside. Wouldn't do for a man to crumple next to his wife's grave. Wouldn't do for a man to cry, period. No, he held it all in until the last scoop of dirt was placed over her, and then he'd taken refuge in his cabin where no one else could hear his sorrow.

"A gathering will take place at the Thompson home immediately following the service," Deacon Fry was saying. "But first, I have an announcement. As you know, our annual Decoration Day ceremony usually occurs in May. I have discussed this with Nell and she agrees that it's only right to go ahead and have it this weekend so that we may honor all of our lost family and friends." A ripple of excitement spread through the cemetery. The deacon hadn't asked Cotton if he minded having the Decoration Day so soon after his Rose's death.

"All of the deacons and male members of the congregation

will be asked to volunteer time over the next few days to clean the cemetery in preparation."

Cotton had been a member of the community long enough to know he'd have to pitch in on the cleaning. It was an unwritten rule that every able-bodied male in town was expected to put in a few hours of labor. The thing he didn't understand was why the deacon was insisting on rushing things. Usually the cleaning took place over the course of a week, and the preparations were begun well before that.

There could only be one reason for the rush: Deacon Fry was testing his bead.

Cotton backed slowly through the crowd to begin making his way down the mountain. If he got out of there, he could avoid an awkward conversation with the other deacons about why he didn't intend to clean or attend the Decoration. Luckily, he had the keys and didn't feel one ounce of remorse about leaving Ruby and the kids behind. They could walk home after the services or catch a ride with a neighbor. But he needed four wheels and an engine to take the logging road up to his shack. Once he was up on the mountain, he could figure out how to get out of town until after the Decoration Day bullshit was done.

He was almost to the cemetery gate when Deacon Smythe caught up with him. "Cotton, Deacon Fry wants a word with you."

Cotton paused and looked over his shoulder. "You tell that son-of-a-bitch he don't tell me what to do."

"Cotton," Smythe whispered, "you know he'll come get you if he has to."

He turned around to stare Smythe in his coward eyes. "Why can't you just leave me alone?"

"Everyone's required to help with the cemetery cleaning, Cotton. You know that."

"Tell Deacon Fry that if he has a message to give me, he can deliver it him-damn-self."

"He'll do that, if you'll just hang back a minute." By that time, Earl Sharps had come up behind Smythe, and that's when Cotton knew they were under orders not to let him leave the hill until Fry had said his piece.

"All right, but this better be quick. I got things to do."

The other men exchanged a look, but Cotton didn't give a shit. He knew they thought he was a useless drunk. They didn't know what it was like, and he was Christian enough to hope they never would.

A few moments later, the mourners started breaking up and making their way to the gate. Smythe and Sharps hung back with Cotton until most of the people had left. Once Sharon Fry walked by, escorting both Sarah Jane and Nell, who seemed to be having some sort of contest to see who could cry the loudest, they pushed him toward the grave for the meeting.

When they made it back to the grave, Deacon Fry was kneeling next to the hole. Cotton couldn't see exactly what he put in the ground, but he'd be damned if it didn't look exactly like a potato. He dismissed the idea. The booze was just playing tricks on him again.

By the time the deacon brushed off his hands and stood, Cotton pushed the strange image from his mind.

Deacon Fry actually stood a couple inches taller than Cotton, but with all that white hair he seemed at least a foot taller than that. "Good to see you, Cotton."

He tipped his chin. "Wish it were for a better reason."

Deacon Fry nodded. "I know it must be hard to be back here so soon."

"Being here ain't what's hard."

The deacon's lips pressed together, as if Cotton's lack of cooperation annoyed him. Good. "I've been real patient, haven't I? Been giving you space to grieve as you see fit."

Cotton shrugged.

"Right. But time's come for you to get back to living, Cotton. Them girls of yours need a daddy and this town needs you to start pulling your weight."

"My girls are fine. Ruby's—"

"Only eighteen," he interrupted. "And she lost Rose, too. Those girls need their daddy."

Blood rushed to Cotton's cheeks and his anger rose with it. "My family's none of your business."

"They are if they aren't being taken care of. Now, I know you're a proud man, and Lord knows you got every right to be, but it's time to let us help you. This community needs to come together now more'n ever."

Cotton drew in a breath, but it caught halfway down before he had to cough. He ain't had a proper lungful of air since he didn't know when, but the air he managed to get down was warm and scented with fresh dirt. Maybe another man might see those things as signs it was time for a fresh start, but not him. His chance at new beginnings was buried thirty feet away. Besides, Deacon Fry didn't care about his family. That man only cared about being in charge, and ever since Rose died Cotton wasn't falling in line like he used to.

"I'll tell you what," he said. "You can take this community and shove it up your ass—"

Sharps gasped and Smythe stepped forward menacingly. Deacon Fry help up a hand to stop them.

"—and I'm gonna go back up on that mountain and find some answers in the bottom of a whiskey barrel."

He turned to go, but Deacon Fry's softly spoken words stopped him. "Whiskey can't bring her back, Cotton."

He looked back over his shoulder at his adversary. "Neither can you—or your God."

27

LOST ON THE RIVER

Ruby

AFTER THE FUNERAL, Ruby needed to be alone. After Daddy took off alone in the pickup, Edna offered to take the girls on to Nell's, which gave her a couple of hours alone to process things. At first, she'd rejected the idea of going down to the river. That had been *their* place. She worried it would hurt too much to be there knowing he wasn't ever going to show up to tell her everything was going to be okay.

But she couldn't think of anywhere she could go where she'd feel better, and down by the river she'd feel closer to Jack's memory. Sometimes even though things hurt they were still worth doing.

As she walked through the woods, sunlight flirted with the leaves and danced across the ground. She'd never hated the sun before, but that day it felt like an insult. It hadn't rained during her mama's funeral either, and she wondered why the sun insisted on being there to make fun of her pain.

But then she passed the red tree and the river rose ahead of her and she got distracted by the rushing sound of it and the way the air felt cooler down there. She went to the log by the bank where Jack had found her after her mother's funeral. She placed her hand on the bark and imagined it still held the heat of his body, the imprint of his weight. Closing her eyes, she inhaled deeply and released the valve on her pain.

The tears came instantly, rushing from her like a downpour on a hot summer afternoon, all angry and hot. Her pain was not delicate or pretty. She cried for Mama and for herself, and for Jack, whose loss had stripped away the last of Ruby's hope. She cried for Sissy and Jinny, too, who would never know a childhood without loss. She even cried for Daddy even though he probably didn't deserve her tears.

She cried so long and hard that she didn't notice when she crumpled onto the log and pressed her wet cheek to the bracken.

Eventually, her list of people to cry for came to Sarah Jane Fry. Standing by the gravesite, she'd looked brittle enough to blow away. Thinking about that now, she realized that she and Sarah Jane now shared a bond, a grief bond, which was as unwelcome as snow on the first day of spring. She hated the idea that she could empathize with Sarah Jane now. She hated that she felt guilty for hating it. But most of all, she hated that she felt sorry for the girl who'd spent so much of her energy making Ruby miserable.

Her grief morphed into anger, and she sat up and swiped at the tears. As she did, the bracelet on her wrist hit her nose. She sniffed and held it up to the light. She'd spent most of the previous afternoon reading her mama's journal, and now, knowing what she knew, the tarnish on the metal seemed more appropriate than ever.

When Granny had told her that Mama left Moon Hollow, Ruby's imagination had offered up idealized visions of her mama on a stage singing to a packed house. She pictured fancy parties and sophisticated clothes, and handsome men who'd wooed her mama with romantic gestures. But the journal had different images to offer. Ones about her mama living in roach-infested motels and waitressing in dingy cafes where truckers pinched her bottom and left bad tips. There had been a romance with a particular man, who in the early pages seemed too good to be true. She'd met him at a party at a friend's house and he'd given her outrageous compliments. Mama had been excited because he claimed to be in the music industry and said he could get her an audition with a big club where lots of agents scouted talent.

Mama had had sex with him in the back seat of his car. Afterward, he promised to get in touch about the audition, but he never called.

After that, the journal entries became shorter and terser, and more days would pass between entries. The last entry happened six weeks after her "date" with the man in the car, and it simply said:

Called Mama Collect today. She's sending me money for a bus ticket. She was nice about it. Didn't even say I told you so. *I didn't mention my little problem, but we'll figure that out when I get there. I wish I'd never left.*

Ruby might be young, but she could do math. That last entry had been dated about seven-and-a-half months before her birthday.

It wasn't every day that a girl found out that her daddy wasn't hers, and that the man who'd made her had been a bastard.

Last night, she'd skipped the viewing because she couldn't handle being in the room with Jack's dead body. Besides, Daddy hadn't come home and she couldn't leave the girls alone at night without a sitter. Instead, she spent the time trying to figure out how she felt about what she'd learned. On one hand, she felt like so much of her life suddenly made sense, at least in terms of how Cotton treated her and why her mama had stayed with him for so long. On the other hand, she couldn't believe the things her mama had done. None of what she read fit with the woman who'd raised her. It had been like reading a story written by a stranger— a dumb one who did everything wrong.

Sitting on the log, she watched that Nashville charm sway in a shaft of light.

Her mama had made lots of mistakes, but Ruby couldn't fault her too much for her choices. She knew that yearning all too well. The fear that if she stayed in Moon Hollow she'd eventually just disappear altogether.

She sniffed and looked toward the river. The mountain wasn't singing to her anymore. Mama was dead and Jack, too. Soon, Sissy and Jinny wouldn't need her anymore. Then what would be left for her in Moon Hollow?

But on the other hand, what was waiting for her off the mountain? Based on her mama's journals, the world beyond didn't hold much for her either. Which left her where?

Alone.

28

THE APPROACH

Peter

THE DAY OF THE FUNERAL, he kept his promise and stayed well away from the church and Cemetery Hill. But about three o'clock, being trapped in the cabin had him so restless he was ready to claw his skin off so he decided to take a walk.

He took off down the road outside the cabin. If he stayed on it, he'd eventually end up in town, but he didn't plan to walk that far. Just a stroll to stretch his legs and get his mind off the lack of progress he was making on the book.

He'd written that morning for the first time in months. It was terrible, of course. His backspace button had gotten quite a work out, but he'd managed a couple of not-too-shitty pages before lunchtime. He reminded himself that it would take a few days to get his rhythm back and that progress was the most important thing. Isn't that what he always told his students? Just keep your fingers moving and eventually something will come. Also, the important thing was to have something, anything to rewrite later. *You can't fix a blank page.*

He chuckled and kicked a pinecone down the hill. It was always so much easier to give writing advice than to take it. But it did feel damned good to get some real writing done. He'd gotten so used to being blocked that he'd forgotten how good it could feel to open a vein and bleed onto the page.

As he rounded a curve in the road that skirted the forest, a flash of red captured his gaze. He stopped walking and squinted. Was it a person in red clothes or—no, it was stationary. He stepped into the soft grass by the road. His right hand grasped a low hanging branch and he ducked underneath and into the cave of leaves and bark. His gaze never strayed from the shock of red, which was like a bloody handprint in the center of a black and white image.

The leaves underfoot made shushing noises, as if warning him to be quiet in this place. It seemed even the birds had fallen silent the moment his eyes lit upon the curious red. He stepped over a fallen log and stopped to reassess his path. Behind him, the gravel road was still visible through the veil of leaves, but he'd gone farther than he'd first realized.

Something held him back from pushing forward. His hesitation seemed primal, from that instinctive part of every human that knows more than the mind can know.

He was letting his imagination screw with him again. Whatever that damned thing was, it had not moved so much as a centimeter since he'd stepped into the forest.

The unease in his center calmed with this realization. He let his fear of the unknown slip away and tried to focus on the new sensation coalescing in his center—a foreign feeling, one that, had he been blessed with a longer memory, he'd have been able to recognize immediately from his childhood from warm summer days spent exploring the forest behind his grandparents' house near Knoxville. But his memory was not long, so he'd forgotten that the name of that long-forgotten emotion he'd taken for granted as a kid: wanderlust.

He soldiered on, stepping high over logs and energetically pushing aside branches heavy with silky leaves.

He was breathing heavily by the time he got close enough to realize he'd been looking at a red tree. He'd seen trees with leaves turned red in autumn, but he'd never seen a tree with a red trunk and branches in the middle of spring.

"Hello."

He spun around so fast he grew dizzy. Sitting not ten feet away was the girl he'd seen on the street the other day—the one Bunk said was *touched*.

"You're Ruby."

"And you're Peter."

He stepped closer and realized that her eyes were swollen and red. "Why are you crying?"

She shrugged. "My friend died."

This was the strangest conversation he'd had in recent memory. "You knew Jack. I'm really sorry."

"It's okay." She picked at some bark and avoided his eyes. "You came instead."

He frowned. "What do you mean?"

She shook her head. "It's nothing."

He hesitated, wondering if maybe Bunk hadn't been wrong. Strangely, he felt like he was the awkward one. "I saw that tree from the road." He pointed to the red trunk. "I've never seen anything like it."

"I don't remember what it's called, but my mama told me when I was little that it's only supposed to be red during the winter. For some reason that one stays red year round. No one knows why."

"Any idea why it doesn't have any leaves?"

"They show up in June, usually. They're black."

His brow dipped into a frown. "Maybe it's a hybrid or something."

She sighed and stood. "Or maybe there's things all around us that don't make a lick of sense because they're not supposed to."

He paused and let that sink in. "How old are you, Ruby?"

"Eighteen. How old are you?"

He laughed. "Forty-three."

Her eyes widened. "I would have thought you were older."

He didn't laugh at that. "Do your parents know where you are?"

Something shifted in her expression. "Daddy don't care, and my mama's not alive anymore."

His stomach dipped as he remembered, too late, that Bunk had already told him about her mother's passing. "I'm sorry."

She waved it off. "Hey, you want to see somethin'?"

Her eyes sparked with mischief he found hard to resist even though he knew he should. He wasn't attracted to her sexually—not that any judge in the land would believe him—but she was irresistible nonetheless. Maybe it was the refreshing lack of guile, or maybe he just wasn't ready to go back to the solitude of his cabin yet. Either way, he nodded in response to her question.

She grabbed his hand in her smaller one and pulled him after her. She led him out of the woods and to the road that led up into the hills where many of Moon Hollow's residents had built their homes. It wasn't a neighborhood but a scattering of ramshackle dwellings with plenty of space between one home and its nearest neighbor. He started to worry she was taking him to her home. Images of her presenting him to her hillbilly father rose in his mind like sharp whiskey fumes. He pulled his hand out of her grasp and stopped walking.

She looked back with mock ferocity. "Well? Come on."

"Where are you taking me, Ruby?"

"It's a surprise."

"You're not taking me to your home, are you?"

She frowned as if he'd said something crazy. "Now why the hell would you think that? My daddy would kill me and then hang you up by your toenails if I brought you onto our land."

For the moment he forgot that he didn't want to go to her house as his pride rose up. "Don't be silly. Wouldn't your daddy be happy to meet—" He caught himself before he could say something like "an award winning author" or something else equally boorish. Instead he just let the end hang there.

She just shook her head and turned away to keep walking. He felt ashamed, as if he'd somehow let her down. He watched her go for a moment, wondering what to do. Then, her voice carried over her shoulder, "You coming or what?"

Five minutes later, they reached a gravel drive. To the right, a yellow mailbox with weeds choking its base stood before a house that looked haunted. Broken toys and car parts littered the yard. Ruby marched right past the property without giving it a look. Peter began to dismiss it as well until he saw the wooden sign hanging from two slender chains from the mailbox that said "Barrett." He glanced up at Ruby but she sniffed and picked up her speed. She didn't want him to know this was her home, or at least didn't want to acknowledge it out loud.

They walked in silence for about half a mile before they reached another house. This one was set farther back from the road, so far he could barely see it through the trees on either side of the dirt track that served as the driveway. Ruby stopped at the gate.

"Here we are." Her eyes were wide and her voice was a bit breathless.

He remained quiet, waiting for her to continue. It felt like a game, coming here. A test maybe.

"That there is the Jessup place."

As if on cue, furious barking carried through the trees separating them from the house.

"Jessup's prize hunting dogs."

"What does he hunt?"

"Bears."

He'd been expecting her to say deer or maybe turkeys, but what did he know? He'd never hunted a day in his life. While other men in his family enjoyed sporting he'd preferred the library and wooing women.

"Isn't that dangerous?"

She shot him a withering look that would have looked more natural on a society maven in Manhattan. "Of course it's dangerous. Mostly for the bears though." Her tone indicated she wasn't a fan of the sport.

When he didn't respond, she continued. "Bear season starts in the fall, though, so he also uses them for hunting coons and jackrabbits. But mostly that's to keep the dogs trained for bears."

He was about to tell her that was all very interesting but what did it have to do with him when she ducked through the gate.

"Ruby," he hissed.

She waved a beckoning hand behind her but didn't stop her progress over the property line. Peter was no expert about small town politics, but he was pretty sure a man who hunted bears for fun wouldn't take too kindly to having a stranger trespass on his land.

"I don't think—"

"Hush."

The barking continued as they made their way through the trees toward the house. He considered—hoped—it was a good sign that no one came out the front door to shout at the dogs to be quiet. He prayed that meant no one was home. The promise he'd made to Ed Sharps rose in his memory. By trespassing he basically ruined his argument that he hadn't broken any laws. But the perverse part of him that didn't like taking orders from anyone pushed all that aside. What Ed Sharps and Deacon Fry didn't know wouldn't hurt Peter.

About halfway to the house, another sound mixed in with the barking—a high-pitched mewling sound, like a fussy baby or a pissed off cat. "What's that?" he called softly.

"You'll see." She burst through the trees onto the circular dirt drive in front of the house. The only car out front was a rusted-out Chevy Pinto that looked like it hadn't run since the Carter administration.

Ruby skirted the house. He crept after her, his eyes always on the road, waiting for a truck to come roaring up that drive.

The barking was louder in the back. He cast one last nervous look toward the drive before turning to take in the yard. Five large dog cages lined one section of fence. Each was filled with a long-eared hound dog and each of those dogs were howling and barking like the devil himself had just stepped on their property.

Ruby ignored the dogs even though several of them lunged at her as she passed their runs. Peter had a harder time maintaining his dignity. He'd never been a huge fan of dogs to begin with, much less ones that spat ribbons of drool as they tried to bite through metal.

Across the yard from the dog runs, another cage sat alone under a tall tree. This one was smaller, and the brown clump of fur inside didn't lunge for the grid of metal. Its body was smaller, too, and covered in matted fur that seemed thicker than the other dog's coats. The animal was huddled in the corner at the back of the cage, and it let out terrible cries that seemed to crawl inside his ears so it could yell directly at his conscience.

"All right, we're here," he said. "Are you going to tell me why?"

Ruby stopped beside him with her hands on her hips. He'd

half expected her to make fun of his obvious discomfort. But with each pitiful cry, her earlier bravado slipped a little more and her complexion grew a few shades paler.

She pointed toward the dark ball in the corner. "That's why we're here."

This close, the overwhelming scent of urine and wet fur nearly overwhelmed him. "What? The dog?'

"Bear."

"The dog's name is Bear?"

"That's no dog." She shook her head. "It's a bear."

As if it somehow knew they were talking about it, the bear raised its head. Now that Peter could see the face, he couldn't believe he'd ever mistaken it for a dog. The face was large as a dinner plate and dominated by watery eyes and a chalk-dry nose. "Is it a pet?"

"Bait."

He turned to look at her, but she didn't return the favor. "Bait? For what."

"When he's old enough, they'll tie him to a stake and let the dogs at him to train them to hunt."

His stomach rebelled at the thought. "How does letting them maul a bound bear train them to hunt?"

"It's something about training them to force a bear into a standing position so they're easier to shoot." She finally looked his way with haunted eyes. "Sometimes they pull out the fangs and claws—or just cut off toes."

He swallowed the hot spit that rose in his throat. The bear's head cocked to the side and he looked into its eyes, as if trying to somehow telepathically communicate his empathy. The impotence of the gesture shamed him. Peter couldn't fathom living the sort of life that involved murdering animals for sport. He was no saint, he knew—he certainly enjoyed steak. But, like most people who lived in cities, he lived in happy denial that the meat he bought at the supermarket had once had a mother. "Why do they hunt them?"

"People used to hunt them for meat, but now?" She shrugged. "Trophies."

"How is that legal?"

She laughed at him. "Mountain folks have their own laws."

He let that sink in for a moment. Hadn't he seen that himself since he arrived? In the city, someone was always around and cops were fairly easy to summon when trouble cropped up. But up here? Hell, Bunk had told them they only had a sheriff and one deputy for the entire county, and their office was forty minutes away. And with a town as tight at Moon Hollow? Made sense no one would be real eager to report infractions like this one and risk being found out as the town snitch. He hadn't met this Jessup, but judging from the man's hobbies Peter was pretty sure he wasn't the kind of man who'd take kindly to having the law called out to his homestead.

"Why did you bring me here?" The questions popped into his head and he spoke it without knowing if he was ready to know the answer.

The dogs had quieted down a bit once they got used to their presence but out of the blue they tuned up again. This time the pitch of their howls was sharper. Ruby turned and stared toward the house with wide eyes. "Shit. He's back." She grabbed his hand and pulled him into a crouch, as if making themselves smaller would also make them invisible.

"Wh—"

"Shh. We need to be quick."

She lunged toward the bear's cage.

"What are you doing? We have to get out of here." He hoped like hell that those dogs had identified the impending arrival of their master from a great distance. Otherwise, they were well and truly busted. He grabbed her arm.

With more strength than he expected from her, she ripped his fingers from her flesh and went back to her fight with the cage. "We have to save it."

The noises roused the lethargic bear into raising its head again. Now, it was hard to see the moisture in its eyes as a sign of illness because it looked so much like tears. He shook off the dangerous pity.

"It's sick, Ruby. It won't survive in the wild." A dog bowl in the cage was filled with kibble. Flies swarmed the milky liquid in the other bowl. None of it looked fresh, which meant the bear wasn't eating. It was only a matter of time now.

"It'll have a fighting chance out there. If we leave it here, it'll be tortured before it dies all alone."

He knelt down next to her. Tears streamed down her cheeks, making her look impossibly young. Something in his chest tightened and pushed away his annoyance and fear of being caught. He placed a hand on her shoulder. "Ruby, look at me."

She kept scratching and pulling at the lock. Blood and scrapes covered her knuckles.

Over the sound of the baying hounds, the dull snap of a truck door closing reached them. "We have to go." He said it as calmly as he was able, but part of him was tempted to just turn tail and leave the girl to face the consequences. Surely Jessup would go easier on an eighteen-year-old girl than he would after finding a strange man on his property. Even if Ruby exonerated him in her scheme, he wasn't naïve enough to believe he'd be free to go.

But even he wasn't heartless enough to leave her to take the blame. He ripped her hands off the lock and dragged her away from the cage. She yelped and tried to scream, but he used a free hand to muffle the cries. Every muscle in her body yearned toward the cage and the bear, who was crying again.

He ran as fast as he could for the rear fence. It only came up to his hips but was constructed of wooden stakes connected together with several strands of barbed wire. "God damn it."

He ripped off his jacket and wrapped it around his right hand. He pushed the wires down as far as he could and all but threw Ruby over the fence. She landed on the other side with a sharp cry, but she didn't try to scramble back over. That gave him just enough time to lumber over the wires. On the way, his jeans snagged on several barbs, one of which punctured his thigh. Pain made him roll to the ground, where he allowed himself only a few rapid breaths before he leapt up again. As he grabbed Ruby off the ground and ran with her toward the tree line, the dogs bayed like demons and the bear cried, and, too soon, the sound of a man's voice hollered for all of them to "shut the fuck up!"

Once they were several yards into the woods, he collapsed against a tree trunk and slid down to the ground. Beside him, Ruby curled up into herself and sobbed like she'd betrayed her best friend.

He wiped the sweat from his forehead and blew out a long breath. When he closed his eyes, an image of that pitiful bear haunted him. On one hand he couldn't blame Ruby for wanting to save it, but on the other, it was such a childish act that he found himself pitying her almost as much as the bear itself.

"What were you thinking? We could have been arrested—or worse." The latter option was clearly the more likely scenario.

With her head bowed, she shrugged.

"Even if you'd gotten it out of the cage, it was too sick to survive in the wild."

"I would have taken care of it."

He shook his head. "Why do you care so much about it?"

She sniffed and swiped at her eyes before answering. "I dunno. I guess, I—"

"Go on." He tried to sound encouraging but the words sounded annoyed even to his own ears.

She huffed out a sigh. "I guess I just felt like we had some stuff in common."

Was he ever that young? Did he ever possess the sort of credulity that allowed children to empathize with beasts? "Like what?"

She snorted. "You'll just make fun of me."

"So? Tell me anyway." The rules of politeness would have dictated he promise her he'd never do such a thing, but he didn't have the patience at that moment.

She took a shaky breath and looked up at the canopy creaking overhead. The scent of dry pine needles and deep green forest mysteries surrounded them. "Every morning, I wake up hearing him cry," she began. "Well, not every morning of my life—just for the last few weeks."

He nodded to encourage her to continue. She stared at him as if she expected him to find meaning hidden in her words.

"I'm sorry," he said finally. "I don't follow."

In an overly patient tone, she said, "It started right after Mama died."

"I see." But he didn't. To him it was the sort of magical thinking preferred by children and women who planned their daily schedule based on their horoscopes.

"I told you you'd think it was silly."

"Look, it doesn't matter what I think. Keep telling your story."

She pressed her lips together for a stubborn second before continuing. "So, the thing is that ever since I was a little girl I could hear things. Songs, I guess you'd call them."

He didn't say anything because there was nothing he could say that wouldn't make him sound like a total asshole.

"Anyway, I've heard them since I was real young. Mama

taught me how to hear them. But ever since she died, the songs stopped and all I can hear is the bear crying all the time. Every morning I lay there thinking it's missing its mama, too."

His annoyance evaporated in the face of such innocent grief. His own father had passed away when he was in college. It had been a sort of relief to know he'd never have to have that dreaded reconciliation with the father figure Joseph Campbell seemed so fond of. He'd spent most of his adult life completely comfortable with the unresolved issues his father had left behind, and unencumbered by the necessity to prove himself.

Liar.

"I guess I figured if I saved the bear that maybe the songs would come back." She wouldn't look directly at him, but he couldn't tell if it was shame or dishonesty causing her lack of eye contact.

In the silence that followed her admission, Peter was keenly aware of the press of the forest around them—that sensation of being observed. But Ruby, who'd grown up in those woods, supposedly hearing mysterious songs, seemed oblivious.

"We should be getting back." He took her arm and helped her rise. He kept his gaze on the ground, but could feel her earnest attention. She was raw, he knew it. She'd just admitted something that she'd probably never tell another human being. But he didn't feel equipped to play mentor to a girl who clearly didn't have the tools to survive in the real world.

"Can I tell you something else?" she whispered.

He wanted to warn her to keep it to herself. In fact, maybe he should tell her never to trust any man with her secrets because they would only make her easy prey. Before he could warn her, her secrets leapt like lemmings from her tongue.

"I'm leaving Moon Hollow." She said it in such a way that he got the impressions she'd only just made the final decision.

"When?" he asked, confused at the strange segue.

"Soon." Her mouth turned up into a Mona Lisa smile.

Talking to this girl was like walking through a room filled with funhouse mirrors. One minute she seemed gullible and the next, a budding femme fatale. Lord help the men of the world if she ever permanently shrugged off her innocence and realized her true power.

"Where are you going?" He felt disoriented, like he'd spun in rapid circles and was trying to locate true North.

"Don't know yet."

He frowned at her. "You don't know when or where, but you're leaving? Why?"

The smile faded and her eyes got this far-away look, as if she'd retreated into the part of her brain that made all her bad decisions. "Because if I stay I'm gonna end up just like the bear, like Jack and my mama, too."

A spike of fear stabbed him just above his heart. "Ruby, promise me you're not just going to take off without anyone and no idea where you're going."

Her attention snapped back to his face. "Well why not? It'll be an adventure. Like Huckleberry Finn sailing down the Mississippi."

"Huck had Jim, Ruby. He didn't set off by himself."

She grinned up at him. "Will you be my Jim, Peter?"

29

COFFIN NAILS

Cotton

THE OPEN DOOR of the cast-iron stove looked like the devil's own mouth. Hungry flames writhed inside like obscene tongues that hissed his name.

Fuckin' people. 'Specially that uppity Deacon Fry.

Cotton fed another stick into the stove. Sparks jumped out and sizzled on his arm. He licked the burnt spot and the flavor of sweat, corn whiskey, and ash bit his tongue. He should've known better than to go to the funeral, but he'd always liked watching young Jack play football. Damned shame.

Life was just an endless string of disappointments. He lifted the plastic milk jug to his lips. The hooch burned and stripped the spit from his tongue. Yes, sir, a damned shame.

The rocking chair had been carved by his pappy's own hand. The woven straw seat creaked as he rocked—the sound like the song of pines deep in the woods on a windy day. He smoothed a finger over the glossy arm, worn smooth from decades of hands resting in that spot. Pappy's hands, Daddy's hands, and now his hands.

Forty-five years ago, he'd sat on Pappy's lap in this chair. He'd been five? Six? Who the hell knew? He still could smell the scent of cigarettes and sweat that clung to Pappy's skin like cologne. He still could see the deep network of wrinkles on the old man's neck and the gray hairs curling out of his ears like smoke.

"Cotton," he'd say, "a man's job is to take care of his family."

Pappy's fingers were thick and tanned, his knuckles permanently rough and chapped; they were strong hands—a real man's tools. Cotton looked at the graying hairs on his own knuckles. The insides of his index and middle fingers were stained permanently yellow and always stank strongly of nicotine.

"A man has to take care of this family," Pappy said, "because without a family, you can't be a real man."

Rose had been his family. Now she was gone and he couldn't even take care of himself.

Was he a real man, anymore? Had he ever been?

He took another swig of his home-brewed therapy.

He ain't felt like a man ever since he saw all them spots on the X-ray and the doc said his lungs was blacker than coal. Hell, he'd barely felt human since Rose died.

"Real men don't cry." This advice, given by his daddy, who'd learned it from Pappy, had been punctuated by the snap of leather on skin and the taste of blood on the tongue as he bit back tears. "Real men ain't pussies, son."

Daddy and Pappy had taught him an ungrateful woman sometimes needed a reminder to appreciate all the sacrifices her man made for her and her children. They'd both done their best to show him how to live a good life. They worked down in the mines and kept working after their own X-rays developed polkie dots. Back then, insurance company lawyers didn't keep a man from workin' just because his lungs weren't pink anymore.

A rasping sound came from nearby. His eyes couldn't focus too good, but he rose and he stumbled to the small window. Outside, tree trunks creaked and swayed in the darkening dusk. No matter how much he squinted they wouldn't stand still.

That noise again—like a hoof on concrete or a match against sandpaper. It made his back teeth itch. He closed his eyes to listen, but his pulse pounded in his ears. He'd had too much to drink again. It meant another night alone in the cabin, but he liked it that way.

The sound didn't come again. He opened his lids and relaxed his eyes until they lost focus, until his vision went blurry, like someone had smeared lard across the windowpane. Through the haze, a shape darted between the trees. The shadow was too large and moved too fast to be anything friendly. He rubbed his eyes to clear them. The trees were still there swaying. The sun was lower now, but the thing—whatever it was —had disappeared.

Craving warmth, he returned to his chair by the fire and his hooch. He leaned back and took a nice long swig before closing his eyes for a catnap.

When he woke, the room was darker. The fire still crackled in the stove, but the air at his back was colder. He wasn't sure what had woken him. On the edge of his brain the misty silhouette of some forgotten dream taunted him. He tried to focus on it to remember, but the more he shined the light of his attention on it, the further the dream retreated into the shadows of memory.

"Hello, Cotton."

The two softly spoken words entered through his ears and seared an icy path straight to his heart. No hooch in the world could warm him now. He jumped from the chair. He clinched his fists and ignored the rush of bile up the back of his throat. "Who's there?"

But no one was there. No intruder stood nearby, no man-shaped shadows darkened the corners of the room, and when he opened the door no one stood on the doorstep. Cotton closed the door and locked the latch. He backed up toward this chair and fought to get his pulse under control.

Still, his skin prickled cold as if he were being watched. The darkened window across the room looked like a dilated pupil. He half expected to see a white face and two red glowing eyes staring at him through the panes, but there was nothing except the nagging dread that he was not alone.

"I say, who's there?"

The only response was the wind outside and a faint scratching.

Dammit, you old fool, you done drunk too much and now you're seeing the boogeyman. It's just the trees.

The old milk jug sat beside the rocking chair. The brown liquor inside was barely two inches lower than it had been when he started drinking earlier that evening. Normally it took at least four inches before he started seeing things that weren't there.

The knock on the door had a familiar pattern to it, and he realized it was the old "Shave and a Haircut" rhythm.

Two bits.

It was only after his brain filled in the missing two beats that he realized he should be worried. "Who is it?"

The knock sound it again—*shave and a haircut*. And again, faster this time— *shaveandahaircut*. Each time Cotton mumbled "Two bits," before demanding again that his visitor identify himself.

Da-dum dum dum dum.

"Two bits," Cotton cried. "God damn it, who's there?" This time he grabbed his shotgun from the doorjamb and unhooked the latch. The door bounced off the wall and hit Cotton on the side. He was only vaguely aware of the pain.

Standing on his doorstep was not the white-faced devil with red eyes he'd imagined.

"Jack," he whispered. "Jack, son, is that you?"

The boy's skin was gray and his cheeks sunken in like a collapsed mine. His clothes, torn and covered in blood. But it was the boy's eyes that shocked the old man. His pupils were as dark and cold as the swimming hole on a January night.

"Jack?"

The boy stared at him for a good minute before moving. His lips were cracked and bloodied, but the inside was worse—a cavern filled with broken-off teeth like stalactites and stalagmites, and a white tongue like a dead grub. No words came out, but a dry click escaped his throat.

Cotton coughed in sympathy. The boy looked like hell, but now that he knew it wasn't a murderer at his door, his pulse slowed and he left behind fright mode in favor of fix-it mode. He pulled Jack's arm to bring him inside, but the boy's skin burned his fingertips like dry ice. He yanked his hand away and stuck it into his pocket. "Hell, son, get your ass in here where it's warm."

His visitor stepped inside the cabin. Cotton shut the door and leaned the gun against the wall. Then, he scooted around Jack to pull a dusty beer cooler from the corner to use as a seat. He motioned to his rocking chair. "Have a seat."

The boy lowered himself into the chair as instructed. Cotton rubbed his hands together. They'd gone numb with cold ever since Jack walked in the door. When that didn't work, he grabbed his milk jug and took a swig. Once the bracing fire seared a path down to his gut, he wiped the opening with his shirt cuff and offered the jug to Jack. "This should warm ya up. My own recipe."

No response from his guest. The only sounds were the crackling of wood in the stove and the creak of the rocking chair's runners on the warped floorboards.

He couldn't look at those eyes. He shrugged and took another drink before capping the jug and stashing it close to his right foot. Three inches down now.

Something tugged at the back of his mind. Like how Ruby used to pull on his sleeve to tell him secrets when she was too young to be scared of him. What was it? Something from earlier that day. Something about Jack.

The rocking chair creaked back and forth.

Jack was wearing a miner's rig. Blue coveralls with neon orange safety tape down the arms. His throwing hand lay bent at an odd angle on his lap. The right sleeve was torn clean away. A black stain covered his chest. His face looked like it had been on the losing end of a humdinger of a fight.

"You all right, son?"

What was it he was supposed to remember?

The stove's heat had chased away the lingering chill. Under the wood smoke and the rubbing alcohol scent of the moonshine, there was now a new smell. A sickly sweet, off scent, like turned meat.

Meat.

Dead meat.

Cotton stumbled over the back of the cooler. He scrambled back until he hit the wall. Only when there was no place left to go, did he look at Jack.

The boy still rocked back and forth in Pappy's chair. A grin spread across the gray face, making him look like some kind of sinister jack-o'-lantern.

"You're—the funeral—Oh, God!" Three inches of moonshine rushed out his mouth like a crowd pushing through an emergency exit. It happened so fast, he didn't have time to turn his head. The front of his good church shirt clung hot and wet to his clammy skin. His brain wasn't working right. Nothing was right. Jack was dead.

Cotton mumbled words he remembered from some psalm he'd memorized in Sunday school as a boy. "Deliver me, oh my God, out of the hand of the wicked, out of the hand of the unrighteous and cruel--"

A mean coughing fit broke off his prayer. He could barely get enough air in to cough back out.

The thing in the rocking chair laughed. "Your God abandoned you a month ago."

The cane seat groaned as the thing rose to approach him. Cotton whimpered and pushed himself sideways into the farthest corner. Jack had been a big boy when he was alive, but dead, with the stink of death on him and the cold eyes, he seemed fifteen feet tall.

The thing knelt. Joints popped like gunshots. "Cotton."

He whimpered again. God damn him—he whimpered like a child.

"Shh," it said. "I'm not here to hurt you."

Cotton wrapped his arms around himself. "Yer the devil!"

The thing's low chuckle sent a puff of putrid breath into his face. Hot spit pooled in his mouth.

"Rose wants to see you again."

Suddenly he felt more sober than he had in months. He sat up and wiped the bile and spit from his lips. "You seen Rose?"

The thing nodded. "You want to be with her again, don't you, Cotton?"

Cotton might be a drunk and a son-of-a-bitch, but he'd grown up hearing stories about what happened to fellas who made deals with Old Scratch. "You ain't stealing my soul, Devil!"

The thing pulled out a packet of Marlboros, not the generic cancer sticks he had to buy because he couldn't afford better, and took its time packing it against bloody knuckles and unwrapping the cellophane. It lifted one to those ruined lips and lit it with a wooden match. Its eyes closed as it inhaled a deep lungful. The scent of freshly lit tobacco and the hints of sulfur and burning wood from the match pushed away the stink of decay and reminded him of his Pappy, who smoked Reds every day of his life.

The thing offered the pack to him. The pristine white tip of the filter peeked from inside its brown wrapper. He needed that cigarette more than he needed another swig of shine, for the moment, anyway.

"Go on," the thing said. "Takin' it ain't a promise."

That voice. His attention moved from the cigarettes to the face of the thing kneeling over him. Only, instead of Jack, it was his Pappy. "C'mon now, son. I promise I won't tell yer mama."

Suddenly he was five again. Pappy stood next to his workbench in the old garage. The scent of motor oil and sawdust. Light spilling in through the open door. His hero had bent down and offered his smoldering cigarette to him. His first drag had burned his tiny, perfect lungs like poison, and he'd coughed for so long he thought he'd die. Pappy had laughed, and pounded him on the back. "That'll put hair on yer chest."

He'd never tasted anything so awful, but the approval on Pappy's face and the pride of being considered a man had imprinted on him so permanently that by the time his balls dropped he had a pack-a-day habit.

"Just one," the thing that looked like his Pappy said. "Here I'll light it for you. That's a good boy."

Then the filter was between his lips. His tongue touched the filter, the soft fibrous circle surrounded by the sharp edge of paper. Pappy struck the match. The comforting brimstone scent pinched at the inside of his nostrils.

"Inhale."

He did. The smoke soothed the rough edges of his nausea

and filled the hungry cells of his black lungs. He could finally breathe again, even if what he was breathing would likely be the death of him.

Death.

Rose.

He held the smoke inside like a secret. "You saw her?" His voice sounded different inside his head.

The face was back. Those shark eyes. The thing held out its left hand. He shook his head and pushed himself up with the cigarette dangling between his lips. Once he was upright, he pushed the smoke out slowly.

The thing sucked down another drag instead of answering. It motioned to the cooler seat. Cotton righted his makeshift seat and settled on top of it. The thing resumed its seat in the rocking chair.

"Do you know the legend of Moon Hollow?" it asked.

"Which one?"

"Jeremiah Moon's deal with the devil."

He coughed up a mouthful of phlegm. Spat it into the corner. Took another drag. "S'pose I might." He exhaled. "Some say that's why we have Decoration Day."

The thing tipped his chin to confirm. "Cemetery has to be reconsecrated every year or the deal is void."

"What did you do to Jack?"

"You don't want to know."

He pondered that for a few moments. Where had his fear gone? He still stank like vomit because he'd been more terrified than he'd been his whole life just a few minutes earlier. But now he felt like he was floating in a warm sea. Felt better than he should after emptying three inches of shine from his belly. Some part of his brain, way deep down and far back, was flashing like fireflies in June, but he didn't care. Didn't care about much, 'cept finding out what this demon man knew about Rose.

"Decoration Day's coming, Cotton."

He put the cigarette between his lips and inhaled long and slow. Best drag of his life. Talking about cemeteries and deals with the devil shouldn't make him smile, but he couldn't fight the urge. The smoke came back out in the shape of a crescent moon. "That so?"

"Play your cards right and sweet Rose'll be back in your arms by week's end."

He ran a tongue over his lower lip and tasted raw tobacco and bile. The cigarette burned to a stub between his fingers. The final drag singed his lips, but he smiled. "Tell me how."

30

CEMETERY MAGIC

Ruby

THE WAXING MOON was the only witness to Ruby's sins.

After her visit to see the bear with Peter where she'd asked him to help her leave Moon Hollow, she'd returned home to an empty house. Edna left a message saying she was going to take the girls home with her for a sleepover. That was just fine with Ruby since she needed time to think.

She wasn't sure what drew her back to the attic, but she'd found herself there anyway. Without Jinny there to distract her, she searched deeper into the boxes until she found a cache of books that had belonged to her mother. The book of spells had been at the bottom of the box. On the inside cover, both Granny Maypearl's and her mama's names were written in different colored inks. Judging from the dog-eared pages, it had been well read by both of them. Mama could sing like an angel and taught Ruby to hear the mountain's song, but Ruby had never seen her mess with potions and spells. Had her magic gotten left behind like her songs when she'd returned home? Or had she left it behind before she'd gone to Nashville?

Intrigued by the mysterious incantations and recipes, she'd taken the book with her back to her room and spent a pleasant hour thumbing through the pages. It made her feel closer to her mama, and Granny, too.

Everything had changed when she came upon a spell for making a man do your bidding. According to the book, the best way to control a man was to make him love you. The process of accomplishing that feat was laid out in detail.

She made the decision without admitting it to herself. But in the back of her mind, she could still see the look on Peter's face when she'd asked him to help her. It had been a mixture of suspicion and worry. Not a good sign. She'd made him promise not to answer right then, but to think it over.

But as she sat on her bed, in her lonely attic room, she could easily imagine him sitting alone in his cabin wondering how he was going to let her down easily. She had a little money saved up, but if he rejected her, she would never leave. It would be too easy to convince herself then that her place was with her family regardless of what that would mean for her own future. Her mama had taught her too well the importance of duty, and without Peter to give her an excuse to ignore everything she'd been taught, she'd surrender. She just knew it.

Her first sin that night was sneaking into Reverend Peale's shed. It was situated at the back of his yard. She knew it well because she and Mama used to help take care of his garden. Judging from the cobwebs sealing the building like a tomb and the weedy garden trying to swallow the shed whole, no one else had stepped in to take over those chores after Mama died. She liked Reverend Peale, and stealing was wrong, but Granny's book had been specific that the trowel needed to belong to a man of God.

The tall trees blocked the moon's view of her progress as she climbed the hill toward the cemetery. The darkness tried to swallow her lantern's light. Taking it from Daddy's workshop hadn't been a sin because she planned to put it back where she'd found it before he realized it was gone. If he even bothered to return home in the next day or so, he'd never notice it missing before she put it back. Near as she could tell he hadn't used it since the time he went to help Mr. Jessup rescue a coonhound that had gotten its paw caught in a bear trap the previous October.

She stopped near the small metal archway leading into the cemetery and tried to remember if the dog had survived that time. Chances were good it hadn't. Mr. Jessup shot his dogs with such shocking regularity that the acts couldn't be described as merciful, even though they usually followed some sort of traumatic injury to the animals. Ruby thought if the man had any mercy he'd have gathered up those damned bear traps so his hounds couldn't stumble into them anymore. For that matter, he should forget about hunting bears altogether.

The spell book had said the rites were supposed to be done with a clear head and a true heart. She took three more breaths, sucking in the moist, cool air and breathing out warm puffs that were visible in the lantern's yellow glow.

Beyond the metal archway a path cut through the tombstones. The mourners at Jack's funeral had upset the white pebble paths that hadn't been cleaned up since last Decoration Day. The messy paths and pine needles that carpeted the cemetery gave it an abandoned appearance, like the graveyard of a ghost town. Ruby turned left down a row that led away from the cemetery's most recent graves.

Her conscience warned her that Mama wouldn't have approved of what she was doing. Would Jack say anything? She didn't know, but she avoided looking in the direction of the mound of fresh dirt behind her.

She checked the time. Her watch had a pink crystal chip over the twelve and a black, fake-leather strap. Mama had given it to Ruby for her seventeenth birthday. The timepiece told Ruby it was already quarter till midnight. She needed to hurry or miss her chance. As she lowered her wrist, the Nashville bracelet slid down her arm and clinked against the watch.

On the eastern border of the cemetery, a large statue of an angel stood over Jeremiah Moon's grave. The angel's left side was dotted with soft green moss, while the right side, which faced west, was decorated with gold-colored lichen. The effect made the angel appear as if her one face was made up of the halves of two separate faces. Like that god she read about in the book on mythology at Granny's house as a girl.

Ruby snorted. Wouldn't the people of town be shocked to hear her comparing their sacred angel to a pagan god? Did that count as another sin? And if so, shouldn't it bother her more?

Behind her, the presence of the particular grave she wanted to forget pressed against her back like a cold hand.

She dropped to her knees in front of the statue and set the lantern by the angel's feet. The stolen trowel came out of her backpack. She held it up to the light, wondering why it mattered that it came from the reverend. But knowing the hows and whys of magic wasn't her job. That was Granny's business, and if her book said it needed to be Reverend Peale's who was she to argue?

Next, she removed a copy of *Devil's Due*. The shipment of Peter's books had arrived that morning at the library. Since Sarah Jane was all torn up over Jack, Mrs. Fry had asked Ruby to stop by the library to collect the mail and make sure everything was locked up. She'd logged in all the copies into the system—

except the one she'd put in her bag. She supposed that counted as a sin, too, but at that point it was getting hard to keep track.

The book had Peter's picture on the back. He looked younger in the photo and his eyes squinted less. She wondered what had happened to him between the shot being taken and his arrival in town.

She touched her lips with her finger and lay the kiss on his face because it seemed like something she should do. Then she lay the book face up in the pool of light beneath the lantern. Then, using the reverend's trowel, she dug a shallow hole and placed Peter's book inside. She removed her bracelet and set it beside the book. She buried them together using the dirt, and then, after a deep breath, she raised the trowel into the air one last time and plunged it into the earth beside the book's grave.

Closing her eyes, she recited the words she'd memorized from the book. "Guardian of the cemetery, heed me," she whispered, adding "please" after a moment. "Make him think of only me."

Opening her eyes again, she rose and looked around. According to the book of spells, if the ceremony worked correctly, the shadow of her desired mate should appear.

She held her breath and stared hard as can be into the darkness. She stared so hard that little circles of light appeared on the corners of her vision. She blinked once, twice. The circles remained, but no shadows appeared.

She licked her lips and closed her eyes to block out the hovering orbs. "Guardian of the cemetery, show me my love. Please!"

In her mind's eye, she imagined the silhouette of Peter West as if that could conjure his shadow. When she opened her eyes again, the glowing orbs hadn't gone away—they'd multiplied. But she didn't care about the lights. She was too busy being disappointed by the lack of shadow to be scared or excited by some stupid lightning bugs.

Muttering to herself, she knelt and removed Granny's spell book from her sack. She knelt down next to the lantern to see the words written on the correct page. "If the shadow of your love appears to the north, there will be great passion. A southern appearance means the union is possible but will require much labor. To the west, you'll be friends. To the east, he will be your enemy forever."

"But what about no shadow?" she asked the book, as if it would respond.

Before she could read the rest of the page, movement captured her attention. Believing her shadow had finally appeared, she looked up. Her breath dropped to the bottom of her lungs. She rose despite the cold shock spreading through her limbs. The orbs had multiplied and flew around the center of the cemetery in a cyclone of light. She stumbled back.

Her shoulder touched stone. Something gave way. A breath passed, followed by a loud crunch. The orbs dispersed like flying sparks.

Oxygen rushed in and out of Ruby's open mouth. Her heart thudded like the knock of an unwelcomed guest against her ribs. She blinked a few times to be sure the lights were truly gone. The air was dark once more, and a few small rays of relief seeped between the lingering shadows of confusion and the echo of fear.

She cleared her throat and the noise was unnaturally loud in the dark and empty cemetery. She looked down. The lantern lay dark on the ground. Her foot must have kicked it. She lifted it and clicked the button a few times, but nothing happened.

Only then did the thought occur to her: It was too early for lightning bugs.

She'd come to the cemetery looking for a shadow, but all

she'd found was light. She looked around for the spell book. She wanted to tear it up with her hands. She wanted to burn it. She wanted to destroy it for making her believe she was capable of magic.

Something to her left caught her attention. Something was different. A void that had not existed a few moments before.

Grey chunks of stone littered the ground. The angel's two faces were divided and two sightless eyes stared up at the moon. Ruby gasped.

Worries about lights and shadows dissolved. If Deacon Fry or any of the other church elders found out she'd destroyed the beloved angel of Moon Hollow, she'd never live down the shame. It was bad enough to be the daughter of the woman who'd died too young and the old-before-his-time man who was trying to kill himself. To be both a thief and a vandal of sacred ground? It was too scandalous.

And what if Peter West found out why she'd gone to the cemetery in the first place? No man could fall in love with such a desperate and silly girl. He'd never agree to help her leave now.

She'd destroyed everything.

She grabbed the trowel out of the ground and picked up the spell book, which lay beside the rubble of the destroyed angel.

"Oh, God—Jesus, please forgive me," she whispered. With shaking hands she shoved the book into her bag of sin and snatched the lantern off the ground.

As she ran from the cemetery, she felt as if she'd forgotten something important, but she'd worry about that later when she wasn't busy running from her mistakes.

31

THE INVITATION

Peter

THAT NIGHT, Peter sat on the porch again. The darkness emanating from the surrounding woods pressed against the meager pools of light spilling from the cabin's windows. He'd sat there every night since he'd arrived, but it had taken him a while to realize it was not the yearning night that scared him. It was the loneliness.

No matter how often he had tried to make friends with the night sounds, his brain wasn't having it. Without the stimulation of lights and sounds to distract it, the bully in his head went looking for trouble. First, it created ridiculous monsters out of shadows. Then, after he was able to logic away the specters, the bully searched for real horrors in the steamer trunks hidden in the back of his brain, and then the cold hands of memory squeezed his throat.

The solitary darkness of his childhood bedroom rose around him. Huddling under his covers with a pillow over his head. Angry voices stabbing through the walls. The crash of glass and the crack of a palm slapping flesh always preceded the brittle sound of his mother's tears. His small heart pounded in his chest, in his ears, in the dark, alone.

He didn't remember the first time he distracted himself by making up a story. Later, he would try to recall those first tales but all the characters he created swirled and dipped through his head like exuberant ghosts distracting him from those early attempts.

No, he didn't remember that first story, but he knew it had been his salvation. His friends who'd come from "complicated" families like his found solace first in rebellion and then in drugs or an addiction to anger. They'd call him the lucky one.

But they didn't know that at some point his savior had evolved into his master. His imagination morphed into a dictator that prevented him from ever experiencing full contact with reality or ever truly engaging with people. This ruler told him that people couldn't be trusted because they couldn't be controlled.

He coughed and spat on the warped boards.

He should be writing. The press of memories was a warning sign. His bully was telling him it was time. Even though he'd written a couple of pitiful pages that morning, he had six months' worth of bile to vent.

At some point, after he'd given up imagining dragons and wizards in the dark and had traded them for fantasies about the girls in his English lit classes, long after he'd written his first trunk novel and then another, he'd learned to control the bully by writing as much as possible. The epiphany had hit him while doing research on ancient medical practices he'd been doing for a book about a doctor-cum-serial killer who tortured his victims using arcane medical procedures. For thousands of years it was believed that the human body was made up of four humors: sanguine, choleric, melancholic, and phlegmatic. It was believed that an imbalance of the humors led to disease, and the best cure was to bleed the patient to purge the bad humors.

Untapped creative energy was like that. It collected inside the body like yellow bile that turned a person restless and edgy. If the energy didn't find release, it would turn against its host and transform into the necrotic black bile of melancholy. A lot of writers he knew turned to pharmaceuticals to tame that energy, but Peter never saw his black moods as psychological malfunctions. Instead, he'd learned that the only cure was the ritualized bloodletting of laying prose on the page.

Even now, the yellow tentacles were squirming up the back of his throat and around the base of his brain. If he didn't get some serious word count soon, the bile would blacken and turn against him.

He rose from his chair, intent on finding paper and his favorite fountain pen. Getting something down—anything—was better than nothing. Refusing to write because it wouldn't be brilliant was like forgoing the temporary relief of his own hand because it wasn't as good as sex with an actual woman.

Before he could pull his pen and notebook from his satchel in the kitchen, tires crunched on the gravel drive out front. He glanced at the clock on his cell phone. He couldn't think of any of Moon Hollow's citizens he'd want to see after midnight.

A few moments later, a knock sounded at the door and as he walked to answer it, he saw Deacon Fry through the window. A panic sizzled in his stomach. Had Jessup found out what he and Ruby had been up to that afternoon?

"Mr. West?" The voice was muffled by the door, but the authority in the deacon's voice was clear.

He blew out a deep breath and opened up because he wasn't a coward. "Deacon," he said, "you're up late."

He hadn't seen the deacon since his first day in town at church, and the changes were remarkable. Dark circles weighed down the skin under his eyes and the wrinkles on the sides of his mouth were deeper, as if he'd spent a lot of time frowning recently.

"Sorry to disturb you at this hour, but I presumed you keep late hours on account of your writing."

Deacon Fry wasn't wrong, so Peter didn't correct him, but it was presumptuous as hell to show up like this. "What can I help you with?" He didn't invite him inside.

The deacon smiled tightly, as if the effort cost him. "I apologize that I was not there for our meeting the other morning, but I assume you've heard about the trouble we had at the mines that day."

"The funeral was today?"

"Terrible business."

"I'm sorry."

"Thank you." The deacon motioned to the chairs on the porch. "May we sit?" He'd obviously figured out an invitation inside wasn't coming.

Peter dipped his head to accept the compromise and stepped out, closing the door behind him. Naturally, his guest took the rocking chair, which left Peter to take the creaky metal folding chair.

Deacon Fry began rocking as if settling in for a nice long chat. Peter suddenly wished he'd thought to pour himself some bourbon first.

"Are you a man of belief, Mr. West?"

As far as opening salvos went, it was quite effective. "I suppose everyone believes in something, Deacon Fry."

"What's your something?"

"What's your point?"

The deacon's lips twitched. "Today I helped bury a boy who should have had a long life. Lot of people would see that as an excuse to question their faith. It's understandable, I suppose. It's hard to remain faithful when bad things happen to good people. But for men like me, faith doesn't make tragedy more complicated—it simplifies things."

Peter leaned forward with his elbows on his knees. "How so?"

When he realized Peter wasn't mocking him, he leaned back with his hands folded across his middle. "Life is a lot easier if you accept that you're not in control."

A startled laugh escape Peter's mouth before he could stop it. "You do realize that you are both the head of Moon Hollow's only church and its mayor, right? This little theocracy you have here is all about control."

The deacon's expression hardened. "Being a leader isn't about controlling people. I'm doing the Lord's work."

"Sure," Peter said. "The Lord's work."

"Do you have something you'd like to say to me, Mr. West?"

"The more important question is, what did you come here to say to me?"

The deacon rocked a bit, looking out into the night. His expression wasn't angry; it was thoughtful. Peter had baited him, and he'd expected a fight in return, but he had no idea what to do with this pensive version of Deacon Fry.

"I'm afraid we've gotten off on the wrong foot."

"Why don't you tell me what the right foot was supposed to look like?"

"Mr. West, I have come to mend fences, but you insist on continuing to bait me. Why is that?"

"Are you aware that Earl Sharps threatened me with arrest yesterday if I didn't agree to stay away from the funeral today?"

His expression didn't change but he did slow down his rocking for a moment. "I regret that Earl took it that far. I simply asked him to inform you that it might be best if you allowed the people of this town to mourn our loss without outside influences."

He made it all sound so reasonable, but Peter wasn't quite ready to become pals. "So how do you explain Lettie trying to cancel our rental agreement?"

Deacon Fry sighed. "Mistakes have been made. I admit that. But I'm hoping we can move forward in a spirit of cooperation."

He wanted something. Peter was sure of it, but he was also sure that if he didn't play by the deacon's rules things would get a whole lot worse before they got better. "I am open to that."

"Excellent. Tell me, have you ever heard of our tradition of Decoration Day?"

He nodded. "I've read a little about it, but I'll admit I've never attended one."

"I might be able to help you with that. Despite recent tragedies, we've decided to move forward with the tradition this year. The festivities will commence in three days' time."

"That's fast."

"We are eager to begin the healing process. The Decoration will provide much-needed closure for the town."

"That's nice," Peter said, "but what does it have to do with me?"

"I came to extend a formal invitation to join our community at the Decoration."

Peter let that sink in for a moment. "What's the catch?"

He stopped rocking. "That when the Decoration is complete, you will pack your bags and leave this place."

So much for cooperation. "And if I refuse?"

"Then my good friend Sheriff Abernathy will arrest you for trespassing."

Trespassing? Shit. "So this is about Ruby?"

Deacon Fry's placid expression deepened into a frown. "What about her?"

The relief he should have felt was displaced by regret over even bringing up the girl. "Oh nothing. I misunderstood." He cleared his throat. "If you have that kind of power and want me gone so badly, why haven't you already had Abernathy pay me a visit?"

"I'm a reasonable man, Mr. West." He nodded, as if doing so might make it true. "You paid good money to rent this cabin. Leaving after the Decoration means that you'll get a full week of time for your trouble. Use the next couple of days to get more writing done, and then go to the Decoration so you have a good story about your time here. But then it's time to go home and leave us in peace."

Peter stood. "It's late."

To his credit, the deacon didn't miss a beat. He simply nodded and stood. "When can I expect your answer?"

"I'll give it to you now."

"All right." He clasped his hands together, the picture of benevolent patience.

"I'm not here to make enemies or upset anyone. I'll leave before the Decoration."

"Oh, Mr. West, please don't feel like you have to rush out on my account. You'll enjoy Decoration Day. There's a picnic."

Peter couldn't believe this man was trying to sell him on a picnic when he'd just threatened him with arrest. Given that he had a teenager pressuring him to spirit her out of town and, now, with the town's mayor/religious despot threatening to have him arrested, maybe the best course of action was simply to leave the next morning and be done with the strange town and its even stranger inhabitants. Still, part of him was intensely curious about attending the ceremony, if for no other reason than to see what the fuss was about. "Either way, you win. I'll be gone by the end of the day of the Decoration, if not before."

The deacon held out his hand to shake Peter's. "If you think that's best."

He stared down at the man's hand. Shaking it would have felt too much like making a deal with the devil. "Good night, Deacon Fry."

"God bless, Mr. West."

32

TENDING THE FLOCK

Deacon Fry

THE MORNING after the funeral and his late-night meeting with Peter West, Deacon Fry paid a visit to the Barrett house.

An old tricycle and a mangled swing set stuck up from the weeds like sculptures done by one of those fancy New York artists who liked to make statements about the loss of innocence or the unbearable passage of time. He didn't know too much about art, but he was pretty sure those fancy boys with their art degrees didn't know a dang-burn thing about innocence. Besides, Cotton's front yard wasn't no work of art. It was proof of neglect, pure and simple.

He stepped over an old, rusted wagon. Old Cotton hadn't been so good at taking care of his home or his family even before poor Rose died, but where the man had simply been lazy after going on disability, now he was downright slovenly. Lord knew poor Ruby had her hands full with those two girls and keeping the household afloat while her daddy was off cooking his shine.

He climbed the steps, careful to avoid the gaps between the boards, and knocked on the door with the torn screen. The sound of a television drifted out of the open windows facing the porch. He mentally shook his head. Television rotted brains, and heaven knew those children didn't have many of those to spare. Ruby seemed to take after her mama with her curious brain and always having her head in a book, but he didn't have a lot of hope for those youngins now that they had to grow up without Rose's influence.

He knocked again.

"Ruby!" a young voice called. He couldn't tell which of the girls had spoken. "Someone's at the door!"

"Well git it!" Ruby's yell echoed down from the second floor.

An argument followed as the sisters argued over who had to answer the door. Deacon Fry prayed for patience. Clearly this house was in need of a responsible adult who could teach these children proper manners. "Hello?" he called. "It's Deacon Fry. I've come lookin' for your daddy."

The argument cut off abruptly, almost as if the children thought if they were quiet he'd just go away. His voice must have carried upstairs because suddenly a pair of bare feet appeared on the top step. Ruby smoothed her hair as she came down in an attempt to look more presentable. Didn't help much seeing how her britches were short enough for the devil to see the Promised Land.

She pasted a smile on her face and opened the screen. "Deacon Fry," she said breathlessly, "I'm so sorry. I was upstairs reading." She said it in a tone that implied she wanted him to believe she'd been reading scripture, but Sarah Jane had already told him that Ruby preferred the kind of books he'd been trying to get banned from town for years.

He smiled his best shepherd-of-the-flock smile. "It's all right, dear. Your daddy home?"

Her guarded expression told him she was considering a lie, but then her shoulders slumped. "No, sir," she said in a reluctant tone. "I haven't seen him."

"Since when?"

She looked up at him from under her lashes. "Since the funeral."

He'd really hoped his talk with Cotton at the cemetery would have helped things, but it appeared that he'd been wrong.

"He up at his cabin?"

"I think so."

Deacon Fry reached out and touched the girl's arm. When she looked up at him, embarrassment was there, but also something deeper—shame?—and a healthy dose of fear.

"Don't worry. I won't tell your daddy you told me where to find him."

She visibly relaxed. "Thank you."

"Now," he said in his get-down-to-business tone, "how are you doing for money?"

She looked at a point just south of his eyes. "We're okay."

He bent down until he caught her gaze. "You know it's a sin to lie, don't you, Ruby?"

"Yes, sir. But Miss Edna brought us some leftovers from Jack's funeral supper and Daddy's disability check is due tomorrow to pay the 'lectricity."

"Good—that's real good. I sure am proud of you for taking such good care of your family."

She tipped her chin to acknowledge the compliment. "What are you gonna say to Daddy when you find him?"

She had no right to ask an elder to explain his intentions to her, but he had a feeling that keeping her thinking they were allies would benefit him. "I'm just gonna check on him, is all. I know he's been hurting ever since your mama went to heaven, bless her. All the help he needs can be found in the Lord." He paused meaningfully.

"Amen," she said on cue.

"You'll see. Once we get him back in the bosom of the church your daddy won't need to find solace in that cabin of his or in the bottom of a whiskey bottle."

Her head jerked up, as if she'd somehow believed her father's drinking was a family secret no one else knew. Poor lamb. Poor dumb lamb.

"Have faith in the Lord, Ruby."

"Amen." Her tone lacked the enthusiasm one might expect from an obedient child of God when discussing faith.

"Say, you haven't been spending time with that author fella, have you?"

She looked down at her dirty feet. "What do you mean?"

"Oh nothing. I was chatting with him last night and he brought up your name."

"He did?" her voice squeaked.

"It's okay to tell me the truth, Ruby. He's a guest in our town. I trust you haven't been doing anything ... inappropriate."

Her cheeks flushed. "Oh no, Deacon Fry. I swear it. I just saw him yesterday after the funeral when he was taking a walk is all. I was pretty upset about Jack and all. He was real nice and told me everything would be okay. That's all, promise."

He gave her the same look he gave Sarah Jane when he suspected she wasn't telling him the whole truth. Ruby met his expression without flinching. "It isn't appropriate for a young woman to be talking to a grown man alone."

She tilted her head. "But I'm talking to you, Deacon."

He resisted the urge to reprimand her. She always seems a tad odd to him, and so he had to be patient. "That's different, Ruby. You known me your whole life. Peter West is a stranger."

She frowned but nodded. "I guess so."

"Anyway," he said, changing tactics, "Mr. West's time with us won't be lasting too much longer. He's decided to leave following the Decoration."

Her skin paled and her face fell. "Really?"

"I know it's been real exciting having a famous author around, but he needs to get back to the city and get on with his life."

"I see," she whispered.

"All right, I need to head out. If I miss him and your daddy comes here, send him up to the cemetery to pitch in with the clean up, will you?"

She nodded but her lip was trembling. "Yes, sir."

He patted her head. "That's a good girl. Everything's going to be okay, Ruby. Trust the Lord."

"Amen," she whispered.

33

HAIR OF THE DOG

Peter

He woke later than usual the next morning. The bourbon he'd attacked after the deacon left the night before had glued his tongue to the roof of his mouth. He stumbled out of bed and gulped water straight from the faucet. His head throbbed, as if overnight his skull had shrunk but his brain had grown. Only, he knew that wasn't right because he'd never felt dumber.

He'd let that man get to him. He splashed some water on his face and spat into the basin. He was tempted to just throw his shit in a bag and take off, but he didn't want to seem like a coward running out of town with his tail between his legs.

Snatching a towel from the hook on the wall, he scrubbed away the moisture. The scent of laundry detergent surprised him. Somehow he'd missed that Lettie had come by to replace the linens. He paused and tried to think back to the night before when he'd passed out in the bed—a vague recollection of cursing the coverlet he'd had to pull out from under the pillows. He frowned at the towel and let it drop into the sink.

Now that he was upright and marginally awake, echoes from his argument with Renee flew through his head. *Peter, why are you calling me in the middle of the night?*

He winced as half-formed sentences paraded through his head. Terrible words he'd spewed at her like venom—accusations and wild theories about why she'd written that damned book.

That warped imagination of yours is telling you lies.

Oh she'd loved his imagination in the beginning, hadn't she? When they'd met in college, she'd read each of his short stories, looking for herself between the lines and hidden among the letters. She'd giggled when he told her he'd named the murder victim in his first published novel after her. He couldn't recall when she'd started to find it less charming. Maybe it had been about the time his advances started slipping. Or maybe it was when her nosey friends started asking pointed questions about why the characters in her husband's books bore uncomfortable similarities to themselves. Or perhaps, after a while, she'd simply grown jealous of all the time he spent writing instead of worshiping her.

She'd never understood his need to prove himself. Beautiful Renee with her family money had never had to worry about working. He still remembered the smug look on her father's face the day he handed them a check for the down payment on their house. He'd called it a birthday present for his little girl. Peter had seen it as a reminder that he'd never measure up, but he'd still cashed the check. Turning it down hadn't been an option. He'd coveted the little guest house in the back because it seemed like the sort of thing a real author would have—a sacred space where a serious scribe used alchemy to transform words and paper into the Great American Novel. From the moment he saw it, he'd begun imagining the photo shoot that would happen when the *New York Times* sent a photographer to capture images of the bestselling author in his habitat.

In the end, he'd gotten the office, but the rest of his vision never materialized.

Which brought him back to the reason he'd drunk-dialed his ex-wife, as well as the reason for him coming to Moon Hollow in the first place. Both choices had clearly been mistakes. At that moment, standing in the little cabin with a hangover raging behind his eyes like a demon, he wondered how long it had been since he'd made a good decision.

He padded from the bathroom to the kitchen. On his way there, he stepped on something sharp. "Son of a—"

He stooped down to see what caused the pain, and realized he'd stepped on the remains of his cell phone.

Oh, right. The ill-fated call with Renee had resulted in yet another terrible decision when he'd thrown the phone against the wall. He vaguely remembered feeling satisfied when he'd heard the loud crunch, but now it was just another reminder of his stupidity.

Now he'd have to deal with the headache of figuring out where to buy a new one. Another reason to just leave that morning. He could buy a new phone on his way down the mountain in Big Stone Gap. If he stayed, it wouldn't be worth the effort. The only person he'd called since he'd arrived was Renee and look at how well that had gone.

In the fridge, he found a Coke and an untouched mystery casserole brought over by the good deacon's wife. He grabbed the soda and turned his back on the other thing, which he was too polite to throw away but definitely was never going to eat. Eventually he'd need food, but for now, he contented himself with the bubbles and caffeine.

He was halfway to the haven of the couch when a knock

sounded at the door. He considered ignoring it and retreating to his room to hide under the covers, but then he saw Bunk's beat-up truck through the window. He padded over to the open the door.

"You look like warmed over shit, son."

"Hi, Bunk." He rubbed at his aching head and stepped back to let the older man inside.

Bunk came in, his eyes doing a leisurely inventory of the space. "Why ain't you dressed?"

"For what?"

"For the cemetery cleaning?"

He frowned and scanned his mental inventory to see if he was forgetting a conversation he'd had with Bunk about it, but nothing came up. "I didn't know I was going."

"Well, 'course you are. Every man in town is required to pitch in with the Decoration Day clean up."

"I don't even know if I'll be here for the Decoration."

Bunk simply watched him, as if he was wasting both their time by arguing.

Finally, he spoke again. "I'm not feeling well."

"Judging from the way you smell, you was drunker than Cootey Brown last night. Best cure for a hangover is fresh air and workin' up a sweat. Run and git yer britches on."

He considered telling the old man to get the hell out. He was in no mood for being pushed around or forced to participate in Moon Hollow's arcane community rituals. But then he remembered the book he needed to write to punish his backstabbing ex. If he left town that day, he'd miss out on the extra material for his story. Spending the day cleaning a cemetery wasn't his idea of fun, but he knew enough about people to know the men would spend as much time telling stories that day as they would pulling weeds.

"All right," he said. "But I'm going to need some food."

Bunk smiled. "Oh, I don't believe that'll be a problem."

BY THE TIME they reached the cemetery, Peter's hangover raged like a hurricane in his head. In the heat of the late morning, his sweat smelled sour and flammable. The dark sunglasses he'd put on before leaving the cabin did little to calm the throbbing behind his eyes. More than anything, he wanted to go back and dive headlong into the couch for a long nap. Warring with that urge was a craving for an ice-cold beer to take the edge off and settle his stomach.

This was his first visit to the top of Cemetery Hill and, despite his sour mood, he had to admit the spot was spectacular. Tall evergreens and shorter hardwoods surrounded the open space as if trying to keep a secret. A black wrought iron fence surrounded the area and an archway over the entrance had a Bible verse painted on it. *He that endureth to the end shall be saved.* —*Matthew 10:22*

Peter stared up at the words, seeing them but not quite processing their meaning. He that endureth—what, exactly? Life?

He shook his head and wiped a sheen of sticky sweat from the back of his neck. Christ, he needed a beer.

"You okay, son?" Bunk didn't try to disguise the humor in his tone. If he'd sounded the least bit sincere, Peter might have taken the chance to beg off and run back to his cabin.

But Bunk hadn't sounded sincere and so Peter swallowed the bile clogging his throat and nodded. "Let's get to work."

The old man looked unconvinced by his bravado but he nodded towards the cemetery gate. Peter walked under the arch ahead of Bunk. Several men had already gathered, but they weren't working. Instead, they gathered in a loose circle around something on the far side of the plot. Each of the men had removed their hats and were scratching their scalps. Earl Sharps stood at the head of the group and stared down at the ground as if it were a disappointing child.

"What's going on?" he asked Bunk. The old man shrugged and brushed past to go find out.

Peter considered hanging back in the shade, but he followed because part of him was hoping whatever had their attention would provide him with the out he was too proud to ask for from Bunk earlier.

"Mornin!" Bunk called. "I brought reinforcements."

Earl looked over his shoulder. "Come lookit this." On the tail end of the invitation, he spotted Peter walking up behind Bunk. "Mornin', Pete."

Having a name like Peter tended to invite all sorts of terrible nicknames, and Peter detested them all. However, the Ed Sharps who called him "Pete" was a lot more pleasant than the one who'd called him by his full name the other day in the diner, so he let slide. He guessed whatever Deacon Fry had told his flunkies following their conversation was to thank for the change, but it annoyed him that his impending exit was the only reason people were being civil.

"What's going on?" he asked as he followed Bunk over.

Sharps stepped out of the way. "See for yourself." A couple of others moved, too, to give Bunk and Peter access.

Bunk gasped. "What the Sam hell?"

Peter looked at the chunks of stone. Most of the pieces didn't have discernible shapes, but one near his foot had an eye carved into it. He realized then he was looking at the remains of some sort of funerary statue. "How'd this happen?"

"That's what we was trying to figure out. It was like this when we got here."

"It was fine yesterday during the funeral," Bunk said.

"Someone must have come up here last night," Sharps said.

Bunk nudged the rubble with the toe of his boot. "Have you told Deacon Fry?"

Sharps shook his head. "He'll be here soon."

Another man, one that Peter didn't recognize, who wore baggy camp pants and a beige T-shirt, spoke up. "When I find out who did this, I'm gonna throw 'em to my dogs."

That was when Peter realized he was standing next to the infamous Jessup boy. Just in case, he stepped to the other side of Bunk, who was rooting through the rubble with his good hand for possible clues.

"Huh," the old man said.

"You found something?" Sharps asked.

"Reckon so," Bunk said.

They all closed in for a better look. Bunk moved several pieces of rubble away. "There's something buried here." He used his pincer to dig at the dirt for a moment before he cleared away an edge of whatever it was.

"What is it?" Earl asked.

Bunk jiggled the item to free it of some of the dirt, and a second later he pulled it free. "Got it."

They all leaned in to see what he'd unearthed. He bent over it and took a moment to brush off the rest of the dirt. "I'll be damned."

"Well?" Junior demanded.

Bunk looked directly at Peter. "It's your book." His face stared at him from the back cover of his last novel, *Devil's Due*.

"What the hell?" He took the book from Bunk and turned it over to the front.

Against the black background, the title had been written in a large, bloody font. His name appeared in a much smaller font below. He'd fought with his publisher over that cover for weeks. In the end, the people who paid the bills got to call the shots, but now, standing in a cemetery with a bunch of small town mountain people, he was grateful that they hadn't gone with his suggestion of a big red pentagram against the black background. Something told him that the satanic symbol would have gotten his three-day reprieve rescinded.

"Were you in the cemetery last night, Mr. West?" Earl's expression had lost its newfound politeness.

"Of course not," he said. "Ask Deacon Fry. He paid me a visit."

"Then how do you explain your book being buried here?" Junior puffed up like he was ready to kick Peter's ass.

"Gee, I don't know, maybe someone else did it?"

Bunk caught his eye and shook his head slightly in warning.

"Most of us were at the funeral dinner last night at Nell's place," Earl said. "But I suppose someone could have come up here after."

"It doesn't make any sense," Peter said. "Why bury the book?"

"Or break the statue?" Bunk added.

The hairs on the back of Peter's neck stood on end. Knocking over the statue could have been an accident, but why in the hell would anyone bury his book? Was it a warning? Did someone want him dead? His imagination ran off in a thousand different directions of possibility and none of them ended pleasantly.

"I think it was him." Junior narrowed his eyes at Peter. "He's doing satanic stuff up here."

This was from a man who had a bear cub caged in his backyard to use to bait dogs. "If I were responsible, why on earth would I have come here this morning with Bunk?"

Junior spit a stream of tobacco juice onto the ground. "I watch them cop shows. The criminal always returns to the scene of the crime."

"What crime was committed here?" he asked. "Are books outlawed in Moon Hollow?"

"Peter," Bunk said, "maybe you should go back to your cabin and get some rest, what with you feeling poorly this morning."

"I think we should wait until Deacon Fry gets here," Earl said.

Bunk stood and brushed his hands on his jeans. "The man just said Deacon Fry visited him last night at his cabin. No, there's some other explanation."

While the other men argued, Peter knelt and fished through the rubble. Something shiny caught his eye. He moved the rock covering it and saw it was a piece of jewelry. He started to open his mouth to call the others over, but then he saw it was Ruby's Nashville bracelet.

He'd seen it on her wrist the day before when they'd gone to Junior's place. She'd had it on when he left her at her mailbox. He'd asked her about it and she said it belonged to her mama.

He shoved it into the breast pocket of his shirt and stood up.

"It could have been Granny Maypearl," Earl was saying. "One of her hoodoo spells."

He told himself that the bracelet didn't necessarily mean that Ruby was to blame for the broken statue or the buried book. Someone could have stolen the bracelet, too. But he knew there was no way he should show it anyone until he'd had a chance to speak with her.

"You okay, Peter?" Bunk said. "You're looking a little pale."

"I just—it's a shock to think someone used my book like that."

Junior spat on the ground. Earl looked away, as if uncomfortable with Peter's admission of weakness. Bunk's eyes narrowed but he nodded.

"Why don't you head back to the cabin? When Deacon Fry

gets here we'll explain what happened. He'll likely want to chat with you a spell, but we've got some investigatin' to do."

"If you think that's best," he said.

On his way down the hill, he told himself there was nothing to worry about. Surely it was all just a misunderstanding. But just in case, he was going to hunt down Ruby Barrett and figure out what the hell the girl had been thinking.

34

SO MOTE IT BE

Ruby

AFTER DEACON FRY VISITED HER, Ruby got the girls ready for school and headed into town to do her shift at the library. Even though she knew no one would be coming in to check out books, she needed something to do to keep her mind off her problems.

As she walked by the church parking lot on the way, she saw several trucks parked in the lot. The men were already up at the cemetery getting ready for Decoration Day. She could only imagine what their reactions might have been when they arrived to find the angel broken on the ground. Would they assume someone had done it on purpose? Would they suspect her?

On the heels of that thought, she quickened her pace. She was suddenly very grateful for the refuge of the library, where she could avoid any of the drama once word spread through town.

Distracted with her to-do list for the day, she unlocked the front door and went inside.

"What are you doing here?" Sarah Jane said.

Ruby yelped and spun around with her back against the closed door. "Sarah Jane! I didn't think you'd be here."

Sarah Jane sat behind the desk as usual, but she didn't look the same at all. Her once glossy hair now hung in dull sheets, and the only colors on her face were the red lines in her eyes and purple smudges beneath them.

"I had to get out of the house." She said it in such a way that it left Ruby wondering if she'd been forced out by her parents instead of deciding on her own to leave.

"How are you doing?"

"Fine."

"I was just stopping in to check on things."

"I have it under control." She looked down to shuffle through some paperwork. "You can leave."

Ruby hesitated. The thought of going back to the house and spending the whole day wondering if anyone would connect the statue to her made her skin feel itchy. "I could stick around and help—"

"I don't want you here, Ruby. Please just go."

Any thoughts Ruby had about Jack's death softening Sarah Jane evaporated. She opened her mouth to say something else, but at that moment the door pushed against her back as someone tried to come into the building. She jumped out of the way in time to see Peter push through the doorway.

"Oops," Ruby said, even though she'd been the one who got bumped. "Sorry."

"My fault," he mumbled.

"Good morning, Mr. West." Sarah Jane stood and tried to smile. "I'm afraid we're closed."

"Oh," he said, "I'm not here to check out a book. I was looking for Ruby."

As heat rushed to Ruby's cheeks, she was also aware of Sarah Jane's surprised glance in her direction.

"Really?" Sarah Jane's surprised tone indicated she'd never heard anything so odd.

Peter looked at Ruby. "Do you have a minute?"

A confusing tangle of emotions rose in her midsection, pleasure mixed with confusion and a little bit of fear. But through it all one thought broke through: *It worked. He's come to me.*

"Uh, sure," she said. Her tongue felt too thick for her mouth and she hated how nervous she sounded. "We can use the back room."

He glanced at Sarah Jane and back to Ruby. "Actually, I was hoping we could talk outside."

Sarah Jane's eyebrows shot up to her perfectly trimmed bangs.

"Okay," Ruby said.

Peter nodded and touched Ruby's elbow to guide her that way. The spot where his fingers touched her skin sparked with sensation.

"Ruby?" Sarah Jane said, looking up from the forms she'd been studying. "Did you order some books?"

Her heart hop-scotched in her chest, but she managed to speak over her panic. "Of course not."

"That's weird. Someone ordered several copies of Mr. West's books."

"Maybe it was your mom." She avoided Peter's eyes.

Sarah Jane frowned. "Hmm."

"Ruby?" he prompted.

"Oh right." She ducked past him and through the door he held open.

"That's the strangest thing," Sarah Jane said as they stepped outside.

Peter followed her out and turned away from the church to

walk toward the diner. He kept looking back over his shoulder as they walked.

"Were you in the cemetery last night?" he said in a low tone.

The question, so unexpected, caught her completely off guard. "I—why?"

He reached into his pocket and pulled something out. When the light caught the Nashville charm, her heart stopped and then tripped into a triple-time pace. "No," she blurted.

Up close, she could smell his scent, which was a mixture of sun and a slightly sour smell that she recognized as day-old alcohol cologne. He smelled just like Daddy after a bender.

He shoved the bracelet back in his pocket, as if it were too dangerous to see the light of day. "Ruby, this is serious. They found the broken statue."

"I don't know what you're talking about." She moved away from him to escape the scent.

"What about the books?"

"I'm sure Sarah Jane's mom ordered them."

He grabbed her arm. They were in front of the closed post office. "Damn it, Ruby. This isn't a game. They found my book buried in the cemetery."

Her mouth fell open. In her rush to leave the night before, she'd forgotten all about burying the book. "I—what book?"

He shook her a little. "Stop it. I know it was you."

Tears gathered in Ruby's eyes and pressure built up inside her until she wanted to scream like a teakettle. "I—" She snapped her mouth shut. If she admitted to everything then Peter would never help her. She'd be trapped in Moon Hollow until it was time to join her mama and Jack up on Cemetery Hill. "I—"

She searched the area wildly for an escape route, but they were in the middle of the street. If she ran off it would attract too much attention. Besides, he'd just follow her.

Down the street, a door jingled as Reverend Peale exited the diner. He was only a few feet away and had already spotted them. He tipped his hat to Ruby. "Miss Barrett, how are you on this fine day?"

"Just fine, Reverend Peale. How are you?"

"Oh, fine, fine." He turned his attention to Peter. "And who might you be, young man?"

Peter held out his hand. "Peter West."

"Ah, yes, I do believe Deacon Fry mentioned we had a guest in town. Why haven't you come to visit with me yet?"

"I don't believe I'd had an invitation."

"Well, consider it issued. You'll come by tomorrow around ten."

Peter smiled, clearly charmed. "I'll have to check my schedule."

The reverend waved a hand. "Oh fiddle, there ain't nothing going on in this town then, anyway. You'll come."

Peter laughed. "Yes, sir. I'll be there."

The reverend nodded, as if to seal their deal. "I look forward to hearing all about this book you're writing about Moon Hollow."

With that, he said his goodbyes and waved off their offers to help him to the parsonage. When he'd walked far enough out of earshot, Peter touched her elbow again. "We need to talk about this somewhere else."

She wanted to tell him she didn't want to talk about it at all. She was embarrassed and worried he just wanted to go talk somewhere so he could tell her he'd never help such a dumb little girl. But running away would only make her feel more ashamed. "There's a spot nearby."

He nodded. "Lead the way."

Ten minutes later, she stopped in the middle of the forest. "Here we are."

He stood beside her and looked around. "What is this place?"

She tried to see the spot through his eyes. The crumbling stones formed a ragged square in the clearing. "According to the stories, this house used to belong to the Witch of Moon Hollow."

He looked at her as if to see if she were joking, but she nodded.

"She was Granny Maypearl's great-great granny."

"Did they burn her?" he asked.

She laughed. "No, silly. She was respected as a healer and midwife in the region. Going back as far as Moon Hollow has existed, a woman has acted as mountain granny to the people here."

"So what changed?"

"Deacon Fry changed it."

He walked toward the ruins of the house. "How?"

"I don't know the whole story, but Deacon Fry started changing things a long time ago—even before he became mayor."

"That's something I've been wondering about him. He clearly runs the church, so why isn't he a reverend?"

She shrugged. "He flunked out of seminary. But since his daddy was reverend for a long time, Deacon Fry's always had a lot of power in town. He's just way more conservative than his daddy was and started making new rules as soon as he got himself elected mayor."

"What sort of rules?"

"Well, for one, music can only be played in church and has to be religious. Used to be everyone in town would gather on porches at night to have sing-alongs, but Deacon Fry said it was sinful to carry on like that."

"You said all the women in your family did mountain magic —your grandmother, too?"

"Granny Maypearl lives way up on the ridge but people still go out to get her remedies, which makes it easier to hide it from Deacon Fry." She smiled and thought back to Granny's voice singing to her as a young girl. "Granny can hear the mountain song. That's the source of her magic."

"And you really expect me to believe that her granddaughter doesn't dabble in magic, too?"

Too late, she realized he'd backed her into a corner. "I can't hear the mountain song," she said. "I don't have no powers."

He looked as if he was struggling to follow all this talk of mountain magic and songs. "That doesn't mean you didn't try to do some sort of spell in the cemetery last night. Come on, admit it." He reached into his shirt pocket and removed the bracelet again.

The charm flashed in the sunlight accusingly. Her stomach dropped about fifty stories and crashed at the bottom. "I didn't break the statue," she blurted. "It fell over."

He closed his eyes and pinched the bridge of his nose. "Why did you bury the book?"

Even with his eyes closed, she still couldn't look directly at him. Instead, she looked down at her shoes. Her canvas sneakers were dirty from the walk out to the ruins and looked childish next to his boots. "I was trying to be sure you'd say yes."

His eyes popped open. "What do you mean?"

The thought of admitting what she'd done aloud made her feel like throwing up right on his boots. "I read in a book that there were some things you could do to make sure a person did what you wanted them to do."

He scowled at her. "Was it a book of spells?"

"Don't make it sound like I was killing chickens under a full moon. It was more like setting an intention." She didn't mention that the book she'd used actually had a spell that involved sacrificing chickens.

"Did it occur to you that burying a book about the devil in a consecrated cemetery might raise a few eyebrows?"

"I didn't think anyone would ever know. I told you, I accidentally bumped the statue and it broke. I realized I'd made a mistake and left as fast as I could."

"Leaving behind my book and your bracelet," he said. "Do you have any idea how suspicious it looked this morning when several members of the Deacon Council found my book buried under the broken statue? They think I was up there last night doing some sort of satanic rite."

Panic welled again. "What did you tell them?"

"The truth—that I had no idea why it was there and that I'd been with Deacon Fry last night."

She paused. What he said tickled a memory of something. "Wait a second, did you tell Deacon Fry we'd spent time together yesterday?"

"Of course not. Why?"

"Because he showed up to my house this morning. Asked me if I'd been spending time with you."

His color went high and his eyes suddenly looked everywhere but at her.

"Peter?"

"Shit," he said. "When he showed up last night, I was worried that Junior might have figured out we'd been on his land. I mentioned your name to the deacon to test the waters, but when I realized he was there on another matter, I dropped it." Almost to himself he said, "Clearly he'd thought it an odd enough comment to follow up with you this morning."

"Don't worry. I told him I saw you after the funeral and we talked for a few minutes but that was it."

He blew out a breath and nodded. "That's good. That's really good."

She chewed on her bottom lip for a moment. "You, uh, aren't going to tell them it was me in the cemetery, are you?"

"Of course not, but it's only a matter of time. Are you sure you didn't leave anything else behind?"

She thought about it real hard before she answered. "I don't think so."

"Any chance someone saw you coming or going?"

"I don't think so."

He braced a foot on a decaying tree trunk that had fallen against the wall. "This isn't good."

"You didn't show anyone my bracelet, did you?"

"Of course not."

"Then I should be okay."

He huffed out an edgy laugh. "You don't get it, do you? When they figure out it was you, all hell will break loose. History is full of small towns persecuting young girls for doing magic."

"But they don't hurt Granny Maypearl."

"Ruby, listen to me, you buried a book about the devil with my name on it in a cemetery and destroyed a sacred statue. No reasonable explanation in the world can compete with the imaginations of people who enjoy nothing more than punishing sinners."

She rubbed her hands over her arms to warm them. "So what am I supposed to do?"

He pushed himself upright and started pacing. Judging by the way he was mumbling to himself he was having quite an argument. Finally, he stopped and said, "God damn it."

"What?"

He sucked in a deep breath and exhaled it slowly through his mouth. "Can you leave today?"

Excitement fluttered in her stomach. "Today? Leave?"

"That's what you wanted, right?" He sounded angry. "Well,

guess what, sweetheart—you got your way. There's no way I can leave you here now."

Her mind spun. This was all so fast. He was offering her exactly what she'd asked for, but it felt wrong. "I can't leave today."

"Why not?"

"I need time to make sure my granny can take care of my two little sisters. Plus, I need clothes and I have to get ahold of some money." She chewed her lower lip and thought it over. "We can leave day after tomorrow while everyone is at the Decoration."

"What if they figure out it was you?"

"That's a risk I'm willing to take. I can't just abandon my sisters, Peter."

"All right. The morning of the Decoration. We can leave right after."

"No, it has to be before that while everyone's at the ceremony." She hated to argue with him when he seemed so close to accepting, but her gut told her it would be impossible for them to leave if they went to the Decoration.

He looked like he wanted to argue, but he sighed instead. "Fine, but don't be late. I won't wait around for you."

Ruby had never been one for dancing but right then she could have jitterbugged her way all the way to New York City. She threw herself at him. His arms came around her to steady her.

"You won't regret this, Peter," she whispered into his neck. He still smelled like Daddy after a bender, but she pretended it was just her imagination.

"Yes," he whispered back, "I will."

35

THE DEVIL'S SPINE

Deacon Fry

REACHING the old cabin where Cotton brewed his moonshine required tromping through acres of woods up to the Devil's Spine. Luckily, the deacon had dressed for the cemetery work that day, so his sturdy boots and work pants stood up well to the briars, mud, and deadfall that formed a natural barrier around the cabin. However, it took him a good twenty minutes to reach it, so by the time he pounded on the door he was in quite a lather.

The cabin wasn't much. Cotton's daddy had built it back in the sixties for he and his fellas to get away from the womenfolk, drink moonshine, hunt, and look at nudie magazines. Deacon Fry had never been invited to these get-togethers, but he knew it well enough because he'd gone up there a time or two to bring Hank Barrett home, just as he now was doing with the man's son.

He pounded on the door three times because he assumed

Cotton would be passed out, as usual. But on the third strike, the door opened inward. He paused with his fist raised against the rectangle of shadow.

"Hello? Cotton?" He took a hesitant step toward the threshold, but didn't cross it. A man who'd been on a bender was likely to shoot first and ask questions later if a man darkened his doorway. "It's Deacon Fry."

Silence from inside the cabin. But outside, three birds leapt into the air, screeching like the devil himself was on the hunt. Were he a cursing man, the startle might have dragged a real string of profanity from his lips. "Dumb animals," he muttered instead.

As he finally placed a foot over the threshold, he convinced himself it was concern for Cotton—not fear, never that— that finally got his feet moving.

"Anyone here?" Light from the doorway revealed the outlines of an old rocking chair and potbellied stove, but the far edges of the room were still blurry and dark.

A smell rushed at him like a fist, punching him in the nose with the stench of rot and the heavy smell of old tobacco smoke. There was no electricity in the cabin, so he pulled his keys out of his pocket. Sarah Jane had given him a small flashlight keychain for Father's Day a few years back. He twisted the base and a weak beam spilled from the tip. He wished he'd thought to grab the large Maglite he kept in his trunk in case he ever had car trouble on the deserted back roads of Wise County, Virginia.

"If wishes were horses, poor men would ride." He started at the unexpected sound of his own voice in the small room. Where had that come from? The proverb was one of his father's favorites to trot out when Virgil or his little brother, Isaac—back before the accident, of course— begged for sweets. He hadn't thought about that for decades. Why had he repeated it now?

He shook off the memories and stepped farther into the

room. In addition to the stench, there was also a nagging sound, a constant buzzing, he hadn't noticed when he'd first entered. He moved the light around to try and locate the source, but it was difficult to see anything with a two-inch band of light as your guide. If only the cabin had windows—

Wait a second. The last time he'd been to the cabin, it had been early morning, and he had a clear memory of watery light seeping through two small windows as he had dragged Hank Barrett out of the cot in the corner. He stepped closer, and realized the rectangle where there should be light appeared darker than the rest of the walls. When his fingertips made contact with the dark shape, they slid across the surface like someone has spread grease across the glass.

He pointed his flashlight at his fingers. The substance coating his skin was oily and black. He lifted it to his nose. The rotten smell forced his head back.

The nagging feeling in his abdomen—the one he'd ignored ever since he'd stepped over the threshold into the dark, foul-smelling space—bloomed into hot panic.

Across the room, a scraping sound exploded into the silence.

He spun and aimed his pitiful light at the far corner. "Cotton?"

Nothing answered.

His chest tight, he sidestepped toward the open door.

It slammed shut.

His heart pounded a painful rhythm in his chest. He lurched toward the door. His greasy—bloody?—fingers slipped against the metal knob.

The air behind him felt like ice tendrils on the back of his neck.

Open, open, open. His fingers grasped for purchase on the metal.

"Cain." A single word, whispered hot in his ear.

"Lord, protect me!" His hand twisted the knob, and, hallelujah, the door finally opened. But before he could run out, a force slammed into his back, pushing him out of the cabin. He fell to the ground and rolled over just in time to see the door slam closed behind him.

36

MEETING WITH THE MENTOR

*Pete*r

AT TEN A.M. the next morning, Peter arrived at the rectory for his meeting with Reverend Peale. Located across the street from the church, the reverend's home was a charming little place with a picket fence and flowers in hanging baskets along the front porch. The mailbox out front was in the shape of a small church with a perfect little steeple and cross. He wondered if it was a replica of the original church before the lightning strike—or the demon strike, if Bunk was to be believed.

He knocked on the front door and waited two minutes before it was opened. Instead of Reverend Peale, Sarah Jane Fry stood across the threshold. He'd seen her the day before in the library, but he'd been so distracted he hadn't really looked at her then. Now, he was shocked to see how different she looked than when he'd first seen her in church. Her youthful shine was gone. Dark circles dulled her eyes and her hair was pulled back in a greasy bun.

"Mr. West?" she said, her voice wasn't welcoming.

"I have an appointment with the reverend." He immediately regretted the words. Surely he should have begun by offering condolences, but something in him wanted to escape her as quickly as possible. Something small and selfish that didn't want to be bothered worrying about how someone so young could live with such loss.

If she'd noticed the slight she didn't show it. Instead she nodded. "He's in the study." She stepped back to allow him entrance, and as he passed he didn't look at her.

"Ruby ordered those books," she said quietly.

He paused, caught off guard by the unexpected change in topic. "I don't know anything about all that."

"Someone's going to have to pay for them."

He looked her in the eye. In mourning or no, he didn't appreciate her tone. "Are you suggesting I was somehow involved in those books being purchased, Miss Fry?"

She shrugged and pursed her lips. "Something's going on. I don't know what, but it ain't right."

"You've been through a lot this week. I'm sorry for your loss, but harassing me seems like an odd way to deal with your grief." The minute the words left his mouth he felt like a grade A asshole.

She was staring at him as if she was expecting something. Instead of guessing, he simply waited. Finally, she spoke. "Why are you in Moon Hollow?"

He hadn't expected her to be so direct. Maybe in her grief she simply had lost the ability to be politely passive. "I'm writing a book."

"About what?"

"I don't know."

Her frown deepened. "Doesn't sound like you're off to a very good start, then."

Part of him admired her chutzpah. He'd written her off as a

vapid girl, but she seemed to have some spunk under all that blond hair and pain. "I'm sorry about your—I'm sorry about Jack."

Something shifted. Her posture stiffened to the point of brittleness and her mouth hardened. He'd seen that look before. It reminded him of the way Renee would look at him when he'd disappointed her, which was most of the time.

"Second door on the left." She turned and walked away.

Watching her go, he wondered when women learned how to make men feel so little. Did their mothers teach them or was it simply part of their DNA? Left with no other option, he walked down the hall toward the study. The door was open, so he poked his head in. "Reverend Peale?"

At first he couldn't locate the reverend in the room. Two large windows let in streams of light that illuminated the bookcases that took up two of the room's walls. Two upholstered chairs sat in front of the large desk, where the reverend appeared to be napping.

"Reverend Peale?"

When no response came, Peter rushed into the room. He was about to call out for Sarah Jane when the reverend looked up with bloodshot eyes. He cradled a tumbler in his palms and a bottle of cheap whiskey stood nearby.

"Are you okay, sir?"

The reverend made an inarticulate grumble.

"I don't know if you remember me—I'm Peter. You asked me to come by today?"

"I'm old but I ain't senile, son." The reverend raised the glass to his lips and drained the last half-inch of liquid. "Get a glass." He motioned toward a sideboard.

"It's ten in the morning."

"You've got some catching up to do, then."

Peter suppressed a shocked smile and grabbed a glass. When

he placed it on the desk, the reverend nodded his approval and poured a couple of fingers for Peter and a few more for himself. "Whatever you do, don't tell the deacon 'bout this. He'd have a conniption."

"Mum's the word." Peter had expected Reverend Peale to be as uptight as the rest of the men he'd met in Moon Hollow, but the good reverend was proving to be a delightful surprise. "Deacon Fry isn't my biggest fan, anyway."

Reverend Peale chuckled knowingly. "The deacon ain't a fan of much except the Good Lord and his own damned self."

"Forgive me, but if you're such a critic of his, why do you let him run the church?"

"As if I had a choice." He chuckled and took a pull of whiskey. "Either way, it don't much matter. I'm an old drunk. I'll be making my amends with the Lord soon enough. Deacon Fry'll have his own comeuppance eventually. In the meantime, I serve the Good Lord and Jim Beam." He paused to take another drink. "Now, tell me about this book of yours."

"The idea is pretty unformed at this point, but I'm thinking of basing it on some of the old legends about this area." Peter set his untouched glass on the desk. "Moon Hollow is a fascinating place."

"You been talking to Bunk, eh?"

Peter couldn't fight his smile. "Yes, sir."

"Did you know his real name is Fred? We call him Bunk because that's what most of his stories are."

"Fair enough. But you have to admit this whole area is steeped in legends."

Reverend Peale took a deep breath and leaned back in his chair. He cradled the glass on his thin chest. The move took him back into a beam of light that highlighted the generous gin blossom on his nose. "I suppose there's a few old stories that get passed on about things that can't quite be explained, but if I were you I wouldn't put too much stock in them old tales."

"With all due respect, Reverend, I'm a fiction writer. The things that can't quite be explained are my stock in trade."

"You think my job's any different?"

Shock struck Peter speechless.

"Don't look so surprised, son. I might be a small town reverend, but that don't mean I don't understand the world. When I was a young man, I traveled all over performing missionary work. I read everything I could get my hands on about theology and science so I could understand the way of things. And you know what I found out?"

Peter shook his head.

"No one knows a damned thing. We're all just guessin'."

He'd expected to hear some epiphany. Instead, he'd managed to find a reverend who was both a drunk and a cynic. "If you really believe that, why did you get ordained?"

"Because a man's gotta choose a doctrine."

Peter had never ascribed to the just-in-case school of faith. "But what if he picks the wrong one?"

"You think you're smarter than me, son?" He leaned forward and pointed his tumbler at Peter. "You think I never questioned my choices? I've lived on God's green earth more'n seventy years. I've had plenty of time to learn and question, and what I've figured out is that the problem isn't religion. It's that men are flawed. They take perfect ideas and warp them by living selfishly."

"You sound more like a philosopher than a reverend."

Reverend Peale's smile was indulgent but genuine. "I might be from a small town, but that don't mean I'm a small man." He motioned to the bookshelves. "You don't have to live in a city to access the world's big ideas. You're a writer. Surely you understand that books hold the key to all of life's great mysteries."

"True enough."

Reverend Peals set his glass on the desk. "Now, why don't you tell me what you really want to know?"

Peter thought about it for a moment. "Honestly? I'm not sure. I've talked to several of the residents about the history of Moon Hollow, and I've heard lots of interesting stories, but something's bothering me."

"What's that?"

Peter shrugged. "It seems odd that such religious people actually believe in ghosts and demons."

"You ever read the Bible, son?"

"In Sunday school. Long time ago."

"You ever heard the story about Jesus in the wilderness for forty days and nights?"

"It's vaguely familiar."

His expression became animated in a way that convinced Peter that Reverend Peale might have been a great college professor in another life.

"The story goes that after he was baptized, Jesus retreated to the desert, and while he was there, the devil tried to tempt the Savior. Is that story any different from the ones Bunk told you?"

"Okay. The Bible is a parable, but some of the people in this town believe that Alodius Fry actually had a confrontation with a devil in front of that building." He pointed out the window and across the street at the church.

"Is the Bible a parable? Don't millions of people around the world believe that the words in the Bible are literally the Word of God?"

Peter nodded to concede the point. "For argument's sake, let's assume they're correct."

The reverend smiled indulgently. "Yes, let's."

"How did evil come into being? I'm no theologian, but none of the stories I ever read addressed its origins."

The reverend opened his hands. "Evil is created when man sins."

Peter blinked at him. "Do you believe that?"

"Of course."

"Isn't that vaguely blasphemous? I thought the Bible said that the devil was a fallen angel."

"Drink up, Mr. West."

Clearly the reverend was done debating theology. Probably for the best, Peter decided, since he was hardly qualified to argue any religious fact with anyone. The last time he'd been in a church was for his wedding, and look how God had punished him for that.

"You know what?" He lifted his glass. "Don't mind if I do." The first sip burned his lips and branded his tongue and throat.

Reverend Peale chuckled at his pained expression. "Good, huh?"

"Yes, sir."

His companion lifted the glass to the light and studied the amber liquid. "Deacon Fry paid me a visit last night."

Peter stilled. "Oh?"

The reverend nodded. "He was asking about demons, too." He made a little life-is-funny sound and drained the liquid. "You heard about the vandalism at the cemetery couple nights ago?"

Peter was glad he'd only had a couple of sips of whiskey since it appeared things were about to get hairy. "Yes, sir."

"Upsetting business. Young people these days ain't got no respect."

"The deacon thinks it was a teenager?"

"Nah. It's just to me, everyone's young." Reverend Peale shrugged. "Doubt they'll ever know for sure who did it."

Peter relaxed. "That's too bad."

"Oh, I don't know. Like you said," the reverend's eyes twinkled, "unexplained mysteries keep men like us in business."

37

PORCH DIPLOMACY

Granny Maypearl

THE ACHING in Granny Maypearl's knees meant rain was coming. She'd have a wet walk home but there was nothing for it. Important business needed tending to, and she meant to get it done.

As she rocked on his porch, her fingers itched for an instrument. She hadn't picked up her mama's dulcimer in months, but, right then, she longed for a connection to the women who came before her something fierce. She needed their wisdom and their strength to know what was right. But she didn't have her dulcimer, so she used her God-given instrument and sang a song she'd learned at her Granny Bell's knee.

She was far enough from town that no one would hear her and tell Deacon Fry on her for singing something that wasn't a hymn. When they were young, the whole town would get together to sing the traditional songs, and everyone knew little Virgil Fry had a strong, clear voice that could make any song sound like a prayer. But for some reason, after the accident, he refused to sing except in church.

She pushed thoughts of Virgil away as she concentrated on singing her song. She closed her eyes and let the melody flow out of her. The breeze picked up and made her hair dance. As she reached the chorus, the trees creaked and moaned like backup singers. The mountain had always liked this song.

Footsteps crunched on the gravel drive. She let the last note trail off before she opened her eyes. The man on the steps paused.

"Granny Maypearl, I presume."

She tipped her chin. "Mr. West."

"To what do I owe this pleasure?" His tone was casual as he continued onto the porch, but his posture was cautious.

She didn't fall for the extra bit of Southern charm he'd used to lubricate his words. "Hmph. Heard you been putting some ideas in my granddaughter's head."

More carefully this time, he spoke. "Ruby?"

She squinted at him. "You thick, boy?"

"No, ma'am." He smirked like he was indulging her. City folk always thought they knew best, didn't they?

"Then come on and sit down. We got some talking to do."

He obeyed, which proved he wasn't all bad. When he was settled in the metal chair across from her, he put his hands up to show he was ready.

"I got a visit from my granddaughter today. Said she was leaving town tomorrow with you."

He leaned back in his chair and sighed. "So much for not telling anyone."

"She did the right thing, telling me."

"Except now you're here to threaten me."

He sounded like such a Pitiful Pearl she cackled. "I ain't here to threaten you, son. What could an old woman like me to do a fella like you, anyhow?"

"I'm sure you still have some tricks up your sleeve."

"Might be true, Mr. West. That just might be."

She rocked for a spell, watching the clouds gather and feeling the pressure inside her joints. Peter seemed content to give her time, and she aimed to take it. Eventually, she looked his way again. "My people been up on this mountain long as memory serves. Most of us 'round here is like that. Families come over from Scotland or Ireland bringing their old traditions to the mountains. Some of our kin people mixed in with the Indians who lived here. Got to be where their ways and our ways mixed to create new old ways. Time marched on and people worked hard to survive. But children? They don't care about tradition. They want everything new."

"Aren't children always like that?"

She gave him the side-eye. "You got children, Mr. West?"

He shook his head. Didn't surprise her none.

"Used to be children obeyed their parents. I blame that dang boob tube. Filling their heads with all sorts of things. Make them get too big for their britches, like they know better than their elders."

"Have you ever left the mountain?"

"Course I have! I ain't been to New York City or Londontown, but the way I see it, people is people. Bigger city just means bigger problems, I reckon, but the problems aren't so different. Hatin' the ones they should love, and lovin' the ones they'd best avoid. Being greedy and small. Wanting what other people have."

He nodded. "I suppose you're right."

"My Rose was like that. Thought she was smarter than her mama. Wanted to live a bigger life. But you know what? That world out there," she tipped her chin to indicate the world outside the mountain, "it uses up girls like my Rose." She looked him in the eye. "It'll use up Ruby, too, and you know it."

Peter leaned back in his chair and looked at her for a long

moment before speaking. "Did Ruby tell you why she's leaving? Not the wanting a big life part, but the other reasons?"

"You mean what happened in the cemetery?" She shook her head. "Damn fool child. Messing with power she don't understand. It's my fault. If I'd been around to teach her the proper ways she wouldn't have done that."

"I don't see how it's your fault. She's an adult."

"You wouldn't understand. It was my job to train her but I didn't. Thought I had all the time in the world, but time is a real bastard. Tricks ya."

"If she told you why she needs to leave, why are you trying to get her to stay? You know what Deacon Fry and his cronies will do to her if they find out."

"Thing is, Mr. West, there's worse things in these mountains than Deacon Fry."

"All the more reason to get her out of here," he shot back.

"Maybe so." She rocked a little faster. Now that they were down to the truth of things, she felt like she had June bugs in her britches. "That's why I'm not here to ask you not to take her."

"Why are you here, then?"

"I need you to promise me that you'll stay until after the Decoration."

"Why does it matter if we leave before or after?"

"It just does. Surely, waiting a few hours won't make a difference for you."

"The real question is: What difference does it make for you?"

She chuckled. "That's a good question, but not one I'm sure I can answer easily. Truth is, if I told you the reasons you'd laugh and call me a crazy old woman. So I'm just asking you to stay as a favor to me."

"Favors usually get paid back."

She sucked at her teeth for a few seconds. This boy was sharper than she'd given him credit for originally. "I promise if you stay, you'll get a story so big you'll hit every bestseller list that exists."

His left eyebrow twitched. "Oh?"

"You ever wonder why Deacon Fry's so het up about doing the Decoration so quick after Jack's funeral?"

"Not especially."

"What do you know about ghosts, Mr. West?"

Peter rose and walked toward the cabin door.

"Where you goin'?"

He paused on the threshold and glanced back at her. "I have a feeling the story you're about to tell me would be best heard with some more whiskey in my belly."

She didn't comment on his use of the word "more." She just smiled and said, "Now you're talking."

38

BLACK

Cotton

GET HER BACK. She's coming home. My Rose. Rosebud. No thorns, my Rose. It'll be easy. Jack promised. *Was it Jack?* Doesn't matter. He said she'd come back. Easy as pie. Just a small thing —nothing, really. He's old, too. Not far from the grave hisself. Just speeding nature along. Sometimes bad things make it easier for good things to happen. Daddy always said, "All's well that ends well."

Jack wouldn't ask me to do something too wrong. Jack's a good boy. *That's not Jack.* He's a good boy. Loved watching him throw that pigskin. Wish he were my own boy. 'Stead I got stuck with three needy things. Rose was needy too. Them tears would dry up right quick after a reminder of who was boss. Yessir.

Gate's open. Too late for anyone to hear anyway. He'll be sleeping. Go fast in his sleep, like a dream and wake up with God. He'll like that. Just 'cause God forsaked me and my Rose don't mean he don't deserve to have that for hisself.

Back door's unlocked. That's what he loves about Moon Hollow. People trust each other.

Inside, the house is dark but there's enough light to get the job done.

Soon, Rose. Soon.

There's the bedroom. Door's already cracked, like a welcome. Won't be long now. Then everything will be okay.

Just don't think while you're doing it. Just don't think—

The shovel makes a funny sound.

Eyes fly open. The blood comes fast and spreads across white sheets.

He raises it again and again. The shovel makes such wet music.

That'll stain.

Someone's hollerin'. "Shhh. Quiet now. It's almost over. Shh." The lips scream under his palm.

Hush, little baby, don't say a word, Papa's gonna buy you a mockingbird.

Press harder against the mouth and nose. Something snaps under the weight—cartilage.

And if that looking glass gets broke, Papa's gonna buy you a —

Legs and arms stiffen, hard as boards. Torso jackknifes up. The eyes open wide enough to see eternity. A gasp, a rattle.

Surrender.

Nothing. No thoughts. No sounds except the drip, drip, drip of blood and Lord knows what else on the floorboards. His own breath whistles between the fingers he clasps over his mouth.

The haze clears long enough to see his handiwork.

He falls to his knees in the puddle of blood. "What have I done?" His hands tremble against the cooling skin of the victim.

Rose. Rose. Rose.

The smell of cigarette smoke overpowers the stench of blood and other body fluids—both the victim's and his own. He breathes in the scent like a drowning man sucks in oxygen. "Marlboro take me away." Did he say that out loud?

"Relax, friend."

The new voice, familiar but not comforting, whispers in his ear. He turns his head but no one is there.

"There's still chores to be done. Then you'll see Rose. Won't that be nice?"

He swallows hard and pulls the pack of smokes from his pocket. Not the generic shit, but Marlboros—the king of tobacco. His new friend gave him a whole carton and now he needs a coffin nail more than he needs the blood in his veins. His fingers slip off the lighter's metal wheel three times. He wipes his shaking hand on his pants. This time the flame catches and he raises it to his face. Across the bed, a bank of windows reflects the red light on his face as he lights the cigarette. The image reminds him of something out of a horror flick.

He sucks the sweet poison into his lungs. On the exhale, a line from some psalm or other flashes like neon through his dark mind.

I am become a stranger unto my brethren.

39

FLY AWAY, PRETTY BIRD

Ruby

That morning, the air smelled different, sweeter.

She chuckled at her whimsical thoughts and picked up her pace. The weathered leather bag in her hand held some of her clothes and a few treasures she couldn't leave behind. She'd considered bringing a bigger bag, more clothes, but she was hoping that it might take Daddy a while to figure out where she'd gone. An empty closet would tip him off too soon. Besides, she liked the idea of traveling with only a couple of changes of clothes because it meant she'd have to buy new ones. Ones made from slinky fabrics in bright colors. Clingy things that gave her curves. The kind of clothes Daddy would hate.

The bag was one she'd found in the attic during her search for Mama's things, and inside she'd found a bus ticket stub from Nashville to the depot in Big Stone Gap, Virginia. She'd taken the stub and the bag as tokens to remind herself to do things different than Mama had. She wouldn't be calling Granny Maypearl in a few weeks for bus fare back. She'd get a job at a bookstore and sign up for college courses. She wasn't leaving to become a star. She was leaving to simply *become*.

Daddy had stayed out all night again so her escape from the house was simple. Granny arrived early so someone would be there when the girls woke up. She hadn't said much to Ruby, but the hug they shared before she left had been fierce.

She hadn't dared check in on the girls. Couldn't risk losing her nerve.

Once she stepped off her front porch, she'd lifted her arms out like wings and spun around. She giggled and placed a hand over her stomach, which swirled like the inside of a snow globe.

Today, I fly.

At the end of the drive, she stopped and looked around. She'd been up and down that old gravel path so many times it had become almost invisible. But now she took a moment to look at the chipped red mailbox with drooping daffodils at the base. She set down her bag and knelt to pluck a few of the weeds out, careful to bring the roots up with them. She tossed them aside, feeling better until she realized no one would be around to make sure they didn't come back.

Just as sadness got its first hook into her, a high-pitched cry ran down the road and grabbed her by the ear.

The bear cub.

She looked left, toward the road she'd need to take to reach Peter and freedom. She looked to the right, toward Junior Jessup's place with its cages and snarling dogs. The old Ruby, the one who shoved her anger down and tiptoed so as not to wake the beast from his hung-over stupor, the her that washed behind her sisters' ears because there weren't any parents to do it, that Ruby would have turned right and tried to free that poor cub. Once she freed the cub, she'd get caught by Junior, who'd take her to her daddy for a whoopin'. Old Ruby would miss her chance of escape with Peter West because she'd be too busy spitting blood in the bathroom sink.

But she was New Ruby now. The kind of girl—no, woman—who was in charge of her own destiny. New Ruby didn't know the weight of duty shackling her feet to the dirt. New Ruby would wear high heels and elegant dresses. She'd read new hardcover books instead of second-hand paperbacks. She'd never have dirt under her fingernails or know the taste of her own blood. Never again.

Never.

She turned left and marched with her head held high even as she ignored the pleading cries of the bear, which sounded a little too much like the pitiful thing was crying, "Stay! Stay!"

BY THE TIME she made it to Peter's cabin, the sun was busy burning dew off the high grasses. The steamy air ruined her carefully curled hair, and made her dress wrinkle and cling in awkward places.

She paused on the bend of the road just before the cabin and took a deep breath. The humid air intensified the perfume of wood poppies and wet leaves. She closed her eyes and listened to the morning song of birds and the chatter of squirrels. She even listened extra hard for a song from the trees or the nearby creek, some mountain melody to bless her journey. When she heard nothing, she sighed and opened her eyes. The mountain had passed on its last chance to ask her to stay.

She stepped off the road and onto the gravel drive leading to the cabin and stopped. She'd expected to see Peter's trunk open and his bags tucked inside waiting to snuggle hers on the long ride. Instead, the doors and trunk were closed tight, and a quick peek into the back window confirmed her worry that he hadn't started loading the car at all.

She dropped her bag by the front fender. On her way to the front door, she resisted the urge to panic. Maybe he'd overslept. Or maybe he was excited too and wanted to wait for her so the packing of the car was an event. By the time her knuckles made contact with the door, she decided she was just being silly. Peter had made a promise. He knew how important it was for her to get out of Moon Hollow. He wouldn't go back on his word. He was an author—their words weighed more than most people's did.

She had to knock three times before he answered. When the door opened, her stomach dropped. His hair stood in tufts as if he'd just gotten out of bed, and, though he wore a pair of jeans, his T-shirt was on backwards, like he'd thrown it on just to answer the door.

"Hey, Ruby." He didn't sound disappointed to see her so much as disappointed in himself.

Gravity doubled. She struggled not let it pull her down.

"Why aren't you ready?" She had no choice but to be direct with her question. Her plan was unraveling between her fingers.

"There's been a change of plan." His expression remained the same, but his body turned away from hers, as if he didn't want her to see all of him as he lied.

"What do you mean?" Her voice sounded foreign, harder, betrayed. "We are leaving this morning. Right now. We're leaving right now." She stepped toward the door with a hand outstretched to … what? Grab him? Slap him? Anything, she realized. She'd do anything to make him stop looking at her like a stranger and admit that he was just fooling around and of course they were leaving. "Peter?"

He flinched as if she had really slapped him instead of

letting her hand fall, useless, by her side. "Relax. We're still leaving."

She looked him right in his lying eyes. "When?"

"This afternoon."

The remaining threads of the plan slipped from her fingertips. "No. It has to be now."

He frowned at her, as if she'd spoken an alien language. "Relax, it'll be fine. We'll leave right after the Decoration."

She shook her head slowly. Some internal knowledge she couldn't explain told her that if they waited all would be lost. "It has to be now." The naked desperation in her voice came from a deep place. It was the same place inside that had heard the mountain's song before Mama died. The place where Ruby stopped being Ruby and became a part of something more.

"I don't see why it's such a big deal to wait a couple of hours."

She couldn't explain it to him. Not the truth, anyway. She didn't understand it herself. Instead, she said, "If Daddy shows up he'll never let me go."

Peter smiled that smile he used when he took on his role of wise old man advising the dumb little girl. But he didn't know as much as he wanted to believe. "It'll be a miracle if your father shows up. And even if he does, he'll be so drunk he won't notice if we sneak off after."

"Maybe so," she admitted, "but Deacon Fry will definitely be there."

He pulled back a fraction, as if the deacon's name was a sudden, strong wind. "Granted, he could be a problem," he said. "But you're an adult, Ruby. No one can stop you if you really want to leave. You know that, right?"

Granny's words came back to haunt her: *The mountain won't let you leave.*

"Please, Peter. Let's go. Okay? Let's just go."

He stepped forward and placed a hand on her arm. He

looked annoyed, as if she were being unreasonable. It made her so mad she was half tempted to kick him in the shins, steal his keys, drive off in his car, and never look back. Let Peter stay and deal with whatever was coming.

"Something bad is going to happen," she whispered. The words felt as if they came from something separate from herself.

He squeezed her arm. "No, it's not. You're just scared of change. It's totally natural."

She pulled away. "You don't understand. This place—it holds on to people. If we don't go now—"

"What?" he interrupted. "We'll never go? That's crazy." He took a breath and when he continued his voice had softened. "I'm finally making some progress on my book. I need to stay to see the ceremony so I can put it in my story."

"I've been to Decorations every year of my entire life. I'll tell you what happens."

"That's not how it works. I need to see it for myself—the smells, the sounds. How the characters behave, what they say and don't say."

"The characters?"

He laughed a little. "The people, I mean."

Her mama always told her that in every woman's life there comes a time when she has to make the decision to be an adult. For Ruby, watching Peter, the man she'd pinned all her hopes on, casually toss aside his promise in order to use her family and neighbors as characters in a dumb book, she realized that time had come for her. Instead of arguing with him further, she marched down the steps.

"Ruby?"

She dipped down to pick up her bag, a souvenir of the time her mama had made her own escape.

"Come on. Don't throw a tantrum," Peter called. "I said we'd leave in a couple of hours."

She stopped and turned to look at Peter, really look at him. "You are a liar, Peter West."

He threw up his hands. "What do you want from me?"

"I want you to get in the car and leave."

"Jesus, I already told you, I will. I just need a little more material for the book. Just one more hour, okay?"

Why did people always do that? How many times had she heard her father say he just needed one more drink? Or her mama swear that she'd give Daddy one more chance after he'd left marks on her ribs?

The thing she figured out standing on that gravel drive watching Peter lie to her and himself was that "just one more" was the universal adult code for "I ain't fooling nobody but myself."

Just like her daddy was addicted to whiskey and her mama was addicted to being punished for her sins, Peter was addicted to pretending the world wasn't real.

"I hope you get what you're looking for," she said. To herself she added, *I hope I find what I need, too.*

"Fine!" he shouted toward her retreating back. "But you're not going to get very far without money."

She smiled a secret smile he couldn't see. Weighing down the right pocket of her coat was the money she'd taken from the bottom of the coffee tin. Over the years, she'd seen Mama stash a few dollars in there every now and then. Mama would always turn to her and put a finger over her lips. "It's our secret." She'd even taught Ruby how to cross her heart and hope to die, stick a needle in her eye. She'd never understood why the needle thing was added at the end since you'd already be dead.

It wasn't much. The night before, she'd counted each coffee-scented bill three times, coming up with three hundred and seven dollars each time. If she hitchhiked all the way to Asheville, she would have enough left over to rent a small room and eat Cup O' Noodles until she found a job waiting tables or something. Despite what Granny Maypearl had claimed when she warned Ruby not to run off with Peter, Ruby's intention had never been to depend on him for money.

Back behind her, Peter cursed and slammed the cabin's screen door. After the slam, more cursing followed, but they were muffled enough for her to know he'd retreated inside instead of following her. Still, she pumped her arms a little faster and turned her indignant march into a speed walk. She wasn't really worried Peter would force her to stay for the Decoration.

He was more worried about his damned story than about her, anyway.

She did have one problem, though. The road from Peter's cabin led straight down into town. If she stayed her course, she'd pass plenty of townsfolk on their way up to the cemetery. Even if she avoided Daddy and Granny Maypearl, there'd still be all those busy bodies that would report to Deacon Fry if they saw her sneaking out before the celebration began.

It was a generally accepted fact that every resident of Moon Hollow was required to attend the Decoration, barring grave illness. Over the years, she'd watched old men in wheelchairs with oxygen tanks attached pushed up Cemetery Hill by a handful of red-faced men, who sweated through their Sunday best before the sermons began. There was even one time when Mrs. Honeycutt made the climb the day after giving birth to that pest Darrell, who liked to look up girls' dresses when he got older. She remembered the women whispering about how poor Mrs. Honeycutt had "torn real bad" during birth because Doc Fortenbury over in Big Stone Gap didn't believe in *peas otomie*s. At the time, Ruby couldn't blame the doc since she'd never a big fan of peas, either, but she never could figure out what they had to do with giving birth. But Mrs. Honeycutt sure did look uncomfortable all day, and, once, after Mr. Honeycutt helped her stand up for prayer, Ruby saw a large dark spot on the back of her blue dress. That morning, Deacon Fry's sermon had been about the blood of Christ washing away the sins of the world.

As she stomped down the road, a new plan popped into her head. It wasn't the first time she'd considered doing it, but after her chat with Peter, things had changed, hadn't they? She checked her watch. The church leaders always arrived at that cemetery early to help set up the stage and set out tables for the food. She'd have plenty of time to do it and no one would find out until the Decoration was done and she was already long gone from the mountain.

Peter might have broken his promise to her, but she'd damned sure wouldn't leave before she fulfilled her own vow.

40

BAD DREAMS

Deacon Fry

THE MORNING OF THE DECORATION, Deacon Fry woke up with the sun. He went downstairs to make some coffee, but on his way he found Sarah Jane sitting by a window in the living room. She didn't move when he approached or respond when he softly called her name. She just stared out as if mesmerized.

The window faced west, and the morning mist still coated the peaks and ridges in the moody color that gave the Blue Ridge Mountains their name.

He didn't want to startle her. Her moods had been so fragile lately. But just as he started to back out of the room, she spoke.

"Jack came to me in a dream last night." She didn't turn to look at him, and the words were spoken so softly that they sounded like a secret.

His hand reached for the back of a chair for support. His own dreams had featured Jack, too, but he didn't dare tell her that. "Oh?"

"He looked terrible." She let out a long shuddering breath

and rubbed her arms, as if chilled. "And he told me terrible things, Daddy."

The distance between them felt farther than just a few feet. He'd never known how to relate to his little girl. She had always been sort of like a living doll—pretty but best kept up on a shelf. Since Jack died, her porcelain had cracked and what was exposed wasn't pretty or easy to ignore.

"It was just a dream, sweetheart." Hadn't he told himself that a dozen times for the last week? He hoped she believed it more than he had.

The back of her head shook back and forth. "He said you did a bad thing, Daddy."

A cold burst of panic exploded in his gut. "Just a dream," he said.

She didn't hear him. "He said you killed your brother."

"Sarah Jane—"

"Did you, Daddy? Did you kill Isaac?"

He closed his eyes and swallowed the icy gorge of panic. "That's enough, Sarah Jane."

"The time has come for revelation, Daddy."

Every hair on his body stood at attention. This time the voice was not Sarah Jane's but a deeper voice, a masculine one that seemed to come from some other place. His eyes flew open.

The chair was empty.

41

JAILBREAK

Ruby

THE DOGS WERE RESTLESS. Instead of snapping at her through the cages when she walked past, they whined and paced. It should have been a relief, but it made her skin tingle like she'd been coated with the salve Mama used to use on her when she got the croup. The dogs might be acting odd, but across the yard, the bear was in the same corner it had been when she and Peter visited.

The backyard smelled of piss and dried shit. She didn't recall that from last time, which meant Junior had been neglecting his cleanup duties. She gripped the bolt cutters tighter. She'd stolen them from Junior's own storage shed. He never locked it because he said the hounds scared off anyone stupid enough to trespass on his property.

She struggled to get the cutters in place, but they kept banging against the cage door. The bear didn't move or look up. She worried she was too late and the poor baby had already died from neglect ... or fear. She stared hard at the ball of black fur. She held her breath and waited for the slightest movement, praying all the while that she wasn't too late. Finally, the bear's side rose a little and fell. She'd never been so relieved in her life.

"Hang tight, little one." Even though Junior wasn't home, this felt like whispering work, like prayer.

She tried again to seat the edges of the bolt cutter in the right spot. This time, it landed true. Luckily the door was low and she could brace herself against the side of the cage. Even with the good leverage, her muscles strained and her palms ached with the effort pushing the handles together. On her third try, the cutters slipped off the lock.

"Damn it," she hissed.

The racket of metal on metal had not gotten a reaction from the bear, but for some reason her hissed curse caused it to raise its head. Its eyes seemed to have gotten larger since her last visit. "Poor baby," she said. "You ain't been eatin' have you. Can't say I blame you." She eyed the dead flies floating in the pan of formula.

The bear just kept looking at her with that hopeless stare.

Were bears capable of hope? She knew they experienced other emotions, like anger. She'd heard lots of stories of mother bears tearing up people and property after someone harmed her cubs. Surely that meant mama bears—and their cubs—experienced love, too.

If Deacon Fry ever heard her talking that way he'd have a stroke.

"He'd tell me I was going to hell," she confided in Bear. "But I don't know why it's wrong to think animals have feelings. My science teacher, Mrs. Price, told us all about how we came from monkeys and stuff. That means we're animals, too."

Bear continued to watch her.

"Anyway," she said, "I think you can feel things. Don't be mad at all people just because Junior is an asshole." She glanced around to make sure no one heard her curse, but she realized that where she was going, people could probably curse whenever they wanted. Ruby had seen lots of TV shows where girls like her said all sorts of curses and were never dragged in front of a church deacon to confess their sins. "Shit," she whispered. "Damn." Then, "God damn it!"

One of the hounds bayed in response. That riled the rest of them up until they were all barking like fools.

Ruby got back to work. "I'll have you out in no time, Bear."

It took three more tries before the clippers finally broke through the lock. The instant it hit the ground, the dogs stopped barking. Just like that. One second they were carrying on and then next, nothing. The hounds lined up along the front of their cages watching her. A sound in the cage behind her brought her attention back to Bear.

The cub's claws scratched at the concrete slab. She realized that it couldn't stand on its own. She debated going in to help it, but hesitated. It was one thing to open a gate door so it could run off. It was something else altogether to enter the bear's den and touch it. She'd lived in the mountains long enough to understand that a scared bear was dangerous, and this cub had lived in a constant state of terror most of its short life.

"Come on, now." She pulled the cage door open. "You can do it."

Bear pawed at the concrete again, but didn't manage to gain any traction. A low whine escaped its small mouth. Ruby's ribs felt too tight to contain her heart.

"All right," she said, "I'm coming in but you behave yourself, you hear?"

Another bleat.

She propped the bolt cutters against the open door. She had to stoop down low to fit inside, but the cage was wide and deep enough to accommodate both her and the cub. Inside, the ammonia scent nearly overpowered her. Breathing through her mouth, she shuffled toward her charge. As she moved, she prayed the bear was just weak from lack of food and not permanently injured. She had no idea what she'd do if it couldn't walk on its own. She couldn't take the poor thing with her when she left.

Once she was closer, she realized the problem. Junior had clipped a collar around the bear's neck and the lead that connected it to the cage was too short to give it enough room to move.

"Bastard." She unhooked the collar from around the bear's neck and stood back. Up close, she realized just how small the little thing was—maybe twelve pounds, fourteen at the most.

Now that the collar was off, it managed to get its paws under its legs and stand. After wobbling for a moment, it took an experimental step toward Ruby.

"That's real good," she whispered. "Good bear."

The dogs tuned up again. The sound spooked Ruby, who thought Junior might have come home. All thoughts of patiently waiting for Bear to walk out on its own four feet disappeared. She snatched its little body up and pressed it to her chest.

The bear didn't fight her or wriggle in her arms at all. As she ran through the yard, she was vaguely aware of the bundle snuggling into her chest. She held on tight and somehow managed to scale Junior's fence without dropping her burden.

Once she cleared the boundary of his land, she ran through the forest. She wanted to get as far from Junior's place as she could before she set her friend free. She couldn't raise it, but she could try to make sure to release it somewhere that it might have a better chance of surviving on its own.

She wasn't sure how much time had passed since she started running, but eventually she reached her destination. The ruins of her great-great granny's house seemed like a good spot for the cub. The ruins provided a little bit of shelter and it wasn't too close to the river or the road, either of which could spell disaster for a tiny bear.

She set it down inside the three partial walls that remained. The bear managed to stand on its own, but it looked up at her and made a noise like a fussy baby. "You'll be safer here."

The bear wobbled forward and pawed her shoe.

"Now, look, I can't take you with me. Where I'm going there won't be any bears allowed. You're gonna have to be brave and make it on your own."

It rose on its two shaking hind legs and wrapped its paws around her leg. It cried again.

"No, stop that," she scolded, gently removing the paws. She kneeled down to look it in the eyes. "You're a bear. These woods are your home."

It whined again and tried to climb up into her lap. She pushed it down. "No, bad bear." Her temper started heating up. "You can't come with me."

She reached into her bag and removed a baggie filled with peanuts and raisins she'd packed for her journey. She dumped the snack on a flat topped rock. Soon, the bear lost interest in her and went to investigate the food. It took an experimental nibble and then it made the first happy sound she'd ever heard from it.

While the bear dug into its food, Ruby petted its back.

The bear looked up to make sure she was still there. She pulled her hand away. It went back to eating.

She backed away a couple of steps. The bear kept eating. "Bye, little friend," she whispered. Then she turned and ran as fast as she could before she could lose her nerve.

42

DIFFERENT PATHS

Peter

By the time he'd climbed Cemetery Hill, the fire of Peter's anger had dulled into a smolder. Small wooden crosses and American flags lined the path just in case anyone forgot that the separation of church and state didn't exist in Deacon Fry's Moon Hollow. The ornaments didn't help his mood, but the climb gave him time to sort through what happened with Ruby.

He refused to feel guilty. Hadn't he told her they could leave right after the Decoration? All that urgency was just immaturity. She wanted to go and so they had to go right that moment. She was too young to understand that being an adult meant things had to be prioritized. His book was more important than her quest for self-discovery or whatever bullshit she wanted to call it.

He remembered being eighteen. Back then his only priorities were getting laid and rebelling against his father's plans for him.

The path was little more than a dirt trail forged by decades of feet trampling the ground until it surrendered and stopped growing green things. He barely noticed his steps as his memory lapsed back twenty years earlier. Like Ruby, he'd been eager to leave his home. But he hadn't grown up in a town as small as Moon Hollow. Unlike Ruby, he hadn't tried to leave a place where everyone in town knew who he was. He'd grown up in Chapel Hill, where his father was a business professor at the university. The college town's population was mostly transient—students coming in droves every fall and deserting the place every summer.

The summer of his eighteenth year, after graduating high school, he dreaded the fall term at UNC. Professors got free tuition for their kids. Not only would he be trapped in Chapel Hill, but his father refused to pay for room and board. The idea of staying in that house for four more years had made his skin feel too tight.

But that summer, he'd been too young and selfish to appreciate the benefits of free tuition or having his mom do his laundry. All he wanted was to escape that stifling house and his father's perpetually disappointed stare. So he took all the money he'd saved up from working at the local bookstore, got in his old Nissan Sentra, and took off for an epic summer road trip. He'd left a note for his parents on the kitchen counter.

As he drove out of town, the road lay before him like a promise. Like every white male aspiring writer, he'd read his Kerouac. He was headed to New York, not California, but he sure felt like a beat poet smoking his American Spirits and speeding up I-85 at ninety miles per hour.

It was a good plan. He'd crash with his friend at NYU and take a couple of weeks to decide if he really wanted to be the man his father wanted him to be or if he'd build a life with his own two hands.

His right rear tire blew just outside of Richmond. Towing the car and replacing the tire decimated his nest egg. He'd barely had enough money for gas to get back home.

He rolled into his driveway around suppertime. His dad had been waiting at the table with his note.

That night, Peter finally hit back.

He'd spent the rest of the summer working a construction job his father arranged. By the time he started school that fall, he had a farmer's tan and more muscles than he'd ever gotten from reading books. His freshman year was a blur of cheap keg beer, drunken hookups, and occasional classes. His dad threatened to kick him out if he didn't get his grades up.

One month later, his dad dropped dead from a heart attack while screwing his mistress. Peter's mother had a mental breakdown and Peter's long-dormant sense of duty kicked in. Between taking his mom to therapy and running the house, he still managed to make the Dean's List.

The following spring, he met Renee.

He finally made it to New York ten years later after his first book got picked up. He'd traveled lots of places since. None of those trips had that aching wildness he'd longed for in his youth. Now he was middle aged and divorced, and he had a hole in his center he worried would never be filled. He wasn't like Ruby. He knew that aborted road trip wasn't the root of his problems.

But sometimes he still wondered if he'd missed out on his real life.

He stopped walking. He'd reached the top of Cemetery Hill and the iron gates were about ten feet ahead of him. Inside, people dressed in their Sunday best milled around. Even before he realized Ruby was not among them, he knew he wouldn't see her there. When she'd marched off after their argument, it had been with the timeless posture of a teenager bent on rebellion. Part of him had been glad to see it. When he'd first met her, she seemed totally detached from reality. She'd had the moony look of someone who believed that fiction's common miracles could actually happen in real life. She'd also been waiting for her Prince Charming, and beyond all reason or logic, she'd decided he was the man for the role.

He wanted to scorn her for being so innocent. But a surprising emotion bubbled to the surface: pity. When he'd done his own disappearing act, he'd had his own car—piece of shit that it was—and money, but he also knew that if he failed he could always come back home. If, when, Ruby failed, would she be able to come back? The little he'd seen of Cotton Barrett didn't give him much faith in the man's capacity for forgiveness. Maybe Granny Maypearl would take her in.

"Peter?" Bunk stood by the cemetery gate. "You comin'?"

He looked over his shoulder, back down the hill. A beat-up Dodge was tearing up the road away from the church. He frowned, wondering who was in such a hurry. The Decoration wouldn't start for another thirty minutes, according to his watch.

"Peter?" Bunk, more concerned than impatient.

Dismissing the truck, he turned back toward Bunk. It wasn't until he took a couple of steps that he realized he hadn't seen Ruby marching up the hill out of town. Either she'd changed her mind and was licking her wounds at home or she'd managed to make her escape and was already well on her way down the mountain. Either way, she wasn't his concern any more.

All he had to do was walk into the cemetery and take notes as the good people of Moon Hollow did their thing. Then he could head back to Raleigh and start writing his masterpiece.

"Coming!" he called to Bunk. He jogged toward the gate. He couldn't wait to see what this Decoration was all about so he could get the hell out of town.

43

STORMING THE HILL

Ruby

FIFTEEN MINUTES after she left Bear, Ruby stopped to rest on a log. The cool morning mists were already turning into humidity that would settle over the valley like warm clouds all afternoon. Since going through town hadn't been an option, she'd followed the paths that ran through the forest behind the buildings on the south side of town. Once she got closer to the hill out of town, she'd leave the forest cover to walk on the road.

Sitting was a mistake because it allowed what she'd done to catch up with her. Tears formed and spilled onto her cheeks. Was the bear better off out of that cage? At least at Junior's place it had food and wasn't having to fend for itself in the wilderness.

A gray catbird mewed from a nearby bush, and a cedar waxwing trilled in response. But the mountain didn't sing to her.

She clasped her hands together over her heart. Granny Maypearl said that the mountain's song couldn't be heard with the ears. *You gotta listen with your heart, girl.*

Ruby blocked out the sound of the birds and focused inward. *Sing to me, Mama.*

Tears stung the inside of her lids and slipped between her lashes to land on her cheeks.

Why did you leave me? Please come back. Just once, before I go. Please?

But her heart just continued its same old rhythm. The mountain didn't sing for her and her mama didn't say goodbye.

She sniffed and swiped at her cheeks. She was being a baby. The mountain had stopped singing to her because it was time to go. Maybe that's why Mama left, too.

She'd worry about the cub, of course, but she knew she'd done the right thing. Bears were meant to be wild. Staying chained up was no way to live. And wasn't that why *she* was leaving? Because she was too wild to stay penned up in Moon Hollow?

She rose and continued through the woods until she reached the place where the hill out of town rose in front of her. The going would be easier on the road.

Once she left the cover of the woods, she looked back toward town. Downtown Moon Hollow spread out behind her. The road pointed like an arrow toward Christ the Redeemer. From where she stood, the warped steeple seemed to point right at her, like an accusing finger. Like God himself knew what she was up to and definitely did not approve.

Well, that was too damned bad. She turned her back on the steeple and the town. This time, when she took a step her foot struck the asphalt with a determined smack. The sun was higher and the heat made little beads of sweat roll down her back. She welcomed the sweat because it came from the honest work of taking her life into her own hands.

Stupid Peter West might be a liar, but she knew now that she didn't need him. In fact, the closer she got to the top of the hill leading out of town, the more she understood that it was only right that she walked out of town under her own steam. It was the act of a woman, walking out on her own two feet. Little girls needed big men to help them do things. As of that day, Ruby resolved to never be a little girl again.

She was almost at the crest of the hill when the sound of an engine reached her ears. She turned to look over her shoulder, fully expecting to see Peter's car. Before she'd even turned around she knew exactly how she'd tell him off—

But it wasn't Peter's car roaring up the hill. It was Junior Jessup's truck.

She started running before she made the conscious decision to flee. But in the end, her resolve and the thin soles of her tennis shoes weren't enough to outrun the horsepower of Junior's truck or his anger.

As he drew closer, the sound of his curses rose over the rumble of the engine and the blood and wind rushing through her ears. She pivoted left to try to reach the woods, but her ankle revolted. Her palms scraped across the road, then her left knee. The impact made her teeth slam together and the concussion rocketed behind her eyes. Through the shock and pain, she was vaguely aware of the truck's tires screeching and the slam of a heavy door.

Before she could recover enough to resume her escape, hard fingers grabbed her shoulder and lifted her clear off the ground. "God damn, girl! If you aren't the biggest pain in my ass." At the end of each sentence, he shook her as punctuation. "Just you wait till yer daddy hears what you been up to."

As he continued to curse and shake her, she looked over his shoulder at the space where the road curved into the shadows. At the end of that dark tunnel, the road would hit the highway. Freedom. That shadow meant freedom.

"... what the fuck you were thinkin' let my bear—"

She slammed the toe of her shoe into his shin. Pain ricocheted up her foot. It should have slowed her, but she took off like a bullet up the hill. The instant she realized the window for her escape was closing, she'd gone numb. Her sole focus was that sliver of shadow that represented the shaded road out of town and her freedom.

"Little bitch." Junior's voice had gone from mad to enraged. She hadn't really hurt his shin, but she'd learned from living with her daddy that the most vulnerable part of a man's body was his pride.

Her legs burned and blood pounded behind her eyes. The shadow grew closer, closer—almost there. She raised a hand to reach for it. Pain exploded between her shoulder blades. Heavy weight slammed her into the unforgiving asphalt.

Junior's big body and the unyielding road crushed her like a fly caught between a swatter and granite. After an agonizing moment, the weight on her back lifted. He didn't give her a chance to take stock of every source of pain. Didn't matter much. Her entire body felt like a throbbing wound.

As she lay on the hard gravel with the scent of tar and blood hot in her nostrils, her eyes sought and found the sliver of shadow. Closer now, she realized that the shadow was not black, but deep green from the tree canopy arching over the road. She imagined the air there would feel cooler and a light breeze would act like a balm on her scrapes. But even as she longed to be enveloped by the deep green like a thirsty person longs for cool water, she knew she'd lost her chance at that benediction.

The looming mass of Jessup kneeling in front of her blocked her view. "Now," he said, his voice low and mean, "if you try running again, I'll lock you in the cage with my dogs, and they're hungry. You understand me, girl?"

She swallowed the blood and bile clogging her throat. She

tried to speak, but that didn't work. So she just nodded her scraped cheek against the hot asphalt.

"That's a good girl." His breath smelled of pickled eggs and stale cigarettes. The bile she'd swallowed threatened to come back up, but before it gained any traction, he jerked her to her feet. She stumbled against him, hating herself for not having enough strength to stand on her own. But something was wrong with her right arm and the right side of her face felt like someone had gone after it with a cheese grater.

He pulled her toward the truck. "First, we're gonna find your daddy. Then we'll see about teaching you a lesson for trespassing on a man's private property."

He shoved her into the passenger seat of the truck. The cracked vinyl seat whined and pinched her like a cranky aunt.

Before he closed the door, she rasped, "What happened to the bear?"

The predatory smile on his thin lips faded into a hard line. "Gone."

That one word, clipped off like a curse, entered her ears and lit up her whole body with a mixture of relief and jealousy. She'd never known that *gone* could sound so much like *free*.

44

DAMSEL'S DISTRESSED

Peter

As they approached the cemetery gate, Bunk pulled Peter to the side.

"Just thought I'd let you know that Junior and Earl are still making noises about how maybe you were the one put your book in the cemetery."

Peter cursed under his breath. "Didn't Deacon Fry confirm he saw me the night it happened?"

Bunk scratched the side of his head with his metal pincer. "That's the thing. When he got here that day, he was real distracted. Told them to just clean up the mess and we'd deal with it after the Decoration. Kind of strange, too. When he first started talking about doing the ceremony this year he sounded like it was the last thing he wanted to do, but then he got here and was real insistent about making sure everything went right."

"That's odd."

"That's not all." Bunk looked around and scooted closer. "He was talking to himself. Kept going on about a potato."

"Had he been drinking?"

"Deacon Fry don't drink." Bunk shook his head. "Maybe it's just stress getting to him, what with his girl losing her beau and all."

"What do Junior and Earl intend to do about their theories?"

"No telling with them two."

"Well, it won't matter much either way because I'm leaving right after the Decoration."

Bunk nodded. "I'll be sad to see you go, but it's probably for the best." He clapped Peter on the shoulder with his good hand. "Just be sure to send me a copy of your book when it comes out."

Peter chuckled because buying the book would never occur to Bunk. "It's a deal."

They turned together to enter the cemetery, but the sound of a car's horn honking over and over caught their attention. They looked down the hill in time to see Junior Jessup's truck fishtail into the church lot.

Junior got out and strode around the truck's fender toward the passenger door. He wrenched it open, reached in, and pulled someone out.

"What in tarnation?" Bunk said, taking a step forward.

It took a moment for Junior and his companion to come around to the front of the truck. When Peter saw Ruby was with him, he cursed. "Damn it."

Bunk gave him the side-eye. "You know something about that?"

"I have no clue." It wasn't the whole truth, but not exactly a lie, either. Bunk had just told him that Junior suspected Peter for the cemetery vandalism, so he had no reason to think the man had uncovered a clue that tied Ruby to the act instead.

"Sure don't like the way he's handling her, though," he added.

"Junior ain't exactly known for his gentle touch."

As they spoke, Junior continued to rant as he pulled Ruby by her arm. Every few feet, she'd dig her heels in, which would only earn her a hard jerk that made her cry out.

Peter took off down the hill before he knew he'd made the decision to get involved. Behind him, Bunk cursed, but footsteps quickly followed.

"Is Cotton in the cemetery yet?" Peter asked over his shoulder.

Bunk snorted. "No one's seen Cotton in days."

They all met up halfway down the hill.

"Outta my way, Bunk." Junior lowered his head as if he intended to bulldoze his way past the other two men.

Peter grabbed the arm that had a handful of Ruby's shirt at the other end. Closer now, he saw the scrapes down Ruby's face and the angry road rash and bruises on her arms.

Rage turned Peter's vision red. He snatched Junior's hand off her arm. "What did you do to her?"

Junior dug his boots into the slope and knocked Peter's hand away. "Get the hell outta my way." The words were delivered in a tone that could have peeled paint off a barn.

Bunk stepped in. "I can't let you continue to manhandle the girl, Junior."

Ruby ripped her arm free. "I got a name, you know."

Peter rocked back on his heels in surprise at the strength in her voice. She looked like a victim of abuse, but she sure as hell sounded like a survivor. "And he didn't 'manhandle' me—he tackled me."

The minute she'd opened her mouth, Junior's complexion had taken on the hard, red hue of a man on the verge of committing a deadly sin.

Peter stepped between them. "You got a lot of nerve—"

A bark of laughter escaped along with a dribble of tobacco-tinged saliva. "Give me a fucking break. That bitch trespassed on my property. She's lucky I ain't shot her yet."

Fear popped like hot grease in his chest. How in the hell had Junior figured out they'd— But before he could finish that thought, Ruby caught his eye and shook her head. Treading more carefully now, he asked, "You found her on your property?"

Junior wiped the tobacco juice from his chin and smeared it on his overalls. "Last week, I got home from a trip to town to find my dogs all het up. I noticed real quick some other things that didn't look right—footsteps in the mud and such." He jutted his chin in the air like a gorilla putting on a display. "Decided right then and there I wasn't gonna risk someone stealing one of my prize hounds so I set up a security system."

Ruby's head shot up but she didn't say anything.

"What kind of system?" Bunk asked so Peter didn't have to.

"Whenever the gate into my backyard opens when I'm not there, security cameras switch on." He pulled a set of keys out of his pocket and showed a fob that looked like a car lock remote. "Went off this morning while I was out—uh, running some errands."

Bunk shot Junior a dubious expression. "Go on."

"So I run home, but by the time I got there she was already gone." He didn't clarify whether the "she" in question was Ruby or the bear. "But I got her on tape, stealing my bear."

"It wasn't your bear," Ruby said. "It didn't belong to you."

Junior lunged at her.

45

LOST LAMB

Deacon Fry

First time in his whole life Deacon Fry was running late. Worse, he was late for Decoration Day.

Where was Reverend Peale?

He passed the church and took the trail out back leading up Cemetery Hill.

Maybe the reverend had gone up the hill early with the help of someone else. He sped up, taking the slope in lunges that ate up the ground and made his thighs burn. He'd been silly to worry. It was all the stress lately—the worry that the Decoration wouldn't go as planned and . . . all the other things he'd best not think about too hard.

The chair was empty.

The Decoration had to go right. It was unthinkable that it wouldn't work.

Halfway up the hill, he came upon Junior shaking Ruby Barrett while Bunk and that damned author hollered at him.

"Junior Jessup, let that girl go this minute." He didn't like to raise his voice, but Junior was hollerin' so loud, it left the deacon with little choice. "I said, let her go!"

Junior fell back, but he his sides heaved and his eyes had a dangerous glow.

"Does someone want to explain why this disgraceful display is happening on one of our town's most sacred days?"

Everyone started yelling at once. He held up his hands. "Enough. Bunk, you tell me."

Bunk nodded, as if it was his due since he was considered the town's unofficial storyteller. "Well, it's like this—Junior here thinks Miss Ruby trespassed on his land—"

"She did!"

"Junior."

Junior's hands curled in to fists. Once Deacon Fry felt confident the man didn't plan on using them to hit anyone, he nodded at Bunk. "Go ahead."

"Seems there's a small matter of a bear cub who's been set loose from Junior's land."

He looked at Junior, who suddenly wasn't looking so eager to fight. "That true? You took a cub?"

"Ah hell, Deacon, I wasn't treatin' it bad or nothing."

"Regardless, it's illegal to separate a cub from its mother."

"The mother was already dead when I found it." The words came out indignant, but his lack of eye contact told the truth of it. "But that don't matter. *She* trespassed on my land!"

"Ruby, what have you got to say for yourself?"

The girl looked like she'd wrastled with a polecat, but she raised her chin. "Oh, I did it," she said. "I marched right on to his property, opened the cage, and carried that cub out."

All four men stared at her like they were worried her head might start spinning.

The only word the deacon could manage in his shock was, "Why?"

"Because it was the right thing to do."

How could he argue with that logic? Still, she'd put him in quite a pickle by admitting to her crime. Junior would never let the matter drop unless she was punished. But he had a Decoration to oversee, which would at least buy him some time to figure out how to handle the situation. "There ain't nothing we can do about this right now. The Decoration's about to begin."

"Like hell," Junior said. "I'm gonna call Sheriff Abernathy."

"No, you won't," he snapped. "You gonna tell him about how you had an illegal cub on your property? Might as well call the department of game, too." He stepped closer to the man and placed a hand on his shoulder. "I ain't saying you don't have a right to be angry. But we got to handle this the right way, you understand?"

Junior frowned as if Deacon Fry had used too many syllables, but nodded. "You ask me, she deserves a few good licks from her daddy's belt—and if he won't do it, I'll will!"

"Is Cotton here?" Deacon Fry asked. Part of him was afraid the answer would be yes after his strange experience at the cabin.

"Ain't seen him," Bunk said, "not that I expected to."

Deacon Fry sighed and blew out a long breath. "All right. Junior, you go see if you can rustle Cotton up at his house—"

"He ain't there," Ruby said. "Least he wasn't when I left this morning. Probably up the Devil's Spine."

It was getting harder to maintain his patience. He glanced up the hill, where the gates of the cemetery loomed, waiting for him to get the festivities underway. "We don't have time to go looking for him now. Once the Decoration is done, we'll go out there and we can resolve this matter."

He marched up the hill before any of them could argue.

Something was brewing with that girl. Normally, she had her nose buried in a book. Far as he knew, the girl hadn't caused a lick of trouble for her parents, and he'd seen for himself how she stepped up to raise the two younger girls after their mama died. But today she'd shown a whole new side of herself—one that worried him. She'd had that same shine in her eyes that Rose had before she ran away. Luckily, that prideful light had dimmed by the time Rose crawled back to Moon Hollow. Wasn't proper for a woman to get rebellious ideas in her head.

"Deacon Fry?"

The voice brought him back to the present, where he realized he'd already reached the cemetery gate. Nell, Jack's mother. He hadn't seen her since the funeral. Now, she stood in a simple blue dress by the gate and she was wringing her hands in a way that signified trouble.

"Mornin, Nell." He went up to her and took those old hands in his own to stop the manic movements. "How are you?" He used his most soothing voice in the hope he could forestall any drama. He knew the poor thing had just lost her son, but she acted like she'd invented grief.

"Not so good, Deacon. Every time I close my eyes, I see my poor Jack's face."

You and me both. He wondered if the one she saw was covered in blood, too.

"I'm just not sure how I'm supposed to go on without him."

She looked up at him with her eyes wide and wet with tears, and he had a sudden impulse to blacken them. *I'll give you something to cry about.* He cleared his throat and pushed down the voice. It was stress. Just stress.

He patted her hands. "Time heals all wounds, and remember, you're never alone as long as you keep the good Lord close to your heart."

He tried to withdraw his hands, but her nails dug into his skin like talons. She moved close enough that her alcohol-scent breath assaulted him. "Some wounds just fester."

Her tears had dried, and her expression had a feral edge. He tried to pull his hands away once more, but she wouldn't release him. "I need to get the prayers underway, Nell."

Closer, she pulled him even closer, until her small breasts rubbed against his chest. There was nothing sexual about it. Instead it felt oddly menacing. "When the chickens come home to roost, the fox is waiting for them."

He pushed her with all his strength. She stumbled back and fell to the ground with a cry. By the time he realized he was free, he also became painfully aware of the unnatural silence that had fallen over the cemetery.

On the ground at his feet, Nell was screaming blue murder. A few of the townsfolk came to help her up. As they worked, they shot him cautious glances that bordered on condemnation. He opened his mouth to explain but closed it again. What could he say? That the crazy woman had threatened him? He wasn't even sure she had been. It was just as likely that losing Jack had pushed her over the razor's edge of sanity.

Long red gashes covered the backs of his hands and across a few fingers. But he couldn't hold those up in his defense, either. A few scratches wouldn't justify him pushing a grieving woman to the ground.

The silence stretched out, and each second raised the tension and lowered the chances he'd be able to explain away his terrible behavior.

Peter West spoke from behind him. "Deacon Fry?"

He quickly surveyed his flock. Just over there, three people held up a sobbing Nell. She was cradling her wrist, as if it had taken on too much weight in her fall. The rest of the town stood in a semi-circle behind those three. There were the other deacons, Smythe in the lead, looking like he'd just watched his mama French kissing Santa Claus.

"What happened?" Peter asked finally.

When Deacon Fry tried to speak, his voice got all tangled up with the guilt in his throat. He cleared it twice just to be sure before speaking again. "Nell tripped over my foot."

A low rumble spread through those assembled.

"He pushed me!"

The familiar red haze rose behind his eyes. This time it was anger mixed with his old friend, the black shadow of shame.

He wanted to scream at her, at all of them. Didn't they know how much pressure he was under?

But he knew how things worked. He was the power in Moon Hollow. No one would believe that he felt threatened by a slip of a woman who wore her mourning like a funeral shroud. "I—I apologize if I accidentally caused you to fall. The ground here is uneven and I'm a bit unsteady after the climb."

A few more mumbles rose, but already he could see the expressions of those gathered begin to transform from suspicious to relieved. How nice for them to be so easily reassured. None of them understood the pressures of a man in his position. None spent sleepless nights worried about five hundred and sixty souls.

"And see there," he continued, pasting on his most benevolent smile, "you're going to be just fine."

He took a few steps toward Nell. She whimpered and shied toward Sharon, who had joined the group. His wife put an arm around Nell, and whispered something reassuring.

Mercifully, Sharon didn't look at him with suspicion. If she'd doubted him, too, it would have been his undoing.

Following his nod, his wife led Nell away toward a bench just inside the cemetery. The mourning woman cast a couple of cold looks his way, but said no more.

The entire time, Peter West hovered nearby. The writer had this way of making you think you were being judged every time he looked at you.

"Now, I know we're running a bit late this morning," he continued, "but that won't stop us from having the best Decoration this town has ever seen."

He paused to give the others time to applaud. When only a few half-hearted claps skipped through the crowd, he knew he had to act fast. "Let's thank the good Lord for this beautiful day on which to celebrate life and the legacy of those dearly departed we love so much."

A chorus of amens rose from all assembled. He smiled. "Now, let's get this show on the road. Reverend Peale?"

That damned silence again. This time it didn't have blame behind it, but it still felt menacing.

"Where's Reverend Peale?" As he spoke, the earlier worry reappeared as a burning sensation under his ribs. Hadn't he been asking himself that same question not fifteen minutes earlier when the reverend hadn't answered his knock on the front door of the rectory?

Deacon Smythe stepped forward. "Ain't no one seen him yet his morning, sir. We thought you was bringing him."

This was not the first time Deacon Fry had faced a crisis. He knew not to panic. He knew that clear heads found solutions faster than ones drunk on adrenaline. However, no crisis he'd ever faced—except one—had ever felt so personally threatening to his own well-being.

"I see," he said slowly. "No one has seen the reverend this morning?" He scanned the crowd, praying to Jesus that he'd see a head nodding instead of shaking. Alas, the good Lord didn't see fit to grant his request.

"Did anyone speak to him last night?"

Glances were exchanged, shoulders shrugged, and more head shaking ensued. He was finding it harder and harder not to start yelling. "Can anyone recall seeing him in the last twenty-four hours?"

"I saw him day before yesterday around five o'clock," said Deacon Smythe. "He was out in his garden."

The deacon nodded. "Did you speak with him?"

Smythe shook his head. "Just waved." He dipped his chin and shoved his hands deep in his pockets.

Deacon Fry fought his frustration. He'd seen the reverend after Smythe had when he'd gone to discuss some of his worries, but he couldn't bring that up now.

"Did anyone see him yesterday?" He tried to keep his tone even.

"I saw him."

Every eye turned toward Peter West.

"Oh?" Deacon Fry said. "Do tell."

"He asked me to come by for tea yesterday around ten. Sarah Jane was there." He nodded toward the deacon's daughter, as if they were on familiar terms.

Sarah Jane wouldn't meet anyone's eyes but she managed to nod to confirm what the writer had said.

"What time did you leave?"

"About eleven."

"It's true," said Sarah Jane. "I made the reverend's lunch and left around one o'clock."

He said you did a bad thing, Daddy.

He cleared his throat. "Thank you, sweetheart."

"Why didn't anyone check in on him before now?" Peter spoke as if he had the right to question the people of *his* town.

"I knocked on his door this morning," Deacon Fry said, "but when he didn't answer I assumed he'd come up the hill already."

Silence reigned for a tense moment. Dread hung heavy over the graves despite the cheerful paper flowers decorating each headstone.

"All right," the deacon said, taking back control, "split up. Everyone grab a buddy and search the town until you find him."

He prayed that the reverend had just got into his spirits and was waiting for someone to come retrieve him from his office in the church. If not, well, if not wasn't something he was ready to think about just yet.

Still, as people started pairing up, he couldn't ignore the cold sensation of doom looming in his chest.

46

FALLOW

Ruby

SHE AND PETER decided to check the reverend's house. Well, she'd decided to check the house. Peter had followed her without asking if she minded.

She was really worried about Reverend Peale. He'd never shown up late to anything. He often showed up drunk, but never tardy.

"He'll be there," Peter said between gulps of air behind her.

She didn't answer because she still wasn't talking to him. Instead, she threw open the garden gate. She veered right, which would take her through the garden and around to the back door.

"I'll try the front," Peter said.

Before continuing into the garden, she looked over to see Deacon Fry running toward the church's front doors. He didn't see her, which allowed her a rare moment to see Deacon Fry unguarded. His cheeks were flushed and his white hair was matted with sweat. His panic was so naked and raw that she had to look away. She plunged ahead into the side yard, hoping to find some comfort in her old kingdom.

When she had been a little girl, Mama often stopped by Reverend Peale's house to drop off pies or supper. While Mama and the reverend chatted over coffee, Ruby would play in the garden. Back then, it was a magical place filled with dragonflies and sweet-smelling flowers. She'd spent hours digging in the rich soil to find earthworms or roly-polies.

After chatting with the reverend, Mama would gather her gardening supplies from the old shed and pull weeds and tend to the plants like they were her own children. Reverend Peale used to joke that Mama didn't have a green thumb—she had a green hand.

While Mama worked in the dirt, Ruby would stage elaborate plays where she was a faery queen and the little creatures were her subjects. She'd always hated visiting in the winter because Mama would tell her it was too cold and make her to sit quietly on a chair in the corner while she and the Reverend talked about boring adult stuff.

On those days, she'd stare out the window at her kingdom, which had retreated under the dirt for a winter's rest. Back then, her favorite story had been about a boy named James who got to go on a big adventure in a giant peach, and in the winter, she imagined that her earthworm and insect friends had parties down there without her.

That morning, as she turned left into the narrow space between the stone wall and the garden, she stumbled on the first paver. The garden she'd once cherished was now a weed-choked rectangle filled with dry, brown leaves and the bruised petals of flowers that had long since died. It hit her like a cold January wind that without her mother around to pull weeds or water, the garden had simply died from neglect. She imagined her little kingdom below the dirt dying, too, without juicy leaves to eat or their queen there to shower them with water and love.

She also realized that she'd failed to notice all of this the other night when she'd snuck into Reverend Peale's shed to steal his trowel. She would have been better off using that tool to dig up weeds instead of doing magic spells in the cemetery.

"Ruby!" Peter's voice cut through her haze of memory and guilt. "He's not answering the door."

"I'm in the garden." She hadn't forgotten that she wasn't talking to him. She'd just ignored that fact because she suddenly felt very alone.

The space between the wall and the garden was barely wide enough for her shoulders. On her right, thorns from the climbing rose vines scratched her shoulders. To her left, the withered stalks of dead sunflowers brushed her cheeks with papery brown leaves. Her mama had always loved sunflowers and had planted a new patch each spring. Each spring until this one, she corrected. That year, Mama had died before she could clear out the winter-dead stalks and replace them with the promise of new seeds.

Up ahead, overgrown grass had transformed the yard into wild place. Before Jack had died, he'd come every week to mow. She'd once heard Sarah Jane brag about how she'd always be sure to stop by Reverend Peale's house on those days so she could see Jack working with his shirt off. She'd wax poetic about his muscles while she stared dreamily out the library window.

One day, Ruby had wandered by when Jack was working. He'd stopped his work to wave at her, but seeing all his muscles hadn't made her feel poetic so much as embarrassed and sweaty.

As she exited the narrow passage, she felt as if weeds were choking her like they choked the life out of the sunflowers. Were Mama and Jack down in the dirt kingdom with her former subjects? The thought gave her a little bit of comfort. The idea that they might be going on adventures along the dormant roots of the plants felt a lot better than the idea that they might no longer exist at all.

The passage ended where the wall veered sharply right to the side yard. The old shed where garden supplies were stored stood ahead of her now. The doors weren't quite closed. The grass tickled her ankles as she moved toward the doors. Her head told her there was nothing to worry about. She'd visited that shed just a few days ago. Maybe she'd just forgotten to close the door all the way.

Built from wood, the structure was shaped like a small barn with chipped red paint and white accents. Black metal hinges and simple latches on the doors were the only decorations. When the garden had been alive, the shed added a whimsical touch to the yard. She shouldn't have had any reason to give it a second thought. But her instincts had a different idea, and her heart, which fluttered like a black crow's wings, agreed.

A rustling sound behind her announced Peter's arrival. Instead of using the walkway, as she had, he tromped through the dead garden.

She decided to ignore his lack of respect since he didn't know he was trampling over her kingdom. Instead, she pointed at the shed in the corner of the yard. They both stared at it for a few moments. Finally, Peter whispered, "What's wrong?"

"Something feels ... off." She'd whispered too, as if they both worried that talking any louder would set off something terrible.

"Only one way to find out." Peter moved toward the shed, but Ruby grabbed his arm. He looked back over his shoulder with a reassuring smile that wasn't at all convincing. But she released him anyway because she wanted the unbearable tension of not knowing to ease up.

As he made his way to the shed, she stayed close because suddenly the entire garden felt threatening.

The tall grass tickled her shins and calves. A bead of sweat rolled down her temple but the base of her neck felt cold. She grabbed Peter's shirt, and his hand came back around, as if to shield her—or pull her closer for his own safety.

Over his shoulder, the thin line of black between the shed's frame and the slightly open door felt as wide as a chasm. Was something watching their approach?

Peter's muscles bunched under her hand as he reached out for the handle. The door opened with the sound of metal scraping against the concrete pad. The scent of grass clippings and gasoline mixed with the stink of her own fear sweat and Peter's aftershave. She peeked around his shoulder into the darkness inside the shed. At first, all she saw was a lawnmower, a red gas can, and a bag of potting soil.

"Oh no, no, no." Peter lunged inside. The fabric of his shirt ripped from her hand. "No!"

She stumbled after him. The fear in his voice should have stopped her, but she needed to see the truth for herself.

Inside, the air was thick with dust and the biting perfume of fertilizer. Peter was kneeling near the back corner, his shoulder blocking her view.

"Get out, Ruby—you don't need to see this."

"What—" Her words cut off as a new detail emerged from the dark.

The bare foot glowed pale against the shadows.

She pushed Peter out of the way.

Reverend Peale's hands were clasped in prayer on his stomach. He wore his black robe and the traditional green stole he'd worn every Decoration Day since she could remember. His chin sat heavily on his chest. She tried to convince herself he'd somehow fallen asleep in the shed. But her lie was rejected by the caved-in skull and the blood.

Peter regained his balance and grabbed her arm even as a scream crawled up her throat. He jerked her away from the body —the body, no Reverend Peale, oh my God, oh my God—and he pushed her until she fell out of the shed. There in the tall grass, with the scent of death and fertilizer strong in her nose—she vomited. At some point the tears began to fall but she wasn't aware of them until the sounds of her own sobs broke through her shock.

"Was—is he—" The words crashed into a new sob and tangled with it until she choked on them.

Peter knelt in front of her and grabbed her chin. It hurt, but she didn't care because that pain was real. It was real and it didn't hurt as much as her chest, which felt like her ribs would crack open and her heart would simply flee to escape the pain she was subjecting it to.

"We need to go," he was saying. "We have to tell Deacon Fry. Need to call the sheriff."

She shook her head slowly back and forth. Her gaze kept straying toward the wide-open mouth of the shed and the grisly surprise it held on its tongue. If they left him, he would be swallowed completely, until it was as if he never existed.

This town will consume all of us, one by one.

Hard hands shook her shoulders. She watched the gaping mouth. Her own tongue felt dry. Dryer than the dust in the shed, certainly dryer than the blood on—

No, don't think of that. It will be real then.

"Ruby? Listen to me." He shook her again. Forced her gaze to turn toward him. "We have to leave."

Peter pulled her up, wrapping his arm around her shoulders to guide her and force her through the tall grass toward the dead garden.

Mama, are you there? Jack? Is Reverend Peale with you? Are you having a party without me?

Peter had to push her in front of him to get through the narrow passage. She stumbled forward, barely noticing the bite of the thorns or the crackle of her mama's dead sunflowers.

47

SIGNS & PORTENTS

Granny Maypearl

As they approached town that morning, Jinny skipped on ahead. The basket in her right hand swung in time with the nursery rhyme she was singing. The older girl, Sissy, held Granny's hand and asked never-ending questions about how to make love potions. That girl would be trouble once she hit puberty. The boys in town wouldn't know what hit them.

Granny smiled and squeezed Sissy's hand, but part of her felt awful bitter. Damn that Cotton for depriving her of the simple happiness of spending time with these girls. At least with Ruby, she'd had a few years before he got wise to Rose's sneaking around. It was later that Sissy and Jinny were born, and now they were virtually strangers to her—precious strangers who wanted to hear stories about their mama.

Although, if she were being honest, maybe she deserved some of the blame. Her own mama always said she had a stubborn streak that made a mule look reasonable. If she were going to be honest, she'd admit that she never got over the fact that

Rose chose Cotton over her. She'd aimed to make her girl learn her lesson by leaving her to deal with that man on her own. She always figured that one day Rose, who'd inherited her own healthy dose of pride, would come crawling back to admit that her mama was right.

But, Lord, how time loved to make fools of the stubborn.

"Granny—"

Muted shouts interrupted Sissy's next question. Granny put her arms out and pushed the girls behind her, like she used to do with Rose when they were driving and she had to hit the brakes. She was halfway down the hill into town, and as she looked down toward the church, she saw the deacon run across the street from the church and into the reverend's front yard. That writer fella met him and they shared a brief but frantic conversation before they both disappeared back around the house.

Her first thought was relief at seeing Peter still in Moon Hollow. It meant he'd taken her advice after all. Ever since Ruby told her that foolish plan to convince Peter to take her away, Granny had known it would never work. But if the writer was still there it meant Ruby was still in town, too.

She started walking again. She'd soon find out what had Virgil and Peter so worried, but for now she wanted to enjoy these moments with her granddaughters. However, she'd barely taken two more steps when she spotted Ruby.

The girl stumbled into Reverend Peale's yard, fell to her knees, and covered her face. Even from the hill, Granny could see how hard the girl was shaking.

She grabbed both of the girls' hands and took off down the hill.

FIFTEEN MINUTES LATER, she'd deposited the girls with Edna, who'd opened her diner to serve refreshments to the search party. Naturally, she'd had to hear an earful about what was happening before Edna allowed her to leave. Apparently, a handful of the menfolk had taken off for Reverend Peale's house a few moments before Granny arrived and everyone else had been told to sit tight.

Walking up the street toward the rectory, Granny's intuition arced like a lightning bolt in her midsection. But it wouldn't have taken a mountain witch reading the signs to know something bad happened to Reverend Peale.

Who on earth could hurt that sweet man? He was one of the few people in town she could stand. They'd spent many a pleasant afternoon drinking tea laced with bourbon on his front porch. He might be a drunk, but he was real.

She swung open the gate. She didn't wonder why something bad happened, though. It was Decoration Day, and given all the bad signs lately, it wouldn't be an easy one. She feared whatever happened to the reverend was just the beginning of the trouble.

Instead of turning right toward the garden, where she could hear the raised voices of several men, she went straight up the front walk to the porch. She was already at the top step when she noticed Ruby in one of the wicker chairs.

"Ruby?"

The girl looked like she'd seen a haint. Her eyes were wide as doorknobs and seemed to be looking into the middle distance instead of focusing on any one thing.

Granny considered trying to coax her out of her shock, but she knew from experience that the numbness could be a blessing compared to the desperate pain of feeling too much, too soon. Besides, what she needed to do would only take a moment.

The front door was unlocked. She paused at the threshold

and was relieved not to hear any footsteps or voices inside. The only thing that greeted her was the metallic stink of blood. Lots and lots of blood.

She walked through the entrance and down the central hall. Past the office, where she and the reverend had debated everything from religion to the best recipe for cornbread.

Best not to think too much about that now, though. She needed to do what needed doing.

At the end of the hall, a long smear of blood went from the bedroom door to the back door further down the hall. Whoever killed him had done it in the bedroom and then, instead of letting the dead rest, dragged the poor man's body out into the elements. That explained why everyone was in the backyard. She blew out a breath as a parade of images swam through her head.

"Enough." She whispered the word, but her voice sounded unnaturally loud in the empty home that used to be filled with Reverend Peale's booming laughter.

She stepped over the wide smear of blood in the doorway. Inside the room, the blood wasn't as polite. The room looked like one of them modern artists had gone hog-wild with a paintbrush. The walls, the floor, the bedspread, even the ceiling were covered in millions of flecks of deep red blood.

She fancied herself a steady woman. She'd given birth and helped dozens of other children enter this world. She'd buried one man and one daughter. She'd cleaned game and euthanized animals that needed mercy. But she had never in her living life witnessed the aftermath of such savage violence. The air vibrated with it, like just after a lightning strike. The energy was so dark and chaotic that it nauseated her. Her gorge rose in the back of her throat, and cold sweat bloomed across her stomach.

Breathing through her nose wasn't an option because here the air smelled not just of blood, but of voided bowels and flop sweat and death itself. She opened her mouth and managed a couple of deep breaths, but stopped when the scents became flavors on her tongue.

She turned her back on the bloody walls and faced the bed, but it was worse than the rest. The quilts that had been made by good Christian women and white cotton sheets that had been washed by hand and hung out in the sun were now stiff with dried blood. Despite the obvious signs of struggle, the Reverend Peale's pillows remained at the top of the mattress. The head-shaped indention in the bloody pillow unsettled her more than everything else.

Swallowing hard, she reached for it, but hesitated. That soft spot was the last bit of comfort Reverend Peale had experienced on God's blue earth. Emotion threatened to bubble up and drown every bit of her resolve. She snatched the pillow off the bed. Kneading it with her fingers, she felt for lumps. When she encountered a hard disk, she froze. "Have mercy," she whispered.

She removed the pocketknife from her skirt pocket. After tossing aside the stiff cotton case, she stabbed the knife into the seam and ripped open the pillow. Blood had dyed the feathery intestines pink. She plunged her hand inside and pulled out a disk of matted feathers nearly as large as her palm. Each of the quills had turned inward and the feathers curled around the central axis to create a firm puck-shaped item.

A death crown.

Lots of folks in the mountains believed finding a crown in the pillow of the deceased was a sure sign that person had ascended directly to heaven. If one were found in a living person's pillow, it was considered a sure sign they'd be dead by sundown on the third day. That's what people believed, anyway.

Granny had other theories—ones that would make the God-fearing people of Moon Hollow shiver in their boots. She, herself, had only seen three death crowns in her whole life, and each of those times it was in the pillow of a person who'd met an untimely end. There was no doubt that Reverend Peale's death was not natural, so in that way the crown fit the template. But the other thing was, in both of the other instances, before they'd died the people had claimed to be vexed by a demon in the weeks before their deaths.

She sucked a long breath through her nose—needing the oxygen more than she wanted to avoid the stink of death—and exhaled slowly. She had to show this to Deacon Fry. The question was, would the old fool finally listen to her?

She went into the attached bathroom and grabbed a clean towel in which to wrap the death crown. As she went back into the bedroom, she thought about how Deacon Fry wouldn't believe her. She worried that the murder would convince him to cancel the Decoration altogether. Without Reverend Peale to do the rites, the ceremony couldn't be done properly. But not doing a Decoration wasn't an option, either. She would just have to make up for the lack of clergy by doing some of the rituals she knew to appease the mountain.

She looked down at the bloody floor. If that didn't succeed, goddess help them all.

48

PARADISE LOST

Deacon Fry

THE LATE-MORNING SUN warmed up the metal shed. The heat wouldn't have been pleasant on the best of days, but on that day, with the body of his dead friend cooking inside, Deacon Fry thought he'd had his first real glimpse of hell.

He had to get out. He swatted at the swarming blowflies, shouldered his way past Deacon Smythe, and escaped into the fresh air of the garden.

He wanted to lean against the wall and cry until his body was emptied of every drop of water. However, his congregation needed him to be strong and guide them through their grief and fear with faith. Carrying on like a woman would only weaken him in the eyes of his flock, and he feared that almost as much he did finding out the identity of Reverend Peale's murderer.

He walked with all the dignity he could muster toward a bench tucked under an arbor of yellowed vines. Most years around that time, the arch would be covered in green leaves and fragrant confederate jasmine blooms.

Sarah Jane had been helping Reverend Peale lately, but she didn't have any talent or interest in gardening and had obviously neglected the whole yard.

On the heels of that unfair thought, he immediately felt guilty. His poor daughter had been trying to help and the Good Lord knew that girl had been through a lot lately. Sharon had been the one to suggest that Sarah Jane spend some time with Reverend Peale to get her mind off of losing Jack. But now he'd have to tell her that Reverend Peale was dead, too.

The time has come for revelation, Daddy.

He removed a handkerchief from his pocket and ran it over his sweaty brow and upper lip. He'd have to be very careful. Betraying even the slightest hint of panic would set off a chain reaction. Luckily, he was still in so much shock there wasn't much of a risk of showing any emotion beyond exhaustion.

Earl Sharps walked over with his hands pushed deep in his pockets. Deacon Fry didn't rise, nor did he scoot over.

"Called the sheriff's office," Sharps began. "Arlene said Deputy Evans was on a call way down in Keokee. Sheriff Abernathy hadn't checked in recently, and when she tried to get ahold of him via his radio, it was turned off. Arlene said it was possible he was out checking on the widow O'Neill up Stonega way."

Deacon Fry primly ignored the implication that the sheriff was engaging in sexual congress with one of his mistresses. "Did she expect him back soon?"

"She said she'd keep trying and send one of them on when they were available."

"Did she happen to mention what we're supposed to do with the body until then?"

"She just said not to touch nothin'."

He resisted the urge to make an unchristian comment. A time or two, he'd caught one of them crime scene shows on the television. If this had happened in Lynchburg or Charlottesville, maybe they'd have the resources to do blood spatter analysis or genetic testing to find the murderer. But this was Moon Hollow. Sheriff Abernathy could take some fingerprints, but he was hardly schooled in forensics.

Plus, considering most of the town had been inside that house at one point or another, it was pretty clear that any evidence Abernathy would find wouldn't amount to a hill of beans, much less a conviction.

"We need to find a place to keep the body cool."

"Edna's got that big freezer."

"Oh, she won't like that one bit."

Sharps shrugged. "Can't say anybody's gonna like seeing Reverend Peale's body bloat up in this heat, either."

Deacon Fry blew out a deep breath. "Go ask her."

"What should I do, boss?" Smythe looked so eager to be useful that Deacon Fry wanted to smack him.

"Find me—"

The backdoor to the house flew open and that shrew Granny Maypearl ran down the steps. With her wild hair flying and her harpy voice, she reminded him of a witch on the way to the unholy Sabbath. The only thing missing was a broomstick. He ground his teeth and forced himself to stay put instead of running the other direction. Besides, it was already too late because she'd already spotted him.

"Deacon Fry, I need to talk to—" She cut off and wrinkled her nose. She looked at the shed, where two of the other deacons were attempting to hang a white sheet over the entrance.

"Oh dear," Maypearl whispered. Her gnarled fingers touched the spot between her clavicles and lifted a shiny pendant to her lips. "May the blessings of light be upon you."

Upon hearing her pagan blessing, the ice of Deacon Fry's

shock melted under the fire of his rage. He was up off the bench before he remembered making the decision. "Don't you dare," he said in a low tone. "Don't you dare use that forked tongue to speak of a man of God."

The men stopped to gape and lost control of the sheet. A breeze snatched it and carried it toward the garden, where it landed over the corpses of sunflowers. He ignored it and continued his advance toward the old hag. Instead of backing up, she placed her hands on her hips and jutted her chin out like a damned mule.

"Don't you dare soil this place."

She pointed toward the shed. The interior was shadowed, except where the sun crept across the floor and spot lit a single bare foot.

"This place already been soiled by murder, Virgil!" She held a bundle of cloth aloft as if to prove a point.

He squinted at the thing, but couldn't make heads nor tails of it. But he was in no mood to play her games. "You better not have touched anything in that house. When Sheriff Abernathy gets here he's gonna arrest you for obstruction."

"Like hell he will," she shot back. "If he puts me in jail he won't get any more of my ginseng tea for his man problems."

For a man widely known for his inspiring oration, it was rare for Deacon Fry to be struck speechless. But having this vile woman talk about the sheriff's virility problems with Reverend Peale dead not twenty feet away managed the trick. He sputtered for a good twenty seconds before he managed to spit out, "You watch your mouth."

She pressed her lips into a thin line and stepped closer until she was so close he could smell the hippie oils on her. "You listen to me, Virgil Fry," she poked his chest three times for emphasis, "you got bigger problems than you know."

Suddenly, he felt too tired to continue the conversation. Not just body weary but soul sapped, too. He sighed and rubbed the back of his neck with a hand. "No, you listen to me," he said, but his tone lacked the heat it had before. "I've got to get the sheriff here and I need to track down your son-in-law before that happens."

She reared back. "What's Cotton got to do with this?"

"Hopefully nothing, but no one's seen him this morning."

"You know Cotton's not my favorite, Virgil, but surely you don't think he's capable of that." She pointed toward the shed.

"I'm not saying he's guilty, but he needs to be found."

She thought it over for a moment before lowering her chin in a grudging nod.

Relieved that she'd managed not to argue for once, he continued. "I also have to explain to the citizens of this town that the Decoration is canceled because their beloved reverend was murdered."

She pulled back. "Oh no, you can't cancel it."

"I can and I will."

She fumbled with the towel in her hand and removed something from inside. "Do you have any idea what this is?" She pushed the clump of fuzz toward his face.

He snatched it from her hand.

"Careful," she snapped.

"A death crown," he said. He knew all about them because his mama had found one in Isaac's pillowcase after he died. She swore it meant he'd gone straight to heaven.

No, he shouldn't think about Isaac.

He shoved it back at her. "That's disgusting." When she took it, he wiped his hands on his pants.

"No, it ain't. It's a sign." She continued in a wheedling tone, "You know where I found that?"

"I don't want to hear it."

"Too damned bad, you old fool. If I were you, I'd be worried less about who killed the reverend and be asking yourself why, on the day of the Decoration, someone would kill the only ordained man in town."

It hadn't occurred to him that the timing of the murder might be an issue, but now that she'd mentioned it, he struggled to come up with a way to dismiss the concern. "Let's hear your theory, then." He delivered this in a challenging tone, which he hoped would disguise the fact he always felt like he was playing catch-up with this woman.

She waved the death crown in the air. "Lots of people think this means the person went to heaven. But we both know that our rites require someone to be properly buried before their soul can ascend."

According to the doctrine of Moon Hollow's church, that was the case. The Decoration Day rites were a way to reinforce the belief that a proper burial was required to achieve Heaven.

"So there's no way the crown would mean what most people believe—otherwise, you'd never find them in the pillows of people who hadn't been buried yet." She paused, as if to let that sink in. "Which leads me to my own belief about the meaning of the crown."

She continued to tell him her theory about how crowns showed up in the pillows of people who claimed to be vexed by the devil. When she finished, he looked around to see the intensely interested gazes of all the deacons resting on him, as if bracing for his reaction.

He was too busy wondering if they'd find a death crown in his pillow after he died, too.

"Deacon Fry?" Earl Sharps said, after a moment.

Right, he needed to keep things calm. So he snorted and slapped his knee. "Hell, Maypearl, you had me until you started talking about possession nonsense."

Her eyelids snapped into a narrowed line. "It ain't nonsense and you know it."

He felt as if there was an invisible wire connecting them that had just grown painfully taut. At that moment, he knew in his bones that they were both thinking about their conversation at her house where he'd all but admitted to being haunted by Jack's ghost.

He was on the verge of pushing her too far to rein her in again. If she wanted, she could tell the deacons why he'd been acting so strange the last few days. Time for some damage control. "Look," he sighed, "I apologize. It's been a stressful week."

Her expression tightened into a suspicious frown and she braced her weight on her legs, as if preparing for a real fight.

"This morning has been especially trying, and we're all upset about the loss of dear Reverend Peale. We can discuss our concerns later. But first, we need to track down Cotton."

All eyes turned toward Maypearl. She pursed her lips while she thought over her response. He wasn't worried anymore because he knew he'd pushed her in a corner. If she continued ranting about devils, she'd lose any chance of gaining allies in town. Especially after Earl and Junior found that broken angel statue and Mr. West's satanic book buried there.

"Hold on," he said. "Where's Peter West?"

"Why?" she asked.

From the corner of his eye, he saw Junior Jessup run out of the garden toward the front of the house, as if going to find Mr. West.

"I want to know where he was last night."

She laughed in his face. "You're not serious. That boy couldn't kill a possum. Besides, he and I were visiting yesterday afternoon. When I left he seemed pretty antsy to get to writing."

"Which leaves his whereabouts unknown for at least twelve hours."

"You're unhinged, Virgil."

"Am I? A couple nights ago someone did a satanic ritual in the cemetery. They broke the angel statue and buried one of Mr. West's devil books in sacred ground. And now our reverend is dead."

"What sort of satanic ritual?"

"Here he is, boss!" Junior yelled, dragging Mr. West into the garden behind him. "He was on the front porch with Ruby."

Maypearl muttered something under her breath and crossed her arms.

"Mr. West—"

"Why are you all just standing around?" Peter demanded. "Where's the sheriff?"

"I have some questions for you."

"For me?" Mr. West's frown transformed as he realized why he'd been summoned. "Oh, no. You're not going to pin this on me. I helped find his body, remember?"

"Maybe because you knew right where to look," Junior said.

"This is ridiculous. I have no motive. I only met with Reverend Peale for the first time yesterday." He pointed toward the shed. "That's a crime of passion committed by someone with a deep well of rage. Hardly the act of a passing acquaintance."

"Virgil, you know he's not guilty," Maypearl said. "We need to find Cotton."

"You think he's the killer," Mr. West said.

"Or another victim," she said in a grim tone.

Deacon Fry wanted to walk away from them all. He didn't want to play referee or detective. He didn't want to do anything but be alone. But he had to admit that Maypearl was right. He couldn't deny his instincts, which were telling him Cotton was tied up in all this somehow.

"All right," he said, "we'll find him." He turned to Mr. West. "But you stay in town, you hear?"

Mr. West looked like he wanted to punch something. "Yes, sir."

He turned to the other deacons. "Y'all spread out to the—"

A scream near the front of the house interrupted him.

"It's Ruby," Mr. West said, exchanging a worried look with Maypearl.

Everyone took off at once. Deacon Fry followed because, for the first time in years, he didn't feel up to leading the charge.

49

FUGUE

Cotton

THE SUN HURT HIS EYES. It seemed too high. Decoration started at ten. He couldn't be late or he'd miss Rose.

Wished he'd had time to shower before, but there wasn't time. He was pretty sure he didn't look too bad though.

He limped down the center of the road. There wouldn't be any traffic that day anyway. Everyone would be up on Cemetery Hill.

He sure hoped Edna made her famous fried chicken for the picnic. He was so hungry, his stomach felt like it might turn inside out.

The scream startled him.

He turned to face Reverend Peale's house.

Something tickled his memory about that place, but before he could figure it out, Rose's daughter screamed again.

"Ruby?" His voice croaked like a frog's. He was thirsty.

She sat on one of the rockers, but she wasn't relaxed. She looked like she was seeing a ghost.

"What's wrong, girl?"

Her hands came to her mouth, as if to hold in yet another scream. But before he could tell her to hush up, a whole group of people ran from around the side of the house.

He wondered if they'd moved the party to Reverend Peale's back yard without telling him.

"Cotton!"

He raised his hand to wave at Deacon Fry. For the first time in he didn't know how long he didn't get angry the second he laid eyes on that man. "Howdy."

"Cotton, what have you done?"

He slowly lowered his hand. On the porch, Granny Maypearl had her arms around Ruby, who was sobbing. "What's wrong?"

Maypearl, that old bat, scowled at him. That wasn't anything new, so he brushed it off, but he couldn't figure out why everyone else was looking at him funny.

"Did Rose come back yet?"

"Cotton, put down the gun."

He looked down. Sure enough, he had a pistol in his right hand. "Huh."

Junior Jessup ran over from the church parking lot with a shotgun in his hands. "Put down the weapon, Cotton!"

He shrugged and set the pistol on the road. "Okay."

Junior stopped running, but he didn't lower the gun. Deacon Fry approached from the yard and a couple of the other men followed him.

"Why's everyone acting so strange?" Panic rose in his chest. "Where's Rose?"

Junior and Deacon Fry froze and looked at each other like they both knew a dark secret. From the porch, Granny Maypearl left Ruby with a fella Cotton hadn't met. Maybe it was that author everyone kept talking about? Either way, he didn't like it, but that old harpy had to say her piece.

"Cotton Barrett, what have you done?" The old bat stepped into the street and approached him.

"God-Ah-Mighty, woman, leave me alone."

He looked down at the pistol again. His fingers itched to pick it up, but then he got distracted by a stain on his jeans. He couldn't remember where he slept last night, but he had a vague recollection of a bedroom with feather pillows. Either way, the stain on his pants sure looked a lot like blood. Now that he was looking, he realized his shirt was covered, too, and his arms and hands. Had he been butchering a hog?

"We're gonna need you to come with us," Deacon Fry said. "We'll get you cleaned up and then we're gonna have a nice long chat."

He shook his head. "Not until you tell me where Rose is."

Deacon Fry exchanged a look with Cotton's mother-in-law. Granny Maypearl was the one who answered. "Rose is dead, Cotton. Remember?"

Electricity jolted his brain, like he'd stuck it in a light socket. His body stiffened and twitched as images flashed through his mind. He couldn't make no sense of them because he kept seeing Rose inside a box.

"But no," he forced the words out, "she's alive. He promised."

Deacon Fry asked slowly, "Who promised?"

Didn't they know? Why was everyone being so peculiar? "Jack, of course."

"Cotton," Deacon Fry said, "Jack's dead, too."

Another shock attacked his brain a moment before the world went totally black again.

50

MOON HOLLOW INTERLUDE

Spring always brought storms to Moon Hollow. When the rain fell, the whole mountain smelled of petrichor and wet pine. A clean spring rain was a baptism, washing away the death of winter so the springtime resurrection could begin. But the rains also brought lightning, which destroyed without remorse. Every Sunday during the stormy season, Deacon Fry preached about how turbulent times could bring unexpected blessings. Not all baptisms happened in water, he'd say. Sometimes fire could renew a soul, too.

The night of the failed Decoration, the sky was bone dry. The lightning came anyway, but not the blessings.

THAT EVENING, Ruby sat alone in the chapel. Deacon Fry had ordered her to stay put while he dealt with her daddy and called the sheriff again.

The pew's edge dug into the backs of her thighs, and the road rash from her run-in with Junior Jessup both stung and throbbed at once. Being in the church brought her no comfort.

With the echoes of her father's screams standing in for the choir and the air all electric with his sins, the chapel felt downright menacing.

She could go. Nothing to stop her, really. She could just stand up, march down that aisle and out the front door. Then she could continue the route she'd been on earlier—the trail to the Promised Land beyond the trees and down the mountain.

Yet something kept her rear end rooted to that pew.

Something her daddy had said when he'd regained consciousness and they dragged him out of the street. "She's comin' home. My Rose is comin' home."

She couldn't figure out how that idea got into his head. Oh, she knew he'd been drinking too much. More than too much. But drunk wasn't the same thing as crazy, and he for damned sure was insane.

Daddy might be an angry man—she knew firsthand he absolutely was capable of violence—but she'd never seen him raise a hand against another man. No, he preferred to assert his dominance over women and children.

Besides, Daddy's anger always struck like lightning—hot and fast. In order to kill the reverend, he would have had to sneak onto his property, get the shovel from the shed, break into the house, see the sleeping reverend, and make the decision to kill him.

Premeditated—was that the word?

Either way, it was planned, which both confirmed and rejected the insanity theory. But if her daddy really was that far gone, how in the world could he plan the murder out on his own?

The idea that someone might have influenced him banged around in her head for a moment, but she dismissed it. Since Mama's death, he'd barely talked to his own family, and he'd pretty much avoided most everybody in town. Besides, who in

Moon Hollow would want Reverend Peale dead? And, if someone really wanted him dead, why would they choose the town drunk?

No. She was just wishing for someone to blame. Someone who could be punished and whose family could carry the shame instead of Ruby and her sisters.

One thing was for sure, her daddy's actions had just destroyed any option of leaving Sissy and Jinny in town when she left. She guessed that once the sheriff carted him off to jail, it would only be a matter of days before the town turned on her and the girls. But she couldn't think about that yet.

The other reason she didn't run away right that second was Granny's worry about the Decoration. The old woman knew things beyond normal ken. And, while Daddy was passed out, Deacon Fry and Granny had turned on each other in front of God and everyone.

Granny said they needed to go through with the Decoration but he'd insisted that they could reschedule. As Granny laid out the reasons they needed to go ahead with it, it was clear all the adults were listening to her. Deacon Fry had seen it, too. After he'd ended the discussion and told Granny to go home, Ruby could have sworn the wind picked up and the leaves rustled a warning.

Or maybe, at that moment, Ruby had missed the mountain's song so keenly, like a bird would miss its wings, that she'd imagined the wind and the leaves to escape the loneliness of her inner silence.

She closed her eyes and clasped her hands together. There, in God's house, where the only songs ever sung were about sacrifice and blind faith, she bowed her head, as if in prayer. But she was not pleading with Deacon Fry's God for help. He reminded her too much of her daddy on a bender, all vengeful and hungry to prove his power.

No, the prayer Ruby Barrett sent out was for her old friend Mountain, and Mountain's children—River, Tree, and Wind. "Please talk to me again. Tell me what to do."

The air crackled with so much energy that her hair raised on end. A bright flash lit up the blood in her eyelids. A split second later, a massive boom exploded. The entire church vibrated from the power of the lightning bolt and its immediate shout of thunder.

Heart pounding—or was it the echo of the thunder?—Ruby realized Mountain had answered her, but she still couldn't understand the meaning of its angry song.

THE SPEED LIMIT in Moon Hollow was twenty according to the sign Peter flew by going fifty miles-per-hour.

After Cotton Barrett showed up covered in blood and was taken into the church, Peter had run down the hill and all the way to the cabin. Not an easy feat for a man with such a sedentary occupation, but what he lacked in physical fitness he made up for with motivation. He wanted to get the hell out of town as soon as possible. He'd packed everything the night before, so it was a simple matter to carry everything out to the car. He'd expected to share trunk space with Ruby's things, but that whole plan had been shot to hell, hadn't it?

They'd taken her off when they took Cotton into custody. By that point, Peter knew there was no use in trying to sneak her out of town. Even if he could manage to get into the church past the deacons that had been posted in front of each exit, he was no longer willing to get tangled in the mess of Ruby Barrett's life.

When he'd originally offered to help her leave, it had been fueled by a rare flare up of heroism. He sort of liked the idea of playing knight in shining armor to the damsel in potential distress. But the instant the damsel's father proved to be an actual murderer, Peter's heroism had dried up faster than a puddle in the Sahara. It was all too messy, and he had no skin in the game. No responsibility to help; no reason to stay, either.

He paused with his hands on the open trunk and lowered his head. Despite his insistence that none of this was his problem, his conscience had other ideas. If he'd just driven her out of town that morning she'd already be free. Instead, she was locked in the church with no hope of parole.

He slammed the trunk. Not his problem. He'd gotten his story. Time to go.

Five minutes later, he sped through the deepening dusk toward town. There were lights on in a few of the buildings, but he didn't see anyone on Main Street. He imagined them all huddled in their homes whispering about poor Reverend Peale and about how they always knew something was wrong with that Cotton Barrett.

He shook his head and pushed the whole thing out of his mind. In a few minutes, he'd be on the main road and on his way back to civilization. How long had it been since he had a decent internet connection or a cup of proper overpriced coffee like a real citizen of the world? He considered stopping in Big Stone Gap for the night, but rejected the idea. He wanted a lot of miles between him and Moon Hollow before he slept. Didn't feel safe any closer.

The thought surprised him. Why wouldn't he feel safe? Cotton was in custody and Reverend Peale's death, while tragic, didn't affect Peter beyond the normal pangs of regret one felt upon hearing of an acquaintance's death. But unsafe? No, that was silly.

On the road beyond town, the trees on either side swayed in a strengthening breeze. He looked up, expecting clouds, but the sky was a clear indigo. Toward the east, the stars were waking up for their evening performance. He never saw many stars in Raleigh, but he wasn't romantic enough to think he'd miss them when he got back to the city.

The road rose ahead of him, climbing toward the tree tunnel that would eventually lead out to the highway. He rolled down his window and let his elbow hang outside the opening. The night air, though windy, was warm. Through his rearview, the steeple of Christ the Redeemer's warped spire scraped the sky, and, behind it, Cemetery Hill loomed like a dark secret.

Tempted by the atmosphere, he imagined himself a character in a movie. An indie, of course, about a stranger who'd come to a small mountain town and was leaving wiser than when he'd arrived. In his version of the story, he was leaving a hero. That's why he preferred fiction to reality—endings were tidy and someone always got to be the hero.

The car finally reached the hill's apex, where the paved road gave way to gravel and narrowed before snaking into the woods. Somewhere in the town behind him, an ear-splitting crack of thunder and a flash of bright interrupted his peaceful drive. He slammed the brakes and turned to look over his shoulder.

There were still no clouds in the sky. No raindrops fell. But he'd be damned if that hadn't been the largest bolt of lightning he'd ever seen. A large plume of smoke rose above the spot on the hill where the cemetery stood.

Shaking his head, he turned back and eased his foot on the gas. No one was left on that hill to worry about.

The car continued toward the tunnel of trees. Through the window, the smell of ozone reached his nose. He reached down to turn on the radio for his road trip. The reception was almost nonexistent except for a couple of local AM stations that played non-stop religious programming. The familiar sensation of dangerous solitude overcame him. Just to have some noise to listen to, he left it on a station where a preacher was reading verses from the book of Revelation.

"But the fearful, and unbelieving, and the abominable, and murderers, and whoremongers, and sorcerers, and idolaters, and all liars, shall have their part in the lake which burneth with fire and brimstone: which is the second death."

Peter laughed out loud. "Ohhh, Lord, kum-bay-a," he sang.

The car was less than fifty feet from the tunnel of trees. The preacher moved on to a new verse, but before Peter could register the message, a flash of light blinded him. His hands jerked on the steering wheel. The car swerved beneath him. He slammed his foot down to brake. The squealing of the tires was drowned out by a boom of thunder so loud that it echoed in his bones.

Still blind, he screamed, but it was more sensation than sound. The car continued its skid until, all at once, the nose tipped down and slammed into something immovable.

When his vision cleared, blood dripped into his eyes. After he wiped it away, he registered that his fender was planted in a giant crack. Groaning, he wiped the back of his hand across his eyes and touched his forehead. His fingertips encountered the gash that had opened when his forehead connected with the garage door opener to his house—no, Renee's house— that no longer was good for anything except to cut gashes in his head.

"Fuck!"

Loud hissing interrupted his pity party. Steam billowed out from under the hood, which had crumpled from its impact into the gap in the road—a gap that hadn't been there thirty seconds earlier. The fractured macadam still smoked from the heat of the lightning's strike.

His head swam and stars danced in his vision as he groped for the door handle. But the door was trapped shut by rocks and asphalt.

The voice of the preacher cut through his shock. "Write the things which thou hast seen, and the things which are, and the things which shall be hereafter."

He snorted more from bitterness than humor. "If I ever make it out of this fucking town, I'll write whatever you want, God." With that, he hauled his bruised body out the open window and fell to the ground. The stars overhead mocked him from the clear night sky.

———

AS THE THUNDER ECHOED OUTSIDE, Deacon Fry paced in his office. On the sofa, Smythe and Earl Sharps sat on either side of Cotton. The latter bent over with his head in his hands while he sobbed like a woman. Before the lightning lit up the entire town, he had been hollerin' and carrying on something fierce. Deacon Fry only had been able to make out every few words, but none of it had made a lick of sense, except the way he kept yelling out Rose's name.

It was pitiful and it made him feel capable of violence. He did not want to feel pity for a murderer.

"You left a message for Sheriff Abernathy?" Smythe said in a low tone.

He stopped to stare at the man. "You heard me, didn't you?"

Smythe shifted on the couch cushion, and his big ass forced a squeal out of the leather. "Sorry."

"What are we gonna do if he don't call back?" Sharps asked.

Deacon Fry turned away from their questions and walked to his desk. The phone sat there quiet and stubborn, like a woman planning to make someone pay. He didn't answer Sharps's question out loud, but inside he debated his options.

Reverend Peale's body had been moved to the diner's refrigerator after a shouting match with Edna. A rotation of men had been scheduled to sit guard through the night.

He'd considered loading Cotton into his Caddie and driving him direct over to the county jail. But it was a good forty-minute drive there and from the sound of the thunder he'd just heard they were in store for a massive gully washer. Not the best time to be out on winding mountain roads with a murderer. Plus, he didn't like the idea of leaving the town alone without a leader.

He shook his head and blew out a long breath. He braced a hand on the desktop, and he willed Sheriff Abernathy to call.

"Uh—Deacon Fry?" Smythe said.

"What?" He turned his back on the traitor phone.

All three of the men on the couch were staring at something behind him. Smythe's face was pale as a bleached bone. Sharps had gone green, like he'd eaten some of Sharon's pork surprise casseroles. But Cotton, well, he looked . . . happy. His puffy eyelids and tear-stained cheeks paled in comparison to the broad smile that lifted up the corners of his mouth, as if someone had used fishhooks to raise them. Then there were those two glassy blue eyes that shone like a devout man on Judgment Day.

"Smythe?" he demanded.

Instead of answering out loud, Smythe raised a single finger to point toward the window behind the desk.

A frozen spot appeared between his shoulder blades, as if someone had poked him with dry ice. The rest of his body broke out into starchy flop-sweat.

He didn't want to turn around, but as if compelled by an outside force, his body disobeyed his mind. As he spun, he saw the painting of John the Baptist, a photograph on his desk of he and Reverend Peale at a previous year's Decoration, and the Bible that had belonged to his father. Some bone-deep knowledge told him none of these totems could protect him from what waited at the other end of his rotation.

There were no streetlights on that side of the building, between his office window and the woods, so at first, the large plane of glass appeared black as the midnight sky. Then his eyes were drawn to the white face pressed against the lower right pane.

His heart tried to climb right out of his chest, but his damned feet were useless.

The face didn't move. The eyes watched him and a sickening smile exposed shadowy gaps in the teeth. What his eyes couldn't make out, his memory filled in from his previous encounters with the demon.

"Wh—what the hell is that . . . is that Jack?" Smythe cried in a high-pitched voice.

The demon smiled wider, as if he'd heard the exclamation, but his eyes never left Deacon Fry.

A screeching sound came from the windows, where the demon scratched his dirty fingernails down the glass.

"Lord Jesus, protect us." He wasn't sure who had spoken. It might have been his own voice. He didn't know anything for sure except fear.

A lightning strike lit up the sky like a giant flashbulb. The glare made the demon's entire body visible. It had shunned clothing altogether, and its nudity seemed the greatest blasphemy so far. But even as he registered the horror of that, he saw the other things the light had revealed behind the demon.

Dozens of corpses shambled down Cemetery Hill.

———

GRANNY MAYPEARL CONSIDERED NOT RETURNING to town. If she

rode out the night in her cabin with Jinny and Sissy, she could guarantee the future of their line, at least.

But even as the thought occurred to her, she dismissed it. Truth was, what was coming was as much her fault as it was anyone's. After her fight with Rose, she'd been too stubborn to mend fences. But, fool that she was, she'd always thought she had plenty of time.

It was too late for do-overs or regrets.

She threw bundles of sage into a canvas bag, and tossed a box of matches on top of those.

"What are you doing?" Sissy demanded.

"Gotta go to town to take care of something." She turned away from her work to look at the girl. "I need you to stay here and take care of your sister."

"I want to come with you."

She placed her hands on the girl's shoulders. "I know you do, darlin', but this is work for grownups. Now, do you know how to shoot a shotgun?"

Sissy's eyes widened and she smiled. "Yes, ma'am."

"That's real good." She pointed to the shotgun by the front door. A box of shells sat on a table next to it. "If anything tries to get in the house before sunrise, you shoot it."

"Any...thing?"

She nodded. "If for some reason, they get into the house, you go out the back to the shed. There's a root cellar underneath. Hide in there until sunrise."

"If who gets in the house, Granny?"

"The haints."

Sissy reared back. "Ghosts?"

"Not exactly. You'll know 'em when you see 'em, though. The shotgun can't kill 'em but they'll sure think twice about trying again. Point is, you gotta hold 'em off until sunrise."

"What are you going to do?"

"I'm gonna go find Ruby and see if we can stop them from taking over the town."

Since it was too late to do the proper rites, all she could do now was minimize the damage. Protect those who deserved it, and get out of the way while the others paid the piper.

"I hope Ruby is ready." Even as she said it, she knew the truth. None of them were prepared for what was coming. Even she'd been in too much denial to act on the early signs.

Sissy launched herself at her legs. "I'm scared, Granny."

She closed her eyes and lowered her cheek to the girl's hair. How many times had she done the same thing to Rose, and how often had she taken the simple gesture for granted. Now she closed her eyes and inhaled deeply. Sissy's hair smelled like strawberries and warm sun, like all the good things. Tears burned her eyes. So much time wasted and now it was too late to linger. "I know I haven't been there for you, but I love you, Sissy."

The girl's hands tightened around her waist. "I love you, too, Granny."

With a sniff, she backed away because she didn't want to lose her nerve. "I need you to be brave. Can you do that for your granny?"

"Yes, ma'am."

Jinny ran out from the kitchen, where she'd been coloring. "Where you going, Granny?"

"Just gonna run to town real quick." She knelt down. "You mind your sister, now."

Jinny sent a resentful look toward her sister, but said, "Yes, ma'am."

She hugged her real hard and quick. "That's a big girl."

She whistled to summon Billy. A swishing sound accompanied his entrance through the dog door in the kitchen. The slow click-clack of his nails on the linoleum followed. Then, finally, he lumbered into the living room.

Her joints popped and groaned as she knelt to talk to him. From her pocket, she removed a small red bag that smelled of bay leaves and black pepper. Billy snorted and shied away from the scent.

"You wanna scare off evil, you gotta smell worse than it does." She patted his head and straightened his collar. "Now, you keep an eye on my girls, you hear?"

The dog dipped his head under her chin and whimpered.

"None of that." But she gave his ears extra skritches. "Granny needs to go. There have already been two thunders."

With one last look at her two granddaughters and her Billy, she grabbed her bag of tools and her trusty dowsing rod, and stepped out onto the porch. "Lock it behind me," she said to Sissy. Then she closed the door.

On the front steps, she closed her eyes and took three deep breaths. Then she raised her hands and faced north. "Gods of the North, where the cold winds blow, lend me your ear. I, your humble servant, am in need of protection and guidance." She turned to the east. "Gods of the East, land of the sun, hear me." She turned again. "Gods of the Southern waters, heed my call." Finally, she faced west. "Great mountain father, hear your daughter, and know that you are heard in return. Have mercy on the sky god's children."

In the distance, thunder rolled for the third time since sundown.

She placed her hands over her galloping heart. "Please don't let me be too late."

―――

As the sun dipped low, the demon some called "Jack" entered

the cemetery. It stood on white pebbles spread over the graves and paths to keep the souls anchored. The fools did not know souls fled before bodies cooled. Humans were so fragile, so simple, so corrupt.

The demon raised its hands toward the pregnant moon. "Return to your flesh, mountain sons. Return to your bones, mountain daughters. There is work to be done."

No humans could hear the words of the demon's song with their ears. Yet, the dark crawled under their skin and caused gooseflesh and made them say things like, "someone walked over my grave."

About that, at least, they were right.

A few moments later, the first blue lights circled down from the sky. The tiny dots came together and swirled around the demon.

"Now," it spoke in an ancient tongue too low for the human ear.

The lights dispersed. Charged from the energy, the demon's vision turned red. All those dots like droplets of blood spatter flying through the air. Each orb found its home and disappeared beneath the rich soil.

The demon listened to the wind, and heard the girl's pleading voice.

Please talk to me again. Tell me what to do.

The demon placed a cigarette between its smiling lips. "As you wish." It lifted its mangled face to the sky.

Lightning arced out of the cloudless sky. It branched like an electric nervous system, striking every grave in the yard and lighting the demon's cigarette.

The demon sucked the delicious carcinogens into its black lungs. It lifted its head to the sky and exhaled thunder.

The ground rolled beneath its feet. The vibrations shook each grave until cracks formed in the earth. When the first skeletal fingers emerged from the soil, the demon let the cigarette dangle from its gray lips and clapped its blood-caked hands.

"Welcome back, sons and daughters of Moon Hollow," it said. "The time for revelation has come."

51

RESTLESS VILLAGERS

Peter

BY THE TIME Peter made it back to town, the dizziness had passed but not the anger. His car was totaled, he knew that much. The chances of him luring a tow truck up the mountain after dark were slim even without the road torn up from a phantom lightning bolt. He was all but guaranteed to spend another night in town.

He limped past the diner's window. The majority of Moon Hollow's citizens gathered around the counter and the booths. No doubt they were gossiping about the canceled Decoration and speculating what would happen to Cotton. Hell, Reverend Peale's murder was probably the biggest thing to happen in the town's history.

Edna was holding court behind the counter. He'd never seen someone look more excited to be in mourning. He couldn't stomach the idea of entering that circus parading as a wake, so he continued walking.

Up ahead, the church's warped cross curled up toward the

moon, and for the first time he thought it looked sort of like an extended middle finger.

He'd sort of liked that car, too. It wasn't as fancy as the one he'd sold to pay for his divorce, but it had been dependable and solid during a time everything felt unstable. Now, the car, like his marriage, was totaled—the damage too extensive to be worth the trouble of fixing it.

He was in front of the library when a loud bang behind him made him stop and turn around. People spilled out of the doorway of The Wooden Spoon. Edna and Junior led the pack, and everyone was talking over each other. The only thing missing from the tableau was pitchforks.

Edna had already spotted him so there was no use trying to hide.

"What's happening?" he asked once they reached him.

"Justice, that's what," Junior said.

"For whom?"

"Reverend Peale!" several people shouted in unison.

"Isn't that the sheriff's job?" Even as he spoke the words, he wished he could snatch them back and swallow them before anyone heard. But he couldn't stop them, and so he had to listen to the gasps and withstand the searing heat of their angry glares.

"What are you still doing here anyway?" Lettie asked from the center of the crowd. "Thought you'd left already?"

He touched his forehead. "Ran into a bit of trouble."

She opened her mouth to say something else, but Junior interrupted. "We ain't got time for more of your tall tales, author man." He elbowed past, holding his shotgun high, like a war flag.

Lettie flashed him an apologetic look before she followed Junior. Edna and the others trailed after them.

Bunk, who'd been at the back of the group, hung back. The old man removed a toothpick from between his lips with his pincers and sucked air at his teeth before speaking. "Might want to get moving along, Peter. Things are 'bout to get out of hand, I'm afraid."

"You should go, too, Bunk. Go lock yourself in your house until it blows over."

Bunk smiled a sad smile. "Afraid I can't do that. Someone got to speak some sense to these fools."

"I—my car, it's totaled. Lightning came out of nowhere and hit the road in front of me." He touched the wound at his forehead again and his fingertips came away wet with blood. "I'm stuck."

Bunk put the toothpick back in his mouth and reached into his pockets. He grabbed Peter's hand and placed his keys in the palm. "Take my truck."

"I can't take—"

"Don't start with me, son. I'm old and ornery. Take the truck. See if you can find Sheriff Abernathy and send him this way. If not ..." He shrugged. "Just get yourself away from this place."

"I can't just leave you here. If it's as bad as you're predicting, you're in real danger."

"That's my risk to take," he said. "These are my people so they're my problem. But this ain't your business or your fight. So take them keys, get in my truck, and get the hell out of here."

Metal cut into his palm. Moon Hollow was on a crash course with its own destiny and he couldn't stop it any more than he could stop the earth from rotating or the moon from causing the tides.

Still, of all the folks he'd met in town, Bunk was his favorite. Bunk and Ruby, he amended. Where was she?

He looked toward the church. Lights along the street pointed up toward the bent cross, which loomed over the heads of the crowd marching up Main Street.

"Ruby's in there," he said.

Bunk's placed his prosthesis on Peter's shoulder. "I'll look out for Ruby. Make sure she's not punished by the town for the sins of her father."

The implication that Bunk believed the town had the right to punish Cotton unsettled Peter. The metal pincer on his shoulder took on new weight, and now, he could see the oddly anticipatory gleam in his eyes.

"Time to go, Peter." The metal tips bit into his flesh.

His conscience balked, but he knew the score. If he stayed, he'd be as much of a target as Cotton. It was only a matter of time until someone tried to connect the trouble to his arrival.

Yes, it was time to leave. This wasn't his battle or his story.

He held out his right hand to Bunk. "See you around."

Bunk smiled, showing lots of crooked, yellow teeth. He lifted his pincer from Peter's shoulder and slapped his good hand into Peter's palm. "Probably not." The punishing handshake was not menacing—just overly eager in the way men had of showing affection through pain.

He shook the keys. "And thanks for the wheels."

Bunk nodded. "Whatever you see in that rearview you keep going, you hear?"

Emotion rose in the back of Peter's throat. He wasn't sure if it was premature grief or delayed fear or both. But it meant all he could do was nod a final farewell at Bunk before he jogged away toward the battered blue pickup parked in front of The Wooden Spoon.

52

ANGELS

Cotton

HE'D NEVER FELT SO hopeless. Until the lightning changed everything. Until the flash showed him that his new friend hadn't forgotten his promise.

Never in his whole life had he felt so relieved to see a face. 'Course the deacons acted like little girls, seeing that face. Sure, it was a little banged up. Sure, the flash of white light had played tricks across its planes until they seemed sort of threatening. But he knew better. His new friend didn't mean no harm. He just wanted to make things right in Moon Hollow, and as far as Cotton was concerned, things hadn't been right in that town ever since his Rose had left him all alone.

But that was all about to change.

He sat up straighter and waved at his new friend and the beautiful angels who stood behind him, like a heavenly choir.

"What the hell are those things?" Smythe yelled.

Cotton whispered, "Friends."

The other men ignored him and started fussing with each

other. They sounded scared. They should be. But not him. He'd never been so happy. He rocked back and forth because he couldn't contain all his joy. As he moved, he chanted in time to his movements, "Roseroseroseroserose."

"Shut up!" Earl yelled.

Pain exploded at his temple, but he laughed. Earl stepped back and looked at him as if he were a snake. He laughed harder.

"Enough, Cotton!" The big deacon this time. The big cheese. He wouldn't be actin' so big when he met Cotton's new friend.

"She's coming home to me."

"Who?"

"Rose."

Deacon Fry shook his head, as if Cotton was the crazy one. They was the ones pretending not to see the angels. The angels who brought his Rose home to him. "Amen," he said.

"Forget him," Deacon Fry said. "We got bigger trouble than him for the moment."

"We locked all the doors and windows, right?"

Cotton laughed. "Can't keep the angels out of church, silly."

They continued as if he hadn't just spoken the truth. "No," Deacon Fry said. "We need to get word out to the others about ... whatever those things are."

"Angels."

"Hush up, Cotton!" Smythe's screech sounded like air escaping a balloon.

Thought they had old Cotton trapped, but they weren't as smart as they thought. Nothin' gonna keep him from his Rose, no sir. Besides, Deacon Fry was gonna git his before it's done.

"There's a couple of shotguns in the storeroom," Deacon Fry was saying. "And extra shells. Earl, go make sure we got every door and window the first time. I'll start calling around."

"What about him, boss?" asked Smythe.

He rocked and smiled up at them. *Roseroseroserose*.

"I'll keep an eye on him. You just make sure this place is locked up tight." Deacon Dickhead turned to address Cotton in a voice that reminded him of his daddy's right before he whooped him. "Now you sit there and behave or I swear to the good Lord I will tie you to a chair."

He shoved his hands under his rear end and rocked and rocked and rocked, silently chanting to himself *soonsoonsoon*.

Deacon Fry issued one last warning look before walking to his desk. After Cotton's new friend first appeared, the deacons had pulled curtains across the big window. But he knew the angels were still out. Could feel them out there, calling to him to come join them. To see his Rose.

"Come on, pick up," Deacon Fry said. "Who's this? Bubba Oglesby, why are you answering the phone?"

Cotton? Cotton, we're waiting for you.

He stopped rocking to listen real hard. The voice in his head sounded like his friend, the new Jack.

Come on out. Rose is here.

His heart just about burst in his chest. "She is?"

Deacon looked over his shoulder at Cotton in a way that reminded him of old Mrs. Murphy, his second grade teacher, who would shake him hard when he couldn't sit still in class. She'd been a real bitch—just like Deacon Fry.

She's here, Cotton. Come on out. Use the door at the back of the church. Do you know the one? By Reverend Peale's old office.

He nodded because speaking would only earn him more looks from Mrs. Murphy. Maybe she'd shake him real hard too and his teeth would snap together like a gunshot. Bitch.

Quickly, Cotton!

Deacon Fry's back was still turned. The office door was to his right. About ten feet. If he was real quiet, he could make it over there and out into the hall before Mrs. Murphy called the diner.

" ... They what? Coming here? Listen to me, Bubba—no, leave him, yes come quickly—"

Now, Cotton!

He rose from the couch and tiptoed toward the door. The outer office door beyond was open. Muted shouting came from the chapel down the hall. He ran the opposite direction. The only light in the dark passage was from an exit sign that cast the passage in a bloody glow.

Somewhere behind him, Deacon Fry was still hollerin'.

Cotton passed the exit door and continued to the end of the next hall. His friend Jack said he should go out the door by Reverend Peale's office. It felt right, too, since old Reverend Peale had given his life so Cotton could have his Rose back. "Rest in peace."

The hallways all looked the same now. All dark except for the red, all empty. He had a sudden feeling like he was moving through a heart, like blood itself. "There's wonderful power in the blood," he sang tunelessly.

Cotton.

"I'm comin'," he said to his impatient friend.

The exit across from Reverend Peale's office didn't look right. The door expanded in and out like a lung filling and exhaling. He stopped to watch it.

"Open up, Cotton." This time the voice didn't echo inside his brain; it came through the breathing door, muffled as if spoken from within a coffin.

"Is Rose with you?"

A pause. "Yes, Cotton."

His fingers fumbled with the latch. Excitement made him clumsy. His brain wasn't working right. It stumbled over words and sped forward over ideas and circled, chasing itself, like a mongrel pup after its own tail. He was afraid of the door, breathing in and out. The sound of the metal creaking in and out, groaning. The muted sound of the demon Jack's voice coming through the distended panel. What if his new friend was lying?

"Cotton," the voice said, "it's time."

He ran his palm down the frigid door until it encountered the hard steel bar that extended across the surface. One hard push and the latch would engage and the door would swing open and there would be his Rose.

"Cotton!" The voice came from inside the building. It was not his new friend's voice, but that of his old enemy, Deacon Fry. If he caught up with Cotton, he'd shake him until his teeth rattled in his skull and his eyes banged in their sockets and he'd kill Cotton.

"Yes, he'll kill you," said his new friend's voice beyond the breathing door. "Come on out. Your life is out here, Cotton. Your life—Rose."

His fingers circled around the handle and pushed with more resolve than Cotton Barrett had ever had in his whole living life. The door stopped heaving and simply swung open into the misty night air. The humidity hit him in the face. Behind him Deacon Fry shouted something. His nose filled with the sweet stink of rot.

Cemetery Hill rose above him, empty.

He stumbled into the wet grass. High above, the moon pressed its face to the glass dome above the hollow, bearing witness. His insides slithered like worms digging into fresh turned earth, excited and seeking.

Behind him, screams from Deacon Fry. "Come back, Cotton!"

But he was too smart to listen. Mrs. Murphy wanted to shake him, shake him until his brain became liquid in his skull and he forgot all about Rose.

The angels, the beautiful angels, lit from inside against the dark backdrop of moody hills. His new friend glowed, too, though brighter than the rest. The new Jack, the one Deacon Fry thought was dead, was a dark angel who glowed with black light and the promise of life eternal. Life he promised to share with Cotton and his beloved Rose.

The screams behind him stopped. Deacon Fry whispered, "God have mercy on you." The door slammed.

His new friend didn't speak, and despite his clumsy thoughts, Cotton understood he should not speak, either, or risk breaking the dark spell.

Jack lifted a hand and purple tracers followed it through the air. The angels, so beautiful—such dark beauty—parted like Moses's sea.

She wore a white dress made of moonbeams and promises. Like a fairy tale princess, she'd escaped the sleeping spell and returned to her prince. The night breeze caught strands of her raven hair and lifted it like birds' wings, ready to take flight. Her skin, paler now, looked so soft, and those lips, those pink petal lips, begged for his kiss.

She looked sweeter than she had that first day he'd seen her on the church steps when they was just kids. He'd loved her—although that word wasn't strong enough ... wanted, desired, coveted—yes, he'd coveted her—for years. It hadn't been until she returned to Moon Hollow that he finally had her. Now, she looked like the Rose who'd returned a little broken and sad, but more beautiful for the pain. She'd wanted him then because she knew how lucky she was to have anyone want her for keeps.

His Rose, his life, his, his, his.

His knees gave out at the relief, the God damned relief of seeing her again after being taken from him for what seemed like forever. Now, thanks to his new friend, they'd be together for eternity. "Rose," he whispered. "My sweet, sweet Rose."

She floated over the grass. Her arms opened, inviting him to commune at her breast. He'd never felt more devout in his whole life.

This is real. This is the realest moment of my life. Now, I am a real man. You hear me, Pappy? I'm a man.

God had just been testing him, see? And his reward was Rose.

"God is good," he said. "Amen, forever and ever."

53

DEVILS

Deacon Fry

THE FOOL. The damned fool.

If Deacon Fry was fortunate enough to make it to the ripe old age of one hundred, he'd never forget the moment he looked through that door and saw Cotton Barrett surrounded by dozens of the most gruesome ... abominations—they were too far decayed to be considered human—he'd ever seen.

Lord help him, he'd tried to convince the fool to come back inside. How that man could stand there with the stench of death on the air and those grotesque faces smiling like diners at an all-you-can-eat buffet he'd never understand. But then, that devil had looked at him with such an expression of ravenous anticipation that he knew if he didn't lock that door, he'd be next on the menu.

"God have mercy on you," he'd whispered. What he'd meant was, God have mercy on us all.

Because it was not until the moment just before he slammed

that door and the lock slid home that Deacon Fry understood that God had abandoned them—him—to these soulless ghouls.

Standing alone in the hallway, behind the locked door, he whispered, "Why hast though forsaken us, Lord?"

The only answer was the sickening growl of those demons.

"Rose!" Cotton's voice sounded so joyous, the Deacon couldn't resist turning to look through the small window next to the door.

Cotton knelt before the semicircle of shuddering and rotten undead. The demon Jack said something he couldn't hear, and the masses of walking corpses made way for a new arrival.

His gasp fogged the window.

Calling the thing a woman would have been a blasphemy. The body bent in odd curves, like a question mark, and limped sideways, dragging its right foot behind it. Black hair, matted with mud and leaves, hung in ropey strands around fleshy planes that used to be a face. Large holes lay moist and open in the gray skin, which gaped at the eye sockets and under the cheekbones. Pink worms hung like gruesome ribbons from the holes.

He realized that this new thing looked so terrible because the rot was so fresh. A recent burial, which could only mean one thing—that abomination was Rose Barrett.

As he watched in horror, the revenant Rose opened her arms and approached Cotton. Her husband raised his face to the sky, as if offering thanks to the good Lord.

"No," he gasped, barely aware that he'd spoken out loud. "Please, God, no!"

He should run. He should run and get a shotgun, help, anything.

But his mind wouldn't let him lie to himself. Cotton's fate was sealed.

Some small voice in the back of his brain whispered something he'd never admit out loud. *His death will be the easiest of us all.*

Cotton's undead bride finally stood over him.

Why wasn't he running? Couldn't he see the rot? Couldn't he smell her? Didn't he know the danger?

In the end, the answers to his questions didn't matter. Because whether Cotton could see and smell his rotten Rose, he still took her hand—the one with strips of skin hanging like fringe from its palm—and stood to embrace her like a man about to kiss his bride at the altar. The couple turned sideways, and Cotton's searching, pink mouth touched the drawn-back gray lips of his love. The kiss lasted mere seconds, but the horror of it made it feel like an eternity to the lone, living witness. When it ended, there was no relief. Instead, his horror only increased as the putrid being that used to be Rose Barrett, opened its jaw wide like a pit viper.

Deacon Fry slapped a hand across his lips to prevent the bile in his throat from escaping.

The monster adjusted the angle of Cotton's face just enough to offer a view of his expression. No man's face in the history of the world had ever borne a look of such sublime ecstasy as Cotton Barrett's in the split second before grey teeth set in blackened gums sank into his shoulder and crushed through bones. As his body went limp, her arms wrapped around him in a lover's embrace. She feasted until every inch of her was baptized in his blood, and, when her demonic cohorts tried to get scraps, she raised her ruined face, pulled the body tighter to her breast, and hissed to warn them there would be no sharing.

The demon joined the bloody Rose and her rag doll trophy in the clearing. Rose didn't hiss at Jack.

She handed over the too-still, bloody body of her husband, and watched as the demon raised a finger and pointed it to

Deacon Fry. And when the demon mouthed, "Revelation," Rose lifted her bloody face to the sky and laughed.

The last thing he saw before he ran away was the way Cotton's head flopped to the side enough to show that, even in death, he looked like the happiest man on earth.

54

PREPARATION FOR BATTLE

Granny Maypearl

WHISPERS DANCED IN THE WIND. The messages arrived so fast she could barely keep up with them.

Picking up her pace, she lifted her bag higher on her shoulder. "Tell Ruby I'm coming," she whispered to the wind. "Help her be brave," she sang to the running water. "Have mercy on us all," she pleaded with the sky.

By the time she made her way down the mountain to the trail leading into town, she was winded and every hair on her arms prickled from the static electricity hanging over the town like a plasma dome. The trail dumped her out just beyond the end of town, down near The Wooden Spoon. Stepping into the road, she looked up toward the church.

A group of townsfolk gathered on the front steps. They fussed and carried on, like they were there on a mission. She shook her head and crouched down so they wouldn't spot her. She needed time to prepare.

She glanced around to take stock, and spied Peter walking toward her. He started to call out, but she waved her hand to stop him. They met up in front of the library.

She pulled him into the shadows. "Where are you going?"

He held up a set of keys. "Bunk's truck."

"You're leaving?"

"Things are getting a little too intense for me." He nodded toward the church steps and the angry people. "Time to hit the road."

"Didn't take you for a coward."

"Pragmatist," he corrected. "Never should have come here to begin with."

"You came to this town looking for something. You told us all you was looking for a story, but I got a different idea."

He made an impatient face. "I really should be going."

"Don't sass me, boy. I got to say my piece." She poked him in the chest, not hard but just enough to make him know she meant business. "You didn't come looking for a story. You came here looking for Peter."

He frowned, but she wasn't done.

"What you got to ask yourself, is if Peter is the kind of man who only writes other people's stories or is he the kind of man who authors his own fate?"

"Peter is the kind of man who wants to go home."

She blew a raspberry. "To what? An empty apartment?"

"What does it matter to you? Ruby's still here. You got your way."

"You don't know as much as you think. What's going on is not my way."

"Don't know what to tell you," he said. "If I were you, I'd head back up the ridge and stay as far away from town as you can until Sheriff Abernathy gets here."

She snorted. This boy had way too much faith in the law. "Sheriff ain't coming here. We're on our own."

His expression changed, as if he finally clued in that she was talking about more than just the angry mob. "Everyone's always on their own. That's why I'm leaving."

"If you leave, this will haunt you," she said. "You won't ever be able to leave it behind no matter how many stories you tell to try to exorcise it."

He stepped back. "Goodbye, Granny Maypearl."

"Good luck, Mr. West."

He muttered "thanks" before he jogged over to Bunk's truck. As he got in and started the engine, she waved but inside she was cussing him seven ways to the Sabbath. Damned coward.

The tires crunched as he pulled out of the space and turned the truck toward the hill out of town. The taillights flashed like a demon's eyes in the dark.

She sent up a quick prayer to the Mountain to allow him safe passage.

The door to the diner opened and Bubba Ogelsby ran out, looking panicked. Boy was barely older'n sixteen.

"We have to get to the church," he said. "Deacon Fry's orders."

She stood her ground. "You go on ahead."

He paused and glanced back toward the diner. "Don't feel right leaving Reverend Peale's body alone in there."

"Did you lock the freezer?"

"No, ain't like he's gonna try to get out." His laughter sounded forced.

A loud crash came from inside the diner.

Bubba jumped. "What the—"

"Run," she said. "Run to the church and don't stop until you're inside and the doors are locked."

He opened his mouth to argue.

"Go!"

He took off like a shot. Once he was safely on his way, she turned toward the diner and removed the tools she needed from her bag. "It's begun."

55

THE SPOOKED FLOCK

Deacon Fry

BY THE TIME he made it into the chapel, he'd gotten ahold of himself. It wouldn't do to let them see him crying like a little child. Yet, that's exactly how he felt—helpless and frightened. What he'd just witnessed, no man on earth could see and ever feel safe again.

The shock of Cotton's death and its implications pierced his brain like an ice pick. The pain was visceral and the hole it created allowed in the idea that if he didn't act, the empty graves up on Cemetery Hill would be filled with new bodies—his body and those of everyone he loved.

Closer to the chapel, raised voices reached him. From the sound of it, Edna and the rest had arrived at the church. He had to be sure the doors were locked before that demon and the rest of his horde made their way around to the front of the church.

When he stepped through the side door into the chapel, he found Edna and Junior shouting nose-to-nose with Smythe and Sharps.

"Hand him over or we're gonna take over this whole damned church," Junior shouted.

It didn't take him more than a breath to realize who *he* was—Cotton.

"And I told you, you cain't have him!" Sharps shouted back.

Edna planted her hands on her generous hips. "He's got to pay for what he did!"

Standing there, watching them fight, the absurdity of it all hit him with brute force. But before he could tell them to stop, Edna spotted him. "Deacon Fry, where you got Cotton locked up? The people of this down deserve justice."

He lifted a hand to his mouth to trap the hysterical giggle that threatened to escape right there in front of God and everyone. His eyes stung from the effort and he shook his head at their questioning looks.

"We demand answers!" Junior this time, but the shotgun in his hand made it more difficult to laugh at him.

By then, Smythe's and Sharps's expressions shifted from confrontational to confused. "Deacon? Where is he?"

It was too much. The pressure valve needed release or he'd explode. He considered just venting his hysterical laughter, but then Ruby Barrett stepped around from behind the quarreling foursome.

She didn't look confused or angry. She looked resigned. The expression was too old for her face, weighing it down, aging it. "What happened?" The words, spoken softly, seemed to reverberate through the church. Everyone, even Edna, shut their mouths and watched her. "Where is he?"

Her calm frightened him.

The dregs of his hysteria scraped down his throat and left a bitter aftertaste, like a too large pill. "I—he—"

He looked around the room, at the people who'd gathered, thinking they were about to see justice served. They had no idea justice didn't exist. Not really. If it did, he would never have to say the words he had to say. If justice existed, Reverend Peale would still be alive, and so would young Jack, with his whole future ahead of him. But the bloody shell that used to be the reverend was sitting in a meat locker. And Jack—

Well.

"Are you okay, Deacon?" Bunk asked. He'd barely noticed the old man with all the shouting, but now he realized that, as usual, he'd been standing on the edges of the drama, waiting to step in when things were about to get out of control.

Good old Bunk. Steady, trustworthy Bunk. Seeing him restored some of Deacon Fry's equilibrium. He nodded and swallowed hard again. His palms were sweating. "I'm okay, Bunk." He licked his dry lips. "About Cotton—well, there's no easy way to say this."

Anxious glances were exchanged around the room. But Ruby stood there looking ancient and too knowing. He avoided looking in her direction, preferring instead to deliver the news to good old Bunk, instead.

"Cotton is dead."

Edna gasped. The deacons in the room each stepped back, as if his words had punched them in their chests. Only Bunk came forward. "What do you mean? You didn't—" He trailed off, as if the next words were too awful to say aloud.

It took a moment for the meaning to sink in. "I didn't kill him." He raised his hands. "I swear on a stack of the deacon's Bibles."

Smythe spoke up next, but he took another step back. "But you was the only one with him, Deacon. No offense."

"Did he kill himself?" asked Junior, sounding hopeful.

Truth was, Cotton *had* committed suicide. He had not delivered his own deathblow, but he certainly had set into motion the events that led to his own demise. His mind's eye filled with an image of Cotton's blissed-out death mask. A tremor vibrated through him.

When he was young, his granny would say that when a person shuddered it was because a ghost walked over their grave. He'd always considered his granny a few drops short of a pint. But now? Now he wondered if maybe that old bird had understood more than he ever would.

"No," he said. "He didn't kill himself."

"Did it have something to do with the lightning?" Ruby said, her voice still low.

The lightning? He'd forgotten all about it. But now that she mentioned it, he realized that Smythe and Sharps had seen the lightning illuminate all those devils.

"It was the others, the ones outside the window," he said, looking at the other deacons. "Cotton ran outside before I could stop him."

All the color drained out of the pair's faces.

"What nonsense are you talking now, Deacon?" Jessup demanded. "What others?"

Three loud knocks echoed through the building.

"Deacon Fry! Edna! Let me in!" Bubba's terrified voice came through the church doors.

Everyone looked to him for guidance.

"Deacon Fry, please!" yelled Bubba.

He nodded to Junior. "Let him in."

Junior took his shotgun and jogged to the door to let Bubba in. The boy slipped through and stumbled.

"Was anyone behind you?" Deacon Fry called.

Bubba pulled himself off the ground. "No, sir." His chest was heaving as if he'd run all the way from the diner.

Junior slammed the door home and locked it. "Who would be out there? We're all in here."

Two knocks boomed through the chapel. Then, three rapid beats in a row. Two more.

Everyone in the church froze. Deacon Fry's heartbeat tripled.

"Y'all expecting anyone else?" Junior asked the room.

"Maybe it's Peter," Edna said. "We passed him on the way over."

"Peter's gone," Bunk said quietly.

Ruby looked toward Bunk like this news surprised her. Deacon Fry didn't see why. From the moment he'd met Peter West he'd known that man was yellow.

"Virgil." The taunting singsong was too loud to have passed through the church's thick doors. "Virgil, it's time."

"Who is that?" Smythe cried.

Junior didn't speak as he turned and marched back toward the door.

"If you open it," said Deacon Fry, "I will not be responsible for the outcome."

Junior slowed and turned to look at him like he'd sprouted horns. "I've gotta find out who's there."

"That's what he wants." His voice sounded panicked to his own ears. People were flashing him worried looks like the ones they used to use when dealing with Cotton. "It's not safe. Do you hear me? Not safe."

"All right," Junior said, propping the shotgun on his shoulder, "I think it's about damned time you explain what's going on."

His heart pounded so hard that the underside of his jaw ached. All that blood pumping through his veins should have made him feel hot, but he'd never felt so chilled in his life. Or so utterly alone. "You won't believe me." He placed a hand over his chest, just in case his heart made a run for it. "But I swear, you can not open that door."

The people who trusted him—the ones who'd followed his

rules and done his bidding for decades—now looked at him with a mixture of fear and doubt.

"Now, Virgil, it can't be as bad as all that," Bunk said in a patronizing tone. "Maybe it's just Peter, like Edna said."

"Or Granny Maypearl," Ruby said, suddenly animated. "Oh God, she's out there with the girls!"

"Granny's back at the diner," said Bubba. "Maybe someone's playing a joke."

Was this what insanity felt like? Or maybe they'd all gone insane and he was the only one left with a lick of sense.

But they aren't the ones who think there's a demon on the church steps.

"It's Jack!" He hadn't meant to shout it. Hadn't meant to say it at all, but just like those hysterical giggles earlier, the information had pressed up against his throat and his tongue until he couldn't stand to be the sole custodian of that information a second longer. "That's Jack out there."

All sound fled the room. The only noise he could hear was his traitor heart against his ribcage.

Finally, it was Ruby who broke the spell. "Jack's dead."

Knock, knock

Knockknockknock

Bunk finished the pattern absently, "Two bits."

"Virgil Fry." That voice, that demon's voice, came through the doors and flew toward him as if carried on midnight black wings. "The time has come for Revelation."

56

JUKEBOX OF THE DEAD

Granny Maypearl

SHE STEPPED into the diner with her dowsing rod in her right hand and in her left, a charm bag filled with a piece of white quartz, a piece of smoky quartz, and a few oleander leaves.

"Spirits of the dead, quit this place. I bind you with light and song to send you back whence you came."

The dark jukebox sprang to life. An old bluegrass song came from the speakers. Something high and lonesome, like the songs from her childhood.

The hairs on her arms stood on end.

A few years earlier, Deacon Fry had made a big stink about getting rid of that thing, but Edna had argued it was an antique. The jukebox stayed, but no one was ever allowed to play music.

A shuffling sound came from the shadows near the kitchen.

She spun in time to see Reverend Peale limp into the light. The right side of his head was dented and bits of brain clung to his temple. The swollen skin around his eyes prevented him from opening his lids all the way.

She held up her charm bag again. "Spirits of the dead—"

"Maypearl." His voice scratched out of his throat. "That you?"

She swallowed hard. Seeing him so ruined and stinking to high heaven made her want to scream and run back out that door and take refuge in the church, but her work was best done away from God's house. She started to call him "Reverend," but it didn't seem right calling that thing—that broken shell of him by that consecrated title. "Harlan," she said, using his given name just like she used to when they were children.

His head tipped to the side. "Mama?"

Her stomach clenched. "No, Harlan, I ain't your mama. It's Maypearl." As she spoke, she set down the charm bag and removed a bundle of white sage from her tote. "Remember me?"

"Maypearl?" he croaked.

"That's right." She set down her dowsing rod and struggled to light a match.

"I don't feel right." He sounded confused and terribly young.

"It's all gone be all right, Harlan. You just hold on." The match caught and she used it to light the tip of the sage bundle. The dried herbs lit and a thin ribbon of smoke rose. The scent tickled her nose.

He shuffled farther into the diner, bumping as he went into the counter. "I'm hungry, Maypearl."

She blew softly on the bundle to encourage more smoke. The ribbon thickened and danced across the room but didn't quite reach him yet. She didn't dare move closer, or make any sudden movements.

He recovered from his collision with the counter and resumed his shuffling progress. An incoherent groan came from his mouth. The closer he got, the more his smell overpowered the cleansing scent of the sage.

"The pact was broken," he groaned.

She waved the sage to encourage it to spread through every corner of the room.

Closer. Now she could see the white pupils and bloated belly pressing against his robe.

She held the sage in one hand and the charm bag in the other. "Come on," she whispered.

"Pact was broken," he growled.

The smoke reached him and curled around his body. He jerked, as if the smoke burned him.

"I bind you with light and song to send you back whence you came."

He made an unholy noise in the back of his throat, but the sage slowed his movements.

She dropped the charm bag and reached back with her right hand to grab her dowsing rod. As the haint growled and sputtered, she opened her mouth and began to sing the words of the ancient song her own mama taught her the year she got her first bleeding. As she sang, she beat a rhythm on the floor with the tip of her rod. The banjo music from the jukebox accompanied her, as if she'd evoked it.

She drew the notes from deep inside, from the place where the Great Mother had placed her power before she was born.

The haint screamed.

She continued to beat her rhythm and sing her song. The door to the diner flew open and a wild wind rushed inside. Her hair whipped around her head and knocked the sage from her hand. The rush of air dispersed the sage smoke.

The haint, free of its sage binding, rushed forward. Its dead white eyes and mouth flared open.

She gripped her dowsing rod and sang on.

When he was three feet away, she swung the rod up to her opposite shoulder. The putrid stench of the haint's breath reached her before it lunged the last few feet. With all her strength, she whipped the dowsing rod across his face.

He stumbled back with a terrible sound.

She pounded the dowsing rod into the floor and resumed her song.

The earth rumbled under their feet. A large crack appeared in the diner floor. Edna would be apoplectic, but a pristine floor would be useless to a dead woman.

The haint stumbled back again.

"I bind you with light and song and send you whence you came."

This time when the haint came at her, she didn't hit it or sing. She opened her arms and reached deep inside to summon her final weapon.

When she opened her mouth this time, the note that escaped was not a part of any song known to man or mountain.

The power of her note arced like lightning toward the haint's body. She held the note until his eyes bulged from their sockets and smoke rose from its ruined head.

The diner's windows exploded. The haint screamed as its bones shattered, too. Heat from the friction built until the flesh turned to ash.

Maypearl stopped singing and tamped her dowsing rod three times on the ground. The ash column that used to be the Reverend Harlan Peale crumpled to the floor.

She stepped to it and whispered, "Rest in peace, old friend."

57

DEMON JACK AND THE CADILLAC

Deacon Fry

THE CHURCH DOORS had red glass inserts that bloodied Deacon Fry's view of his town.

Demon Jack stood in the road on the roof of the deacon's Cadillac. The spotlights that illuminated the church's façade now acted as spotlights for the demon's wicked production.

He whispered under his breath, "Bastard."

Behind him, in the church, the others had all run to the windows to see what the commotion was about.

"It's Jack!" Nell screamed.

Deacon Fry tried to block out the sounds but failed—just as he'd failed to save Cotton. Just as he feared he'd fail at saving them all.

"Sir?" Smythe's fear sweat smelled like rotting potatoes in the small vestibule.

He pushed his elbow back into Smythe's soft belly. "Give me some room, Smythe."

"What do you see?"

Deacon Fry blew out a long breath that fogged up the red window. More than anything in his life, he wished he could just write this entire situation off as a nightmare. He longed to be a child, curled against his mother's soft breast, and her whispering, "It was just a dream, Virgie."

Virgie. How long had it been since someone called him that silly name? Sharon called him "Father," and Sarah Jane called him "Daddy." His flock called him "Deacon" or "sir." Even his mother stopped calling him by his pet name after Isaac—

"Come on out, Deacon Fry."

He was almost thankful for the demon Jack interrupting his mind's attempted stroll down memory lane. Almost. Because that same interruption also confirmed his worst fear—this was no dream, but very real—too damned real.

"Good people of Moon Hollow," Jack called, "if you want to survive the night, send the sinner out here to face his punishment." He opened his arms wide and his small army of undead raised their terrible voices like a devil's choir.

The church fell silent. He turned away from the door. They wanted guidance. Impatience expanded like hot air in his chest. These fools were so used to taking his orders they needed him to give them permission to hand him over to the demon.

Disgusted, he started to turn back toward the window, but the sound of someone racking a shotgun made him freeze.

Junior Jessup stood in the doorway leading into the chapel. The aim of his double barrel shotgun took away any question about his goal.

"Now, Junior—"

"Move it." Junior's right eye twitched, but the gun's aim didn't waver.

He threw his arms out to grab the jambs. "You're going to have to kill me here, Junior."

The twitching right eye narrowed and the gun raised a fraction of an inch. "If that's your choice."

"Daddy?" Sarah Jane's scream ripped through the cold night air and through the doors, where it took aim like an ice arrow that embedded itself in his heart.

"Daddy, help!"

"Virgil!"

He turned and looked through the windows, praying it was a trick. It was not.

The monsters circled his wife and daughter. Jack stood on the hood smiling like a snake. "Virgil, we have your women."

Sarah Jane craned her neck. The instant her eyes landed on Jack's ruined face, she let loose a screech that crawled up his spine and exploded at the base of his brain. "Jack! What's—Daddy, what's ... " The rest of her words dissolved into sobs.

Sharon put her arm around their daughter, but tears were streaking down her face too.

His hand tightened until the doorknob dug into his palm.

With everything happening, it hadn't occurred to him to check on Sharon and Sarah Jane.

He closed his eyes and swallowed hard to dislodge the taste of copper on his tongue and the hunk of bile wedged behind his Adam's apple.

Sarah Jane's hysterical babbling continued.

Hard metal at his back indicated that Junior had made his decision. "Time's up."

This is Gethsemane, and my Judas has a shotgun.

"Go on." The lack of emotion in Junior's tone barely registered.

His fingers wouldn't work right. The metal at his back pushed him forward until his face crushed into that red glass.

Finally, the latch gave way and the doors swung open. Cold night air rushed in to surround him.

A hand shoved his back. His feet missed the first step and lurched forward. The world became a riot of color and pain. It happened so fast that he barely registered the fall until he'd skidded to a stop at the bottom. It took an extra couple of seconds before the hot pain on his palms and the sounds of the demon's laughter cut through the shock.

Behind him, Junior's footsteps echoed as he came to help the deacon rise with a surprisingly gentle grip. As he rose from the ground, something hard and cold pressed into his hand.

"Wait until I say," Junior whispered.

Schooling his features, he turned to face the demon, and he held the gun behind his back until Jessup *said*. Sarah Jane sobbed and clung to Sharon as they were each tugged apart by two skeletal creatures who probably had once been members of his church. The demon who looked like Jack stood on the roof of the car like the cock of the walk. His heart pounded so hard, he could barely catch his breath.

Anger and fear, a caustic elixir.

Jack executed a mocking bow. "Now the real party may begin."

58

FAMILY REUNION

Ruby

RUBY WATCHED her neighbors run out of the church. After Junior pushed the deacon out the door, they'd argued about locking the doors tight or going out to help. In the end, it had been Bunk who convinced everyone to go see if they could help by saying, "Deacon Fry's been trying to save us for years."

Now, she stood alone by the altar. She looked down the red-carpeted aisle, and had the strange sensation of staring down a long, empty throat. At the other end, where the church's double doors lay open, a bright light beckoned her.

She shook off the feeling because it was a trick. There was no salvation at the end of that tunnel. She'd seen the monsters outside. They were not angels come to save them.

Daddy's out there. Mama, too.

The thought popped up so unexpected that she jumped a little. When Deacon Fry had told them her daddy was dead, she'd felt almost nothing—except for a small spark of relief. But thinking Mama might be out there somewhere filled her with both hope and dread.

In that moment, she'd realized something simple but earth-shattering. Cotton Barrett was a man who'd spent his whole life blaming the world for his self-hatred. Every time he struck her mama or started a fight or drank until he blacked out, he was begging to be put down. She didn't know exactly what happened to cause his death, but she understood that her relief was tied to knowing he'd finally gotten his wish.

As this simple truth settled into the center of her being, tears sprang to her eyes. She looked up at Jesus up over the altar. Through the watery film of tears, the Savior seemed to shimmer in the red light.

We nail ourselves to our crosses, but we know nothing of forgiveness.

The demon's voice sounded happy. Real joy, she realized, required a total lack of empathy.

The corner of her ear caught the tail end of something else. Not shouting—whispering. She cocked her head and tried to hear them underneath the shouts. But every time she thought she almost caught one, its tail slipped through her grasp. The only thing she knew for sure was that they had been spoken by Granny Maypearl.

She turned and looked back down the tunnel of pews toward the bright lights outside. Knowledge that came from her gut instead of her head told her that Granny Maypearl was out there somewhere with the shouting devil and her dead daddy, and that, if any of them were going to survive whatever was coming, she needed to be there, too.

Instead of going out through the church's front doors, she ran down the hall to a side exit. On her way, she grabbed the axe from the fire emergency box. She felt better with the weight in her hands, safer, but that part of her that had told her Daddy was outside also told her that normal weapons would not win this fight.

Outside, the air was warm and dry despite the earlier lightning. The door dumped her out on the parking lot side of the church. Up ahead familiar trucks lined up side-by-side in the lot. She briefly considered trying to find keys and speed as fast as she could from town. Go get some help.

That thought reminded her of what Bunk said about Peter's earlier escape. Would he bother trying to find the sheriff? She dismissed that idea since he'd left before the real trouble had begun. She imagined him driving blissfully unaware down the winding mountain passes with the window down and the wind blowing through his hair. She hated him for his freedom, for having the choice.

Which brought her back to the trucks. She realized she had a choice, too. Hadn't she always? How many nights had she lain in her bed wishing someone would come along to save her, when she should have been saving herself. She'd had a hundred opportunities to go before now, but she'd never taken them. To leave now, when her sisters and her town needed her most felt like the coward's choice.

She came around the corner of the church building and stopped short.

The being Deacon Fry kept calling "Jack" loomed on the hood of the deacon's Cadillac. He had Jack's build and voice, but his face was not right. It was bruised and rotten, like a piece of overripe fruit.

She searched the faces of the dead-eyed beings around them for something familiar.

She saw Daddy first. His head jutted at an unnatural angle and the side of his neck was a gaping wound. But it was the smile on his face that made her gasp. He'd never once in his living life ever looked that happy.

The reason for his joy supported his weight. Mama's dark hair was matted with leaves and her face—sweet Jesus—the face that had kissed Ruby every night before bed looked like some sort of blasphemy. Worms hung from holes in her once warm skin. The eyes that had looked at her with such love were now as emotionless as a shark's.

The scream began deep inside, down below her heart, and rose like steam from a boiling kettle up her throat before exploding from her mouth.

59

PEERING INTO THE WELL

Deacon Fry

THE GUN in Deacon Fry's hand was a warm, reassuring weight. He stood as straight as he could, just like when he stood before his congregation and delivered the Lord's good news. The demons before him had no interest in lessons from the Bible, but he had to believe that even evil responded to authority.

"I'm here," he announced, "let Sarah Jane go." He couldn't look directly at her or risk weakening his position. But he couldn't block out her sobs or the way she kept chanting, "Daddy, Daddy, Daddy" like a prayer.

"Do you know why you're here, Virgie?"

Something in the pit of him—the deep, dark cave he kept covered up with prayer and good deeds—something shifted, an awakening. It was that infernal nickname. Could the demon read his mind?

"No." He forced the word out like a curse.

Jack laughed, a low, ominous rumble that seemed to bounce

off the hills and return to assault him all over again. When the humor died, the demon spat, "Liar."

He wanted to scream at the demon. How dare something so evil accuse him of sin? "You have me at a disadvantage, Jack."

Sarah Jane's knees buckled, as if hearing the name confirmed what she'd already tried to deny. How could the boy she loved turn into this monster?

A chuckle. "You keep calling me that name. Why?"

A trick question. "Of course. That's who you are—were, Jack Thompson."

The demon leapt off the car's hood and landed without a sound on the sidewalk. "Then you are not just a sinner—you are also a fool."

Nothing made sense. None of it. His carefully constructed world of rules and disciplined living was crafted specifically to prevent this sort of chaos. Hadn't he done everything right?

Not everything.

Hadn't he been a good role model?

Not always.

Hadn't he protected the people of this good town from their own immoral natures for decades?

But not your own.

The demon, who claimed not to be Jack, watched him. Those white eyes had begun to rot since the first time he'd seen it in the woods. The pupils shrank back in the sockets and the skin around had buckled until it was like looking into bottomless wells.

Wells. The well. Oh God, the well.

He couldn't think about that now. Wouldn't.

"Why not?" the demon said. "Why not think about it?"

He opened his mouth to answer before he realized that he hadn't spoken those words out loud. The thing, the demon, the evil thing could read his mind. "I—I can't."

That ruined mouth with its mealworm lips curved into a grotesque smile. "Sure, you can. Think back to that day fifty-seven years ago. Think about walking in the woods with Isaac."

That name entered his head and exploded behind his eyes. The concussion threw him back across the years to that cold winter morning by the river.

60

REVELATION

Winter, 57 years earlier

THE TREES ARE SO tall above him, and he's reminded of the ceiling of the church, which seems to reach right up to heaven. Daddy's always saying that the forest is like church, and that it's a good place to talk to God.

"Virgil! Wait up, Virgie!" Isaac's voice comes from far behind him.

"Dear Lord, please let my little brother learn not to be so annoying. Amen." He continues farther into the woods without calling back.

"Virgil!" Isaac's voice grows more panicked each time. The cold air sharpens the sound.

Good. Maybe he'll get scared enough that he'll learn to stop being such a pain in the rear.

The wintry temperature has the river shuffling sluggishly along the bank. The first snow is expected any day now. He has a sudden, intense longing for the spring, and imagines what this will look like in April, when the dragonflies tap dance along the water's surface. But today, the forest is so cold and quiet, it feels like he's the only thing alive on the whole mountain.

"Virgil!"

Make that him and Isaac. Dumb crybaby Isaac who wets the bed and steals his baseball cards and rips them. Mama's boy Isaac. God's little blessing, she calls him. Why hadn't he been enough to make her happy?

One time, he overheard her and Daddy talking about how something was wrong in her belly so she'd never have another child and then the sound of her tears had cut right through his middle. And then Isaac had come along and you'd think he was the Messiah from all the celebrating and *Praise the Lords* they cried on the day he was born. Did anyone have a party when he came along?

The riverbank squishes under his boots. The leather is wearing away on the side of his toes, allowing cold water to seep into his socks. Mama will lay them near the fire when he gets home. He wiggles his near-numb toes, imagining the moment later when he'll slip the fire-toasty cotton on his feet.

"Come on, Virgil! I'm cold!"

He doesn't respond. He knows he should. Not saying anything makes his chest tight, but he fights the urge to speak. It's nice here all alone in the cold. At home, he has to share his room with the pest Isaac. He never even gets to be alone in the tiny bathroom because Isaac always decides he needs to go, too, and insists on standing in the doorway doing his pee-pee dance like a dumb little kid.

He squats down on the bank. Closer to the river, the cold, clean scent of the water is stronger. He looks upstream and wonders where the water came from and where it's headed. A sudden urge overcomes him to jump in the river and let it carry him along. He closes his eyes and imagines floating on his back with the tree limbs and steely gray sky speeding by overhead. He imagines Isaac reaching the riverbank miles behind him and crying because he suddenly realizes he was so annoying he forced his brother to jump in the river to escape. Mama would be so sad, then. She'd say, "Oh, if only I'd appreciated my darling Virgil more." They'd all think he was dead, but he'd really be off on a grand adventure farther downstream. Maybe the water went all the way down to Florida and he could start a new life living on the beach. He'd never seen a beach, but if Isaac wouldn't be there it had to be a pretty nice place.

He opens his eyes again and stares down into the water. His reflection is broken up and wavy, as if someone broke a mirror and the pieces became liquid. For a terrible moment, he imagines this image is what he really looks like on the inside. But before he can dismiss the idea as silly, a flash of white on the bank catches his eye.

The moth's wings are white as the snow that soon will come to Moon Hollow. He stares at the open wings and tries to understand why he feels so unsettled by its presence. Then he realizes that he's never seen an insect in the winter.

He picks up a stick.

"Virgil!"

He presses the tip gently to one of the wings. The moth flails in the mud, too stuck to dislodge itself. He smiles and pokes it harder.

"Virgil!" The call is growing closer now.

Too fascinated to care, he pins one wing into the mud.

A shadow passes over him, like a cloud blocking out the sun. But there is no sun that day. The sky is a steel blanket covering the moody ridges. He squints up from his project and sees no birds in the sky that might have caused the shadow. Yet the shadow seems to loom over him and with it comes a deep chill that seeps through his coat and sweater and even his skin, down to his bones.

He turns slowly, not because he wants to, but because he has to. What his eyes see, his mind cannot understand. They ache, his eyes, like the time he ignored his teacher's warning and looked directly at a solar eclipse. In that brief second of time, he'd actually seen pain. This is like that, except this time he feels fear, too.

From inside a black hood, a too bright and too dark face of the being seems to be staring back at him, though he can see no eyes or really even a face. But he knows he is being watched, and somehow also that he is being judged.

I am seeing the face of evil.

The words do not register with any accompanying emotion, as if the simple truth of it is absolute and undeniable.

Evil does not move. But he sees it. It makes no sound, yet he hears it. It makes no sense, but he understands.

As if through a long tunnel, he hears the voice of his brother calling his name, but the sound is warped. Everything is warped.

The static enters through his eyes and invades his head until his thoughts are a riot of black and white spots and a sound like a waterfall blocks out his hearing.

IT IS ALREADY DARK when he wakes. Pinpricks of frost stab at his cheeks. His lids flutter open. White flakes dance against the inky night sky. The snow is finally here.

He blinks twice more. Something about the points of white against the black tickles the edges of his memory, but it's elusive and he's so tired and cold he gives up.

Why is he alone in the woods at night?

He sits up slowly. He trembles. The wet ground has pushed moisture into his clothes.

Something solid presses into his side. His hand touches the

familiar curving stone wall. He uses the wall to leverage himself upright. Squinting, he looks around, trying to confirm his location. Sure enough, he can just make out the warning sign bearing the name of the mining company and the large "caution." The sign marks one of the abandoned mines that dot the mountain ridges around Moon Hollow. His daddy told him that he should never play near them holes because if he fell in there'd be no finding him again. He'd always obeyed the rule and he surely had never gone there in the dark. *So why am I here now?*

He limps toward the sign and the opening of the old shaft. There's a smell he doesn't like here. It smells like dirty pennies and rotten leaves. Even snow that's covering up everything and making it seems clean and brand new can't erase that smell. He looks down at his hands. There's something dark there. Something slick. He smells the pennies on his fingers, too. His knuckles are so sore he can barely bend them.

Why am I here?

He backs away from the opening, but his feet stumble over something on the ground. He bends down and picks up the thing that tripped him. It is a shoe. A small shoe.

He knows that if he had a flashlight and he shined it into that shoe, he'd see the neatly written letters of his own last name in the sole. He knows because he'd worn these shoes until they'd pinched his toes and Mama was forced to go to town to buy him a new pair.

Isaac had looked so proud to be stepping into his big brother's old shoes.

His vision swims and the bottom falls out from under his cold, damp feet.

———

HE WALKS FOR HOURS. It gives him time to cry and, once the tears have dried, it gives him time to think. Thinking helps him not feel so alone. It keeps his mind off the snow that rises an inch every hour.

He still isn't sure exactly what happened. The last thing he remembers clearly is the Evil appearing by the riverside and then the static. Flashes of sound and color— screams followed by dreadful silence and alarming flashes of red—break through, but when he focuses on them he starts crying again. So he thinks about what he will say. He repeats his story over and over until it feels like the truth. Until it is his new truth. The truth is important.

The Bible says, "Thou shalt not bear false witness."

He did not witness what happened. He does not know anything except that Evil lives in the woods, and that he does not know where his brother went.

Thou shalt not kill.

He shivers, as if someone chose that moment to dance across his grave. He stops and looks up. There is something about the way the moon catches snowflakes and lights them from inside. The forest, which had been dark when he woke, now glows like the surface of the moon. Overhead, the trees raise their charred branches toward the sky, as if in prayer. He raises his arms, too, and makes his plea and his promise. When the voice tells him his penance, he does not hesitate. He walks to the nearest tree trunk and rhythmically strikes his forehead thirty times into the rough bark.

Afterward, he wipes the blood from his eyes and whispers, "Thank you, Jesus."

Then he pushes himself on through the snow toward his parents, and his new life as an only child and the most devout citizen in all of Moon Hollow.

61

THE ROAD BACK

Peter

GRAVEL PINGED off the truck's undercarriage as he sped away from town. He refused to glance into the rearview mirror.

His headlights illuminated only twenty feet at a time. He flipped the button to engage the brights, but the dark hills absorbed the extra light. His entire world became focused on that bright sliver cutting through the shadows.

He told himself he'd left to find the sheriff, but he had no idea where to start looking. By the time he'd see another car much less the lights of the city the entire population of Moon Hollow would probably be—

Never mind that.

But he got one hell of a story, hadn't he?

It just needed an ending. Maybe he'd conjure a *deus ex machina* to swoop in at the last minute and save everyone. Maybe he'd make the handsome author the hero.

The truck bounced over a dip in the road and its tires slammed down hard on the other side and skidded before grabbing asphalt again. The impact jarred him out of his daydream. There was no God in this machine, and he was certainly no one's hero.

He was a coward.

Something wasn't right in Moon Hollow. He'd convinced himself that the problem was the angry mob headed toward the church when he left, but he couldn't get rid of the image of Cotton Barrett in bloodstained clothes shuffling down the center of Main Street with a smile on his face. The gash on Peter's forehead throbbed. Where had that lightning come from? Why was Granny Maypearl so scared when Deacon Fry decided to cancel to Decoration Day? No, something wasn't right.

He pressed his foot on the gas and took a curve too fast. The tires gripped the road and carried him safely around the bend. He needed to get far away. Once he was off that damned mountain he could find a motel and lock himself inside with a six-pack so he could drink away his urge to think about what was happening behind him.

On second thought, no, he wouldn't stop. He'd go back to Raleigh the more direct route, not through scenic Asheville but through Greensboro. If he kept his foot down on the gas he could make it in less than six hours—home before sunrise.

For some reason the thought of the rising sun filled him with dread. No, he liked the dark. The shadows hid his shame.

The headlights reached through the inky night, yearning like a hand out of a grave. It touched tree stumps and rocks and things that looked like bent human forms but couldn't be because who would be out in the woods this late?

He didn't realized that the twin silver circles in the middle of the road weren't coins but eyes until he was almost on top of the animal. His foot punched the brakes, but they protested and locked up.

The truck skidded sideways toward the place where the road

gave way to air and the air gave way to gravity. He might have screamed. He kept his foot glued to that brake pedal and cried out a prayer that only elder gods could understand. The shock of time slowing down. Noticing everything and nothing at once —the lights shining on the small bear, the sound of crunching gravel, the whack-a-mole thumping of his heart. He braced himself for oblivion, was sure that at any second those squealing tires would slide right off the road and carry him down the mountain to crash in the valley below.

But oblivion never came. A plume of dust rose around Bunk's old truck, blocking out the light and the dark, trapping Peter inside with his heart pounding like wild drums. He gulped air and chanted nonsense to calm himself.

When the dust cleared, the bear he'd been trying to avoid hitting still sat in the center of the road. Even with all the racket, the thing still hadn't moved. Despite its bravery, a bear that small could never survive on its own—especially if it made a habit of sitting its ass in the center of winding mountain roads in the dark.

"Dumb animal," he muttered, not really meaning it. He was glad he didn't hit the cub. Of course he was. He could have done without the near-death experience, though. "Gonna get yourself killed."

The cub sat on its round bottom in the road, looking up at him with those unblinking nickel eyes.

Peter froze. Now that the panic had subsided, he could remember what happened earlier that day, the argument between Junior and Ruby on Cemetery Hill. Junior accusing Ruby of releasing his bear, and her standing there looking like defiance personified.

The truth slammed into Peter like a revelation. This was Ruby's bear.

He started to laugh, but the sound ended on a sob.

When he stopped crying, he opened the door and went to collect the cub. The animal didn't fight him, and settled into the truck's bench, as if it belonged there. Peter put the old truck in Drive and turned it back toward Moon Hollow. The bear made a chuffing noise that sounded a lot like approval.

THE RIVER SONG

Granny Maypearl

FROM HER POSITION on the street corner, crouching behind a trashcan, Granny Maypearl listened to the deacon's story. She should have used the distraction to get to work on the proper rites, but once she realized what he was talking about she couldn't help but listen. Despite her nausea at hearing the details of what had really happened to poor Isaac, she also felt oddly vindicated.

She remembered that time like it was yesterday. Virgil had been three years behind her at school, but back then all the kids had been taught in the same small school building. Unlike the rest of their classmates, who cowered under Virgil's bullying and accepted his story, she'd never believed his claims.

They'd found him near sunrise on Cemetery Hill. All the men in town had spread out just after dark when the boys hadn't returned. Granny, who, at the time, was called "Maypole" by the school bullies, remembered how her mother had gotten on the party line with all the other mothers to cluck like chickens about how the sky was falling. Wild theories had been tossed out. Her mother believed the boys had accidentally come across a bear's den and disturbed an ornery mama bear from her winter's nap. Other people thought maybe a mountain lion had gotten them or that they'd fallen in the river.

When Virgil had returned with that terrible wound on his forehead that never quite healed right and a story about how he'd tripped and passed out, the fathers had gone back out in the woods to try to find poor Isaac. According to Virgil, the last time he'd seen his brother was down by the river.

When daylight came, they discovered footprints down by the water's edge—along with a single, small shoe and some blood mixed into the snow.

The town went into mourning for months. Virgil was treated not as a hero, but as a martyr of sorts, which to Maypearl's mind was far more dangerous.

Not long after they'd held a memorial service for Isaac—a funeral wasn't possible without the body—she'd gone out to the woods and down to the spot by the river. She'd sat on the bank for what felt like hours, listening to the river's song. Usually the water greeted her with banjos and lively fiddles, the water's traveling music. But that day, it was all violins and cellos in minor keys.

It had taken longer than usual that day for the river to open up enough to sing its song, and when it did, Maypearl surely did wish it hadn't. Rivers—or mountains for that matter—sang in emotions that, when heard by the right heart, had more meaning than words. And that day, the emotion lyrics were all about betrayal and mourning and unbearable memories of pain.

Even though Maypearl had suspected Virgil hadn't told the whole truth about what really happened with Isaac, she knew better than to manipulate the river's song to mean what she wanted it to mean. After all, Isaac's drowning could have been the source of the river's dirge. So she sang a song of her own and sent it down the river for it to swirl among the eddies and find the river's heart.

The next time the river responded, the song wasn't strings, but menacing percussion, crashing symbols—the river's anger song. The song pounded like a savage heartbeat. She'd never felt fury that strong, chaotic and powerful, like a sudden thunderstorm. The worst part was the emotions arrived with a clear feeling that the vessel for all that rage had been Virgil Fry.

When the waters fell blessedly silent again, she sat for a long time thinking about what she'd learned. The song's terrible energy didn't fit with the idea that Isaac had simply tripped and fallen into the river. At best, he was pushed. At worst, well—

The worst wasn't comprehensible.

As much as she disliked Virgil Fry and his hordes of followers, she couldn't believe he was directly responsible for Isaac's death. She preferred to think that what happened here was a tragic accident.

The other thing she realized was that the river hadn't answered part of her question. She'd specifically asked it to reveal the location of Isaac's little body. She wasn't sure how she'd tell Reverend and Mrs. Fry if she found out, but she thought at least in this she could offer some comfort. She couldn't imagine not being able to know for certain he was dead and always wondering if there was more they could have done. Some other place they could have looked.

The river had never ignored one of her questions before. Deep down, she knew this meant that the river did not know where Isaac was, which meant he'd never fallen into the river at all.

As the years passed, her copper bright suspicions about Virgil had patinated into general distrust. She didn't know if he ever guessed that she knew he'd lied, but he'd done just about everything in his power to doom her to always be on the edges of Moon Hollow society. In the end, the joke was on him because she preferred life on the fringes. Meanwhile, the center of Moon Hollow, the man who railed against man's sinful nature at his pulpit every Sunday, had committed the foulest sin possible.

If she hadn't been so horrified by the truth, she might have felt smug. Instead, she felt sad and scared.

The dead had risen to punish the entire town for Deacon Fry's sins.

63

UNBURDENED

Deacon Fry

FOR DECADES, Deacon Fry's secret had weighed him down like a stowaway hiding behind his heart. The purge had been painful, yes, but now, he was alone in his own skin for the first time since that awful wintry night.

He closed his eyes and tried to treasure the inner silence, but the demon who'd been vexing him for weeks was now lecturing him on sin.

He was no fool. He was not an innocent man, but he was a penitent one, which was more than most people could say.

He lifted a hand to touch the scar on his forehead. He'd stared at that puckered skin so many times over the years, not shying from its ugliness because it was proof of his atonement.

"Are you listening?" Jack said.

He opened his eyes and looked into the milky pupils of his enemy. With his soul laid bare on the steps of his beloved church, he felt invincible. They had a pact, he and God. It had been the good Lord who'd made sure Junior had a gun to place in his hands. It was the good Lord who made him admit his greatest sin as a sort of baptism that would allow him to rise victorious over the devils on his doorstep. Just like his great-granddaddy Alodius Fry, he would face down this evil and save his town. He just needed an opening.

"I'm listening," he said.

The demon paused, as if surprised by the lack of fear in his response. But like all devils, he was too proud to believe a mere man posed any threat to him. The demon's hubris would be his downfall.

"I have a question," Deacon Fry said. "If you don't mind."

The demon's head tilted to the left, but he didn't say no.

"Why now? After all this time, why am I being punished now?"

The demon chuckled. "Justice has no statute of limitations, old man."

"I suppose not. But why are you my judge? Wasn't I kind to you, Jack?" He tried to smile at the rotten face of the boy he'd once known. "Didn't I help you get your job? Didn't I give you my blessing to marry Sarah Jane once you had some money saved up?"

"For a soul to ascend, the body must be buried with the proper rites."

"Jack had a proper funeral. I saw to it myself."

Instead of answering, the demon looked him deep in his eyes and showed him a series of images. Jack in the mines, looking impossibly young and out of place. The older miners playing a joke that got the boy turned around and lost. Him taking wrong turn after wrong turn. Tripping and falling down a side shaft. Heavy weight slamming into him. Red eyes in the dark. Pain, fear, and then nothing.

When the images ceased, he shook off the lingering memory of Jack's terror. "You—what?"

The demon leaned forward and whispered, "When a soul is unleashed on a dark moon, it can take any shape it wants, *brother.*"

A scream ripped through the air.

The demon's attention jerked away. Deacon Fry should have taken his shot. He should have emptied the chambers of that gun right into the demon's black heart. But the word "brother" ricocheted through his skull, creating its own shrapnel. *Brother.*

He blinked once, twice. Swallowed hard. Looked at the demon and, for the first time, saw through the scars and bruises, through the decay, and recognized the somber brown eyes that had always looked too old for his brother's young face.

"Isaac?"

64

HOPELESS

Ruby

THE SCREAM CAME from deep inside Ruby, and as it rose, it gained momentum and so much power she couldn't dream of stopping it. It was an awakening of sorts, that sound. It signaled the moment she could no longer pretend that everything was going to work out. That sort of optimism belonged to girls whose mamas baked cookies and didn't have bruises on their cheekbones. It was for girls whose mamas were alive.

Ruby's mama wasn't alive, but she was standing there, anyway. Her time underground had not been kind to her beauty. The bruises of living were gone, but decayed skin and milky pupils had taken their place. The pretty yellow dress Ruby had chosen for Mama to wear for her funeral was in tatters, a victim of the struggle to escape the coffin.

Her daddy, also not alive, slumped against Mama's side. The wound at his neck no longer bled freely, but it glistened red and angry in the moonlight.

She couldn't speak and she was all out of screams.

"Ruby." The voice that came out of that putrid mouth sounded like Rose Barrett was talking through a sewer pipe. "Ruby, darlin', it's Mama."

Ruby stumbled back with her hands raised. "No. N-no."

Her daddy's head rolled back so he could look at her, too. His rapidly bluing skin contrasted with the yellow of his nicotine-stained teeth as he grinned at her. "She's home, Ruby. Mama's home. Just like we wanted."

"I didn't want this. Not this."

Mama limped forward. "Come here, little one."

The wind picked up and brought with it the coffin liquor scent of the grave. Bile burned the back of her throat, but the rest of her froze.

"Come to your mama and we'll be a family again." That voice crawled into her ears and skittered into her brain, where it burrowed into her gray matter. "We'll be together forever, Rubybug."

She struggled to move, to run, anything. She'd had nightmares before where she'd been frozen in terror, but she never knew until then that real terror was so much worse. Real terror wasn't one-dimensional. It attacked all the senses: the darkly sweet scent of death, the flavor of copper on her tongue, the sound of her pulse thrashing in her ears, the icy dread coating her skin, the sight of her corpse-parents lumbering toward her with deadly intent.

Her knees gave out. If she'd had any hope left, it would have given out, too.

She looked up past the heads of her mama and daddy to the crooked cross looming over them. She'd always found the warped symbol of Moon Hollow's faith sort of whimsical, like something from a fairy tale. But right then, she saw it for what it really was—a symbol of abandonment. There was no God in

Moon Hollow. Maybe there never was, but if He'd ever been there, He'd abandoned them long ago.

"Ruby," Mama sighed. She smiled, exposing blackened gums and gray teeth. The tatters of her yellow dress exposed swatches of gray flesh underneath.

"Mama?" she whispered.

"Yes, darlin'. Mama's here. It'll only hurt a little."

She closed her eyes and let herself believe it would be better to surrender.

"Ruby!" The new voice sounded angry and afraid.

She opened her eyes and looked around, but all she could see was that yellow dress and all that blood on her daddy's shirt.

"Ruby! God, no. Hold on, Rubybug!"

"Stop her," Mama said.

Daddy turned with a growl, and as he moved it allowed her to see that Granny Maypearl was running across the street toward them. She had something in her right hand that was letting off plumes of smoke, and she hefted a large bag in her other.

Mama drew closer to Ruby, blocking her view of Granny. "When we're done," Mama said, "we'll go find Sissy and Jinny."

Ruby blinked. "Sissy and Jinny?"

That rotten smile again. "We'll be one big happy family. Forever."

A sound broke through the haze of fear and confusion. She saw her daddy moving toward her granny, who stood her ground on the sidewalk in front of the church. Holding her smudge stick high like the Statue of Liberty's torch, she sang in a loud, clear voice. The words of her song didn't sound like English. They sounded older than that, ancient, but even without recognizing them with her ears, Ruby knew them by heart.

Pain bit into the flesh of her arm. She looked down to see her mama's hand with its exposed bones clawing at her. "No singing," she hissed. "No songs."

Granny's voice got louder, and Daddy started groaning and writhing where he stood. The wind picked up and thunder boomed somewhere far off in the mountains.

Ruby ripped her arm from Mama's grasp. She stumbled forward two steps, but Granny held up a free hand to halt her advance.

Daddy's body was dancing in bizarre jerky movements that reminded Ruby of her mama's death throes a month earlier. She looked at Mama, who had started moaning, as if to drown out the song.

Most of the town had gathered on the front steps of the church, and surrounding them were more of the dead things—most of whom had been dead so long they were little more than skeletons dressed in rags. Deacon Fry was staring at the demon who looked like Jack Thompson, whose attention was on Granny Maypearl as she sang to Daddy.

Time slowed. The words of Granny's song dissolved into the wind that made Ruby's hair whip around her face like a white flag. Her mama lunged at her, those milky eyes flaring. Granny Maypearl's song reached its crescendo. Daddy's body convulsed once, twice before his body exploded into a cloud of ashes.

Ashes to ashes, dust to dust.

The demon took three steps. Behind him, Deacon Fry pulled his hand from behind his back.

An animal sound beside her, a blur of motion. Mama stumbled toward the ashes that used to be Cotton Barrett.

It all happened at once.

Ruby stumbled after her mama.

A terrible explosion that could only be a gunshot ripped through the chaos.

The bullet went through Jack's body and continued its deadly trajectory right into another target.

Mama raised her face to scream at the sky over Daddy's ashes. A flash of blinding lights from the road, the screech of tires.

The truck jumped the curb.

Ruby ran to help the too still body on the sidewalk.

The truck barreled right into Mama and kept going until it pinned her body between the fender and the marquee church sign, which read, "Christ the Redeemer Church: Jesus Loves You."

In the aftermath, the only sounds were the angry ticking of the truck's engine, the hiss of steam from under the crumpled hood, and the hot sobs ripping from Ruby's chest as she fell to her knees beside her wounded grandmother.

65

GOD IS A BULLET

Deacon Fry

THE BULLET. The bullet went right through—

"Oh God, no." Deacon Fry fell to his knees. "Please, no, no, no."

Chaos all around him. The women were crying and screaming. Bunk and Earl went to help Peter West out of the truck. But the good deacon's attention was on the tragedy unfolding on the sidewalk, where Ruby knelt over her grandmother's body.

The demon—oh, good Lord, please don't let that really be Isaac—watched the madness with a smile on his face. Only that ruined face he'd come to know and loathe was no longer that of Jack Thompson. Now, he was shorter and younger and the side of his head was a bloody crater.

His hands wouldn't stop shaking.

"Help!" Ruby screamed. "Someone help her!"

Peter West broke from the men helping him and ran toward her. In his wake, he left a confused Bunk and Earl staring between Peter's retreating back and the tiny bear cub yowling in the front seat of the truck.

"Deacon?" Junior said from near his shoulder. "Why did you do that?"

There was no sense pretending he didn't know what Junior meant. "You saw me. I was trying to get that damned devil!" He pushed himself off the ground and turned to face Junior. "I didn't know the bullet would—" He cut himself off because giving voice to what had happened would make it real.

Desperate for support from someone, he turned toward Edna. "You saw me, right?"

But she wouldn't look at him either. Instead she waddled off to go see if she could help Ruby and Peter.

"Daddy?" Sarah Jane whispered. Her voice sounded too young, like when she was little and woke up from a scary dream and needed him to check under the bed for monsters.

"You killed your brother," she said, "and now you killed Granny Maypearl." The words were spoken as a verdict.

"No," he shook his head. "I didn't kill anyone."

The little boy with the bashed-in head cackled.

"You said you killed Isaac." Sharon looked at him like he was a stranger. "That's why all of this is happening."

"It was the evil," he said, desperate. "The evil thing did it." He pointed toward Isaac. "I didn't kill him."

"The evil is you." With that, his wife and daughter turned their backs on him and walked toward the church.

Isaac sing-songed in a mocking tone, "Virgil is evil."

"Shut up! Why didn't you just stay down where you belonged?"

"You'd best hand me that gun, Deacon Fry," Junior said.

He frowned at the man and then looked at the gun in his hand.

"It's over," Junior continued, "you've done enough damage."

"You've doomed them, Virgil," Isaac said.

He looked up. "I was trying to save them. Us."

Junior sneered at him. "You kilt that old woman, too."

"I was trying to stop them." His voice sounded wild.

"Granny Maypearl was stopping that devil with her song and you shot her."

He felt like he was going crazy. "I shot Jack—I mean Isaac."

"No, you beat Isaac," Isaac said. "And you sent Jack down into the mines."

"That wasn't my fault. I didn't know!"

"You need to atone for your sins, Deacon," Junior said.

Deacon Fry pulled the gun to his chest and backed away, shaking his head. "No, it's them that's evil, Junior. Can't you see it? They're turning you against me."

Bunk and Earl and several of the other townsfolk were closing in on him with determined expressions on their faces.

Father, forgive them, for they know not what they do.

His heart sank and the gun in his hand was a heavy, inevitable weight.

"Save them, Virgil," Isaac said. "Save them."

He glanced at his little brother and remembered the day when he'd been born. It had been a spring day, and Mama and Daddy acted like Isaac was the Savior. That had been the first time Virgil felt the white hot arrival of his rage. He realized now Isaac had been the snake that introduced evil to Virgil's Eden. He thought he'd disposed of that evil on that cold day fifty-seven years earlier, but now, by some mystery of God's design, the snake was back and the only way to purify his Eden once again was to make the ultimate sacrifice.

"The time has come for revelation," he whispered.

He lifted the gun to his temple.

Isaac looked into his eyes and smiled.
"Lord, forgive me."
Deacon Fry pulled the trigger.

66

LAMENTATIONS

Ruby

THE CREPE-PAPER SKIN of Granny's cheeks was the color of the mountain mist. The paleness made the blood glistening on her lips seem impossibly red.

"Ruby." The word was barely above a whisper. "It's over, darlin'."

"No." She hated how petulant the word sounded.

Peter had taken off the shirt he'd been wearing, ripped it two, and handed it to her. "Use this."

The blood covering her hands nearly soaked the fabric before she could place it over the wound on her grandmother's left breast.

"Pressure," Peter said in an apologetic tone.

"Sorry, Granny." She pushed hard.

A gasp rushed from Granny's mouth. "S'all right." She swallowed audibly. "Listen now, girl, 'cause we ain't got long."

The way the words slurred from her bloody lips made Ruby's insides feel like they were coated in the menthol chest salve Mama used to spread on her chest when she had the croup.

Peter took her hand and squeezed it. His hand felt big and warm, which was good because she felt so small and cold.

"You're gonna have to be real brave, Rubybug. There ain't no one else who can do what needs doing but you."

She shook her head. "I'm afraid."

"I know, darlin'. Being scared is just your mind trying to protect you, but you got to ignore it and listen to your heart instead. Your heart knows the truth."

The weight of all those years that she'd been robbed of pressed down on her—the years they'd already lost and those yet to come. So much time wasted.

Tears spilled freely now and distorted her vision. She swiped at them, not wanting anything to get in the way of seeing Granny's face. "I love you, Granny Maypearl."

"Ah, Rubybug, I love you, too. Ain't nothin' ever gone change that, you hear?"

She wiped away more tears. "I don't know what to do."

"When the time comes, you will. That heart of yours been hurt real bad, but it's not so broke it can't sing again."

All this talk of hearts and songs while her grandmother bled out in the street made something inside Ruby snap. "You're wrong!"

"Ruby." Peter's warning tone only made her angrier. She shrugged his steadying hand from her shoulder.

"I didn't stop listening to the mountain. It stopped talking to me. If it wanted to save us it already would have."

As she spoke, a gunshot exploded followed by the sounds of screams. Peter jerked and cursed as he looked toward the front of the church, but Granny tightened her grip on Ruby's hands and captured all of her attention.

Granny wanted her to believe that faith was enough to save

them. But she'd lived her whole life watching Deacon Fry use faith to control the people of Moon Hollow, and where had it gotten them all? The way she saw it, Granny's faith and the deacon's were two sides of the same warped coin. Either way you flipped it, it was a loser's bet.

"You're going to leave me just like Mama did, only this time it'll be worse. Mama left me alone with Daddy and his fists, but you're leaving me alone to face something no one can handle."

Granny had listened to her up until that point, but now, despite her obvious pain, that old steel came into her expression. "Hush up and listen to me, young lady. You don't know as much as you think you do. The women of our family been saving this town's goose for more years than you can count, and as long as we been saving it, the men of this town been taking the credit. Alodius Fry?" She snorted. "It was my great-grandmother, Yona, who fought back the devil that bent that cross. Don't tell me that you're facing something you can't handle. Just 'cause you ain't done something before don't mean you can't do it now." Granny's cold hand found hers. "You got strong blood in your veins and a heart that's filled with songs you ain't sung yet. You just gotta get out of your own way." A coughing fit interrupted whatever she'd been about to say.

Peter moved in and placed a hand on Granny's forehead. "Easy now." He looked at Ruby and shook his head, a warning that time was almost up.

Ruby took a deep, centering breath. She was scared as hell, but she refused to send her grandmother to the beyond the same way she'd sent her Mama—begging her to do something she had no power to do. To stay and protect her.

She wrapped both hands around Granny's and leaned in close. She placed a kiss on Granny's forehead. "Thank you for believing in me." Granny's pupils were so large it seemed to

Ruby that she could see the whole universe inside there. "I'll try to do you proud."

Granny's chest pumped up and down rapidly, almost as if someone was opening and closing a bellows too quickly. Ruby leaned down to catch the words from her lips. "Own your magic."

A rush of breath rattled against Ruby's cheek, cooling the tears. The erratic beat under her hand stuttered and then stopped altogether.

Granny Maypearl was no more.

HOMEWARD

Granny Maypearl

STEEL BANDS TIGHTEN around her chest. Sweet Ruby's tears drip onto her cheeks, but she doesn't complain. If she has to go, best to do it with the baptism of salt water to send her off.

Oh, Ruby, I have so much to say. So much more I wanted to teach you, but we've run out of time.

It feels like someone is playing hopscotch on her heart.

Ruby is closer now. Good, words require too much air. She whispers the words her own grandmother said to her on the day she initiated Maypearl into the art—the initiation she was never able to give her Ruby. "Own your magic."

The last of her precious air rushes from her, along with her soul. *Now I return to you, Mother.*

She caresses Ruby's cheek for the final time as she rises.

She is light, now. She rises like a warm breeze on the night air. Above, Mother Moon glows bright to welcome her to the beyond. Below, Ruby's grief is a lonely song.

Moon Hollow unrolls beneath her. There, the house where

she was born during the worst blizzard on record. Over there, the general store, where she'd buy penny candy with her allowance. Farther, the hill where Ian first told her he loved her. Up on the ridge, the first house they'd lived in as man and wife —the home where they'd made her sweet Rose. And there, looming over it all, was Cemetery Hill, where just that afternoon she'd placed a small white anchoring stone on his grave.

Goodbye, town. Goodbye, hills. Goodbye, beloved river and whispering pines.

And there, beyond the town and the hills and everything, the Blue Ridge Mountains stretch into the Appalachian range.

The supple curve of the horizon spreads out like the hip of a lover. The dark of the eastern seaboard fades across the Atlantic to the bright line of sun heralding the tomorrow that Moon Hollow might never see.

She looks up at the stars and the great beyond, where wait the open arms of her mother and grandmother, all the way back to great-grandma Yona and her mother, the beloved Gigahu, Galilani.

Finally, she is home.

PROMISES

Peter

RUBY PLACED a final kiss on Granny Maypearl's forehead. Peter helped her rise and then knelt to cover the body with his jacket. He should have come back sooner. Hell, he never should have left. She'd asked him to stay but he'd refused to listen. "I'm sorry," he whispered. "I'll watch out for her."

He wasn't sure how he'd accomplish it, but he meant his promise. The least he could do was make sure Ruby had a fighting chance of walking away from this—-whatever the hell this was.

By the time he turned around, she had marched off.

"Ruby?" He grabbed Granny's bag of supplies and jogged after her.

She didn't stop to wait for him. Next to Deacon Fry's body, a boy laughed and pointed. Peter had seen the deacon kill himself while Ruby said goodbye to Granny Maypearl. The last thing she needed now was to see another corpse.

He caught up with her and took her arm. "Hold on."

She didn't fight him and allowed him to turn her body away from the crowd. "What?"

He looked at her, really looked. Her bottom lip was pinned between her teeth and her eyes wouldn't quite meet his. "You okay?"

She raised a hand and slapped him so hard his head whipped to the side. "You left us."

He raised a hand to his burning cheek. "I did, but now I'm back." He nodded toward the truck. "And I brought your bear."

Her mouth fell open and her eyes filled with tears. "Why? Why did you bring her back here? She was safe." Ruby beat at his chest but he grabbed her hands and pinned them to her sides. "She was safe." She fell into him, sobbing.

Peter looked over her head toward the animated corpses closing in on the group near the deacon's body. He might write about demons and ghosts for a living, but he'd always been a skeptic when it came to stories of the paranormal in the real world. To him, people who believed in haints and hauntings were more likely to need the help of a psychologist rather than that of a psychic. But in the last fifteen minutes, he'd run over the corpse of Ruby's mother and watched her grandmother sing a magical song that made the corpse of Ruby's father explode into ashes. Thing like that tended to make a man reassess his beliefs.

"Listen to me," he said, "there's a reason that bear stopped me on the road as I was trying to escape." He put his hands on her shoulders and pushed her back enough to look into her eyes. "For some reason, that bear needed to be here and so did I. I suspect it has something to do with helping you, but we'll never know if you don't get ahold of yourself and do what Granny Maypearl told you to do."

Ruby sniffed and shook her head. "It's no use. She was wrong. I don't have any power."

"How do you know if you've never tried?"

She laughed bitterly. "I've been trying to hear the mountain's song for weeks. It's gone, Peter. I can't sing its song like Granny did."

He looked her in the eye. "Then don't try to sing the mountain's song. Sing your own."

She opened her mouth to argue, but the shout of a shotgun ripped through the air. Peter looked over in time to see Junior Jessup aim the shotgun at an approaching skeleton and pull off another shot. The skeleton exploded into a cloud of bone fragments.

"Everybody in the church," Junior shouted.

"Let's go." While Junior provided cover fire, Peter pushed Ruby ahead of him toward the church steps. On the way, he grabbed the bear from the truck.

69

MAMA'S SONG

Ruby

ONCE INSIDE THE CHURCH, Peter handed Ruby Granny's bag. "Maybe something in here will help."

She doubted it. How could anything help now?

The bag was filled with a collection of small jars filled with herbs and a random assortment of snail shells and what appeared to be beetles. She shook her head. "I don't know how to use any of this stuff."

He placed a hand on her shoulder. "Remember, she had a chance to tell you the secret recipe if there was a potion that would win the day. Instead, she told you to use your own power."

She opened her mouth to tell him Granny hadn't been in her right mind at that moment—she didn't have any power at all—but the church doors flew open. Junior stumbled inside, dragging Bunk and Nell with him. Behind them, Lettie and Earl Sharps came through. Sharps slammed the doors and slid the lock home.

Everyone talked at once until Peter whistled. "Hold on, where's everyone else?"

"There ain't anyone else!" Sharps shouted.

"We're here." They all turned to see Sharon and Sarah Jane enter from the side room Reverend Peale used to use to prepare for services. "Virgil?" she asked.

Earl shook his head.

She took a shuddering breath and mouthed something that was probably a prayer, and Sarah Jane deflated sobbing into her mother's side.

"Those things are gonna kill us," Edna said. "I just know it."

"Like hell." Junior lifted the barrel of his shotgun to his shoulder. "We just need ammo."

Lettie wiped the back of her hand across her forehead. It left a red streak of Deacon Fry's blood. "Them bullets ain't done a lick of good besides slow 'em down, Junior."

"What do you want us to do then? Sit in here until they find a way in?" Junior asked.

Bear chose that moment to growl from his spot at Ruby's feet.

"What the hell?" Junior said, coming to investigate. Once he saw the bear, he cursed and his face went a dangerous shade of red. "You gotta lotta nerve, girl."

"Leave her alone," Ruby said. "She's not hurting anyone."

"Maybe we should throw her out to them devils, huh?"

"That ain't a devil," Nell shouted. "That's my Jack." The woman burst into tears, and crumpled into one of the pews.

Junior lunged toward the bear.

"Get away from her!" Ruby wrapped her arms around the bear, who snuggled into her throat.

"You little bitch," he shot back. "If it weren't for your daddy none of this would be happening. Maybe we should throw you out there, too."

Peter stepped in front of Ruby and the bear, blocking them from the heat of Junior's anger. "Fighting each other won't accomplish anything. Back down."

Junior spit on the floor. "Who put you in charge, author man?"

"I'm not in charge, Mr. Jessup. I'm just trying to be sure we don't kill each other before they do."

Lettie came forward. "You heard the man, Junior. Sit your ass down." She turned to Peter. "What you thinking?"

To Ruby, he said, "Granny seemed to think there was a way to send them back where they came from."

"Oh no," Junior said, "I ain't taking part in no devil magic."

Lettie snorted. "What the hell do you think them things are, Junior?"

That shut him right up.

"Ruby, do you think you can try, if we can create a diversion?" Peter asked.

She lifted her head from the musty fur. "Try what?"

"To sing."

Junior made a sound, but Lettie barked a low word to shut him up.

She threw up her hands. The movement scared the cub, who cried and scampered away down the pew. "There has to be some other way."

Silence greeted her words. Her chest felt tight, like her ribs were constricting her lungs, keeping them from drawing in enough air.

"Your grandmother seemed to think you had some magic in ya," Edna said.

"She wanted to believe that, but Granny didn't know me. We didn't see each other for ten years. Truth is she needed to believe I had her power so she could die in peace."

A new voice jumped in and said, "That's not true."

Ruby spun around to see Sarah Jane, her face tear-stained and swollen, coming forward. "You're lying, Ruby, and you know it."

She stood to face down her old enemy. "Shut up, Sarah Jane. You don't know nothing about it."

The other girl crossed her arms and glared at Ruby. "I saw you."

"What?"

"One day down by the river when we were about eight. I was out collecting flowers and you were there, down by the old red tree. I saw you, Ruby. I saw you."

The blood drained from Ruby's face. "Shut up."

"What did you see?" Lettie demanded.

Sarah Jane turned to address the whole group. "She had a dead bird in her hand—a blue jay, wasn't it?"

Ruby clenched her jaw and refused to answer. She was too busy trying to figure out how she could have missed Sarah Jane watching her.

"Anyway, Ruby was singing to the bird and at first I thought maybe it wasn't dead, but I swear it didn't move at all. But then the wind picked up and the river started rushing louder. The Ruby lifted her hands and threw the bird in the air and it flew. The bird flew on its own."

"Oh come on," Junior said, "You expect us to believe that girl brought a dumb bird back to life. It probably was just sick."

Sarah Jane shook her head. "I would not lie in the house of the Lord, Junior Jessup. Not about something like this." She rounded on Ruby. "I knew then you were a freak, just like your grandma."

"Sarah Jane," Sharon said in a scandalized tone.

"She is, Mama, and you know it."

Ruby wanted to deny it. She wanted to call Sarah Jane a bully and go rock in a corner until she woke up from this terrible nightmare. But she couldn't deny it or run from the truth. "That's why you were always so mean to me? Because you saw that?"

"I told my daddy about it and he said it was because all the women in your family is touched."

"They may be touched, but the only one of all of us whose managed to make a dent in the monsters outside was Granny Maypearl with her singin'," Bunk said. "And Peter there with my truck," he shot Peter a wry smile.

"Sorry about that," Peter mumbled.

Bunk waved his metal pincer to dismiss the apology. "My point is if what Sarah Jane is saying is true then Ruby does have some of her granny's magic in her."

"It doesn't matter," Ruby said. "Ever since my mama died I haven't been able to do any of that stuff."

The bear on the pew mewled.

"The mountain doesn't sing to me anymore. That was the real source of Granny's magic—being able to hear nature talking to her."

The bear cried louder.

"Hush, Bear," she snapped.

"Ruby," Peter said, "when did you start hearing the bear cry?"

She frowned at his odd question. "First time I remember it was the morning after Mama died." She'd never forget waking up with her head on a pillow wet from tears to the sound of that pitiful little cub hollering for its mama.

Peter exchanged a look with Bunk and Lettie. "Did it ever occur to you that maybe the mountain was still singing to you but just in a different way."

"What?" She paused. "You mean through the bear? That's ridiculous."

The bear growled.

She tilted her head and really looked at the cub's face. Its eyes were still crusty and the body too thin, but she couldn't deny feeling a strong pull towards the creature, a responsibility.

"I know you're scared," Peter said, "we all are. But if there's a chance that you have that magic somewhere inside you, we've got to try."

She pulled her gaze away from the cub's sweet face and looked at Peter's solemn one. "How?"

"You're going to have to try to sing."

Instead of balking, she asked herself what Granny Maypearl would say.

Be brave.

She took a deep breath, pulling the air deep inside and then releasing all of it—the fear and the regrets and the confusion over the crazy things she'd seen that night. She released her anger at her daddy and her rage at her mama for leaving her. She let go of her grief, too, but just for now. Later, if she survived, she'd honor Granny's memory properly. For now, she needed to focus on being present so she'd have a chance at a future.

When she breathed in a second time, her chest felt more open, like she'd made some space in there once more for hope. "I'm going to need some music."

Bunk winked. "Now, that I think we can manage."

While Bunk ran off with Earl Sharps to rustle up some instruments, and Lettie and Edna went to go comfort Sharon, Ruby walked over to Sarah Jane.

"What do you want?" the other girl snapped.

"To thank you."

Sarah Jane's expression became guarded, like she suspected a trap. "For what?"

"For reminding me that I'm a freak. I'd forgotten there for a while."

"I don't know what's so good about that."

Ruby smiled at the girl who she once believed had everything in the world. "You might be pretty and your daddy might have been powerful, but you've got an ugly heart, Sarah Jane Fry. And the truth is, when things need fixing, it's never the mean, pretty girl who gets things done. It's always the weird girl with the good heart who saves the day."

"You been reading too many fairy tales, freak." Despite her toxic words, her bottom lip trembled. "None of us is going to survive the night."

It must have been hard to hide all that fear behind such a hateful mask.

"Maybe not," Ruby said, "but if I'm going to die anyway, I'm not going out like a coward."

THIRTY MINUTES LATER, Sharps called from the window. "They're moving around again!"

While the rest of them worked, he'd stood watch and reported that about every five minutes or so, the undead would shift their positions. The most troubling report had been that the little demon boy who called himself Isaac was nowhere to be seen.

Bunk took up the fiddle and looked to her. "What do you want us to play?"

Beside him, Lettie had a banjo in her lap. They'd found the instruments in an old storage room from back before Deacon Fry took over the church and banned all music, except the religious piano tunes allowed at Sunday services.

Ruby sat on the steps of the altar and looked out over the church, where people were busy making makeshift defense weapons in case she failed. "Do you know the 'River Song'?"

"I'm afraid I don't know it."

She wasn't unsurprised. Back when Ruby was little, Mama would sing her that song every night before she went to sleep. Knowing what she knew now, she wondered if her mother had written it during that time in Nashville or if she'd heard it in a smoky bar on Beale Street, but back then Ruby thought it had to be a real famous song 'cause it was so pretty. "I'll start singing and you just play along, okay?"

She closed her eyes and cleared her throat. It had been a long time since she'd sung anything, and she was worried that keeping her eyes open would allow her to see the shocked and worried expressions on everyone's faces. She licked her lips and began.

OH LORD, *take me down.*
I say, Oh Lord take me down.
Take me down to the riverside
Where the water's cool and the shore is wide.
Oh Lord, take me down.

THE FIRST HALTING notes of Bunk's fiddle and Lettie's banjo joined in, picking up the simple melody. With each new word, the rust shook off her voice.

TAKE *me down where the water's clean*
Where the saints give blessings and the current's mean

AS SHE SANG, she remembered back to when she was little and her mama would turn on the radio in the kitchen and they'd dance around together. She thought about those sunny days on the riverbank with Granny Maypearl when the whispers of the trees would tickle her ears and the river sang its secrets. She sang for the proud and lively women they used to be instead of the sad and tragic memories they'd become so recently.

OH LORD, take me down.
  When the waters rise I won't run away
  'Cause we'll all be a'swimmin' come judgment day

HER BODY SWAYED in time with the melody. She imagined the notes dancing in a circle around her. She willed them to enter into her ears and down her throat. She urged them to circle her heart and remind it how much it used to love to sing.

The song reminded Ruby of longing and loneliness, which was to say that it reminded her of herself.

OH LORD, take me down to the river wide
  And carry me away on your righteous tide
  Oh Lord, take me down.

AS THE LAST note left her mouth, she finally opened her eyes. Everyone in the church had stopped what they'd been doing to listen. The final notes of Bunk and Lettie's music echoed through the chapel and disappeared, and the entire room fell silent.

She realized that tears were flowing down her cheeks, and delayed self-consciousness overtook her. She swiped at the tears, feeling like a fool. There was Peter in the front row of the church staring at her like she was some sort of alien. Edna sat nearby crying into her apron. Ruby figured they were tears of surrender as Edna realized that Ruby's terrible voice couldn't save them after all.

Peter stood and said, "Damn it, Ruby."

She flinched.

"Why have you been hiding that voice all this time?"

Bunk hooted and grinned at her, and Lettie dabbed at the corners of her eyes.

"Like an angel," Edna said. "Just like her mama."

Her temporary relief tumbled like a stone into a deep well. Mama's voice hadn't been powerful enough to make her dreams come true. Would Ruby's be strong enough to save them all?

"Oh shit!" Sharps looked over from the window. "He's back."

Peter ran over. "Who?" But he reached the window before Sharps could answer. "Damn."

"What's wrong?" Ruby asked, even though she was afraid to know.

"Ruby Barrett!" It was *him*—the ringleader. "I hear you singing in there!"

She jumped up from the step and clasped her hands together. The idea of that demon listening to her sing her mama's song made her sick.

"Easy," Peter said. "He's trying to mess with you."

"Too bad you don't have your granny's power, girl. Might as well come on out and pay the piper."

No one moved. No one said a word.

The demon tried again. "I've got your friend out here."

Ruby looked around quickly to count heads. She didn't see anyone missing—

The cry cut through the air like a missile.

"Oh no," she breathed. "Oh, God, please no." Another scan of the room confirmed her fear—bear was not there.

Peter came to the same grim conclusion as she did. "God damn it, Junior."

The man in question picked at his teeth with a toothpick as he leaned against a pew. His shotgun hung from his left hand. "Had to be done," he said in a tone that other men might use to share the weather forecast. "Always knew that bear would be good for bait."

Ruby had never wanted to punch another human more than she did at that moment.

Luckily, Peter did it for her. "You son of a bitch!"

Junior took the hit and spit blood on the chapel floor. He didn't bother wiping his lips, choosing instead to grin at Peter with teeth stained red.

Something inside her cracked and, from that single crack, fractures spread through her, destroying the fragile parts and revealing a steely core that had lain hidden behind her insecurities.

She marched to the door and threw the bolt.

"Ruby, no!"

She walked out before he could stop her.

The undead surrounded the poor creature, taunting it. Ruby ran down the steps before her instincts could tell her to go back into the church. She'd survived a lot of horrible things on that cursed day, but she was damned sure not going to stand by while poor Bear, who she'd barely just freed, became the plaything of such evil.

The demon, who still looked like a little boy, stood with a hip cocked beside the Cadillac. She wasn't sure if she should feel relieved or horrified that Deacon Fry's body was gone. Best not to think about that now.

She stopped on the steps so she could look down on the demon child. "You let him go right now."

He laughed and the sound had an otherworldly quality, like

it rose from a deep cavern. "Only if you let us play with you instead."

She put her hands on her hips even though they trembled something fierce. "You get out of this town."

He pulled back with his eyebrows raised. His body morphed from the little boy back into the larger form of Jack Thompson, only now he didn't look as he had when he died. Instead, he looked like he had at the peak of health.

She gasped and stumbled back.

"Well, now," he drawled, "if I'd known you were such a spitfire, I would have given you what you were begging for when I was alive."

Her courage drained out of her like dirty bathwater. "What?" she whispered.

"You were hot for me, Ruby Barrett. Practically panting for me." He slid a hand along the hood of the car. "I know you used to wonder what I did to Sarah Jane in the backseat of her daddy's big Cadillac."

She shook her head because she was too horrified to speak.

"Poor little Ruby, always imagining everyone else's lives and never having one of your own. It's sad." He exaggerated his pout. "Who do you think you are?" He lurched forward, raising his voice. "Who the fuck do you think you are challenging me?"

She stumbled back until her heel struck the hard stone of the step. Her arms windmilled as she struggled to maintain her balance. This amused Jack, who brayed like a donkey.

The sound acted like a splash of cold water on the heat of her shame. "We don't want you here. Leave this place."

Jack placed his hands on his hips to mockingly mirror her posture. "Make me, you little bitch."

He turned his back on her and sauntered toward the cub. Ruby went still, knowing one wrong move could mean terrible things for her friend. He knelt down. His joints popped like gunshots. He clucked his tongue at the bear. "Come 'ere, you little shit."

Bear growled and swiped a paw in the air. Ruby took two steps forward.

"Careful," Peter said behind her.

"Come here!" Jack shouted and took a swipe at the cub.

"I told you to leave her alone." Her voice was strong, but she did not shout.

He leered at her over his shoulder. "I'm going to rip this cub apart while you watch. Then I'm going to kill all of your friends. Once that's done, I'm gonna march up that mountain and find those two brat sisters of yours and make you watch while I bury them alive with your mama."

He waved at the flailing corpse of her mother, who was still pinned between the church sign and the truck fender. Terrible growls emerged from that ruined mouth that used to sing her lullabies.

The demon thought he was being shocking. He thought she was a baby who would run and cry if he said mean things. But Ruby had seen things that night that strengthened her heart. Made her realized she'd been pretending to be a girl when she was really a woman who didn't know her own power.

The demon lunged at the bear and laughed like a schoolyard bully.

Poor little Bear. She hadn't asked to be taken by mean old Junior Jessup. She hadn't done anything wrong to cause her own mama to die. It just happened because sometimes in life, awful things happen. There's no reason for it.

After Mama died, Ruby had made the mistake of closing down her heart and trying to escape her life altogether. But if she'd been successful in her original escape plan, she never would have been able to save Bear. She also wouldn't have had the honor to help her grandmother move into the beyond, and she never would have had the chance to show all of the people of Moon Hollow—least those who were still alive—that she might be touched, but she was no goddamned coward.

She stepped forward again. Ahead, Jack had one of the bear's paws in his disgusting hand. The cub mewled pitifully.

She closed her eyes and took a deep breath. The damp night air felt good in her lungs, full of mountain mist and the promise of the coming dawn. She breathed slowly until she could hear her own heartbeat in her ears. As she listened to the primal rhythm of life, she thought about the things she loved in Moon Hollow. The way the sun kissed the ridges in the morning, and hugged them at dusk. The way the fireflies danced through the graves on Cemetery Hill in June. The smell of wood smoke in the winter and the taste of cold creek water in the fall. She opened herself to these sensations and memories and expanded her consciousness to include the whole mountain and everything in it.

Home. This was her home. Often it was a dysfunctional home. Sometimes it was a painful one. But laughter also lived in this home, and joy. She didn't need to leave Moon Hollow to find herself. She just needed to allow herself to be at home here.

The air shifted. She suddenly felt that something was coming over the mountain. It flew through and around the trees, it danced across the river, and it dove off the ridges. It collected energy as it traveled, like a gathering storm. Because it felt right, she lifted her arms above her head to welcome it.

When it arrived, it plowed into her like a wall of sound. Her heart churned, trying to absorb all the music. It filled her head and her mouth and her chest. It packed into her arms and legs. It distended her belly.

The intensity frightened her. A million voices all sang at once, the notes slippery like eels so she couldn't use any of them to anchor herself.

But then, a single thread of music shone inside her brighter than the rest. The sound was so pure and clear that she knew instantly it could only have come from one place. She mentally plucked the chords from where they had wrapped around her stomach and redirected it to her heart.

The instant the melody entered the chambers, her eyes popped open.

The area was silent, and no one moved, not even the haints.

With the notes of the song echoing inside her, she finally smiled. This wasn't the mountain's song or granny's song. It was Ruby's song.

She turned her back on the undead and looked up at the crooked steeple. Thunder rolled across the mountain and wind whipped through the hollows.

"What are you doing?" Jack's voice demanded behind her.

She braced her feet and let loose her song.

The words manifested as lightning from her lips. Branches of pure energy spread out and found the unwelcome visitors. Their screams were drowned out by the thunder crashing overhead.

She held the note until her eyes rolled back in her head and she saw images of the mountain carrying back through years and decades and centuries. She saw primordial forests and ancient waters and stones that carried the secrets of the ages.

"No!" The sound of the demon Jack screaming broke through the static of energy and the killer melody thrumming in her blood. "You broke the pact. You will pay."

A voice inside her whispered, "Mountain owes no debts."

70

THE ARRIVAL

Peter

HE'D SEEN many uncanny things that day. Things he'd never be able to put into words if he managed to survive the night. But as he watched Ruby stand her ground in front of a demon, he realized he'd never witnessed true power until that moment.

And that was before she started singing her lightning song.

The instant the bolts escaped her, the air became blindingly bright and the smell of ozone nearly overpowering. He dove to the ground with Edna and Lettie, Bunk and Earl Sharps. The bear scrambled under the truck.

Lying on the church steps, Peter peeked through the arms covering his head to watch the show.

Ruby's hair stood in a halo around her head as the force of her energy crackled through the air. The words of the song hurt his ears, but it made his chest expand and tears come to his eyes at the same time. It was at once both the most beautiful and terrifying thing he'd ever witnessed.

"No!" The demon screamed. Its body distorted from that of Jack Thompson into something bent and twisted and horned. It raised its head to the sky and roared. But the lightning's power didn't let up. It cooked him even as he raged.

The air pressure dropped so low that Peter had trouble hearing and breathing properly. But he kept watching because he needed to see it end. One by one the corpses exploded. The older ones—the skeletons—went first, followed by the more recent dead. When Rose Barrett's corpse finally immolated, she screamed Ruby's name.

Demon Jack was last. Chords of lightning whipped around his body. The sound of his agony sang the unbearable melody to Ruby's killing song. Finally, her voice reached a deafening crescendo. The demon's blackened corpse exploded.

Unlike the others, his body hadn't burned to ash, but had hardened into black glass that fractured into brittle shards.

Ruby collapsed to the ground. Her clothes were gone, and her hair and skin smoldered. Angry red lines covered her skin in a branching pattern, as if the lighting branded her.

Peter ran to her and knelt next to her smoking body. He tried to figure out how he could help, but touching her was out of the question.

"What can I do?"

Smoke escaped her mouth when she tried to speak. She ran her tongue over her blistered lips. "Be ... here."

Her body spasmed. Peter cursed helplessly. "I'm here, Ruby. I'm here."

She tried to smile, but before the expression could manifest, she passed out. Overhead, thunder rolled and rain poured from the cloudless sky.

Peter looked up and let the rain wash over him. A sound caught his attention and he looked through the pouring water to see a small bundle of brown fur emerge from under the truck. The bear rose on its small hind legs and raised its muzzle to the sky. This time when it cried, the sound wasn't sad—it was triumphant.

71

RETURN WITH THE ELIXIR

Peter

SCREAMS STILL WOKE him at night, and whispers haunted him during the day. He tried to keep busy, but the memories always found him.

He'd lost a lot of weight. His blazer hung off him, like a boy wearing his father's clothes. When he could stand to look in the mirror, the planes of his face reminded him of ridges of scorched earth.

He splashed water on his face and used the tail of his shirt to dry off. The *before* Peter would have been careful to tuck in the shirt. He would have sprung for a new blazer—one that fit— but the *after* him didn't care. After a man had looked into the face of evil, it was hard to muster concern for trivial matters anymore.

He exited the Wicked Ink bathroom. An employee stood in the dark little hallway waiting for him.

"Mr. West? I was hoping you wouldn't mind signing some stock after the talk."

He recognized the kid as the one who'd worked the coffee

stand the last time he'd been there. The day when Renee's news had sent him off like Quixote to chase windmills in the mountains. Unfortunately for the kid, he'd found his patience for pleasantries had died around the same time he realized that demons were real. "Sorry but I won't be staying that long."

The kid's face fell. "Okay, maybe some other time."

He didn't bother telling the guy there wouldn't be a next time. Once he sent off the manuscript he'd spent the last two years writing, he was retiring from writing for good. He simply nodded and eased past the kid to go join the audience.

"Mr. West?"

Peter turned with his eyebrows up.

"For what it's worth, I think it's pretty cool you showed up for her signing, considering what she said about you."

He chuckled more at himself than the kid. "If I hadn't wanted her to write about it, I shouldn't have done those things." With that, he left the slack-jawed kid behind and took his place at the back of the signing area.

Renee was already at the front of the room talking. She hadn't seen him come in because the crowd was standing-room-only.

She looked tired. Not a good sign. According to her website, this was the first stop in what would be a twenty-city signing tour. The book had come out the day before—six months later than the original release date after they'd had to push it back due to some writer's block—and he'd bet the two hundred bucks left in his bank account that she'd been up all night refreshing her sales rank.

A woman in the third row was asking a question. "You must be so proud of all the support your book is getting from other women who've survived tough divorces?"

Renee's smile was tight. "I'm happy anyone is reading the book," she said. "Writing is a tough, solitary endeavor. It's incredibly gratifying to know your words are helping other people."

Another hand shot up, this time from a woman standing very close to Peter. Renee called on her. He didn't bother trying to hide, and he knew the second she spotted him. Her eyes shot to him and then away and then back again. He didn't smirk or wave. He just stood there.

"Has your ex read the book yet?" the oblivious woman asked, sounding giddy.

Renee shifted uneasily. He tipped his chin and smiled at her. "Uh," she said, "I think he has."

"Well? What did he think?"

Renee was still watching him. All around, people had begun whispering as they recognized him, but the woman who'd asked the question was still clueless. "Was he mad?" she demanded. "I bet he was mad."

Peter looked at the woman who'd suffered under his ego for more than a decade, shook his head, and mouthed "no." A shocked laughed escaped Renee. Now people in the audience were really catching on. Some even pulled out their phones to grab pictures.

"You know," Renee said to the woman in the audience, "something tells me he's okay with it."

Peter put his fingers to his lips and saluted her before he turned and walked out of the store.

He got into his shitty car and looked at the box covered in brown paper. Before he'd left his apartment that night, he'd printed the whole thing out and wrapped it up. It had taken a dozen stamps to make enough postage. It reminded him of the early days of writing when he had to send manuscripts to publishers and they required that writers include pre-stamped envelopes to pay the postage for the rejection letter they'd inevitably send.

Things had changed so much since he'd sent his last unsolicited manuscript. Everything was digital now. Anyone with a word processor and an email program could call themselves a novelist. Hell, maybe it was better that way. Who was to say one story was more valuable than another anyway?

He patted the package. He hadn't included a return envelope in this package because there would be no response required. He'd finally written a story just because it needed writing.

72

THE CIRCLE UNBROKEN

Ruby

BEAR WAS CRYING for her breakfast.

"Hold on, you big baby," Ruby mumbled through layers of pillows and blankets.

She hauled her legs over the side of the bed. A hiss escaped her mouth as her toes made contact with the frigid floorboards. She considered climbing back under the covers, but Bear's bellyaching would soon wake up the girls, and then, they too would be crying for their food.

Besides, she had work to do. Yesterday she'd seen the brilliant green shoots of the season's first ramps on the hillside. In the next few days, the crocuses would join them. Warmer weather wouldn't be far behind. Hard to believe it already had been two years since the spring no one talked about.

Downstairs, she added a new log to the potbelly stove in the living room. Then, shuffling in her slippers, she entered the heart of the home. The kitchen looked almost exactly as it had two years earlier when she'd moved in. She'd only added three items to the room since then.

The first thing was a small radio that she listened to while she cooked. She'd been methodically making her way through all of the recipes in the journals Granny had left behind, and found that listening to CDs of old Appalachian ballads helped her connect better to the work. Now that the mountain sang to her all the time, she found herself seeking out music everywhere she went. She'd even found an old dulcimer in a spare closet, and practiced it on the front porch when the nights weren't too cold. She must be getting pretty good, too, because the night birds had been showing up to sing along.

The second item she'd added was her mama's embroidered hand towels. Besides her clothes and the girls' personal items, the towels were pretty much the only things she'd saved before selling her daddy's house. The money that had been left after paying off Daddy's debts had gone into an account for Sissy and Jinny's schooling.

The third item she'd added was the framed photograph of Granny Maypearl she'd found a couple years earlier in the attic. The mischievous smile on Granny's face was so perfect it always caused a catch in Ruby's throat. Every time she passed it going in or out of the kitchen, she touched the frame. It had become such an automatic response that now even the girls had picked up the habit. She liked to think Granny, wherever she was, appreciated the acknowledgment.

While the kettle heated up, she pulled the container of frozen berries from the icebox. Bear had shown up a couple weeks earlier. She'd been emaciated from hibernation, but she'd brought back three rambunctious cubs—two males and a female. Ruby didn't mind the extra mouths to feed one bit, especially since she knew once Bear and the cubs regained enough weight, they'd go deeper into the woods and she'd only see them every few weeks. Ruby wasn't surprised to see Bear be such a good mama. She made sure to spend a good bit of each day training the cubs to hunt and survive in the woods, and, while she allowed Ruby and the kids to touch them, she was careful not to spend too much time with them so the cubs wouldn't lose all fear of humans.

Through the window, she spied the four dark shapes—one large and three smaller—lingering on the edge of the woods near her outbuilding. Bear had excellent manners and wouldn't come closer until Ruby stepped onto the porch and invited them to come eat. Still, she saw Ruby moving around in the kitchen and stood on her back legs to extend a good morning growl.

Ruby smiled and shook her head as she poured the hot water over the tea bag in her favorite mug. That morning called for Granny's favorite, rose hip tea. She bent over the steaming mug and inhaled the tart red scent.

Before she could gather everything and take it out on the porch, Jinny came into the kitchen. She wore her sister's hand-me-down flannel pajamas, which were blue and decorated with moons and stars. Her hair looked like someone had rubbed it with a balloon, and she yawned so big that her jaw cracked. Ruby laughed. "Morning, Sleeping Beauty."

"Can I help you feed them?"

"Sure." Ruby held out an arm to welcome the girl in for a hug. That was something they'd never done *before*, but over the last couple of years, a delicate sort of loving had blossomed between all the girls. Maybe it was living in Granny's house that did it, or maybe they simply had more space to love in their hearts now that their days weren't spent being so afraid. Either way, Ruby loved each of them in their own way. Sissy wanted little to do with mountain music or root work. She preferred more domestic arts, and took after their mama with her delicate hand for embroidery. She even made clothes for the three of them, which was a good thing since neither Ruby nor Jinny could sew a stitch.

She couldn't help but think of her love for Jinny as a more personal sort of love. Hard not to love her, when she reminded Ruby so much of Granny—and of herself. The girl loved to spend hours in the stone shed helping Ruby concoct tinctures and soaps to sell at the farmers' markets and county fairs. Ruby didn't go to these fairs herself, of course. But Edna had agreed to take a cut of the profits in exchange for running the booths and selling to the customers. Ruby could have done it herself, of course, but she wasn't sure anyone would buy anything if they knew they'd been made by the Witch of Moon Hollow, as people in the region had taken to calling her.

Ruby had even caught Jinny out by the creek at night surrounded by fireflies as she stared up the mountainside with her head cocked, like she was listening to someone whisper in her ear. Ruby had been careful about pressing her for details about what she heard. She knew from experience that the mountain sometimes shared very personal things, and it would be angry if it felt that confidence was betrayed.

Eventually, Sissy would run off with a boy, and then it would just be Jinny and Ruby up on that ridge. She hoped by then she'd know enough to properly train Jinny. She knew better than to wait too long. Granny thought she'd had plenty of time, too, and look what happened.

"Ruby?" Jinny prompted.

Outside, Bear whined loud enough to communicate that she wasn't happy with the delay. Ruby grabbed the container and handed it to her sister.

"Of course you can help," she said. "Just remember, if you're not careful, Curly will steal all the food before Mo or Mary get any."

Ruby went to open the door, but Jinny made a sound that

had her turning around. "What's wrong?"

"I forgot to tell you. Reverend David came by yesterday and dropped something off for you."

Ruby's cheeks immediately heated at the mention of the town's newest reverend. He'd arrived the previous fall to take over at Christ the Redeemer.

"You're blushing!" Jinny said.

"No, I'm not." She tried to look stern, but failed miserably. "What did he leave?"

Jinny shoved the container at Ruby and ran out of the room. Ruby sighed and set the berries on the counter. Bear could wait if Reverend David was involved. She and the girls attended services every Sunday, and Jinny and Sissy always loved to tease her on the way home about how the young reverend kept stealing glances at Ruby. The way she saw it, there weren't too many people in the pews to look at anymore, but she still felt a secret thrill every time she caught him looking.

After the event, Sarah Jane and Sharon had moved away to live with some family down in Florida, and Nell Thompson had to be put in the state mental hospital so she couldn't hurt herself or anyone else when she started ranting about the demon who appeared in the shape of her son, Jack. Lots of people stayed, but those that did weren't too keen on going back to the church, even after Reverend David ordered a proper cross to be installed on the roof. Now, it looked as if nothing terrible had ever happened in Moon Hollow, but a pretty cross couldn't protect them from real evil.

"Here it is!" Jinny ran in with a large package wrapped in brown paper. "I think it's a present."

"Why would he bring me a present? My birthday isn't for months."

"Maybe it's a love present," her sister said.

"Hush you!" Ruby snatched the package and looked at the

front. "Hey, this isn't a gift—it's mail—" She broke off as the Raleigh return address registered. "It's from Peter."

The sounds of feet on the stairs echoed through the house. A moment later, Sissy walked in, yawning. "Y'all are loud enough to wake the dead. What's going on?"

"Ruby got a package from Peter," Jinny said in awed tones.

Sissy froze. "What is it?"

After the event they never spoke of, Peter had hung around for several days helping to get everything sorted out. After all the funerals, he'd helped the girls move into Granny's house. Every now and then, she'd hear from him. A time or two he'd offered to help her move away, but she always refused. She could hardly believe it had only been two years since she was that young girl asking him to help her run away like Tom Sawyer.

"I'm not sure," Ruby said. "He didn't tell me he was sending anything." Last week, he'd called to tell her he was moving out to California. He'd gotten a job as a professor at a school out there, teaching English at an all boys' school.

"Well, open it," Sissy said.

She cradled the package to her chest and shook her head. "I think I need to open this alone. Can you two handle giving the cubs their treat?" As if on cue, a chorus of impatient mewls came from the yard.

Jinny whined, "I want to see—"

Sissy elbowed her. "We'll take care of it, Ruby. You go on."

She smiled at her sisters, now so grown it hurt her to think that one day they'd leave her. "Thanks."

She took her jacket from the hook and threw it on as she walked toward the front door of the house. If the cubs saw her come out the back, she'd have to stop and spend time wrestling with them before she could go. But something told her that whatever Peter had sent in that box was too important to put off.

She patted Billy on the head as she ran down the porch steps and to the old truck she used to make runs into town. The engine growled in the cool morning air, but soon enough she was on the old fire road. Every now and then, she'd glance at the package and the neat script written at the bottom, "For Ruby Barrett's eyes only."

Fifteen minutes later, she parked the truck and got out. She grabbed the bag she always kept in the truck for emergencies that had a spare blanket, a few snacks, and a pistol just in case. When she reached Crying Rock, she stopped to visit Granny Maypearl's grave. Everyone had argued that she should be buried on Cemetery Hill, but Ruby had insisted she would have wanted to be high above all of it, so she could keep an eye on everyone.

She knelt down and pulled a couple of stray weeds from around the gravestone. "Morning, Granny," she whispered. "We got a package from Peter."

Placing her hand over the warm earth, she closed her eyes and let the moment envelop her. A breeze passed over her skin, and it was scented with rhubarb pie and rosewater. She missed Granny so much it burned sometimes. On lonely nights, the worries found her. They tried to tell her she wasn't up to the task of filling Granny Maypearl's shoes. They told her that eventually the evil would come back stronger next time. They told her she wasn't powerful enough to win a second time. But right then, with her hand over the grave and Granny's name on her lips, the worries seemed a thousand miles away.

One day, the people of Moon Hollow would call her Granny Ruby, and she intended to be worthy of the title. Until then, she'd do her best to ignore the needling voice of worry and keep her hands busy learning her craft. She couldn't control the future, but having a purpose made her feel important and worthy of the air she breathed. She supposed that was about the best anyone could hope to do with the time they had on earth.

After giving the dirt an affectionate pat, she stood again and went to the edge of the bluff, where she could see Moon Hollow far below. On a clear day, she swore she could see all the way to Kentucky.

She sang a little song to greet the mountain and a light breeze answered by dancing through her hair. She smiled and looked down at her hands. The backs still bore the faint pink lines that covered all of her body, the only evidence that remained of that night no one spoke of anymore.

What was in the box?

Unable to stand the suspense any longer, she grabbed the package and the bag from the truck. She spread the blanket out on the rock and settled in before carefully tearing into the brown paper. Inside was a white box, like one of the shirt boxes Mama had always filled with socks and underwear at Christmas, only this one didn't have any clothes inside—it held a large stack of paper.

An envelope was paper clipped to the typed pages. She ignored that for a moment and read what she realized was the title page of a book manuscript. The title was *Lightning's Daughter*, but there was no author's name listed. Frowning, she went back to the handwritten note inside the envelope.

DEAR RUBY,

For a writer, an untold story sits on the soul like a curse. But this isn't my story to share—it's yours. What you do with it from here is up to you. Be well.

Your friend always,
Peter West

SHE TURNED the page and started to read.

DEDICATION

This book is dedicated to the wild hearts whose songs are too loud, too dark, or too true. They'll tell you good girls should be seen but not heard. They'll tell you good boys should be strong but silent. Sing anyway, brothers and sisters. Your music can change the world.

Acknowledgments

It generally takes a lot of support to write a book, and, with *High Lonesome Sound* in particular, it took a village.

This novel was my thesis project, which earned me a Master of Fine Arts degree in Writing Popular Fiction from Seton Hill University. During the course of that program, it was workshopped by dozens of my cohorts and several professors and mentors. In addition to the help of my Seton Hill family, I also had assistance from colleagues and friends, who acted as experts, fresh eyes, and cheerleaders.

First, thanks to Clarissa Yeo at Yocla Designs for the gorgeous cover. I gasped when I saw the finished product because it was just perfect. Lillie Applegarth's keen eye handled the proofreading.

Timons Esaias and Shelley Bates were my mentors in the MFA program. They indulged my quirky writing process and *laissez faire* approach to punctuation, but mostly they offered support as I tried to find my new song.

Huge thanks to Tiffany Trent for her beta reading, and her expertise on bears and southern Virginia. Molly Harper also beta read the novel, and, as a result, reports that she is now terrified of looking out windows during rainstorms. Higher praise could not be wished for nor offered.

A debt of gratitude is owed to my Seton Hill cohort for their insightful critiques on different sections of this novel: Jamie Henry, Tricia Skinner, Tracy Douglas, Jay Smith, Caleb Palfreyman, Jeff Evans, Chad Pritt, Luke Elliott, Chris Phillips, Sarah Tantlinger, and Tasha Kreger.

As always, I owe so much to Mr. Jaye and The Kid for their unwavering support, preternatural patience, and good humor. ILYNTB

ALSO BY JAYE WELLS

The Prospero's War Series

Dirty Magic

Cursed Moon

Deadly Spells

Volatile Bonds

The Sabina Kane Series

Red-Headed Stepchild

Mage in Black

Green-Eyed Demon

Silver-Tongued Devil

Blue-Blooded Vamp

Meridian Six Series

Meridian Six

Children of Ash

The Murdoch Vampires

The Art of Loving a Vampire

The Taming of the Vamp

ABOUT THE AUTHOR

USA Today Bestseller Jaye Wells is a former magazine editor whose award-winning speculative fiction novels have hit several bestseller lists. She holds an MFA in Writing Popular Fiction from Seton Hill University, and is a sought-after speaker on the craft of writing. When she's not writing or teaching, she loves to travel to exotic locales, experiment in her kitchen like a mad scientist, and try things that scare her so she can write about them in her books. She lives in Texas.

Find out more about Jaye Wells
www.jayewells.com
jaye@jayewells.com

facebook.com/authorjayewells

instagram.com/jayewells

bookbub.com/authors/jaye-wells

youtube.com/jayewrites

Get a FREE book

Sign up for Jaye's newsletter to get a free book. You'll also receive exclusive access to giveaways, excerpts, and release and event news. Each monthly newsletter also includes a recipe from Jaye's kitchen and the Fur Fan of the Month.

Sign up now!
JayeWells.com/Newsletter

Printed in Great Britain
by Amazon